A Walk Round London's Parks

A Walk Round London's Parks

HUNTER DAVIES

with photographs by Mark Fiennes

HAMISH HAMILTON

LONDON

First published in Great Britain 1983
by Hamish Hamilton Ltd
Garden House 57–59 Long Acre London WC2E 9JZ

Maps drawn by The Kirkham Studios

British Library Cataloguing in Publication Data

Davies, Hunter
  A walk round London's parks.
  1. London (England)—Parks   2. London (England)
  —Description—1951-—Guide books
  I. Title
  914.21'04858   DA689.P2

  ISBN 0-241-11040-8

Typeset by Wyvern Typesetting Ltd, Bristol
Printed in Great Britain by
Biddles Ltd, Guildford, Surrey

Contents

Introduction

This is my fourth walking book. I started with Hadrian's Wall, then the Lake District, then Disused Railway Lines and now the London Parks. It seemed at the outset to be the easiest project, limited to one town, restricted to a certain sort of landscape, with little distance to travel between each walk, all of which is true. I have followed the same system as before, devoting roughly half my time and attention to the past, explaining what has gone before, and the other half to the present day, to the people and places and the problems as they are now, trying to fashion the two strands together into a coherent narrative, to make a flowing story, a travel adventure in the heart of London, so that you will want to keep turning the pages, to learn more and find out what happens next. Or so I hope.

The problems which arose, on a walk which was supposed to be so easy, were unexpected. For a start, where are the London Parks? I could find no book which covers *all* of them nor any published list. I had imagined when I was walking the country's old railway lines, an apparently exotic and eccentric subject for a book, that I was venturing upon virgin territory, yet to my surprise two other books on the same subject were published when I was writing mine. The London Parks, which had seemed so obvious, as well as easy, turned out to be in one way a new subject and they presented an unusual challenge.

The Parks are London's greatest glory. I should have said that in the first sentence, but I now take it for granted, just as all London's millions do, knowing that they have within walking distance of wherever they live a green and open space. It is only when you travel abroad, to New York or Europe, that you realise how fortunate we are. They are unique. No city in the world is so endowed. And yet because of their complicated history, especially in recent years, no one has actually got round to compiling details of them all.

Official visitors come from all over the world, sent by the planning or parks departments of their respective cities, drawn by the fame of the London Parks, then hold up their hands in horror as they try to make sense of all the different facts and figures which are thrown at them by the different authorities. The first shock is that around forty separate bodies own the London Parks. Visitors go home, unable to cope, having missed out some vital parks, which they know exist, because they heard the names, but they have been completely unable in a short visit to track down the owners or assemble any information.

The Royal Parks, now they *are* easy. No, the Queen does not run them any more, though that need not worry any stranger, but the Government in the shape of the Department of the Environment. There are ten of these ancient and very beautiful Royal Parks in London, or seven main ones if you join some smaller bits together. I have walked all of them and they make up seven out of the ten chapters in this book. They are probably the finest metropolitan parks in the world and they have been well written about over the years. But, they make up only a small proportion of the London parkland. Greater London contains 45,000 acres of parks and open space out of which the Royal Parks have 6,000 acres, or almost one eighth of the total parkland area.

The Greater London Council owns almost the same amount of parkland, some 5,500 acres, and it includes some parks just as famous and as popular as the Royal Parks, such as Hampstead Heath or Battersea Park. The City of London owns more parkland space than either the Royal Parks or the GLC, which naturally confuses the visitor, struggling to work out how an institution only one mile square can have acquired so much. The City owns 7,000 acres, though over half of that is just outside the Greater London boundary. The Royal Parks, the City, the GLC, these then are the Big Three owners of the London Parks and the ones I have dealt with in the main chapters.

Then we come to the 32 different London Boroughs, which is when most people give up. In 1971, the GLC transferred the ownership of almost all their local parks to the local boroughs, and the records and details moved with them. You now have to contact each one individually to find out what they own and how they go about running them. Between them, the London Boroughs own 28,000 acres, about 60% of the total.

Finally, there is a group of smaller owners. Certain open spaces are owned by themselves, or at least by the residents who live on the boundaries, such as Wimbledon Common which is controlled by an elected body called the Conservators. The National Trust, so huge in the country as a whole, is another owner, managing some 890 acres of London's open space.

All of these various bodies work independently. There is no connection between them, no contact or communication. There is not even an informal sub-committee, an ad hoc guiding body, looking after the interests of all the London Parks. They are on their own, and so is any investigator, researcher or writer, trying to work out what is going on.

In the end, the Parks I have chosen to write about at length are well known, except for the last one, in chapter ten, which appears in a book for the first time. Several of them have already had whole books devoted to their history, and they will again in the future. It is the attempt to bring them all together in one book, and especially their life today, which turned out to be unusual. Most of all, it is that grey-looking appendix at the end, which tries to list all the Parks, despite their different ownership, that breaks new ground. It certainly broke my phone bill.

The ordinary visitor, and the ordinary Londoner, does not really care who owns what. The pleasure is in the Park, not in the committee room, in walking on the grassy slopes, able to believe for a moment that urban life is a hundred miles away, or sitting in a rose garden tended by unknown hands, or admiring a stately home, enjoying free entry to some priceless treasures. Dr Johnson could have said when one is tired of the London Parks one is tired of life. They do offer so much, from playgrounds to palaces, Wren to Rembrandt, mausoleums, to mosques, ponds to polo.

The present-day ownership is interesting, and how it all came about, but I have tried to keep background politics to a minimum, concentrating more on the individual Superintendents at work, the unseen, unsung stars of the London Parks. In almost all books about London Parks, they seem to be ignored, as if Parks look after themselves. I made it my business to seek out each one. At the same time, I found the history of the London Parks of endless fascination. The story of the Parks is the story of London, of its growth and social history, of the monarchy and Parliament, and in fact at many vital moments it is the story of the nation. The London Parks, after all, are national monuments, there for everyone to enjoy, pleasures for all the people.

Hunter Davies
London NW5
1983.

CHAPTER ONE

The Royal Bailiff, St James's Park and Green Park

It seemed only proper to begin with the Royal Bailiff. Parks people have a keen sense of hierarchy and they like the rules and courtesies and formalities to be observed, just as they like their flower beds to be neat and orderly and well arranged. The Royal Bailiff is the gentleman responsible for all the Royal Parks and it is the Royal Parks which most people think of when they think of the London Parks. They tend, in the main, to be the famous parks, the ones most visited by outsiders, the ones which contain some of our best known national landmarks. They happen to be very well tended parks, places we should all be proud of, though the majority of resident Londoners probably know their own local parks much better. London is full of these work-a-day, local parks, and several of them are just as historic and as interesting and as well cared for as the Royal Parks, but the Royal Parks are *all* show case parks, the leaders in the field. The Royal Bailiff, therefore, would be hard to ignore. What a grand title. What an important job. What a boring beginning it turned out to be.

This is not to insult the present incumbent but to register my disappointment at having to begin my walks, desperate for all those outdoor delights, by visiting him in his dismal place of work, which is far from Royal and totally un-Park-like. The Royal Bailiff is today an official of the Department of the Environment and his office is in one of the Government's monster high rise office blocks in Marsham Street in Pimlico, part of a series of anonymous tower blocks filled with anonymous civil servants. The corridors go on for ever and every room and every door looks the same and there is no trace of the sylvan nature of his job. The Royal Bailiff, to his own regret, never gets his hands dirty. When he goes out and about the Royal Parks, he is careful these days not to bend down and pick off a dead rose, or even to tell a gardener to pick off a dead rose. As a Senior Civil Servant, he observes the correct protocol. He informs the local superintendent, should he notice anything untoward, and then the order filters down to the relevant foreman and then at last to the gardener on the beat, which is what he himself used to be.

The Royal Bailiff is Ashley Stephenson and he is responsible for

St. James's Park and the Green Park

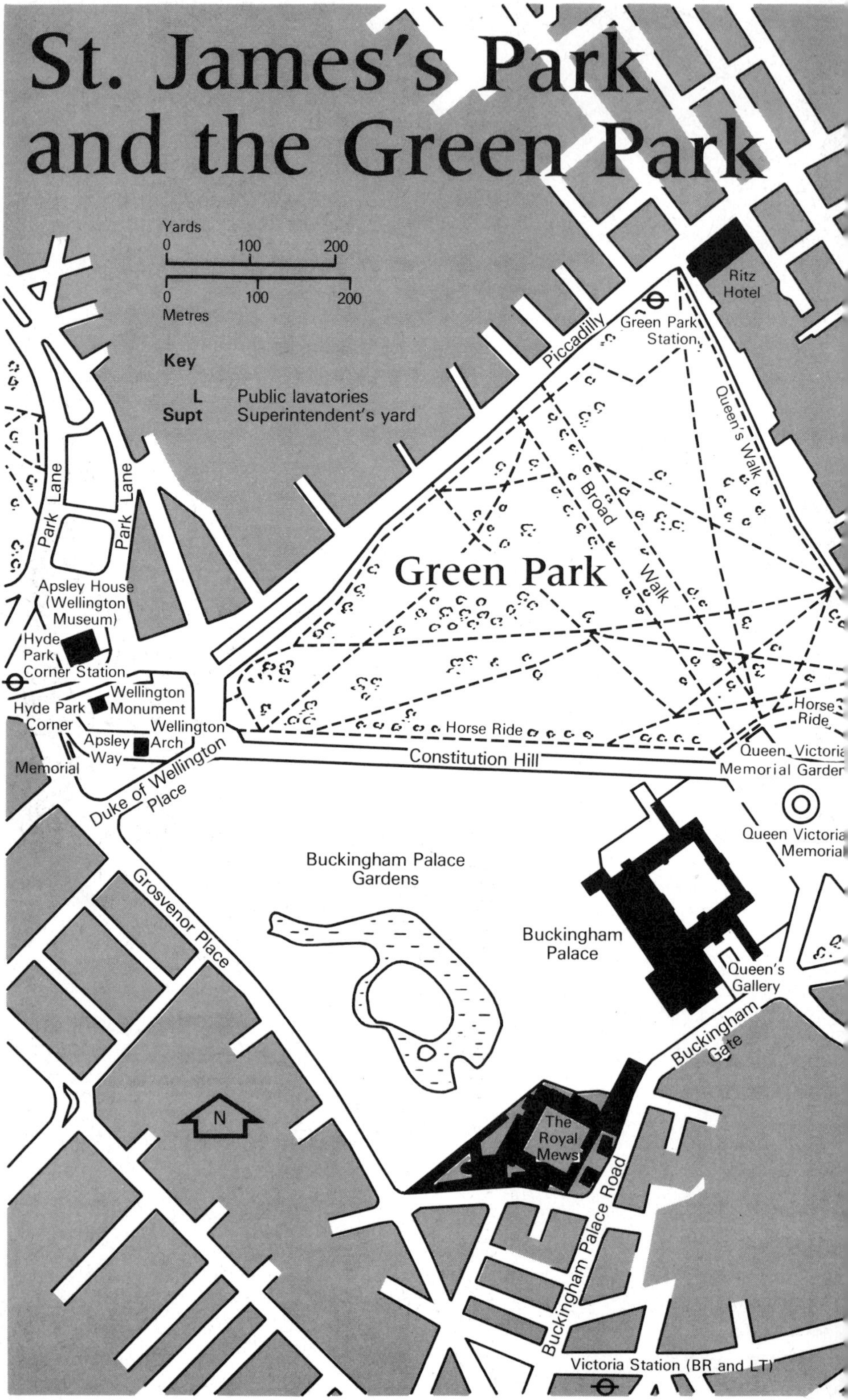

Yards
0
100
200
0
100
200
Metres
Key
L Public lavatories
Supt Superintendent's yard
Green Park
Piccadilly
Green Park Station
Ritz Hotel
Queen's Walk
Broad Walk
Park Lane
Park Lane
Apsley House (Wellington Museum)
Hyde Park Corner Station
Wellington Monument
Hyde Park Corner
Wellington Arch
Apsley Way
Memorial
Duke of Wellington Place
Horse Ride
Horse Ride
Constitution Hill
Queen Victoria Memorial Garden
Queen Victoria Memorial
Buckingham Palace Gardens
Buckingham Palace
Queen's Gallery
Buckingham Gate
Grosvenor Place
N
The Royal Mews
Buckingham Palace Road
Victoria Station (BR and LT)

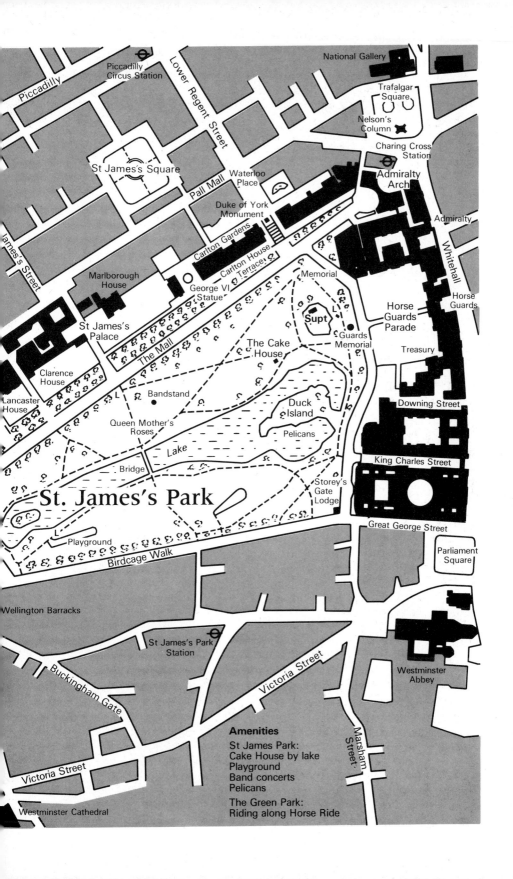

The Royal Bailiff, Ashley Stephenson: the first Bailiff to have risen right through the gardening ranks

everything in all the Royal Parks, for anything that grows, flies, walks or swims. His budget is £5.5 million a year. Then there are the human beings. His staff numbers 550 and they are responsible for an area of over 7,000 acres, though not all of it is in London.

He controls firstly what they call the Central Royal Parks, which means St James's Park and Green Park, Hyde Park and Kensington Gardens. Then there is Regent's Park which is neither classed as Central nor Outer and is considered in a class of its own. And there are the Outer Parks which means Richmond, Greenwich, Hampton Court and Bushy. These are his main concern, the parks everyone thinks of when they think of Royal Parks. But he also has a whole host of other bits of greenery, Government or Crown property, which for various reasons have ended up in his ample department, with him as the senior civil servant finally responsible for them, and they include the gardens of Buckingham Palace, 10 Downing Street, the Tower of London, Clarence House, and Marlborough House. Outside London, he looks after the gardens at Walmer Castle, Dover (where the Queen Mother stays in her position as Warden of the Cinque

Ports), and Osborne House on the Isle of Wight (formerly Queen Victoria's, now a convalescent home).

He does have some grand-sounding places to care for, to go with his rather grand title, and the responsibility that goes with his office is certainly impressive enough for you to expect the holder to be some scion of the aristocracy, a member of the Royal Household perhaps, or maybe a retired General or Admiral.

Mr Stephenson left school at fourteen and has a strong Geordie accent and is very proud of the fact that he is the first person in the history of the position to have risen completely from the bottom. Until 1972, for the previous hundred years or so, the Royal Bailiff had had no training in gardening or horticulture, the position usually being filled by a career civil servant, on the way to somewhere else, or by a retired military gentleman. Before that, the position (then called the Ranger) had indeed been held by a member of the Royal Family. It was Mr Stephenson's predecessor, John Hare, who broke the pattern in 1972 by being a trained horticulturalist, though he had arrived in the Royal Parks at a fairly senior level. Mr Stephenson came right through the ranks.

He was born in Heddon-on-the-Wall, outside Newcastle, and joined Newcastle Corporation Parks Department at 14, thanks to having an uncle who worked in the corporation parks at Whitley Bay. He served 3 years of his apprenticeship before being called up for the army. He returned to gardening and was in private service with a family in Gosforth, then moved to a landscape gardening firm near Ponteland. At the age of 24, he decided to apply to be a student at the Royal Horticultural Society's gardens at Wisley, which in those days took on eight student gardeners a year.

'It was very competitive. I don't know how many applied, but I do know they spent five days, full time, interviewing people.' After two years, he left with a Wisley Diploma and could now call himself a horticulturalist. Until then, he had been simply a gardener. All the same, when he applied for his next job, which was at the Royal Parks in London, he started in October 1954 as a Gardener, Grade 2, the lowest grade of gardener on a salary of £7 a week. His first job was in the greenhouses at Hyde Park, propagating geraniums.

'It was the loneliest few months of my life. I had a single room in Paddington and for months I didn't know anybody and nobody spoke to me.' In 1955 he got married to his girl friend from home. When his promotions came, he moved into a park house.

His first step-up was to be in charge of a propagating block in the green house, with three other gardeners under him. He was soon promoted to Gardener Grade 1 and then to Foreman. 'This was the big step. After just three years, I'd moved into the management grade. I must have been marked down for quick promotion. I think it was my previous experiences in the North-East which helped me, having been in different sorts of gardening work.'

He then became Assistant Superintendent in charge of Kensington Gardens, then a Grade III Superintendent, and so up to a Grade 1 Superintendent in charge of the Central Royal Parks. From this exalted position, after just seven years, he was promoted in January 1980 to be Royal Bailiff, in charge of all the Royal Parks.

As you walk round the London Parks, there might seem a motley collection of gardening folk, working quietly away, with no apparent hierarchical marks, but behind the scenes a strict grading system operates. Could that humble digger have the next Royal Bailiff's baton in his knapsack?

'My biggest problem today is staff. Because of Government economies, recruitment has not been possible recently, so if staff leave for another job or retire or even when they're ill, we have to manage without them. Standards have had to drop, I'm afraid. It won't be apparent to the general public for a while, and perhaps never, we hope, but we have had to look at what our priorities are and how we can save money.'

He is determined that their number one show piece, the spot he considers their prime horticultural display in the whole of London, will never have its standards lowered. I did not dare guess where this might be, otherwise I might have got it embarrassingly wrong. Their most important single scheme, so he said, is the Queen Victoria Memorial Garden outside Buckingham Palace.

It is a wonderful statue, and I have passed it many a time, usually with my head down, avoiding the traffic, but until then I had never considered it part of London's greatest floral display. If asked, I might even have said it didn't have a garden beside it. In my mind, I see it for ever surrounded by people during some Royal Occasion such as Prince Charles's wedding. You must have seen it often enough on television. But did *you* notice the flowers?

Every Year Mr Stephenson's men put 25,000 tulips into that little stretch of garden opposite the statue, facing the Palace. At the end of May, just before they begin to drop, they are taken up by hand and 14,000 geraniums are put in their place. Mr Stephenson is very proud that the tulips are removed on the Monday and that by the Friday every geranium is in flower. Casual passers-by hardly notice it being done, yet it takes 12 gardeners to do the change-over, working flat out all week, with everything carefully streamlined. One man spends the whole week picking up the empty geranium pots. They produce all their own geraniums, either from seed or from cuttings. Mr Stephenson had recently done a cost analysis and found that raising them from seed cost 3p each while from cuttings they cost $5\frac{1}{2}$p each.

In the old days, not so long ago, in their prime show case positions, they would make up to *eight* changes a year, leaving some of the plants in for only three or four weeks. This was when they had ample labour. In the winter, there would be flowering heather with early spring bulbs planted amongst it. When the bulbs had finished, in would go the calceolaria or cineraria, followed by begonias, then chrysanthemums, dianthus impatiens. Now, they have to make do at best with only three changes a year, usually bulbs, begonias and then geraniums.

'It was nice to be able to grow such a variety of plants. It kept the staff keen and interested. Now we concentrate on geraniums and produce them in huge quantities, about 80,000 a year. They're nice enough, but, well, it's not the same. The main jobs in the Central Parks are now maintenance gardening – watering, feeding, spraying. But you still have to attend to them, to keep them looking nice.'

He was concerned that day with grass cutting. It was once a week in the old days, throughout the Central Parks, but now they are trying to get it down to once every ten to fourteen days. 'Only the real professional can tell the difference. Most people in their own gardens do it once every two or three weeks anyway.' With doing it less frequently, they therefore need machines which can cut longer grass. Their big mowers, which they call their gang machines, with five grass-cutting units being pulled by a tractor, can't cope as efficiently with longer grass. He was considering completely different types of machinery to cope with the new system.

'It's untidiness which gets me most of all. I hate to see beds looking tatty, dead roses not picked, or daisies where there should be none. I can accept having only two changes of flowers, but I can't accept things like rubbish, tin cans, litter baskets not emptied.'

He thinks you can teach gardening, but most good gardeners begin with an instinctive gift. 'You must have the right feeling for plants. A good gardener can look at a plant and see that something's wrong with it and know how to put it right. You can tell by the way he picks up a plant, how he handles it, the way he pots it, if he has the right feel.'

Mr Stephenson lives in a rather grand Georgian house, Ranger's Lodge, right in the middle of Hyde Park. From his bath he can see the boats on the Serpentine and from his bedroom he can see Marble Arch and the lights flashing on the Odeon. On the open market, it would doubtless cost around £1 million. He has two children, a girl who is married and a boy about to go to college. He has taken the precaution of buying his own house, a bungalow on the Sussex coast, and tries to go there with his wife at weekends. As with all tied accommodation, you can be homeless when the job finally finishes. He has one extra income which came his way in 1982 when he was appointed gardening correspondent of *The Times*.

Is it not really a caretaker job, running a Royal Park, with little scope to be creative? After all, few major changes can be made. They are historic landmarks, just as much as the famous London buildings, and any alterations would cause a national outcry.

'If a shrubbery was laid out by William Kent, for example, as in Kensington Gardens, then it's true we're not going to be able to move it elsewhere. Avenues of trees can't be moved either, or footpaths. They're all part of the historic landscape. But we can change the shape and content of flower beds and I like each Superintendent to display his own personality as much as possible. It's vital that all the parks don't look alike. Just as long as they're all tidy.'

I then headed for the nearest Royal Park, shaking off the concrete dust and the smell of the filing cabinets, the glare of the office blocks and the noise of the traffic, encouraged by the Bailiff's promise that I would find a different personality to every Royal Park in London.

Of all the Royal Parks, St James's is the most royal, right in the heart of the Empire, within genuflecting distance of Buckingham Palace. No wonder the Bailiff cares so much about that show case garden. The Mall slices through St James's Park, and is technically part of it, then there's Horse Guards Parade at one end of the Park, with Downing Street and Whitehall behind, not forgetting the magnificence of Carlton House Terrace with Clarence House and St James's Palace. One could go on for ages listing all the famous buildings, household names all Britishers have known since childhood, even if they have only ever seen them on television or on the lids of biscuit boxes. On a sunny day, the vista around St James's Park can look totally unreal, a stage setting, created specially to celebrate our wonderful island heritage. Which is precisely why it was created.

Would I see the Queen? That's what all children and most visitors ask. And why not. It can happen all the time. She was due the next day to process down the Mall with the Sultan of Oman, available for all to gape at. It was a wet, blustery morning in early March, so I hoped the weather improved, if only to help the gapers. The flags for the next day's State visit were already being hoisted along the Mall. I watched a couple of Japanese tourists on a bench, trying hard to extract some sense from their map, holding it down against the wind and the rain.

In St James's Park itself, there seemed not to be a solitary soul. Out there, ten million Londoners had all decided not to come into the park that misty, moist morning. I could wander, lonely as a daffodil, and have it all to myself and pretend perhaps that I was in the Lake District, with a bit of careful imagination, not in Central London's most walked few acres of greenery.

I headed first for the Guards' Memorial, outside the main gate which leads into the Park. The five First World War guardsmen shown on the

The Guards' Memorial, outside St James's Park: soldiers at attention, cast in bronze from captured German guns

Memorial are cast in bronze which came from German guns captured by guardsmen during that war, but I didn't study it for too long. I didn't want to arrive soaked for my first appointment in the Parks which was to see the resident superintendent of St James's.

As in all Parks throughout the country, the private parts where the parkies gather are hard to find, tucked away behind shrubs or fences or other obstacles, keeping their covens hidden. The public, even the hardy regulars, go past these secret places all the time, often unaware of the lives being led, of buildings and huts and offices where dozens of people work and sometimes sleep. I suppose we should really avert our eyes, should we stumble on these private places. It is the public park which has been set out for us to enjoy.

For most of its 450-year life, St James's Park has been a very public park, a platform around which many events in our royal and political life have taken place. Most political personages have at some time taken a brief walk through St James's Park, before some vital Whitehall meeting, prior to a Parliamentary speech, on the way to announce the Budget, or simply en route for a quiet word with the Monarch or with the Minister. For one monarch, it turned out to be his last before going to get his head chopped off.

It was Henry VIII in 1530 who first fenced off these few acres. He had decided he fancied them for his own, seeing the site as a handy park for his new palace. The land had belonged until then to a hospice for poor leprous maidens, a religious foundation dedicated to St James, who had owned it since the 13th century. Henry VIII sent them packing and proceeded to drain the land, which had been very marshy, and used part of it for his deer, and the rest he laid out as a garden. For the next hundred years, it became a luxury adventure playground for the Royal families, with cock fighting, shooting, bowling, drinking, relaxing, walking, playing games, watching military reviews, most of the usual mundane things our monarchs still like to do. Almost from the beginning, it seems to have contained a royal menagerie and there are records from 1626 of a keeper being paid to look after the beasts and fowls.

There were at that time three Palaces round the Park. The Palace of Whitehall was where the Monarch held court, till it was burned down in 1695. There was the Palace of Westminster, which became the Houses of Parliament, and the Palace of St James where the Monarch normally lived when in London. The fourth Royal Palace, Buckingham Palace, the one we all think of today as being *the* London home of the Monarch, is a relatively modern creation, as the Royal Family did not move there till 1837, when they decided that St James's Palace had become too dusty.

Charles I was the unfortunate monarch who walked through the Park on his way to be executed. This was in 1649, after his defeat in the Civil War, but he went proudly to his death, dressed in a black coat, preceded by soldiers with banners flying and drums rolling.

Charles II, on the restoration of the Monarchy, made the Park look much as it does today. He had been exiled in Paris and decided on his return that he would turn St James's into a miniature Versailles, with formal flower beds, straight walks, and, most important of all, a long canal, 100 feet wide and 2,800 feet long, on which he could feed his ducks and beside which he could exercise his spaniels.

Charles II was very fond of all exotic animals and birds and he set up a series of aviaries on the south side of the Park, along the stretch now known as Birdcage Walk. He was a keen sportsman and played a type of bowling game he had picked up in France, *paille maille*, and he eventually laid out a special surface near his Palace where it could be played, known today as Pall Mall.

Charles's mistress, Nell Gwynne, acquired one of the new town houses which were soon being built beside the re-designed Park, near the Royal Pall Mall alley. It was exceedingly handy for her as she could look over her garden wall into the King's St James's Park. John Evelyn, the diarist, was shocked when walking with the King in the Park one day to hear the rather personal nature of the comments exchanged between them. 'A very familiar discourse . . . Mrs Nelly, as they call the impudent comedian, looking out of her garden. I was heartily sorry at this scene.'

King Charles welcomed his citizens into his private garden and they were allowed to wander round freely. Samuel Pepys often took a constitutional walk in St James's Park and on July 15, 1666, finding it 'mighty hot and himself weary', he 'lay down upon the grass by the canale and slept awhile'. Pepys was a civil servant, working as a naval administrator, and it is reassuring to realise that 300 years later St James's Park is still the haunt of civil servants, taking a break from affairs of state, from the lowest clerk to senior Minister, each able to walk straight out of his office and into his local park. And have a sleep? Certainly not. But, at any lunch time, probably 75% of the people in the Park are Government officials, resting the while.

The present officials who actually run the Royal Parks are also Government workers. Since 1851, the management of all the Royal Parks has been in Government care, firstly by the Ministry of Works, now by the Department of the Environment. Legally, the Crown is still the ultimate owner, and the Queen could remove you at any time. She won't, of course, if you are good and behave yourself and keep the place tidy.

I found the Superintendent's office, following a sign-post to the Royal Parks Constabulary, and came to a large courtyard containing several sheds and offices. Fred Mitchell is technically an Assistant Superintendent, as far as the hierarchy goes, but is the man in day-to-day charge of St James's Park and Green Park. He was sitting in a corner of a rather dark little office and looked suspicious at first, alarmed almost at being tracked down to his lair.

He was born in Chiswick and left school at 14 to become a tool maker. After the army, he decided he wanted an outdoor life and in 1950 he joined the Royal Parks as a labourer on £4.2.6 a week. 'I was only going to stay six weeks, as a fill-in job, but I've stayed 32 years so far. I just carried on. I got Park Rot, that's what we call it, don't we Jock.'

I hadn't noticed that there was another late middle-aged gentleman sitting in the corner, the Park's foreman, second in command after Mr Mitchell. He grunted some reply and smiled enigmatically.

As a labourer, back in the early 1950s, Mr Mitchell worked in Kensington Gardens, picking up paper, clearing out drains, and after four years he was promoted to Grade II Gardener. 'I was lucky in working with people who were interested in their job. I picked things up from them!' He worked his way through the gardening grades to become a charge hand foreman in Kensington Gardens. In 1971, he took over St James's as Assistant Superintendent.

'I'm not interested any more in promotion. I've told them that. I don't want any more paper work. I'm happiest when I'm outside. I still go round picking up litter. Take Charles's wedding, what a day that was. It took us four whole days, just to clear up, didn't it, Jock.'

He has a staff of 43 to look after St James's Park and Green Park but he is also responsible for the gardens at St James's Palace, Marlborough House, 10 and 11 Downing Street, Parliament Square, House of Commons, Tate Gallery and National Gallery. He feels that he and his men are permanently on display, always being inspected.

'Every MP walks through our gardens. Some of them every day. They all have their say and none of them is slow to write a letter. It's like having 600 Clerks of Works.'

That day, his main problem was not the political scrutiny, or the next day's State Visit, but the mess left behind by some outside contractors. Most specialist jobs are done by outside firms these days and he hadn't been free of at least one outside firm for the last two years. He still had gas men laying pipes, sewage people working on the pond and construction men on a building, all of them driving their machinery across his immaculate grass or digging trenches in his paths. In almost all such cases, the turf has to be completely relaid, after they have finally finished.

'There's also outside men doing the flags for the State visit. The Mall will be closed during the procession, so I'll have to tell my men to stop out all day, till after lunch. They won't be able to get back. Then I'll have people complaining they've been trapped in the Park and want to get out.'

'We usually have two State Visits a year, plus Trooping the Colour. Then you've got your EEC Conference at Lancaster House, and the Commonwealth Conference, oh, it goes on all the time.'

All these great and joyful ceremonial occasions look impressive on the television news, but for the parkies they are just another headache. They are expected to have the gardens on their best behaviour at that precise hour when the world is watching. Then, afterwards, there is all the mess to be cleared up, caused either by the public or by the temporary buildings put up for dignitaries or the national media.

'I think Charles's Wedding was the worst in recent years, don't you think so, Jock? They were out all night singing and dancing in the Mall on the Eve of the Wedding. We had two emergency toilets in the Park, but the women decided to take over the men's toilets as well, so I had to get up at midnight to sort that one out. I said to the wife, "We've had it tonight." Then both toilets got blocked. I only had two hours' sleep that night, didn't I, Jock?

'The police hadn't told us they were going to allow sleeping in the Mall overnight, so we'd cleaned up everything the night before. At 4.30 on the morning of the Wedding, I spent one and a half hours, all on my own, sweeping up the pavement in front of Buckingham Palace. I had no staff on at that time of the morning. We'd finished the day before, hadn't we, Jock, thinking, well, that's it, all lovely and clean for tomorrow. The mess was terrible, absolutely terrible. If I see it's wrong, I have to do it myself. You can't live with yourself otherwise.'

All the year round, litter is still the biggest problem in St James's Park. In the summer, Mr Mitchell and his men spend from 7.30 to 10 every morning picking up litter. 'That's 2½ hours wasted time when we could have been gardening.' Every day in summer, a lorry takes away eight tons of rubbish from the Park's waste paper bins. They're not allowed to burn it in the park itself but store it in a special clearing, hidden by some shrubbery.

Most of the litter is dropped at the Horse Guards Parade end of the Park, near the little cafeteria, known as the Cake House. People buy cakes and tea and then go and sit down on the grass and listen to the music from the nearby Bandstand where from June to September a band plays twice a day. Mr Mitchell was very pleased that the Bandstand was about to be moved to the middle of the Park. He hoped it would cut down the litter and at the same time make his private life more comfortable.

'My lodge is only 50 yards away from the Band. You can imagine what it's been like for the last eleven years. Twice a day! My God, I dread that first note. I'm so sick to death of *The Sound of Music* and *South Pacific*.'

All the same, he enjoys living in the Park, and so do his two children, but his wife is not too keen. She misses having neighbours, being cut off from all shops and community, enclosed behind a fence, even if beyond that fence is a lovely park. 'People say how marvellous, living in a Park, but there are disadvantages. Even now, I don't let my children come home across the Park at night on their own. I avoid the Park myself at night if I have to, and walk round the side. I know too much about the muggers and attempted murders.'

It seemed to have been mainly a tale of woe so far, not the idyllic life that one might have imagined, living and working in such a delightful place. Perhaps it was the dull, rainy day, skulking in the corner of his little office, the paper work in front of him which he never likes doing. But once we went outside and started walking round the Park itself, he cheered up immediately.

The Park for centuries has been notorious for footpads, as have all the central London parks. Muggers are nothing new, except in name. In the 18th century, St James's was noted for a special breed of muggers known as 'Mohocks', after a cannibal tribe in India, and Dean Swift wrote that it was no longer safe to go there even in daylight. For a long time, it was a haunt for prostitutes, of both sexes. James Boswell was accosted in the Park one evening in December 1762 by several ladies of the town. 'There was one in a red cloak of a good buxom person and comely face whom I marked as a future piece, in case of exigency.'

St James's Park was also noted for its duels, all of them illegal, when one gentleman, often on a dopey point of principle, would challenge another gentleman, then the winner would have to flee the country afterwards.

Thinking about it carefully, considering all the activities of the past, Mr Mitchell decided that in recent years things had improved. 'Vandalism is not as bad as it was. It's a while since we came on duty and found a dozen seats thrown in the Lake.' The Park can never be properly closed, as the fence round it is very low and easy to cross, but a new regulation now officially 'closes' the Park from midnight till 5 every morning which discourages a lot of intruders, and makes it easier for the parks police to chuck out any who do get inside. They still do of course, especially in the summer. 'Before the law changed, it was like a dormitory some nights.'

We walked round the northern shore of the Lake, with the Mall to our right, and he pointed out the new site for the Bandstand, then led me to five newly-planted beds of roses, put in to commemorate the Queen Mother's 80th birthday in 1980. She personally chose them – Congratulations, Just Joey, Scented Air, Young Venturer. The Royal Parks people were pleased to have them. In an age of staff cuts and other economy measures, it is much cheaper to have a rose garden than a flower bed which needs constant changing. They look after the Queen Mother's own gardens at Clarence House, although she herself is a keen gardener. She has a very old plane tree, with its branches right down to the ground, obscuring a gravel path, but she won't let them trim it back. Royal Parks gardeners are always very keen on trimming back and having things neat and tidy.

We came to the end of the lake, right under the jowls of the Buckingham Palace roundabout. The Park ends in a very high wall and I noticed that the stones had been shaped to look like a quay with stone mooring rings where boats, in the architect's imagination, could tie up. At one time, the lake did lap against the quay side, but now there's a path all the way round. You have to climb up to road height to see directly across to Buckingham Palace and Constitution Hill.

'I once got a call from Parliament after an MP had stood up in the House and asked why the clock was slow in Constitution Hill. I said there was no clock in Constitution Hill. So they rang off. Half an hour later, they rang back. The Minister had been officially asked and he had to give an official reply. I repeated there was no clock. Half an hour later, I was told to go down Constitution Hill, look around, and make *sure* there is no clock. So I went, knowing there was nothing to look for, then I rang back and told them. After that, I never heard anything about it ever again.

'You have got to be very careful, working in this Park. You never know who you might be talking to. I tell my men to make no comments to the public, not to stop and have a smoke, or stand still admiring their work. They might have been digging solid for two hours, and taken only two minutes off, but someone passing by doesn't know that. He might be a Sir, you never know, and the letters come in. We do get some thanks, well, now and again. It happened yesterday. Some ladies went over and thanked the gas contractors for the lovely crocuses. The gas men! After all our hard work. The gas men thought it was very funny.

'Mr Maudling was very keen on all our flowers. He'd have a walk through the park, then someone would ring up from his office and ask the name of a certain shrub. Mr Callaghan, he was keen as well, and Lord Home. President Carter, he also made a point of walking through the flowers.

'It's always a fight between the Ducks and the Flowers. The people that come just to see the ducks think we waste too much time on the flowers, and the flower people dislike the ducks. The ducks can be a nuisance as they eat the plants. I thought I was being clever last year. I put some netting down on a new bed to keep the ducks off, till an irate man came in to say a duck had got caught under the netting and he was going to report me to the RSPCA.'

We then walked back through St James's Park, this time on the other side of the Lake, past the children's playground, and stood on the bridge over the Lake, which divides it almost in half. The present bridge is made of concrete and was put up in 1957, replacing a 100-year-old iron suspension bridge. The bridge before that had been the work of John Nash. He was called in by the Prince Regent in 1829 to re-design the whole Park and it is very largely his influence which gives the Park its present appearance. He softened the harder, more geometric lines which had been laid down by Charles II during his Versailles phase. Nash turned the canal, which had been man-made in the first place, into a more natural, curving lake, as it is today, introducing an island, now called Duck Island, at one end. It is only when you look at the Lake carefully, on the map or in situ, that you can see that one bank still betrays the straight lines of its formal canal days.

The bridge is probably the nicest part of the whole Park. The view is spectacular, in every direction. Looking towards Horse Guards Parade, the view is totally surprising, as if for a moment one was in St Petersburg or Istanbul, with strange turrets and minarets on the Government buildings dominating the skyline, exotic formations that I had never noticed before when going past by car or bus. In the other direction, down the Lake, the view of Buckingham Palace is more familiar, but nonetheless attractive. In either direction, the views are enhanced by clever fountains and by lights in the water which come on at night.

'I do get a lot of pleasure out of my job,' said Mr Mitchell. 'The main

Whitehall from St James's Park Lake: Istanbul or St Petersburg, with strange turrets and minarets

pleasure is in seeing the pleasure other people get, as they take photographs of the flower beds, rush to see the Changing of the Guard, or stand and admire the ducks. You feel then you're giving something to the community.'

He returned to his office so I set off alone to look at Green Park, which he had not managed to take in on his little introductory walk. St James's Park and the adjacent Green Park are always lumped together and cared for by the same staff. Each has a similar history and in many reference books St James's Park is taken as including Green Park, with little distinction being made between them. They are both very small, compared with the other Royal Parks. St James's covers 93 acres while Green Park is only 53 acres. In character, however, they are totally different.

Green Park is simply a green park, a triangular strip of undulating grass, crossed by various paths, plus quite a lot of trees, mainly limes, planes and hawthorns. There are no flower beds, lakes or fancy ornamentations as in St James's Park. Green Park managed to escape the rash of statues and monuments which the Victorians scattered over all the then central Royal Parks. I did come across one little statue, with no clues to its history, which was surrounded by a little pool of rather stagnant water. Green Park never seems as kempt as St James's, with quite a few barren patches and mounds of left-over soil. The parkies would seem to be too much in love with St James's to have much time to fuss over Green Park. Some of them tend to dismiss it. I met one gardener later who referred to Green Park as dog shit island.

It was enclosed by Charles II, who roped in some former waste ground, and for many years it was known as Upper St James's Park. He built for himself in the middle of the park a so-called Ice House which sounds like a form of early refrigeration. A pit was dug in winter, filled with snow and ice, covered in thick straw and bracken to insulate it, and then used in summer for cooling wines and other drinks.

In the 18th century, Upper St James's was used for military parades and exhibitions, perhaps the most exciting being the Royal Fireworks display of 1748 to celebrate the Peace of Aix-la-Chapelle. It was described at the time as the grandest and biggest fireworks show the world had ever seen. Handel, who was living in Brook Street, was asked to write some suitably impressive and resounding music to introduce the Royal Fireworks. He had an orchestra which included 40 trumpets and 20 French horns who knew they would have to work very hard to be heard above the sound of 100 cannon which were timed to go off as his great overture began. That first performance ended in some chaos as a fire broke out, several buildings were damaged, one person died and many were injured, and the Park for a while was in total confusion. The music, at least, survived intact.

Benjamin Franklin, the American scientist and statesman, gave one of his personal demonstrations in Green Park, pouring oil on the troubled waters of a little pond, just to prove its soothing effect. Sir Robert Peel had what turned out to be a fatal accident in the Park, being thrown from his horse and dying a few days later. And it was in Green Park that the young Queen Victoria was shot at by a lunatic as she was driving past with Prince Albert in 1840. In 1842, and again in 1849, two other attempts were made on her life in Green Park, again by people who were later found guilty but insane. Perhaps there is something unsettling about all that stark grass and utter plainness.

The main attraction of Green Park today, apart from its convenience for dog owners, is that it is an easy and quick escape from the noise of Piccadilly. It is also very handy for the Ritz, the perfect place for breakfast after an early morning in the Park. It has its own tube station which is simply called Green Park, according to London Transport, despite the fact that the Department of the Environment always strictly refers to the Park itself as The Green Park.

It does provide a pleasant little walk, at least for local office workers, but for real walkers it is best to tie it in with an exploration of the rest of the area round St James's Park, or most exhilarating of all, to stride on and find the underpasses at Hyde Park Corner. By doing this, you can walk directly across Central London, from the far end of St James's Park to the end of Kensington Gardens, a distance of some three miles, a walk almost totally on grass, with only two public roads to cross. But that excitement was for another day, another walk, another park.

To finish off St James's Park and Green Park, I returned to the Lake in St James's, looking for the ducks. After all, they are probably the most famous feature of St James's Park, even more so than the flowers. Duck Island is not quite an island, being joined by a short isthmus to the mainland of St James's Park since 1829 when Nash un-formalised the Park and made the Lake a much more natural shape. There was talk the day I was there of removing the isthmus and making Duck Island into a complete island.

The island is not open to the public, as it is a bird sanctuary, but you can easily stand on the banks of the lake and look across and admire all the birds, both on the island and on the water. Except that there was no water round Duck Island that day. They were draining the end of the Lake, having put up a canvas dam to stop the flow, and the bare concrete floor of the Lake was revealed. Workmen in wellingtons were standing in the bowl of the Lake sweeping up the mud and leaves and piles of rubbish. St James's Park Lake is completely artificial, in every sense. The Round Pond in Kensington Gardens, or the Serpentine in Hyde Park, are both man-made, but they have at least got clay bottoms and a bit of water does come in which helps them live and breathe and stay fresh. In St James's, they have to empty and clean out the Lake every two years. Otherwise, the smell would become overpowering. The Lake is only three feet deep, which I could now see quite clearly. The man-made rocks on which the birds usually display themselves were left isolated, sticking up in the air as if marooned on stilts.

There is a little Lodge on the island, built by Nash, which in recent years has been used for the band as a changing room. Workmen were also working on this as it had begun to fall into the Lake – more contractors for the Superintendent to worry about. Right in the middle of the island is an Artesian well, one of nine in St James's Park. A little pumping station sends water into the Lake and also to the Serpentine and the Long Water.

But the dominant feature of the island is the bird colony. There have been birds on the Lake since Charles II introduced his aviary, over 300 years ago. Today, there are around 1,000, all resident, plus an unknown number of wild birds who come and go with the seasons. The residents have not much choice, as they have been pinioned after hatching. It is a simple operation, done by the time they are four days old. Their wings are clipped in such a way that they can never properly fly. Why should they want to leave St James's Park anyway? Think of all that fussing and loving attention and those politicians just wanting to send letters of complaint, should they ever be injured.

Hidden amongst the trees in the island is a bird hatchery which contains numerous buildings and huts, scores of wooden bird boxes and two full-time bird men, Malcolm Kerr and his assistant Martin Bodill. Mr Kerr is the official Royal Parks Bird Keeper and is responsible for the birds in Hyde Park and Kensington Gardens, as well as St James's. (Regent's Park has got its own Bird Keeper.) His father also works in St James's. He turned out to be Jock, Mr Mitchell's foreman.

Malcolm is 29 and started as a gardener in Regent's Park, tree-lopping and driving tractors, till 1975 when the Bird Man needed an assistant and he decided to apply, partly because he felt that if he eventually became Bird Man he would get a tied house. He had always been interested in birds, and had bred canaries and parakeets for his own amusement, but thought he would not be considered knowledgeable enough to be the official Bird Man. But he got the job and was sent on a course to Slimbridge, Peter Scott's bird sanctuary. Six months later he became the Bird Man.

It was he who told me the new plan to make Duck Island a real island. He had been most alarmed to hear of this proposed scheme as it would mean him using a punt to sail across to work each day. 'I have to hump 23 bags of wheat every month, each weighing 25 kilos, and 24 stones of fish. I'm not managing that in a punt. I'm hoping they're now going to leave me a little bridge to get to work.'

I joined him in his own cabin for a cup of tea and it was like entering a distant world, perhaps somewhere in the Rockies, a backwoodsman, cut off completely from all civilisation, alone on an island in the middle of a lake in the middle of a green expanse which just happened to be right in the middle of a city of ten million people, some of them, and their beastly cars, only a hundred yards away. It felt very strange, as I am normally one of those out there, but he was obviously oblivious, living his own life in his own way with his birds and animals. I kept looking round, staring at the door, knowing what was outside, but in his mind the real world was miles if not centuries away. It was so warm and cosy and inviting, insulated from the concrete city, with various birds and animals pecking around him, bags of corn lined up in one corner as if ready for a hard winter, frozen fish gently left to thaw in another corner, waiting for the next feed. On the wall was a dead fox, not one from St James's Park, though Malcolm has seen them there, but one given to him by a friend who works at Kew. This friend at Kew, said Malcolm, once shot 28 foxes, all in the same winter. His assistant nodded to confirm the figures and we all paused, letting the birds and their scratchings take over the silence.

That season he was breeding 36 different varieties of ducks, geese and other birds. He promised to send me the final list, at the end of the season, so I could see what success he had had. Being March, it was a hectic time for him, with the eggs soon to be laid.

He took me into his incubator room, where the first eggs would go and where he would 'candle' them to find out which were fertile. This is his own, home-made device, consisting basically of a light bulb in a little dark box. The light shines right through the egg so he can see the contents. Fertile eggs then take 28 days to hatch out and, although he has an ultra-modern incubator which automatically controls the heat and humidity and the turning of the eggs, he had not had much success with it the previous year. As with all sophisticated modern machines, a simple thing like a power failure, especially in the night when he is off duty, can ruin everything. His more old-fashioned incubator, which needs the eggs turned by hand, had proved more successful over the years. We then went outside to see his most successful method of all – hens. He keeps a flock of them specially to act as wet nurses, if that's the word, or perhaps it should be midwives. 'You have to be quick to get in when the eggs finally hatch. The hen gets confused to find she's hatched a duck and the little duckling thinks he's a chicken.'

He has had great success in recent years with breeding North American Ruddy Ducks, a delicate operation as they need water to swim in as soon as they have been hatched. He has built an ingenious tank with special slopes which provides some water, but not enough to let the new ducklings drown. A duckling has no natural oil for its first six weeks, but in the natural state, brought up totally by its mother, it shelters under the mother for comfort and so picks up the mother's oil, until its own oil glands start working. 'If ours had to fall into deep water in those first six weeks, then their feathers would soak up the water like a sponge and they'd sink.'

His big ambition is to breed Black Swans. He has tried for several years without success. One year the male died. Another year the female disappeared. Another year, when at last he'd got them to lay, some boys, so he suspects, stole the eggs.

The best-known birds on his Lake are the pelicans. They have been

Pelicans on St James's Park Lake

present on the Lake since the 17th century when the Russian ambassador first donated a pair from Astrakhan. In 1977, the Russians presented another pair, named Astra and Khan, but one died and one went to London Zoo. We went to look at his present pelicans, two pairs which have come from South Africa. They were being kept in an enclosure that day, as their end of the Lake was dry, and didn't look too happy. Pelicans are expensive, around £1,200 a pair, and can be difficult to keep. 'People will feed them things like bread, although our notices tell them not to. The bread swells up in their stomachs, then they won't eat their fish and they can get heart complaints. We have to give them protein tablets, Vitamin A, with their afternoon fish.'

He thinks they were upset that day through being kept in the enclosure. They had been sick for most of the last few days. 'I think it's fear, not a stomach upset, that's what's made them sick. When they get chased by predators in the wild, they do sick up their food. It makes the predators stop and eat it.'

As for the visiting wild birds, his duties consist mainly of caring for any injured ones. He has to go across to Hyde Park three or four times a week when some member of the public, or a gardener, has spotted an injured animal. 'A lot of the trouble is caused by fishermen leaving bits of nylon line around, but it's better than it was. At one time I used to have to go to Hyde Park every day.' Other troubles are caused by those metal bits you pull off when you open cans of drink. 'The swans pick them up by mistake, when they're feeding at the bottom, and they get them stuck in their bottom bill. You can see a swan in difficulties, trying to get its foot in its bill to release the ring. But it can't. Swans aren't very good with their legs. They haven't got hands.'

It is one thing to spot a wild bird in distress, but another thing to catch it. He and his assistant were currently stalking a wild herring gull in St James's Park which they had noticed was wearing a plastic ring round its neck, the sort which goes over a four-can pack of beer. They had tried for two weeks to catch it and release the plastic, but had failed so far.

His home is a few hundred yards away, on the Mall, in a little lodge which is part of Clarence House. He can therefore honestly say that his next-door neighbour is the Queen Mother. It means of course that he is on call all the time, whenever any bird does something silly with a beer can.

'I *like* being on call. I prefer being outdoors. I specially like being called out at six on a summer morning. That's the best time in St James's Park, when the day has dawned but the general public haven't yet arrived. You get quite a few regular bird watchers at that time. They live miles out in the London suburbs, but come in early just to see our birds, have a quiet hour or so bird watching before going to work. We get things like woodpeckers, woodcocks, red wing, things you don't often see in the suburbs. And we've now got kestrels. They nest in the Government buildings, but swoop down into the Park to kill the sparrows. Oh, it's a wonderful sight, early in the morning in the Park.'

I left by the Horse Guards Parade entrance, where I'd come in, and saw behind me a notice overlooking the Lake, warning the public not to feed the pelicans. 'Death is often caused by the wrong feed.' Very true. Even humans, whether suburb or city dwellers, know that.

CHAPTER TWO

Hyde Park

Hyde Park is the People's Park. By comparison, St James's Park seems rather exclusive and formal with a carefully discreet aura which it has picked up from all those civil servants and terribly important politicians. It can often look like an adjunct of Buckingham Palace on Garden Party days when the nation's toffs stroll through St James's and Green Park, proudly clutching their heavily-embossed invitations from the Lord Chamberlain. It is hard to imagine tickets or invitations ever being required for anything in or around Hyde Park. The world and his wife are more than welcome there.

All classes have for centuries come to enjoy themselves in Hyde Park and it has a vast range of recreational facilities. It is also where public demonstrations are held, where people assemble before their marches, or where they march to in order to publicise their cause. In the 1960s, the CND marches massed crowds of 200,000 in Hyde Park. In the 1850s, even bigger crowds came for the Great Exhibition. You can get permission to hold almost any sort of meeting in Hyde Park, apart from religious. They try not to get involved in that. Down with the Queen, out with the Bomb, in with Feminism, away with Abortion, all those sorts of things are perfectly possible. But don't start on God.

On a fine summer's day you can get up to 50,000 people using Hyde Park. There's enough space for them all as it is four times the size of St James's, with 360 acres, and is the biggest of the Central Parks. It is near the major shopping centre of Oxford Street, as well as the rather smarter shops in Knightsbridge, very handy for all tourists and visitors to London, but it is in itself a prime tourist attraction.

For many years, the Park's first visitors each morning have been the swimmers, arriving about 5.30 and heading for the Lido on the Serpentine for an early-morning dip, breaking the ice in the winter when necessary. There is some doubt at present about the long-term future of the Lido. It has been costing the Royal Parks £118,000 a year, to staff it full-time, maintain it and put chlorine in the water. Since the Government economy cuts there has been no resident attendant. It is to be hoped they can find a way of keeping it properly open again in the future.

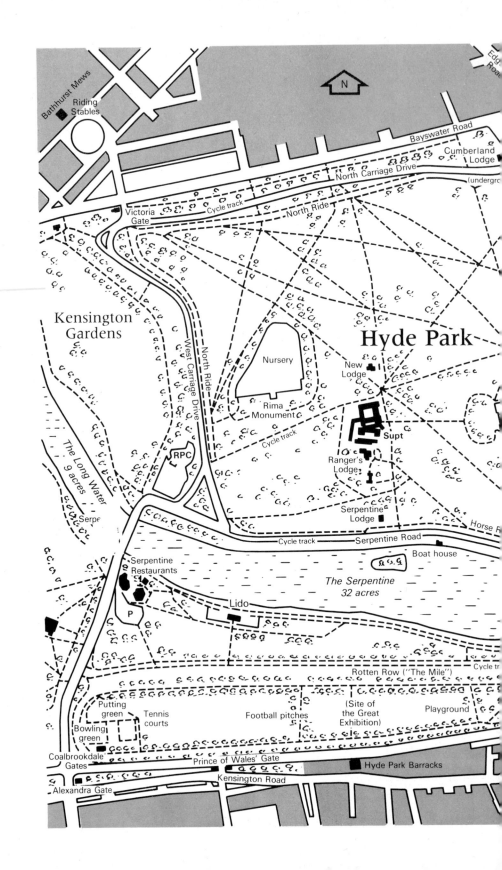

N

Bathurst Mews

Riding Stables

Bayswater Road

Cumberland Lodge

North Carriage Drive

(undergro

Victoria Gate

Cycle track

North Ride

Kensington Gardens

West Carriage Drive

North Ride

Nursery

New Lodge

Hyde Park

Rima Monument

Cycle track

Supt

RPC

Ranger's Lodge

The Long Water 9 acres

Serpentine Lodge

Horse R

Serpe

Cycle track

Serpentine Road

Boat house

Serpentine Restaurants

The Serpentine 32 acres

P

Lido

Rotten Row ("The Mile")

Cycle tr

Putting green

Tennis courts

Football pitches

(Site of the Great Exhibition)

Playground

Bowling green

Coalbrookdale Gates

Prince of Wales' Gate

Kensington Road

Hyde Park Barracks

Alexandra Gate

Edg Roa

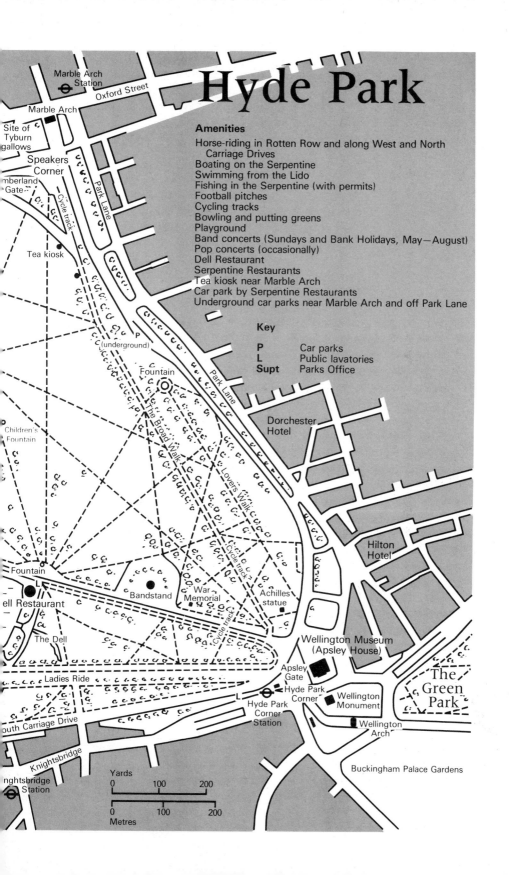

Hyde Park

Amenities

Horse-riding in Rotten Row and along West and North
    Carriage Drives
Boating on the Serpentine
Swimming from the Lido
Fishing in the Serpentine (with permits)
Football pitches
Cycling tracks
Bowling and putting greens
Playground
Band concerts (Sundays and Bank Holidays, May—August)
Pop concerts (occasionally)
Dell Restaurant
Serpentine Restaurants
Tea kiosk near Marble Arch
Car park by Serpentine Restaurants
Underground car parks near Marble Arch and off Park Lane

Key

P	Car parks
L	Public lavatories
Supt	Parks Office

Marble Arch
Station
Oxford Street

Marble Arch

Site of
Tyburn
gallows

Speakers
Corner

mberland
Gate

Cycle track

Park Lane

Tea kiosk

P
C (underground)

Fountain

Children's
Fountain

The Broad Walk

Lovers' Walk

Park Lane

Dorchester
Hotel

Hilton
Hotel

Fountain

L
ell Restaurant

The Dell

Bandstand

War
Memorial

Cycle track

Achilles
statue

Wellington Museum
(Apsley House)

Apsley
Gate

Hyde Park
Corner

Hyde Park
Corner
Station

Wellington
Monument

The
Green
Park

Ladies Ride

outh Carriage Drive

Knightsbridge

nghtsbridge
Station

Wellington
Arch

Buckingham Palace Gardens

Yards
0   100   200

0   100   200
Metres

Hyde Park: famous for centuries of demonstrations

Around six o'clock, the runners arrive. There have always been a few, but the few have become swarms in the last ten years since the mania for jogging began. It is an ideal park to jog in, as it is all so flat with lots of wide open stretches of grass where you can plan your own individual route and be undisturbed. There are few flower beds or park-like bits to be negotiated, unlike Kensington Gardens or St James's.

At seven o'clock, you see the first of the dog-walkers, soon followed by a stream of commuters who criss-cross the Park for the next two hours on their way to work. Hyde Park is so central, right in the middle of the capital's main hotel and office areas, such as Mayfair, Knightsbridge, Kensington, Bayswater. The quickest, easiest, nicest way to and from these districts is by crossing the Park. Public transport round the outside is very difficult, especially in the rush hour.

From 10.30 to 2 o'clock, the Park is taken over by visitors, most of them from overseas, and then at 4 the first of the commuters re-appear, on their way home, followed at about 6 by the locally based joggers who have already arrived home, but have now turned out for their second dose of punishment.

Until relatively recently, Hyde Park's evening visitors included scores of prostitutes, who have used all the central London Parks for several centuries, but since 1956 the laws have forced them elsewhere. A lot of people still sleep overnight in the park, most of them foreign students – or try to, until the police move them along. (Hyde Park is patrolled by the metropolitan police.)

There is one activity, however, which really distinguishes Hyde Park from all the other London Parks. It is just one of the many sports which the Park caters for, along with rowing, fishing, cycling, bowling, putting and swimming, and it is a sport which is also offered by several other parks across London, but somehow Riding in the Park has always conjured up an image of Hyde Park, ever since the quality first cantered there along Rotten Row.

One fine spring morning I set off to capture the day's first rider, hoping I could apprehend a suitable specimen without doing myself any injury. The Park seemed so wonderfully fresh at seven in the morning, that sort of

Rotten Row in Hyde Park: once the 'Route du Roi', now for commoners as well as Kings

freshness which you can taste and feel, which takes over your whole body and being and which you can remember hours later, when the city day has arrived and such senses become dulled and tainted. It is not simply a feeling. You could prove it. The grass is damp and fresh, having been bathed by the morning dew, and the air has been cleansed by the trees which have able to breathe their best at night when the traffic fumes have gone. Pity the poor New Yorker. I have been in Central Park at seven in the morning and still tasted concrete.

Early morning is the time real riders love best. You can sometimes see up to a hundred horses at one time in Hyde Park, some of them going quite fast, though technically, so the notices warn, no galloping is allowed. But in the early morning stillness, with no humans in the way, there are those young cavalry officers who break the rules, just as they have done for the last few hundred years.

I eventually got talking, early that morning, to one of the riders, a young lady called Marion Eason. She goes riding in Hyde Park once a week and has done so for four years. She grew up on a farm in the Cotswolds, where she rode all the time, and was determined to keep it up when she came to London to work as a picture researcher. Her country friends can't believe her when she tells them she can get two miles of perfect riding, right in the heart of London.

'The incongruity of it all is marvellous – being able to ride in beautiful parkland, yet know that modern life is all around. Some of the facilities are *better* than the country. There's an all-weather riding track just beside the Serpentine, so you never get bogged down in mud the way you can do in the country. The Mile ride is so wide that there's space to do dressage practice.'

'The Mile' is what the regulars call Rotten Row these days. All the other stretches have their own names, such as the Ladies' Ride, which is the lower, narrower part of the Rotten Row circuit. Then there's the North Ride which runs parallel with Bayswater Road.

'You don't have pheasants flying up when you ride past, or see any cows coming to the gate to watch you, but you can spot members of the Royal Family being driven through the Park, or gun carriages, or a troop of the Household Cavalry. Life in the Park is never dull. There's always something to see.

'We vary our route each day. Horses can go flat and stale and nappy if you make them do the same things. Nappy? That's when they won't go forward. You're not a rider, are you? When it's *very* early morning, and I'm not being observed, and I feel I'm alone in the world, I might go quite fast. I don't call it galloping. Just a pipe-opener. To open the horse's pipes. You say you've never ridden?

'The exercise is terrific, especially if you've got a hangover from the night before. "There's nothing better for the inside of a man than the out-side of a horse." I'm not sure who said that. I'm always quoting it. Was it Churchill? Jolly true anyway. Does wonders for the liver. Really shakes you up.'

In order to find the stables she uses, I had to follow her and a little group of riders out of the Park, wondering where they could all be going, never having noticed any stables anywhere near Hyde Park before. They left the Park at Victoria Gate, crossed the Bayswater Road, and in minutes disappeared down a mews I never knew existed, Bathurst Mews, one of those hidden-away, bijou London mews, with a spattering of bow windows and lines of window boxes, generously loaded. There was a white Rolls Royce outside one house, with the letters DC, standing for Dave Clark, so I was told, the Sixties pop musician. There seemed no sign of any stables till I came across two girls in jodhpurs who were mucking out and sweeping up manure from the cobbles. Near where Marion stopped was an old blacksmith, unbelievably dirty with charcoal, as if rented from the RSC, getting ready to light his fire and start work on his anvil. This was Old Wally the farrier who visits the stables once a week to shoe the horses. The whole mews looked like a stage set, a scene that had been painted on, only to be removed after the performance. Towering over it all was the vast bulk of the Royal Lancaster Hotel, but of course they wouldn't show that in the film version.

Marion hires her horse for £7 an hour from the Ross Nye Riding Stables, one of three commercial stables open to the public around the Park, two of which are in Bathurst Mews. Between them they have 48 horses. Then there are three private stabling establishments which also use Hyde Park – the Civil Service Riding Club which has about 12 horses, the Royal Mews which keeps 20 and then the biggest of all, the Household Cavalry, which has 130 horses. Altogether, there are about 200 horses who regularly use the Park. Any other rider can of course use the Park as riding in Hyde Park is open and free to all. You often see horse boxes standing on a parking meter while the horse and rider have gone off for a quick trot round Rotten Row.

Almost all the customers at Ross Nye's Stable are regulars, although he will give a casual customer a ride, if he has a gap. He has sixteen horses and four full-time staff, which includes one of his two daughters. He goes out with almost every party, keeping them in a group, for safety and for insurance purposes. There are usually three daily rides, starting firstly at seven in the morning. At 11 there is what he calls his 3M ride – Mid Morning Mums – then at 4.30 he has the after-school ride. On Saturdays and Sundays there are four rides a day. Monday is the day off, for the horses and the staff.

That morning, for the 7 o'clock trot, he had five riders – an Argentinian lady lawyer, a Canadian academic, an English TV producer and two girls, including Marion. He has slightly more female customers than male, but he maintains they come from all classes. Until recently he had a dustman's daughter.

'The price is very reasonable for an hour's exercise,' said Marion, getting off her horse and going upstairs into Ross's private quarters for some morning toast and coffee. He likes to treat all his regulars as family friends. 'I could have my hair streaked once a week – but that would cost me £30. Riding is a much cheaper pleasure.'

Ross Nye is an Australian from Queensland and grew up with horses on his grandfather's 700 square mile cattle station. He came to London in 1964 with his wife Ruth, a well-known Australian concert pianist. At the time, he was acting as her manager, fitting his life to her career. They had gone first to New York where she studied with Claudio Arrau, then had come to London to give some concerts. They decided to stay on, though as her manager he personally didn't have a lot to do. 'I was also her secretary, doing her letters, answering her phone. Secretaries don't get to sleep with the artists, so that's why I always called myself her manager. It sounded better.'

But there was still too little to do, so for a year he took on various part-time jobs, as a labourer, as an exerciser of people's horses, thinking perhaps he might be a farm manager, but he soon found that sort of job harder to come by than in Australia. One day in 1965 he saw some riding stables advertised on a short let in the *Horse and Hound* and bought the remaining lease. The premises were pulled down five years later, but on January 1, 1970, he moved to Bathurst Mews.

His wife is still a concert pianist, though she doesn't do as much travelling these days. She has a few pupils who come to her from different parts of the world. I could hear her practising in the next-door room as we sat eating and talking in the kitchen. From down below, came the sounds of the horses being fed. They get their oats, chaff, bran, sugar beet and pony nuts three times a day, at 8, 12 and 5 o'clock. Lucky horses. Their quarters are immaculate. 'You might see some droppings in the Royal Mews,' said one of his staff, 'but *never* in our stables.'

The previous year had been the poorest for business since he began. The winter had been hard, the recession had hit people's pockets while his rates went up all the time. He'd fought his own little battle to stop the clocks being changed, even badgering his own MP, but without success. He argued that his after-school rides are now impossible from October to March because of the dark evenings. All the same, he seemed cheerful enough, and his hospitality was generous, even to a stranger who had just arrived. All he hoped was that next year would be better. Whatever happens, he will always work with horses. He is particularly proud of his riding lessons for disabled children, sent by the ILEA, which he gives on Thursdays, a scheme under the patronage of Princess Anne.

'I think riding in the Park is *safer* than riding in the country. You quickly get used to the traffic. Crossing the Bayswater Road is remarkably easy. In the country, you never know if there's going to be a speeding van coming down the next lane, late for some appointment, thinking the way is clear. That's how you *do* get accidents. We've had a few sprains, a couple of broken wrists, that's all. The only serious incident was a horse which got loose one day in the park. That could have been nasty. Luckily he came home on his own, uninjured.

'We all say hello to each other when we pass other riders. Being an Australian, I've always done that, though some of the young cavalry officers might be a bit stand-offish.'

I then walked back into the Park looking for a second breakfast, a treat for myself for having made such an early and successful start to the day. I crossed the Serpentine and made for the new restaurant at the end of the bridge, a very modern building with six glazed pyramids on top. I had always imagined they were sheer decoration but on close inspection I could see that they contained bars and eating areas, all with splendid views right up the Serpentine. The building was much bigger than I had expected with several floors and several sorts of restaurants. I followed directions to a cafeteria on the lower floor. It was a dull morning and the place was almost deserted, except for a few isolated couples, staring out at the Lake, as if at a seaside resort out of season, waiting for the weather, or their life, to improve. In one corner, a middle-aged couple held hands shiftily under the table. Two young mothers were deep in conversation while three younger children ran around noisily. An old man in another corner was talking to himself. Nearby, a dotty-looking man, this time quite young, was arguing with a blank wall. London Parks do get their share of loonies.

It was all clean and bright, despite the main colours being a rather lurid yellow and sickly red, but somehow it was soulless, like a motorway café. I had a coffee, which was fresh and quite pleasant, and examined the Black Forest Gâteau, price 65p, but decided against it. The world seems full of Black Forest Gâteaux these days. There must be a mine somewhere, with Trust House Forte owning the British concessions.

I went upstairs and explored the rest of the building, and that was much more interesting, if very much like a Hilton hotel. The restaurant looked a good place for Sunday lunch, as a new place to take my family, so I decided to ask for a menu and prices. There was a chef standing at the bar counter, in his chef's outfit, eating an early lunch, before the day's work began. He told me to wait. The manager would talk to me, but he was just finishing his lunch. It was about 12 o'clock.

The manager came across at last, in his jeans and jumper, not yet in his managerial finery, and said please sit down, what did I want, and proceeded to be very pleasant and helpful. He said he was called Abdin Nasralla but I could call him Toto. He explained that the building contained five units – a first-class restaurant; the Pergola restaurant which could be hired out for special parties; a public bar; a cocktail bar; and the self service buffet down below, the one which I'd just been to. He asked if I had admired the self-service bits. 'No queues, you see, yet in the summer we can serve 5,000 people there in one day!'

There is a staff of 124 in the height of the summer, which seemed enormous, but it reduces to 60 in the winter. 'In the winter, we are dead. In the winter, we are nothing. But in the summer, phew, you should see us in the summer.' He was very proud of the whole building, which he said had been built by a very famous architect. (Patrick Gwynne in 1963.) He was also proud, justifiably, of his own success.

He came to London on holiday nine years ago, from Egypt, with no English and no knowledge of the restaurant business. He was a student, planning to be a surveyor, but he fell in love with London and decided he must find work here and stay. He got a job in the restaurant he now runs, starting as a commis chef, the lowest grade in the kitchen, cutting up onions and peeling potatoes for eight hours a day.

'I had no English so I read the newspapers in my spare time and then I went to night school to learn. Then I go to Ealing Technical College to learn catering. I have my diploma, you know, HCIMA. I'm still studying and will have the highest exam this June.' Meanwhile, working hard every day, he rose in turn to be pastry chef, head chef, store manager, beverage manager, manager of the buffet, then finally manager of the whole complex.

Most customers, he said, come by car or taxi, which seems a shame. 'We get very busy in an evening when the Royal Albert Hall finishes early. Prince Charles's wedding, we were very busy that day. You know, we have a lady guitarist who sings in seven languages.' He's only sorry that most people in London, and visitors to the Park, still don't know they exist. They are not allowed any large signs outside, as it might interfere with the traffic going past.

He loves the Park and has taken advantage of it throughout his nine years in the restaurant. With only two hours off each afternoon, before the evening session, not much can be done, so when he wasn't studying he went for a walk round the Park or played tennis or football. Until recently, his waiters used to have their own team.

'My favourite bit is Kensington Gardens, the Round Pond I like very much. I had a flat in Queensway and I used to walk to work with my wife that way. It was beautiful. Now we live in North London. I like the Lido very much and the Bandstand and the Playground at Victoria Gate. I often bring my little daughter to play there.

'The Park is so big it amazes me. I talked to a workman painting the fence one day outside and he said it takes a whole year to paint the Hyde Park fences, then they start again. The horses, I like them very much. The roller skaters, I don't like them. They are dangerous for the traffic. We have a car accident outside the restaurant once every two weeks.

'People in London love their parks. All people need parks. People without parks are like plants without water. They will die without water as English people will die without green. They love green. They do appreciate it.

'When I first came from Egypt I could not believe all this green in London. We don't see green in Arab countries. There are no parks and the houses don't have gardens. There is no interest in gardening in Arab countries. When I see old people of sixty in England digging in their garden I think this is terrific. To be interested in one little flower, this is terrific. Nobody is asking them to do it. They just like to see the flowers coming up. It is a great thing. The English people keep the park tidy. They like tidy gardens. It's the tourists who drop litter. They don't read notices. The English look after it. It is a big credit to London.

'In Egypt, when I go home, they ask me about this Hyde Park. They have heard of it, oh yes. Everyone in Egypt knows about Hyde Park. They know it is where English people can stand up and swear about their Queen. They think that is interesting. That's the little bit they know. But I tell them all about the *green*. They don't know about green.'

I then walked back over the Serpentine Bridge to start my walk around the Park itself. So far I had met an Australian and an Egyptian, both now resident Londoners and both passionate enthusiasts for London and its parks. Before the day was out I was bound to meet some native English people at work in their own park.

The Serpentine Bridge, which is in excellent condition, is Scottish. It was the product of that remarkable East Lothian family, the Rennies, who were amongst the outstanding civil engineers of the Victorian era. Father John had the distinction of putting up three bridges across the Thames – Waterloo, Southwark and London Bridge – now all replaced or removed. (In the case of London Bridge, it has crossed the Atlantic and was last sighted alive and well in Arizona.) Sons George and John carried on the business, which included docks, harbours and canals, as well as great bridges. The Serpentine Bridge was the work of George Rennie and completed in 1826. It is now the last of the Rennie bridges still in use in London.

Not far from the bridge is something called the Rima Monument which was fenced off. I wondered if anybody these days ever looks at it. It is a statue by Jacob Epstein of what appears to be a naked lady doing something strange with birds and was put up in 1925 in memory of the

Boating on the Serpentine Lake

writer and naturalist, W. H. Hudson. His books are hardly read today, though *Green Mansions* is at least remembered by an older generation. Rima, apparently, is a goddess figure from this book and when Epstein's statue of her was first unveiled there was something of an outcry and she was repeatedly daubed with paint. It is hard now to imagine what all the fuss was about. Behind the statue, amongst the trees, is a bird sanctuary, which is why it is closed to the public.

The first grass mowing of the year had begun so I could feel a fresh, sharp smell in the air as I walked over the broad, grassy, empty expanses of the Park which border the Bayswater Road. In the distance I could hear the motor cars, but as I wandered alone, deep in my own green tundra, the traffic seemed remote and abstract. The Royal Lancaster Hotel came in sight again, the tallest building along the road, and then, as I got nearer Marble Arch, the GPO Tower took over, dominating the whole London skyline. Buckingham Palace stays still but the GPO Tower is everywhere. You catch sight of that familiar phallus in so many unexpected places, down narrow alleyways, through sudden windows, at the end of hidden streets, as if it has a life of its own and is wandering out and about the London streets in its seven league boot. Being so tall and thin, the GPO Tower must only have one leg. I refuse to call it Telecom Tower.

Marble Arch, the chunk that is an arch, as opposed to that dreadful roundabout and traffic bottle-neck, is indeed made of marble and was designed by John Nash in 1828 as the main gateway to Buckingham Palace, part of some general fancy landscaping that went on around the Mall and St James's Park to make Buck House suitably impressive as the monarch's main palace. The Arch was removed to Hyde Park in 1851, to act as an entrance to the Park, but it has subsequently been divorced from the Park by all the road and traffic changes. Today, Marble Arch houses a little police station. So are the mighty fallen, or at least demoted to the ranks.

It is hard to appreciate, as one views this mad maelstrom, London's second busiest traffic bottle-neck after Hyde Park Corner, that it is basically a simple crossroad, a junction of two straight routes which have been in use since Roman days. The north-south route was once Watling Street, now divided into Edgware Road and Park Lane. In a car, the connection between them is tortuous, thanks to all the one-ways, but on the map you can see it is really one straight line. Similarly, there seems little direct connection between Oxford Street and Bayswater Road today, but they too make a straight line, an east-west route known by the Romans as the Via Trinobantina.

The junction was therefore always an important one, even when it was for long inhabited by wild deer and wolves. With the growth of London, it became a convenient place, just beyond the town, to drag out baddies and hang them up for all travellers to see. The first recorded execution on this spot, using the Tyburn tree, named after a little stream called the Ty-burn, was in 1196. From 1571 to 1759, permanent gallows were set up, still known as the Tyburn Tree. Over the centuries, some famous and infamous bodies have been hanged, drawn and quartered, on this very junction, where now the mighty roar of the Cortina would be enough to drown the sound of any final agonies. Perkin Warbeck, who thought he could claim the throne of England, departed here in 1499, as did Edmund Campion and other Jesuit martyrs in 1581. Oliver Cromwell's body was gibbeted and beheaded here in 1661, on the restoration of King Charles II, after it had been exhumed from Westminster Abbey. The body was buried under the Tyburn gallows while his head was stuck on a pole at Westminster Hall.

In 1783, London's public executions were moved to outside Newgate Prison, a more suitable setting, or so it was thought. By this time, there were smart houses and smart people living all around Hyde Park and they did not care to have the hangings taking place on their very door-step. They were not necessarily against the actual principle, and many people, such as Thackeray and Dickens, have written vivid accounts of going to watch the hangings in London, but it was the noise of the rabble who attended these spectacles which they considered had become rather unseemly.

How strange that today on almost the same spot we should have Speakers' Corner. Could there be a connection? Were the condemned allowed some final words, a farewell to their executors? It seems unlikely as Speakers' Corner is a Victorian creation, which grew up long after the gallows had moved to Newgate. It was an unofficial meeting place at first, for those wanting to express their views. The police broke up the meetings if they could, but this led to so many riots, and even more trouble, that there was a movement to make it legal, allowing the public to speak freely 'in their own park'. In 1872, the site for Orators, or Speakers' Corner, was officially assigned. Every Sunday morning, you can still exercise the British right of free speech and stand there and pour out your grievances, undisturbed by the police and even these days by few hecklers. It has become a rather tame spectacle dominated by cranks, of interest to tourists rather than real revolutionaries. No sensible fanatic would bother straining lungs in the open air when there are TV and radio chat shows which will willingly have on almost any fluent loud-mouth . . . and pay them good money.

Emma Goldman, the American feminist, realised the truth about Speakers' Corner as long ago as 1895, so she reported in her autobiography. 'Outdoor meetings in America are rare, their atmosphere always charged with impending clashes between the audience and the police. Not so in England. Here the right to assemble in the open is an institution. It has become a British habit, like bacon for breakfast. It was a novel experience to talk out of doors, with only a lone policeman placidly looking on. Alas, the crowd, too, was placid. It felt like climbing a steep mountain to speak against such inertia. I soon grew tired and my throat to hurt.' She did eventually get some lively hecklers, but they were in it for the sport, and her attempts at a reply 'kept the crowd in spasms', so she gave up, defeated, and never appeared there again. 'My work meant too much for me to turn it into a circus for the amusement of the British public.'

Is Speakers' Corner a cunning Establishment plot, designed to take the wind out of the wild, let loose the lunatic on an uncaring world?

I headed south from Marble Arch, following the line of Park Lane, which formed a new and different sort of boundary, the view this time dominated by smart hotels, Grosvenor House and the Dorchester, and tallest of all, like a slab of cheese turned on its end, the Hilton, from which a good view can be obtained of the gardens of Buckingham Palace, for those unfortunates without Garden Party tickets.

I came to a meeting place of ten paths, all converging near one junction which did not appear to have any distinguishing features, surrounded only by acres of empty, treeless grass. There is an underground car park below, which now precludes any tree planting. Yet, historically, this was a very important assembly point. Elizabeth I reviewed her troops from here and Charles II promenaded with the ladies and gentlemen of his court. There was one recent enormous gathering, in May 1979, when a children's party was held to celebrate the Year of the Child. I had forgotten about this until I came to a little fountain which had not appeared on any of the Royal Parks' leaflets I had read so far. It was just outside the WCs, an oddly shaped statue, with lots of childlike designs and figures peeping out, animals, aeroplanes and boats, and on the top a lady with a child. I have called it a fountain but, even though I pressed several knobs, no water emerged. The writing on the side was hard to read, considering how recently the statue had been erected. Mrs Thatcher, the Prime Minister, unveiled it on December 4, 1981, so it said, to mark the party which 180,000 children attended. The Queen came, and so did the Duke of Edinburgh, Princess Anne and other well-known people of the day. Could this be the most recent statue in any of the Royal Parks? It is not a thing that happens much these days. As we know, it was the Victorians who were so keen on statues and drinking fountains and shoved them up all over the place. I made a note to find a statue expert from the D. of E.

I went into the WC, observing that I would not have been allowed in if I had been wearing 'Roller Skates and Skate Boards', which a sign said were strictly prohibited. I wonder what Victorian children were not allowed to do in the Park? Cycle probably, play with hoops, hop scotch, skipping. They would not have known what skate boards were, nor would we, just ten years ago.

When I reached the Serpentine Road, I turned left and headed for the Bandstand. Since leaving the horse riders, I had passed only two people in the Park all morning, a lady with a dog and a suspicious-looking man hanging round the lavatories, perhaps a secret roller skate freak, looking for his chance to get inside. It had become overcast and, as I approached the Bandstand, the heavens opened and down it all came, so I rushed quickly to get some shelter. Below me on the grass, just outside the Bandstand, lay a tramp, resting amidst his bundles, his back to the Bandstand, a newspaper on his knees in front of him. He seemed to be asleep. I thought about telling him the rain had started, but decided not to.

'What a beastly day.' A very smartly-dressed man had suddenly appeared out of the bushes, raced up the steps and was standing on the Bandstand beside me: a businessman from the City perhaps, wearing a crombie coat with a velvet collar. He certainly did not look like a humble clerk who crosses the Park every day, more a tycoon with a Rolls Royce parked in Park Lane, awaiting his pleasure. He said he was on his way from the Hilton Hotel, where he'd had one business meeting, and was about to go to the Dorchester Hotel, where he had another. He ran a factory out in the suburbs, something to do with printing machinery. When in London on business meetings, he always tried to walk everywhere, especially across the Park. Kensington Gardens was really his favourite, especially the Flower Walk. As a bachelor, he'd had a flat in Kensington and had courted his wife in Ken Gardens, so it would always be a romantic place for him.

We chatted while the rain fell and when it had stopped we shook hands and said goodbye, never to meet again, but we'd shared fifteen minutes together, as if alone in the universe, except for that tramp below. Had he heard our conversation? Was he a spy, waiting for his contact? An Irish bomber, preparing some devastation? Had the posh gent really been in printing or had he been about to deliver something to the tramp and I had ruined everything by being there and being nosey and asking him all sorts of questions?

At the far corner of Hyde Park, right beside Hyde Park Corner itself, is the massive bronze statue of Achilles, one of London's most impressive, and strangest, monuments. It was the work of Sir Richard Westmacott, RA, erected in 1822, and was known at the time as the 'Ladies Trophy'. Its origins go back to 1814 when during some celebrations in the Park to honour Nelson and Wellington, organised by the Prince Regent and attended by Foreign Monarchs and English Bishops, a lady got so carried away by all the festivities that she decided to strip off and have a swim. She was encouraged by some men nearby, but just as she was about to plunge in, some older ladies rushed forward and hurried her away. (Could this have been the first recorded public streak in a London Park?)

Not long afterwards, a Committee of Ladies, so upset by this disgusting incident, decided to open an appeal to raise money for a suitable monument to the Duke of Wellington, a fitting but tasteful tribute to his greatness. Subscriptions poured in and they raised in all £10,000, enough to let Westmacott do it in style, as the world can see to this day. So big was the statue that part of the Park wall had to be knocked down to let it in. The collossal male body striking an heroic pose, now known as Achilles, was based neither on Achilles nor indeed Wellington but taken from the statue of a horse tamer in Rome, but to please the ladies Westmacott made the actual head look a bit like the Duke. Lower down, alas, it was obvious that for the statue's fine muscular frame he was decidedly under endowed. What an offence to the ladies, to see such a naked sight, let alone an affront to Wellington's pride. Naturally, Cruikshank and the other cartoonists of the day were quick to ridicule it. In 1850, a French soldier, a veteran of Waterloo, exclaimed in glee when he first saw it. 'Enfin, on est vengé.' Today, an oak leaf covers the vital part.

The sun was trying to come out so I went to look for the Dell, the only bit of flower gardening inside Hyde Park, just at the eastern end of the Serpentine. It is in a deep little dip so you can't see it till you are upon it. It looked nice enough, full of spring flowers with a stream and little waterfall and a chunk of rock which looked as if it could be something left over from Stonehenge. Some people do assume it is prehistoric, but I found out later it is the remains of a vast Victorian drinking fountain, put up in 1861, then later removed. This bit of Cornish granite, weighing over 7 tons, was too heavy to move.

South of the Serpentine, running almost parallel with it, is the broad, tree lined mile-long sandy track known to the world as Rotten Row, though, as I had discovered that morning, the riders who actually use it today call it The Mile. The name is said to come from 'route du roi', in the days when the King took this route between his palace at Westminster and Kensington Palace. It became a popular rendezvous for the fashionable to preen themselves and, so they hoped, to be seen.

Between the main road and Rotten Row, in an area now covered with football pitches and tennis courts, was the site of the Great Exhibition of 1851, one of the most successful exhibitions London has ever seen. It was Prince Albert's idea and over six million people came to see it, ensuring a profit of £165,000, enough being left over to set up the museums in South Kensington. The poor old Wembley Exhibition of 1924, an equally ambitious attempt to show the work of our wonderful Empire, lasted for two years, but ended in bankruptcy. Those Victorians certainly knew how to project themselves.

The Exhibition centred on a magnificent Crystal Palace, designed by Sir Joseph Paxton, who had previously built the glasshouse at Chatsworth. It measured 2,000 feet by 400 feet, but it was dismantled after the Exhibition and rebuilt at Sydenham in South London, in the area now known as Crystal Palace, though there's not much of the Palace to be seen today. It was destroyed by fire in 1926.

The Serpentine looked rather stormy, with some very convincing waves ebbing about the boathouse. The weather and the earliness of the year were keeping away any crowds and the whole length of the water seemed absolutely deserted, yet in the long history of Hyde Park the Serpentine has seen some of its most exciting and dramatic moments.

There was no lake of any sort when the Park was first begun, back in Henry VIII's day. He had already created for himself St James's Park, just six years earlier, but in 1536 he decided that 600 acres or so of land belonging to the Abbot of Westminster, in the old Manor of Hyde, would do him very nicely for another deer park. His idea was to give himself a continuous stretch of hunting territory going almost all the way from his Palace at Westminster to the slopes of Hampstead. Some sort of high fence was put round it, the public kept out, and a Ranger appointed. It remained a Royal Park, kept for hunting, for the next century, until James I and his son Charles I opened it to the public.

When Cromwell and the Commonwealth Government took over, it was decided to sell off most of the old Crown lands. Hyde Park, which was then 621 acres, was sold in three lots for £17,000. John Evelyn, according to his diary of April 11, 1653, found that he now had to pay for admittance. 'I went to take aire in Hyde Park, when every coach was made to pay a shilling, and horse sixpence, by the sordid fellow who purchased it off the State.'

With the Restoration, and the return of Charles II from France, the whole of Hyde Park was taken back into royal control, and it was opened to the public once again, without any charges. By 1663, Pepys recorded that it had once more become a popular meeting place.

It was Queen Caroline, wife of George II, who did most to alter the face of Hyde Park, and the adjoining Kensington Gardens, and her most ambitious project was the creation of a large lake, right through the Park, now known as the Long Water in Kensington Gardens and the Serpentine in Hyde Park. There had been a little stream coming into Hyde Park, near the present Lancaster Gate tube station, the West Bourne, which led into various little pools, but the whole scheme was man-made, a piece of romantic fantasy, designed to look as 'natural' as possible. The fashion for perfectly straight, ornamental canal-like ponds, in the old Dutch style, had now gone, denounced as old-fashioned by William Kent, the latest arbiter of what was good taste. The banks gently curved and a long, serpentine bend was put in the middle.

Over 200 workmen were employed on digging out the Lake and the total cost was £6,000. For the opening ceremony on May 1, 1731, two yachts were launched, for the amusement of the King and Queen and their children and important guests. It was an international occasion and presents arrived from abroad. The Doge of Genoa sent the Queen a large number of tortoises to put in her newly-designed Park.

Later on, Hyde Park was used for various national celebrations and rejoicing, and the Serpentine always played a major part. In 1814, with the end of the Napoleonic wars – or at least Napoleon's exile to Elba – a mock battle was staged on the Serpentine with fireworks going off and the 'enemy' being ceremonially sunk.

In the summer, the water often became rather smelly and foul, especially with the growth of all those large houses and terraces around the Park, many of them using the little West Bourn as a sewer. In 1820, Princess Lieven wrote to Prince Metternich about the sort of people who now used the Park. 'Good society no longer goes there, except to drown itself. Last year, they took from its lake the body of a very beautiful woman, expensively dressed, who had probably been a whole week in the water.' The lady referred to was probably Harriet Westbrook, the first wife of Shelley, who committed suicide in the Lake in December 1816. Others, alas, have since followed her tragic example. Each year, there are around four suicides, or suicide attempts, in the Serpentine.

With such sombre thoughts I walked over to the boat house, hoping to talk to someone in charge, as the season officially had begun, if only just, and I could see a few empty boats tied up, bobbing in expectation. There was a lady sitting on her own behind a little grille, waiting to take money from prospective customers, but as there were none she was knitting and at the same time watching a little colour TV beside her on a table. She allowed me through, into the back parlour office of Ron Bullman, the boatman in charge.

He always tells people who see him taking the cash by the handful in the height of the summer that they should see him now, stuck in the depths of March. That is when they always open, but not much business is ever done till after Easter. Even then, hiring out boats is not, on the whole, the big business it once was.

Mr Bullman is 47, tall and burly with a gold necklace, an earring, and fair hair that might have been bleached, or could it have been all those seasons of Hyde Park sun. He started in rowing boats 32 years ago as a boat boy in Greenwich Park at £2 a week, working for a firm called J. and T. Maxwell which at one time had 10,000 boats for hire, throughout all the Royal Parks and around many of England's seaside resorts. 'We used to take a bomb.' Now the firm has just 300 boats and they concentrate only on the Royal Parks – and even then they serve only three parks. Hyde Park is their main concern, where they have 120 boats, followed by Regent's Park with 100 boats and then Greenwich where they have 50. They did Bushy Park till a couple of years ago but gave up, despite the Royal Parks people asking them to continue. 'The pond at Bushy is small and hidden away. It just wasn't worth it.'

He blames TV for hitting rowing boats, especially at the seaside. Holiday-makers now go back to their digs and watch TV in the evening. At one time, people took out a rowing boat all evening, till dark. 'It happens in the Parks as well. They are empty at six, at least that's the British people. We're lucky here in that in the season 90% of our trade is with foreign tourists. They'd rather have a row round the Serpentine than go back and watch British TV.

'Arabs love it. So do the French. The French are usually the first each season, around April and May, then the Germans in June, and July it's the Italians and Spaniards. The big day for Arabs is a Sunday. They seem to take over the park on a Sunday evening. They have a row, then they sit around on the grass and the head man gives them a story. It's a fantastic sight to see.'

Mr Bullman is now a director of the firm. At Hyde Park, in the season, they have 12 men, at Regent's Park 8 and 4 at Greenwich. Prices, in 1982, were £1.80 an hour for a rowing boat which takes up to four people. They also have a motor launch at Hyde Park, which tours the Serpentine, and this costs 50p each. 'I still think it's the cheapest hour's entertainment in London. What we're praying for now is another heatwave like 1976. From June to September that year we had no rain and we did amazing business.'

His biggest problem is safety. You can't row under the Serpentine Bridge and into the Long Water any more. There was a fatal accident recently which helped to stop all that. It means that Mr Bullman and his men can now keep an eye on all the customers. Once they went under the Bridge, and round that serpent-like bend, they were lost to sight. There is still enough space to get a good row. The total area of both waters is 40 acres, stretching for almost one mile. The Serpentine section is the larger, covering about 30 acres, and it takes a good hour to row round its circumference.

'The water's 20 foot deep in some parts, so we have radio control on our three big motor boats, for use in any emergencies. Life jackets are provided for all rowers. You'll always get a few yobboes, but it's not as bad as it was. I think the deposit puts a lot of them off doing anything stupid. I don't stand a lot of nonsense, not on my boats. In 1962, the deposit was only 2/6 and you often found some yobbo had put his oar through the bottom. Now it's £2 deposit. The most unruly people today are the French students. They row out to the island and mess about. I've been to Paris and the police there are very quick to run them in. They think they can let their hair down, now they're in London.'

The Superintendent of Hyde Park is considered the number two in the whole of the Royal Parks' hierarchy. The present incumbent is Bob Legge, Superintendent of all three Central Royal Parks, and his office is not far from the Boathouse. He has a staff of 100 to look after Hyde Park, plus 45 in Kensington Gardens and he is also responsible for the 43 in St James's and Green Park. The total was 250 until the last year or so, but now it is down to under 200, as retirers and leavers have not been replaced.

He is aged 45 and comes from Torquay where his first job was as a garden boy for the local Parks Department at £2 a week. He had set his heart on being a gardener from the age of ten, promising himself he would be a Head Gardener by the age of 30. He did it in 1967, aged 29, when he arrived in London to be Deputy Superintendent. He was offered two jobs that year, the other being at a slightly higher salary in Liverpool, where he could have earned £1,300 a year. His wife preferred the Royal Parks in London, even though it was only £1,100 a year.

I was amazed by the lowness of the salaries, even though the year was 1967. You will never get rich in gardening. At the top of the ladder, the Royal Bailiff in 1982 was on a salary of some £18,000, followed by Mr Legge on £14,000 while an Assistant Superintendent earned about £9,500. At the bottom the lowest grade of gardener was on £100 a week and a labourer £87. A selected few do of course get accommodation in the Parks, but they still have to pay rent, which they all say is not cheap. Mr Legge was not complaining. 'I get paid for doing my hobby.' But he does get upset when gardeners these days are still classed as semi-skilled people. 'It's not fair. Plumbers, electricians, carpenters, they're all classed as skilled. We have a three-year apprenticeship, and lots of courses to do if you want promotion. To be a good gardener, you have to be a horticulturalist, botanist, entomologist, physicist, oh, you have to know about 20 different subjects. And don't forget, we're the world's oldest profession. Adam, after all, was the first gardener.'

Hyde Park's own Nursery is a short walk from his office, but it is very easy to go past and be unaware of its existence. It looks from the outside like a large shrubbery and you are guided round it, without realising, by following various curving paths. There is not the slightest hint of glass. Once inside, you come to 12 immense greenhouses which together cover three acres. The St James's Bird Man was living his own, isolated, remote life. But his slice was miniscule, just him and one assistant on a toy island. When you enter the Hyde Park Nursery you enter another world.

The man in charge is Jack Brown, an Assistant Superintendent. He comes from Blackpool where he joined their Parks Department as a boy of 15, then went into the Navy, worked at Wisley, Kew Gardens, then the old LCC before coming to the Hyde Park Nursery in 1969. They are responsible for supplying plants to all the Central Royal Parks. He has a staff of 26, all of them based solely in those hidden greenhouses.

He was sitting in a large, spacious, rather empty office, typing at a little yellow portable typewriter. Mr Legge had said he would ring and warn him I was dropping in, but the message had apparently not come through. Conversation proceeded very slowly. I felt like a specimen being suspiciously examined. Perhaps few strangers from outer space, from the

Nannies and children in Hyde Park

so-called real world out there beyond the greenhouses, ever venture into his private place. The superintendent figures I had met so far had betrayed their strong regional or grass root origins, from the Royal Bailiff downwards. Mr Brown seemed more of an officer figure, cool, calm and very organised. His office was artistic, if sparse, suitable for a very smart architect in a clever conversion in Covent Garden. Most Superintendents crouch in dark huts, skulking amidst the dusty and yellowing papers.

No, he couldn't think of any problems in his job. Things happen very smoothly. No, they don't suffer from much disease. Their hygiene is so good, washing out every pit, so it doesn't spread. And no, insects can't get a hold. They attack them before they can strike.

He handed me his 1982 order for plants, the numbers required by all the different departments he grows for, which included
St James's Park, 45,273,
Kensington Gardens, 40,855, and
Buckingham Palace, 8,885.

The grand total came to 120,000, a little less than the previous year and about half the total of ten years ago. The economy cuts, as we have seen, mean that flower beds are fewer and those that remain are not changed as frequently. All the same, it was an enormous amount of plants. Buying on the open market would probably cost them £1 million a year. They produce 300 different species, with geraniums being the most common, growing 30,000 a year. Begonias come next (25,000), followed by petunias (20,000), then asters (16,000) and marigolds (15,000).

Apart from those 120,000 bedding plants ordered by the various Parks, they also have to grow for decoration purposes, indoor as well as outdoor plants, for displays which are trundled round the various Government and Royal households. Some are for ordinary day-to-day use, to brighten up the Corridors of Power, or for more public occasions like State visits or events like Garden Parties or Trooping the Colour.

'If Buckingham Palace wants 500 begonias, I grow 1,000. If Number 10 Downing Street wants a special display for their entrance hall, or the staircase, I grow double whatever they might ask for. You can't afford to fail, not when you're dealing with those sorts of places.'

In the old days, they got lorry-loads of soil every season, all of which they carefully and richly treated with fertilisers. These days, soil has almost vanished from sight. Instead, they live on peat, Universal Peat Compost, which arrives ready mixed and disease-free, thereby reducing labour, time and expense. 'When we used soil, we would start the begonias in November in soil. Now we use peat and don't start until February. I'm talking about *semper florens* begonias of course. With peat, you can sow everything much later. It has revolutionised the growing process.'

I suggested, therefore, that there was no longer any need to have greenhouses on the ground. If soil has become obsolescent, their greenhouses could be anywhere, on top of Marble Arch or the roof of the Hilton Hotel, and we would have more space in Hyde Park for walking. Mr Brown said the future was even stranger than that. There would be no need one day to have sun or even light.

'One day, we will have growing rooms, with no windows at all. If you think about it, glass houses are very awkward. In the winter, the glass makes them terribly cold, and then too hot in the summer. What you want is *controlled* heat, an environment where you can create the perfect atmosphere.'

The problem of giving them light has been solved by the development of special fluorescent tubes which provide the necessary infra-red content. These window-less growing rooms can be much more easily insulated than a glass house. The walls are lined with silver paper to reflect the light, so saving more electricity. They have tried it out, at the Hyde Park Nurseries, but only for a short period. Apparently, the Department of the

Environment thought they should not be in the business of experimenting, but in America they have almost solved all the minor problems.

'It will mean that if you want a 30-acre nursery, you can do it on a one-acre site just by building a 30-storey building, piling the growing rooms on top of one another. In this overcrowded world, it will bring enormous savings in space and expense.'

We might have started our conversation rather coldly, and I had of course arrived out of the blue, but I left Mr Brown's office rather inspired by things to come. I then moved into the Nursery proper, to see how old-fashioned glass houses were coping.

Going under glass was like stepping into a vast and airy sauna bath. It was so hot and humid with a strange atmosphere and a dead, echo-less sound. I could see figures working away quietly at benches, as if cut off in time and space, filling pots with peat, taking cuttings, each isolated, lost in their own activities. I noticed several girls working away, and I talked to one of them, Helen Shaw, aged 22, from Dewsbury in Yorkshire, who was meticulously taking cuttings from a little bushy green plant which she said was a pilea, a type of fern-like greenery used mainly for sticking in display boxes at places like Number Ten.

She has seven 'O' levels and one 'A' level in biology, and left school at 18 to work in the local Water Authority's greenhouses. She was now part-way through studying horticulture for her diploma. Each morning she rises at 5.30, in a room she has found in Uxbridge, and spends an hour on the tube getting to work in time to start at 7.30. In the Royal Parks, they all start early, then finish at four, with just half an hour for lunch. Her back was still aching from bending over so much, but it was getting better. She had sniffed a lot in the early weeks, feeling the cold whenever she went out of the glass houses, but now she always put her coat on.

'We're hot house plants ourselves,' said Brian Batten, one of the senior gardeners who was supervising her work, a young man of 33 with a naval beard. 'I don't personally care for fresh air. A bomb could go off outside, and we'd never know. I don't actually like all those people outside. I prefer our silent world. At four o'clock, when I leave to go home, I'm always surprised in the summer to find there have been thousands of people outside in the park all day long. I feel like coming straight back in here again.

'When you work out in the gardens, the public just interfere with you. They call you over when you're planting something to ask what it is. You tell them. Then they say no it isn't. The older chaps, they just ignore the public.

'I am never ever bored or tired, not when I'm in here involved with plants. I can spend three weeks solid potting geraniums and never be fed up. I keep talking to them, you're going to be flowering for me, oh yes you are. I like to go like the clappers and set myself targets, see how many I can get done in a day. If someone else is on the same job, I like to compete with him or her, see who can be quickest.

" 'You've got two chances,' so I always say if I happen to knock some over and I'm putting them back in their pots. 'Grow or die.' "

I suppose we all have, plants as well as humans. Personally, I'd rather use up my chance in the open air, but in the Parks it does take all sorts, even those stuck willingly inside, to make life a pleasure for us all.

CHAPTER THREE

Kensington Gardens

You get a nicer class of person in Kensington Gardens, so all the locals say. Even the park keepers are proud that they have the Quality living on their doorstep. Kensington Gardens is the only London Park, either outer or central, Royal or Municipal, which contains a real, live Royal Palace, full of real, live Royal personages who can often be spotted out in the Park itself, or at least their appendages, being pushed in their prams.

On the map, Hyde Park runs straight on into Kensington Gardens, but of course maps give you facts, not flavours, measurements not mannerisms. Most visitors to either Park, even native Londoners, probably can't tell exactly where one ends and the other begins. They doubtless hardly care. It is all one continuous walk, full of variety, flowers and fun, trees and statues, boats and babies.

Once you have crossed the Serpentine Bridge road (on the West Carriage Drive, as it should be called) which bisects the two parks, you are in Kensington Gardens, and the atmosphere is very different. There is no public road in Kensington Gardens, no horse riding or football playing, no rowdy public meetings. In the Gardens, which is the term the regulars always use, becoming aghast if anyone refers to Kensington Gardens as a *Park*, there is an aloofness, a feeling of reserve, of being on a private estate.

The early history of the two parks (perhaps if I use a small p no one in Kensington will object) is linked. It began as part of that same tract of land which Henry VIII took over as his deer park, and made into Hyde Park, but it was with the arrival on the throne of William III in 1689 that the separate character of Kensington Gardens was created. He decided he did not fancy living in the Palace of Whitehall, right beside the river, as he suffered from asthma, and anyway he wanted to be able to get away from all the crowds and the courtiers. He inspected the little village of Kensington, at the far end of his park, where the air seemed fresh and the land a little higher, and he bought an old house called Nottingham House, along with an extra 26 acres of land, for £18,000. John Evelyn was rather scathing about it, dismissing it as a 'patched up building with gardens'.

Sir Christopher Wren was commissioned to rebuild and enlarge the property, to make it suitable for the Monarch, and from it emerged the

Kensington Palace we see today. To help the King's journey to work each day, from his new Palace to Whitehall, a road was cut along the side of Hyde Park to what is now Hyde Park Corner and then to St James's Park. It was called 'The South Carriage Drive', which is what it is called today. It was lit in the winter by 300 oil lamps, probably the world's first illuminated highway.

His wife, Queen Mary II, was very keen on gardening, especially the formal Dutch style, and she started to lay out the gardens around the new Palace. The next Queen, her sister Queen Anne, extended the gardens considerably, and created two features which are well-known today – the Orangery and the Sunken Garden.

It was, however, Queen Caroline, wife of George II, to whom we should be most grateful to for the grandeurs of Kensington Gardens, not just for the Serpentine in Hyde Park. She planted some magnificent avenues of trees outside the Palace gardens, taking in parts of Hyde Park, wide and straight with splendid vistas. The most impressive was the Broad Walk, 50 feet wide, which went right past the Palace. Near the Broad Walk, she decided to dig out a circular basin and fill it with water, creating a pond which would be viewed from the windows of the Palace, known today as the Round Pond. Nearby, her protégé William Kent put up a little temple-like building where she could sit and take tea.

The transformed Kensington Gardens were opened to the public at weekends, when the King and Queen were elsewhere, but formal dress had to be worn and all soldiers, sailors and liveried servants were excluded. This was greatly resented by some of the public, accustomed to walking at will in the adjoining Hyde Park, and bands of them gathered at the gates to mock the properly dressed gentlemen and ladies as they entered the Gardens.

The total cost of Queen Caroline's creations for the Gardens came to over £20,000. This was in 1730s currency. Today, such work would run into millions. George II must have been an ever-loving husband, or terribly wealthy, to have allowed such extravagance. In fact he didn't know how much had been spent. He thought she was using her own money and it was only after her death that he discovered the total and that it had come from royal finances.

Hyde Park had always been popular with footpads from earliest times and although Kensington Gardens were not as open, and were usually well guarded, the pickings could be much better. King George himself fell victim when an impudent highwayman climbed over the wall at Kensington and 'with a manner of much deference' relieved the King of his purse, his watch and his buckles.

The death of George II in 1760, from a heart attack as he was about to take a walk in the Gardens, marked the end of the first important stage in

Kensington Gardens

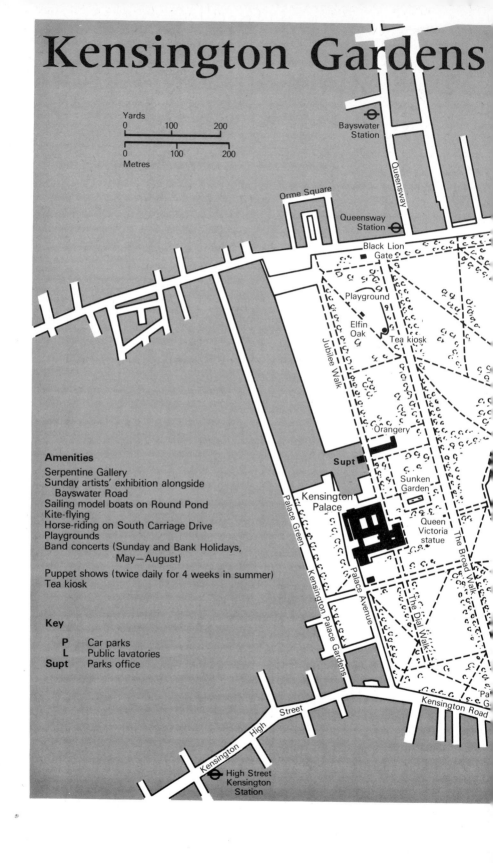

Yards
0   100   200

0   100   200
Metres

Bayswater
Station

Orme Square

Queensway

Queensway
Station

Black Lion
Gate

Playground

Elfin
Oak

Tea kiosk

Jubilee Walk

Orangery

Supt

Sunken
Garden

Kensington
Palace

Palace Green

Queen
Victoria
statue

The Broad Walk

Kensington Palace Gardens

Palace Avenue

The Dial Walk

Amenities

Serpentine Gallery
Sunday artists' exhibition alongside
  Bayswater Road
Sailing model boats on Round Pond
Kite-flying
Horse-riding on South Carriage Drive
Playgrounds
Band concerts (Sunday and Bank Holidays,
                May—August)

Puppet shows (twice daily for 4 weeks in summer)
Tea kiosk

Key

P   Car parks
L   Public lavatories
Supt Parks office

Kensington Road

Pa
G

Street

Kensington High

Kensington High Street

High Street
Kensington
Station

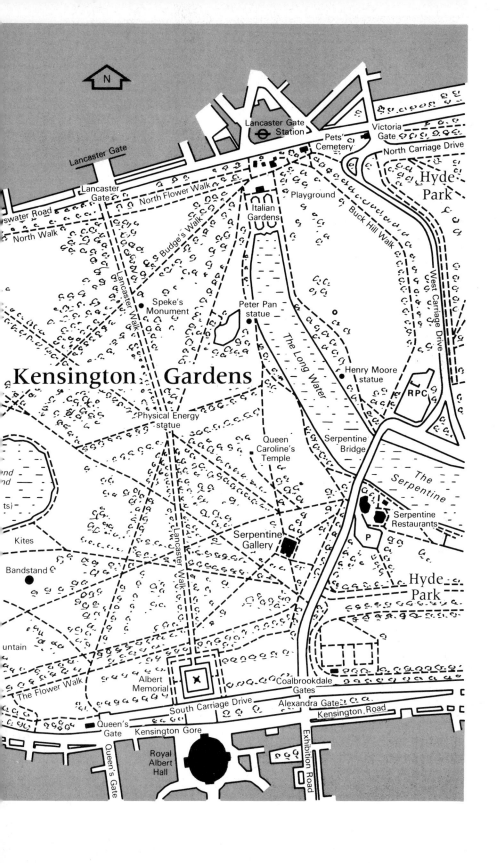

N

Lancaster Gate

Lancaster Gate Station

Pets' Cemetery

Victoria Gate

North Carriage Drive

Hyde Park

Lancaster Gate

North Flower Walk

Playground

Italian Gardens

Buck Hill Walk

Bayswater Road

North Walk

Budge's Walk

Speke's Monument

Peter Pan statue

Lancaster Walk

The Long Water

Henry Moore statue

West Carriage Drive

RPC

Kensington Gardens

Physical Energy statue

Queen Caroline's Temple

Serpentine Bridge

The Serpentine

...nd ...nd

...ts)

Kites

Lancaster Walk

Serpentine Gallery

Serpentine Restaurants

P

Bandstand

Hyde Park

...untain

The Flower Walk

Albert Memorial

Coalbrookdale Gates

South Carriage Drive

Alexandra Gate

Kensington Road

Queen's Gate

Kensington Gore

Queen's Gate

Royal Albert Hall

Exhibition Road

the Palace's history. Subsequent Monarchs no longer made it their main residence and the Gardens were eventually opened to all 'respectably dressed persons' all the year round.

I set off on my walk quite reasonably dressed, for the time of the year, walking once more over the Serpentine Bridge, but this time crossing into Kensington Gardens. I was aiming for the Serpentine Gallery, a building which used to be the Refreshment House. Now that they have the modern Serpentine Restaurant complex just across the road, they don't need it any more, but it does mean that Kensington Gardens has no eating place, apart from a tea kiosk, which is a shame, as the London Parks generally are badly served when it comes to good food.

For a hundred years, this topic has been coming up, ever since 1883 when the Duke of Cambridge, Ranger of the Royal Parks, first allowed food in the Parks. He had been forced to give in, though he put up a strong fight, with Queen Victoria supporting him. 'I have invariably, as Ranger, set my face against the erection of any places for *Refreshment* in the Royal Parks, as I consider that these Parks are for the enjoyment of *fresh air*, and are not to be turned into Tea Gardens. If we ever allow one or more stands to be erected, depend upon it we shall have many more, and the Parks, already overcrowded in the summer, will become intolerable.'

He was persuaded to change his mind by the Commissioner of Works who feared trouble from 'the poorer visitors to the Park' if facilities were not provided. They thought in the end it was better to control what was being demanded, and offer limited refreshment, than have undesirable elements setting up their own unofficial stalls, perhaps even offering 'intoxicant refreshments'.

When at last I got there, the Serpentine Gallery was closed, though I could see people inside getting ready for a new exhibition, about Indian art, to open in a couple of days. I walked on across the grass and came to a strange-looking little building, facing the Long Water, which in the distance had looked like a miniature Indian temple. It was open and empty, no doubt providing good shelter in inclement weather, but the smell inside was most unattractive. Tramps had been dossing down and hooligans using it as a lavatory, judging by the graffiti, most of which I could not understand, though the words themselves made sense. 'Bristol halfbreeds generating hate.' It looked like the end of some slogan, with the rest of the sentence missing. A little plaque explained that the building was part of Queen Caroline's original ornamental gardens, later used as a park keeper's lodge. It had been restored by the Department of the Environment in 1977 and was in excellent condition, despite the scribbles and the smell, with the rounded ceilings in fine condition and the lead on the roof still intact. I wondered how much longer that would remain.

In the middle of Kensington Gardens, standing full square at the focal point of six tree-lined paths, is a huge statue called 'The Statue of Physical Energy', the work of G. F. Watts. It must win some sort of prize for the most boring title of any statue in London, although the subject matter is rather handsome and impressive. It depicts a horse rearing up while the rider, who appears to be naked, is leaning back on the horse, his thumb on his forehead, staring into the distance. It could be some sort of rude sign, or a bit of ham acting, or simply someone who has lost his way.

The history of the statue is rather complicated. Mr Watts, as far back as 1870, thought he was doing it for the Duke of Westminster to celebrate the achievements of one of his ancestors. In 1902, when Watts got the OM, it was sent off instead to Cape Town where it still stands, a memorial to Cecil Rhodes. The cast in Kensington Gardens was put up in 1904, after Watts's death. Who would now think of a horse when they think of physical energy?

There was a young Korean couple photographing each other beside the statue and they asked if I would take a snap of them together. He was studying metallurgy in the USA, but fitting in a week's tour of Europe. They were not quite sure how they came to be in the middle of Kensington Gardens. I was asked to point them in the direction of the Victoria and Albert Museum, which I did. I could see a connection between Physical Energy and Metallurgy but wondered what they wanted to see at the V. and A. Perhaps they really wanted the Science Museum? They smiled as if they had a secret I could never fathom. No, it was the Victoria and Albert. They both liked looking at clothes.

'We have read so much about your Hyde Park,' said the young lady. 'We get it in our text books in Korea.'

I walked with them down one of the paths, Lancaster Walk, which leads to the Albert Memorial, pleading with them not to leave the Park without seeing it, the most amazing statue in London, in the country, in the Universe. They must not miss it. But they went on straight across the main road, hand in hand, searching for the V. and A.

There is a very early issue of *Private Eye* magazine where they put the Albert memorial on the cover and made it look like a rocket being launched into space. It has been constantly ridiculed over the years, even by contemporary Victorians who dismissed it as an 'overgrown reliquary', but I find it totally fascinating, so exotic, so fanciful, so rich and complicated. Basically, it is a statue honouring one man but in glorifying him it was turned into a massive memorial which glorifies a whole age. We see not only what the Victorians considered good sculpture and design, which is interesting in itself, but what they thought about themselves and the world in which they lived.

Prince Albert died from typhoid in 1861 and the desire for some suitable memorial came originally from his grief-stricken widow. The entire nation

The Albert Memorial: Smile please, we are all amused

rallied round and £56,000 was raised by public subscription. An all-star committee, which included the President of the Royal Academy and the Lord Mayor, considered various schemes and chose Sir George Gilbert Scott to be the overall designer.

The total cost of Scott's masterpiece, or folly, depending on your point of view, came to £120,000 and it took nine years to complete. The builders were Lucas Brothers, who had recently done the Royal Albert Docks and Liverpool Street Station, and during the work several dinners for the workmen were given at which 80 or so men sat down at improvised tables to eat beef and plum pudding and hear speeches complimenting them on their temperate habits and for the fact that so 'little swearing was heard' during the building work. Dear Albert would have been pleased.

You need to stand back, as far as possible, to take in the overall shape of the memorial, to fix the outline in your mind, to realise how much there is on top which you can't possibly see, and to wonder at its height, over 173 feet, and its majesty, soaring up in triumphant stages to the heavens.

The lowest stage consists of four large marble groups of figures which represent the four continents. The first is marked Europe and the main element is a Britannia figure riding on a bull surrounded by four other queen-like ladies wearing crowns. If you were looking for a symbol to represent Europe, would you choose a bull? Why did the Victorians choose it? There is probably some learned study somewhere, explaining exactly what every little piece of decoration represents. I suspect the bull comes from classical mythology.

Moving round the base – and it is about 200 feet to the next corner – you come to America. The main symbol here is easier to understand as it shows a Red Indian on a bison. Then there is a frontiersman firing a rifle, objects which, if pressed, most people would agree do conjure up an image of America, even today.

Africa has a camel and another animal with a sphinx-like head and a naked Negro who appears to be a slave, not exactly the symbols we would choose today but, yes, one can see where they have all come from and why Victorian schoolchildren would recognise them. Asia appears to feature a hippie in dark glasses who looks as if he's just taken an overdose. That's clear to us, but what did the Victorians think it meant? There is also an elephant, so that's easy, plus a Buddhist figure, a Chinaman with a pigtail and an Indian goddess with very ample breasts. On the whole, three out of the four continents still make sense, but perhaps they should have been made to re-think Europe. Incidentally, what happened to the fifth continent, Australia? Did the Victorians pretend it did not exist?

Climbing the steps, you come to the second stage which is a gigantic frieze going right round the podium like the decoration on a Christmas cake. There are 169 life-size statues in the frieze, lined up in formation, side by side, all of them striking a suitably impressive pose, with or without some accessory, such as a book or instrument, to give you a clue to their occupation or claim to fame. These are the 169 figures whom the Victorians considered to be the world's all-time greats, people of genius in the arts, music, science, architecture. I walked round them for a long time, recognising faces, recognising names. Shakespeare is up there, and Beethoven, Michelangelo, Titian, Goethe, Purcell, Turner, but who on earth were Vischer, Bushnell, Roubiliac, Pugin, Thorpe, Chambers, or Barry? Only the surnames are given, as presumably they were all household names, at least for educated Victorians, which makes it even harder to know who some of them were. With the help of an encyclopaedia, I have decided that Thorpe must have been Sir Thomas Thorpe, a Victorian chemist. Barry was presumably Sir Charles Barry, architect of the Houses of Parliament, and Pugin his assistant, A. W. Pugin. Was Chambers the dictionary man or possibly Sir William Chambers who designed the pagoda at Kew Gardens? I thought Roubiliac could have been a paint manufacturer, till I decided he was probably the French sculptor, Louis Roubiliac, who did the statue of Newton for Trinity College, Cambridge.

The next layer of the cake, which again consists of four groups of symbolic figures, one at each corner, represents four great human activities. Agriculture consists of bits of corn, a scythe, sheep and a lamb and half-naked shepherd boy who looks as if he's got a miner's helmet on. Engineering is a spade, telescopes and some figures looking busy and thoughtful. Commerce also has some figures, all of whom seem to be talking, with a woman in charge, while Manufacturing has God in the prime position, though he's very busy, looking after some bales of cotton and clutching an hour-glass

Then at last we come to Dear Albert himself, fifteen feet tall, dressed as a Knight of the Garter, with the Garter artistically placed above a very muscular left calf. He is shown seated, as Sir George thought the sitting position was best 'for conveying the idea of dignity befitting a royal personage'. In his hand he has a book, not the Bible, as many thought at the time, but the catalogue for the Great Exhibition.

There is much, much more to admire and to decipher above Albert's head, more sculptures, decorations, mosaics, allegorical groups, reaching in further stages up into the sky, but I had no more time to spare. The Memorial is by far and away the most complete expression of the Victorian age and worth an expedition in itself. In one single object, the Victorians tell us who they were, what they did, what they believed in, what they liked.

My final thought, as I eventually dragged myself away, was to wonder what symbols we would use to represent our age. The Victorians made a spade and a telescope stand for Engineering. Think how boring for a modern sculptor to have to carve a micro chip. Present-day symbols for America might be fun, such as a skyscraper or Mickey Mouse or a hamburger, but Europe would probably present a problem. There is still not one symbol we could all agree on. Most interesting of all would be to list our 169 heroes in the arts and sciences. Could we even reach that number?

I slowly walked down the Flower Walk, a 500-yard-long path which leads from the Albert Memorial towards Kensington Palace. There were lots of nannies around, though few in uniform, mostly either elderly, perhaps grandmothers, or young au pairs from abroad, some sitting on the benches, chattering away to each other, stopping occasionally to check their charges. Each side of the path is lined with flower beds and flowering shrubs and roses, and I found the effect slightly claustrophobic. It is one of the famous attractions of the Gardens, loved by many, but I felt somehow hemmed in by the rather prissy railings which keep the public from getting too near the flowers themselves. I was quite pleased to come out at the end and turn into the space and light of the Broad Walk.

The Broad Walk, which is about 50 feet wide, was another of Queen Caroline's creations and until recently it was tree-lined all the way, but now the elms have gone. It begins on a slope and you can't see over the top, just the horizon, which gives a feeling that the open sea might possibly be over the brow. For such a grand and important avenue, it is a slight disappointment to find it leads nowhere in particular, cutting through the edge of the Gardens, not leading to the front door of the Palace as one might hope. It does, however, take you past the seven-acre Round Pond where the nannies have always pushed their prams and where generations of small, and big, boys have sailed their model boats and yachts. (No engines are allowed.)

You could possibly walk straight down the Broad Walk and not realise the Kensington Palace was to your left, just a hundred yards away. It is all so discreet, hidden away, and it is not clear which bits are which and where, or if, the public are allowed. It is of course the focal point of Kensington Gardens, past and present, and where the Superintendent has his yard.

There seemed to be a great deal of work going on as I started poking around, trying to find the Superintendent's office, with lorries and excavators digging and clearing and painters rushing around. 'Charlie Boy's coming,' said a workman. 'He's moving into apartments seven and eight. This will be his lawn when we've finished. It used to be a car park.' It turned out that that day they were getting ready for the arrival of the Prince and Princess of Wales. How fitting that Kensington Palace should once more be the London home of a future Monarch.

In recent years, it has been more of a Royal lodging house, an apartment block arranged specially to house various members and relations of the Royal Family, plus a few chosen courtiers, such as the Queen's Secretary. It looks like one building from afar but on close inspection you can see how the various wings and sections have become self-contained, with their own little front doors and porches.

The main part, where the Royals enter, is at the other side, carefully kept from the public view, and you have to pass a police guard at the gates in Palace Avenue. Princess Margaret has lived there for several years with her children, while in other apartments live the Duke and Duchess of Gloucester, Prince and Princess Michael of Kent, Princess Alice of Gloucester.

Mick Crane is the Assistant Superintendent in charge of Kensington Gardens. His office, when I eventually found it, was more charming and cheerful than some other parks' offices I'd been in, and so was he. A notice on his desk read 'Illegitimus non tatum carborundum' which he maintained meant don't let the bastards get you down. He had not long returned from a nine-month absence due to open heart surgery. He comes from Suffolk, the son of a head gardener on a private estate, and came to London in 1959 as a Grade 1 Gardener at Regent's Park, where he spent nine years before becoming head gardener at the Tower of London. He came to Kensington Gardens in 1977 as Assistant Superintendent.

'The Royals keep us on our toes,' he said. 'But they are so nice and kind, all of them, and very interested in the Gardens.' Princess Margaret's children, when young, used to play on their bikes in his yard, though never in the Gardens, where cycling is not allowed to Royals or anyone else. Unlike those MPs who are forever walking through St James's Park and spotting something they don't approve of, the Royals are not complainers.

'I've only had one complaint, if you can call it that. Princess Margaret's Secretary once rang to say that Cleopatra's asp on the Albert Memorial was missing. Statues are not my problem. I passed the news on to the Ancient Monuments. The Royals are very correct. If they want to take any visitors into the Sunken Gardens, they always ring up first for permission.'

He has a staff of 46 to look after the Gardens, including a tree gang of six who are based in his yard but look after all the Central Royal Parks. He searched for a recent tree survey which had been done on the Gardens, but could not find it at that moment. He is very proud of the large number of ancient trees they have in the Gardens. There's a sweet chestnut which dates back to 1700. He was rather hurt that I had not been thrilled by the Flower Walk, but he agreed that the railings were not very attractive. 'I had a great struggle to get them put up two years ago. People were always going on the grass to feed the birds or the rabbits and ruining all the flowers.'

Like all Superintendents, he likes it best when he has an excuse to get out

Gardeners at work in Kensington Gardens

of his office, so we set off for a short walk round the Palace gardens. We sat in the sun on a bench in the Broad Walk for a while, at a spot where he often sits, early in the summer before he starts work, and he pointed out the numerous vistas which can be seen from the windows of Kensington Palace, looking across the Gardens to the Long Water and Hyde Park. Some had now been obscured by trees becoming too tall, but the main grassy avenue, from the Round Pond to the Physical Energy statue, was still clear enough. Every day, Mr Crane feels fortunate to be back at work.

He was once told, so he said, that the reason the Broad Walk was kept so broad and so clear was in case the country was ever invaded. The Royals could then be taken off easily in a light aircraft. He didn't really believe it, but if you study the surface of the Broad Walk, you can see it would make an ideal little landing strip.

We then headed for the Sunken Garden which he had been saving, promising me delights to come. I had to admit I had never seen it, despite having had the occasional walk through Kensington Gardens over the years. If only it was clearly signposted, more people might find it. In the middle of the Gardens, there are a few ornate signposts, with crowns on top, pointing in the direction of Kensington Palace and elsewhere, but when you set off to try to follow them, the signs run out. 'We like to surprise people. Signposts anyway are so untidy. I'm always being asked if that building over there is Kensington Palace.'

He pointed up the Broad Walk to a large building with red turrets. It was the Coburg Hotel which stands on Bayswater Road, and from that angle it did look rather stately, whereas Kensington Palace, partly hidden behind trees, is easy to miss. The Sunken Garden is even easier to miss, being sunken, which was how I had been unaware that it existed.

The original Sunken Garden, very formal in the Dutch style, was created for Queen Anne in 1722. The present one is quite near the original site and was laid out in 1909 on similar, mathematical lines. The focal point is a large rectangular pond, about fifty yards long, sunk into the ground. Rising up and around it, in increasingly large rectangles, are three series of flower beds. I had noticed on Mr Crane's office wall a complicated chart for that autumn's flower beds and his ground plan looked like a military manoeuvre. The three levels contain respectively 36, 44 and 64 flower beds, making in all 144 different flower beds. The same species is often repeated in opposite corners, but if that happens they make sure they are in slightly differing varieties or different colours. That particular spring, the garden had contained 30 different plant species. Each year, there are two complete changes, plus two other partial changes.

There is a tree-covered bower all the way round the brim of the Sunken Garden, which makes it even harder to see from outside, a cloister-like walkway of lime trees which have been plaited and trained to form arches. 'Pleached limes' is what gardeners call it. At intervals along the walk, little windows have been cut in the limes so you can look down into the Sunken Garden. The general public can't get *into* the Sunken Garden itself, as the gates are kept locked. Every day of the year, whatever the season, there are always one or two people standing in meditation, looking through at the flowers. One elderly lady, who lives locally, comes once a week to paint them. 'She always does the same scene and it's strange to look at it sometimes, especially when she is finishing off an arrangement we have already taken out.'

If, like Princess Margaret, you make a special request, you might possibly be allowed into the garden at certain times. I was with the Superintendent, so naturally he took out his large bunch of keys and ushered me straight in. Such privilege. On the surface of the pond were several ducklings. There had been eight this morning, so he said, now he could see only two. The magpies must have got them.

It was what was below the surface which he was most keen to show off. A couple of years ago, before the economic squeeze had begun and all luxuries were stopped, Mr Crane had been allowed to stock the pond with 70 carp, special Koi carp from Japan. Over the recent winter, alas, the ice and frost had killed most of them and now there were only 13 left, but they

The Sunken Garden, Kensington Gardens: the Superintendent waits for the carp to come

looked strong and healthy enough, flashing just under the surface, gold and silver or multi-coloured, all of them beautiful and exotic. They were following him round, so Mr Crane boasted. I stopped, to test his claim, and they did seem to be swimming in time to his steps. 'I get livid if anyone else feeds them instead of me. My ambition is to be able to stamp one foot, very gently, and have them all rise to greet me. I love them. I can watch them for hours.'

Isn't that small one over there, that rather gaudy little reddish thing, isn't it a goldfish, the sort which comes from fun fairs?

Mr Crane affected not to see it at first. 'Oh that, I told her not to put it in. It was one of the girl gardeners. She found it in a plastic bag on the Broad

Walk. Take no notice of it. Just look at that Koi carp over there, isn't it magnificent . . .'

I thanked Mr Crane for all his help and then went to find the public entrance to Kensington Palace, the part which you can enter, for a modest fee, and view several of the state rooms. I ended up first of all at the Orangery, built to the design of Vanbrugh for Queen Anne, often used today for concerts and parties, and stared through at some painters working away. I then realised that a door I'd looked at earlier, which had appeared locked, was the entrance to the State Apartments. No one had been coming in or out, which was what had misled me. Once I pushed the door open, two uniformed security men jumped upon me, as if they'd been waiting, tipped off that an intruder was approaching. They inspected my little haversack, which contained guide books, maps and some uneaten sandwiches, and beckoned me through to another room. I came to a long counter, part of a little souvenir shop, where I bought a ticket, and went up a staircase to inspect the 15 or so rooms and galleries which are open to the public. There was still very little sign of the public, but guards were everywhere, patrolling each room and corridor. Perhaps Prince Charles's arrival in the building had increased their numbers. They were all very friendly, especially with each other. I could hear their laughter and chatter echoing down the long corridors.

Queen Caroline, to whom we Park lovers owe so much, used to lie in bed in Kensington Palace and listen to Lord Hervey, one of her court favourites, telling her the latest chatter and gossip. He was not *in* the bedroom, of course. Perish the thought. It was 'contrary to queenly etiquette to admit a man to her bedside whilst she was in'. Lord Hervey therefore had to stand for two hours at a time, unseen, stationed outside the bedroom door. Quite a feat, but then he was a very fanciful and imaginative gossip. Talking to an unseen audience is an art that can be acquired. People do it on TV all the time. Lord Hervey would certainly have been given his own programme.

The room which most visitors to Kensington Palace want to see is the one where Queen Victoria came into the world on May 24, 1819, along with the room where she was christened, known as the Cupola Room. There was some argument and haggling at the christening ceremony as her Christian names had not been finally decided, even while the Archbishop of Canterbury held the baby over the font. Her father, the Duke of Kent, fancied Elizabeth, while the Prince Regent (later George IV) preferred Georgiana, after his own name. They compromised on Alexandrina as her first Christian name, in honour of her chief sponsor, the Czar Alexander of Russia, and then Victoria, her mother's name. It is strange to think that if there had not been that minor disagreement we might never have called a whole way of life the Victorian age.

Victoria became Queen on June 20, 1837, aged 18, on the death of

William IV. She was in Kensington Palace at the time, asleep in her bedchamber, when the news came through. Her mother woke her with a kiss, then she went alone into a room where several officers of state were waiting and descended the King's Staircase (another of the areas open to the public) and into the Red Saloon to hold her first Privy Council.

She held court for a few weeks at Kensington Palace, the last reigning sovereign to have resided there, then she was driven to the newly-completed Buckingham Palace. She made her farewell on July 13, recording in her diary that she had said 'adieu for ever, that is to say, for ever as a *dwelling*, to this my birth place'.

I looked out of the window of her bedroom where she was born, which has a fine view of the Round Pond and of the Gardens beyond. Most of the apartments where the present Royals live, even Prince Charles, are on the other side of the Palace, overlooking Millionaires Row (Kensington Palace Gardens), a view not half as romantic or anywhere near as rural. Outside the Palace, on the Broad Walk, is a statue of Queen Victoria which was unveiled in 1893, a gift from her 'loyal subjects of Kensington to commemorate 50 years of her reign'. She was over 70 at the time, but the statue shows her as a slender young woman of 18, the age she was when she took over the throne. As all stamp collectors know, she also remained a young girl on all Victorian postage stamps right to the end.

There are few vandals in Kensington Gardens, as one might expect for such a salubrious area, but when any pranksters do decide to have a bit of fun, it is often this statue of Queen Victoria, standing so prominently in the Broad Walk, which is a popular target. Mr Crane the superintendent recently came to work to find a flower pot on her head and a bunch of pampas grass stuck in her hand.

It is an excellent statue, capturing the nervousness yet resoluteness of the new young queen. She has some of the looks of a modern young Kensington lady, perhaps of a Sloane Ranger, with a trace of haughtiness, but the overall impression is of youth and delicacy. If you look carefully at the inscription you will see that the sculptress was one of the unsung artists of the Victorian age, her daughter, Princess Louise. The statue depicts her mother at an age she herself never knew her. Louise was a talented sculptress and artist and had a private studio in the walled garden of her own apartment. She had been taught by Sir Joseph Edgar Boehm and in 1890 she had the rather nasty experience of finding him dead in his own studio. But for her Royal position, Princess Louise might have achieved greater public recognition as an artist, perhaps even ending up with the great and good on the Albert Memorial.

I left Kensington Palace and continued round the northern glades of the Gardens, wandering through the trees and paths, till I came to Speke's Monument. As far as I am concerned, this is unspeakable. It is simply a blank column of polished granite, undecorated, unexplained, unadorned, which comes to a point at the top like a needle. That's all. I advise no one to even try to find it. I can appreciate that the Albert Memorial might not be to everyone's aesthetic taste, but no one could say it is not interesting. Speke's Monument, which was put up at exactly the same time, must surely be the most boring statue in London. Only its title is interesting, although utterly mystifying for most people today. A simple inscription beneath reads: 'In Memory of SPEKE. Victoria, Nyanza, The Nile, 1864.' Was Speke a place, a person or a language?

This elliptical wording hides a Victorian mystery which has still not properly been explained. John Hanning Speke was a celebrated explorer who claimed he had discovered the source of the Nile. He died tragically on the eve of a meeting with his rival, Sir Richard Burton, who was going to challenge his discovery. Speke was said to have killed himself accidentally while hunting, although some alleged it was suicide. Hence those few brief, confusing words on his blank memorial, giving nothing away, giving offence to no one.

Not far away, just on the shore of the Long Water, is another monument, though this one has been called the 'most beautiful statue in London'. That was what the readers of *John O'London's Weekly* voted in 1912, the year the statue was erected. I had to queue up to get a good look at it. It is rather small, compared with the Albert Memorial or even Physical Energy, yet there was a large group of people round it. The whirl of their cine cameras drowned their excited chatter and made it hard to decide their nationalities, but they could have been South American.

Peter Pan is still one of the best loved and best known statues in Kensington Gardens, perhaps in the whole of Great Britain. It is one of the very few statues anywhere in London erected to a fictional character, unless you consider gods and angels and mermaids as fictional creations. Peter first appeared on the London stage in 1904 and, despite some early worries, he proved an instant success and has appeared annually ever since. His creator, Sir James Barrie, loved Kensington Gardens and wrote about them in various plays and books.

'The Gardens are bounded on one side by a never ending line of omnibuses over which your nurse has such authority that if she holds up her finger to any one of them it stops immediately. She then crosses with you in safety to the other side,' so he wrote in *Peter Pan in Kensington Gardens.*

Barrie himself commissioned the statue of Peter Pan from Sir George Frampton and unofficially arranged with the Commissioner of Works where it should be erected. A question was later asked in Parliament, when this was discovered, but the site had become an immediate tourist attraction and nothing was done to change it.

When I eventually got close enough to touch and feel, as millions before have done, judging by the high gloss on the rabbits' ears, I could see that Peter is on top, blowing his pipes, while below, in a rather sickly art nouveau formation are various other figures with Wendy, presumably, the main figure, trying to reach up to Peter. There are lots of birds, rabbits and fairies popping out of holes and children with wings dressed in Liberty frocks and 1920s hair styles.

Kensington Gardens have for long been associated with fairies, a tradition which goes back beyond Peter Pan. Near the Palace, there is the Elfin Oak, a dead oak tree, carved with twee fairies and goblins, which probably originates from a poem Thomas Tickell wrote in 1772 about an Elfin King who had his home nearby. This fairy mythology was perpetuated by Matthew Arnold in 1852 in his poem, 'Lines Written in Kensington Gardens'.

In my helpless cradle I was breathed on by the rural Pan . . .
Could this line have sparked off Barrie?

The Long Water ends, or begins, depending on where you start from, in a formal arrangement of four rectangular ponds known as the Italian Gardens. There are several fine urns and some fancy balustrades, but everything looks rather shabby, as if it is somehow *too* fancy for its setting, right under the eyes of the Royal Lancaster Hotel with the Bayswater Road roaring not far away. Even the gardeners don't seem to lavish the same attention on it as at the smarter end of the Gardens.

There were a few people sitting around the ponds, enjoying the tea-time sun. An Indian gentleman, with his trousers rolled up on his bony thighs, was listening to a horse race on a transistor radio which was tied with elastic bands. On his knee was a carefully folded morning paper and the list of runners. He was sitting on the ground, leaning against a statue of Edward Jenner, the doctor from Gloucestershire who in 1798 discovered vaccination, a development which eventually saved millions of Indian lives.

The statue was originally in Trafalgar Square, but it was decided to move it. There were long discussions about finding a suitable new site which led to one wit writing to a newspaper, pretending to be Jenner himself. 'If I saved you a million spots cannot you find me one?' In 1862 it ended up in its present position in the Italian Gardens.

At the end of the ponds is a building which is trying hard to look like an Italian Pavilion, hence the name for the gardens. Two tramps were sitting at their ease inside, looking very philosophical, obviously in the middle of some long conversation, though one with enormous, timeless pauses, as if they were waiting for Pinter to supply the missing dialogue.

'Then I had to get out of Dublin,' said the slightly younger one, with a broad cockney accent. They both stared at the ponds, heads in their hands.

'Why was that then?' said the older one who from his voice could have been a Geordie.

'Dublin was too rough for me. Know what I mean.'

Prince Albert is thought to have dreamt up the design for the Italian Gardens, hoping to create his own Petit Trianon, as seen at Versailles. Would he have approved of his proud Pavilion becoming a shelter for dossers?

The Pavilion has been very cunningly constructed and at the rear it hides an old pumping station, used at one time to supply the fountains and ponds. I went round to see if I could get in, but the door was locked. Right behind the building, though, I could see a trickle of water coming through a low brick arch, from underneath the Bayswater Road. This must be the original West Bourne, the stream which Queen Caroline used to produce the master plan for the Serpentine and the Long Water.

To the right of the Pavilion, there is an enormous wood-panelled alcove seat, created for another Queen, Queen Anne, by Sir Christopher Wren and originally elsewhere in the Gardens. On the other side, I stopped to look at a little fountain which at one time was described as the most immoral statue in London. It shows two bears in a passionate full frontal embrace, with their eyes closed and a look of utter bliss. I made a note to look up an animal book on intercourse between bears. It could, of course, just have been a kiss.

Near the Victoria Gate exit is something I had been greatly looking forward to visiting, the Pets Cemetery. It was started in 1880 by the Duchess of Cambridge, wife of the then Ranger, who as a personal favour was allowed to bury her favourite dog in a little stretch of garden. Naturally, others wanted the same privilege and by 1915 there were over 300 little gravestones, each in memory of various dearly loved, sadly missed dogs, cats, and birds, all with suitable inscriptions.

> I faithfully loved and cared
> For you living. I think we
> Shall surely meet again.
>
> Sleep little one sleep
> Rest thy head
> As ever thou didst at my feet
> And dream that I am near.

The cemetery is now full, just in case you want to give your favourite pet a decent burial, and it is not even possible for the public to look at the little graves. The area is fenced off, though if you were lucky, or persuasive enough, you might talk the park keeper in the nearby lodge into opening a gate and letting you have a quick look.

As I was gaping over the fence, with the roar of the traffic only ten yards away, charging through Victoria Gate into Bayswater Road, I noticed that at my feet was a baby rabbit. I thought perhaps I'd imagined it at first, my mind wandering with all those thoughts of Elfin Oaks and Peter Pan's little winged friends. It was munching away at some wallflowers. It stopped and stared at me, close enough for me to touch it, then continued munching, not at all concerned by me or the traffic. Like Peter Rabbit in Mr McGregor's garden, he had perhaps become somnolent with all that guzzling.

I turned back towards the Long Water, following its banks on the other side this time, quickly losing the traffic noise, heading once more for the Serpentine Bridge. Through gaps in the rather overgrown shrubbery I could see glimpses over the Long Water of crowds still taking movies of Peter Pan.

There was a sudden clearing, recently made by the look of it, perhaps in the last year, and I came to a massive concrete arch, a pale cream colour, like a bit of left-over motorway bridge which had buckled under the strain and been dumped till someone decided what to do with it. I had thought

Kensington Gardens: families are allowed

the Speke Monument was pretty boring, but this seemed even more pointless.

I got nearer and lined up my eyes and realised it had not just been dropped there by some mad helicopter pilot but that it was indeed a new statue. Through the arch I got a nicely framed view across the Long Water towards Physical Energy and beyond towards the Round Pond. As vistas go, it was quite impressive, but I still found it hard to admire. Then I noticed a little plaque and to my surprise discovered it is a work by Henry Moore, carved in 1979, a recent gift of the Henry Moore Foundation. Should I now

Henry Moore statue, the Long Water, Kensington Gardens: (Known more rudely by gardeners as the 'Arse on Stilts')

re-align my thoughts and my eyes in order not to appear a complete philistine?

I talked to a park keeper later and he said that they had christened it the *Arse on Stilts*, which was rather unkind. It will doubtless improve with age, as our eyes get used to it and nature starts working and that starched, bleached look begins to fade. In the meantime, if you come across it on that empty path, which is in Kensington Gardens (though most people assume that once the Long Water is crossed Hyde Park begins), then consider it as a Viewing Station, the sort of platform which all gentlemen who loved the picturesque had in their gardens at one time. No need to strain and try to work out what Mr Moore was on about. Simply look through it and you will see what I have now decided, after great consideration, is the best single view in Kensington Gardens. Perhaps that was the intention.

CHAPTER FOUR

Regent's Park and Primrose Hill

John Nash was a funny-looking fellow. His own description of himself was not exactly flattering. 'Thick, squat, dwarf figure with round head, snub nose and little eyes.' His career was equally peculiar and for most of his working life he was known as a minor architect of some flair but also as a gambler, someone who took risks and was careless of regulations, for which he had paid the penalty. He had had to suffer several disasters in his professional life. He was almost sixty years old, having done little of distinction, when he embarked on his life's work and became responsible for the development of a London Park and a style of architecture for which the world will always remember him.

He was born in the Isle of Wight in 1752, trained as an architect and then set himself up in London after an uncle had left him a legacy. He involved himself in various speculative building ventures which succeeded for a time but in 1783 he went bankrupt and he retired to Wales, rehabilitating himself and re-thinking his career. Slowly, he began again, this time as a country house architect, concentrating on landscape rather than urban developments, becoming a practitioner of the 'Picturesque', then a fashionable concept amongst poets, travel writers and architects, all of whom put Nature first.

In 1798, Nash married a handsome young woman called Mary Bradley and it was through her he met the Prince of Wales. His wife's relationship with the Prince – who became Prince Regent in 1812 and then King George IV in 1820 – is alleged to have at one time been rather intimate and the scandal of the day was that five children she had 'adopted' were really the Prince's. Whether or not she had been his mistress, she was still close to the Prince and Nash in turn became a friend, which was fortunate as George's chief interest in life, apart from the ladies, was architecture. The two men spent a great deal of time together, planning and altering houses for the Prince or for his wealthy friends.

In 1811, the Prince had to make an important decision about some extensive Crown lands just to the North of London, the so-called Marylebone Park. Henry VIII, once again, had originally been responsible for taking them over, during the dissolution of the Monasteries, and had added them on to his other hunting estates in and around London. They had been sold off during the Civil War, for £13,000, then taken back into Royal ownership on the return of the Monarch. The other Royal Parks were kept intact but it was decided to split Marylebone into little farms and lease them to separate tenants and for the next hundred years these farms became important suppliers for London, particularly with fresh milk and hay. The original name came from the Parish Church of St Mary, built in 1400, by the stream known as the Tyburn. St Mary by the bourn became, over the centuries, St Marylebone.

Almost all the leases held by the individual farmers came up in 1811, by which time the London sprawl had reached the edge of what had once been remote farm land. It was an area ripe for development and for some years there had been discussions, and even a competition, about what to do with it.

Nash put forward a plan which was expensive and grandiose and it delighted the Prince. He wanted to treat the whole area as a garden city, with fine houses for the wealthy, linking it by a grand processional way from the Prince's existing Whitehall house to a new country home which would be built at the heart of the new estate, in the prime position. This entrance route would use Portland Place, which had already been built, and was admired by Nash, but would include a new and equally grand connecting road, now the road we call Regent Street.

Nash's master plan included fine terraces all the way round the Park, containing shops and little factories and markets, with artisans' dwellings hidden on the edges to supply the needs of the big houses. He also included a canal through the estate, in which he happened to be an investor, yet another of his speculations, but he also saw the canal as part of the landscaping, using the water as a picturesque background.

As with most master plans, endless changes had to be made. Nash had originally envisaged 56 large villas, each one set in the Park in such a way that it would look as if the Park was its own private estate. Only eight villas were ever built. The Prince Regent's house never even got off the drawing board. The canal, which was seen as a major feature, was shoved to one side, and made to run along the edge of the scheme so that the rude shouts of the bargemen would not upset the sensitive tastes of the wealthy villa owners, but the terraces were finished and the parkland in the middle, including a new artificial lake, were all completed over the next two decades, being finished by around 1830. There were various financial troubles along the way, when one of Nash's main partners went bankrupt, and costs escalated, as they always do, but in the end the scheme was a triumph, the world's first attempt at residential landscaping on such a scale.

Henry Crabb Robbinson predicted in his Diary in 1818, well before the

Regent's Park

and Primrose Hill

Amenities

Regent's Park:
Zoo
Open Air Theatre
Boat Hire
Children's boating pool
Playgrounds
Puppet shows (weekdays for 4 weeks in summer)
Golf and tennis school
Tennis courts
Running track
Band concerts (twice every weekday, May—early
    August)
Q.M. Rose Garden Restaurant and cafeteria
Refreshment pavilion by Broad Walk
Tea pavilion by tennis courts

Primrose Hill:
Playground and open-air gymnasium

Key

P   Car parks
L   Public lavatories
Supt   Parks office

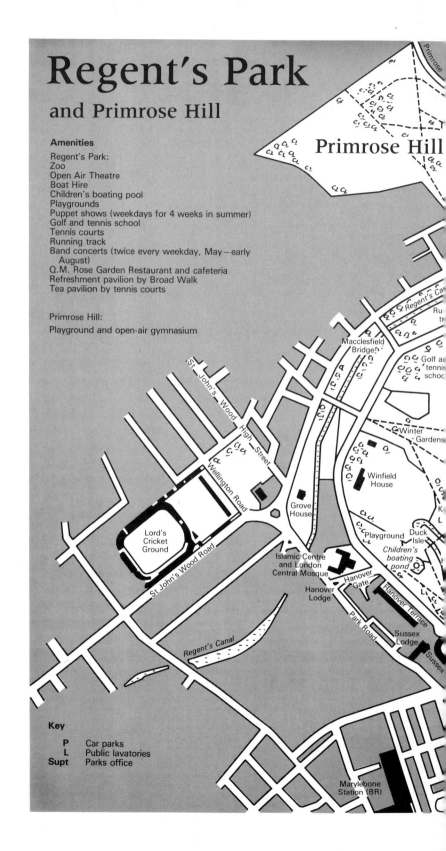

Primrose Hill

Regent's Ca

Macclesfield
Bridge

Golf a
tennis
schoo

Winter
Gardens

Winfield
House

Grove
House

Playground   Duck
Isle

Children's
boating
pond

Islamic Centre
and London
Central Mosque

Hanover
Gate

Hanover
Lodge

Hanover Terrace

Park Road

Sussex
Lodge

St John's Wood High Street

Wellington Road

St John's Wood Road

Lord's
Cricket
Ground

Regent's Canal

Marylebone
Station (BR)

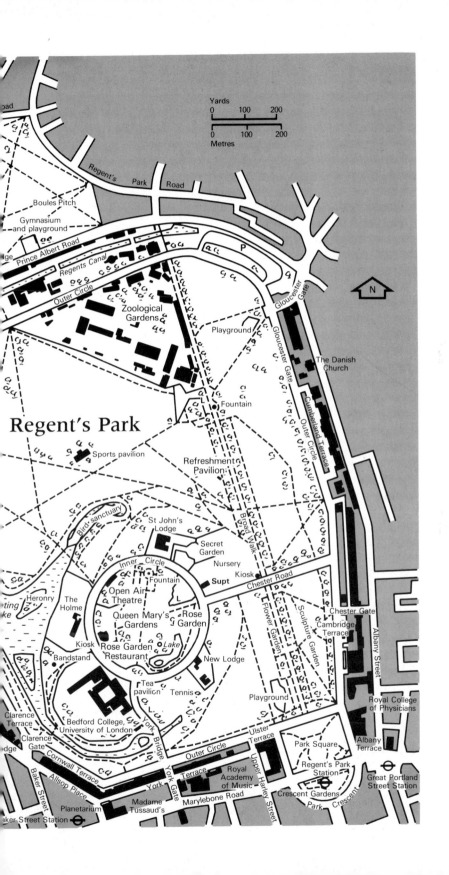

Yards
0   100   200

0   100   200
Metres

Regent's   Park   Road

Boules Pitch

Gymnasium
and playground

Prince Albert Road

Regents Canal

P

Outer Circle

N

Gloucester Gate

Zoological
Gardens

Playground

Gloucester Gate

The Danish
Church

Cumberland Terrace

Fountain

Outer Circle

Regent's Park

Sports pavilion

Refreshment
Pavilion

Broad Walk

Bird sanctuary

St John's
Lodge

Secret
Garden

Nursery

Kiosk

Supt

Chester Road

Inner   Circle

Fountain

Heronry

The
Holme

Open Air
Theatre

L

Queen Mary's
Gardens

Rose
Garden

Flower Garden

Sculpture Garden

Chester Gate

Cambridge
Terrace

ting
ke

Kiosk

Rose Garden
Restaurant

Lake

New Lodge

Albany Street

Bandstand

Tea
pavilion

Tennis

Playground

Royal College
of Physicians

Clarence
Terrace

Bedford College,
University of London

York Bridge

Clarence
Gate

dge

Ulster
Terrace

Albany
Terrace

Cornwall Terrace

Outer Circle

Park Square

Allsop Place

Terrace

York Gate

Royal
Academy
of Music

Upper Harley Street

Regent's Park
Station

Great Portland
Street Station

Baker Street

York

Planetarium

Madame
Tussaud's

Marylebone Road

Crescent Gardens

Park   Crescent

ker Street Station

work was all finished, that the scheme would 'give a sort of glory to the Regent's government which will be more felt by remote posterity than the victories of Trafalgar and Waterloo, glorious as these are'.

Those famous battles have not been forgotten, but we associate the names of Nelson and Wellington with them, rather than the Prince Regent. His name lives on however in the Park named after him, and in a style of architecture which also bears his name, both of them the inspiration of his friend John Nash. The Regent's Park was opened to the public in 1835, five years after his death, and has been open ever since. Nash's Regency terraces are still there for all to see. But what else has remained?

If you walk down Regent Street today, into Portland Place, along Park Crescent and then into the Park, you can see what a magnificent route it still is, if of course you can close your mind to the traffic. The route was meant to enter straight into the Park and then proceed along the Broad Walk. This walk through the Park still clearly stretches ahead, the final section of the ceremonial way the Prince would have taken to his 'country' retreat, if it had ever been built.

I entered the Park and made first for the Broad Walk which at this end is now laid out as a Flower Walk, broader and less hemmed in than the Flower Walk in Kensington Gardens, with some large handsome flower urns. There's a feeling of a seaside esplanade rather than a Prince's grand country garden. To the right, amongst the lawns and clumps of bushes, lurk some modern pieces of sculpture, a recent attempt at creating a Sculpture Garden. None of the pieces I found had any titles or authors. Perhaps they'd all fallen off the back of some modernist's lorry. One of them, made out of two large red metal plates, had been covered in graffiti. 'Cumberland Rules' said one. All the Nash terraces were named after the Prince's brothers. Could the Duke of Cumberland have left a visiting card?

I turned left at Chester Road (which is open to traffic) and headed for the Inner Circle, inside which Nash was going to create the Prince's own little home. He also envisaged a ring of terrace houses round the Inner Circle, which were never built, making in effect two Parks, which is still the case. Many people, while wandering in Regent's Park, often miss completely the inner Park, thinking that when they come to the Inner Circle road they are about to leave the Park. This inner Park, known generally as Queen Mary's Gardens, is one of the best-loved features of the Park. The Regent's Park gardeners, naturally enough, consider it the finest garden in all the Royal Parks.

The Superintendent, David Caselton, has his office and yard on the Inner Circle. He comes from Cheshire where he left grammar school with three A-levels and later studied horticulture at Pershore College, coming out top student. He does look prefect material, being young, smartly dressed and very neat. Some of the older Superintendents tend to wear rather shabby clothes and could easily be mistaken for their own gardeners.

Mr Caselton came to the Royal Parks in 1977, after several years of horticultural work for the National Trust and other bodies. He took over Regent's Park in 1980 as a Grade Two Superintendent. (There are only four of these – the other three being at Richmond, Greenwich and Hampton Court.) He has a staff of 100 at Regent's Park, which is half what it was just ten years ago. Even five years ago, they had 150. He hopes not to relax their activities in Queen Mary's Gardens and along the Broad Walk, but fears that the ornamental flower beds at various entrances to the Park will have to decrease.

He thinks his Park is the most *rural* of the central London Parks, thanks to the hedges, the hidden gardens and the vast amount of bird life. (The nearness to the Zoo helps the wild birds as they can drop in and steal the animals' food.) 'The gardens are in a modern taste compared with the ancient gardens in say Kensington Gardens where the lines have been laid down and can't be changed. We're basically a Victorian park, but with lots of recent additions. We reflect more what people like today. We're very aware of plant relationships, how they look with each other, creating pleasing combinations. All the same, people like a lot of colour in their park gardens, especially if they have no gardens at home. We still have to try to provide that.'

I left his office, crossed the road and went through some massive wrought-iron gates, gold-painted at the top and dated 1933, and so into Queen Mary's Gardens. For almost a hundred years, the Royal Botanical Society of London had 18 acres inside the Inner Circle and their summer Flower Shows were a big attraction of the London Season, but their lease ran out in 1932 and the Royal Parks' gardeners took them over, naming them after Queen Mary, wife of George V, who was a keen gardener.

Thousands of visitors come every year, from all over the world, to see the roses, but there are also many other flower beds, lawns, shrubberies, wooded areas, a waterfall and a little ornamental lake. For such a small, circular garden, with a radius of only 300 yards, there is an enormous amount to see and admire. I climbed a little mound behind the waterfall and sat on top and felt completely cut off from London, the first time that this has happened. There was absolutely no traffic noise to be heard. The Inner Circle road helps to deaden the noise, because it is lined with hedges, as is the Outer Circle: two lines of defences to keep out the world.

I had got the name of the Foreman Gardener, Doug Richardson, from the Superintendent, and managed to find him at an entrance to his Rose Garden, building a little wall. He was tanned and muscular, not a gentleman to argue with, with long bushy sideboards. I asked him how long he'd been here. 'Too bloody long . . .,' he said, continuing to build his

Overleaf: Regent's Park line-up: Royal Bailiff in front, with the superintendent and other staff behind in their respective working groups

Queen Mary's Gardens, Regent's Park

little wall. 'And here I'm going to stay, unless they have other plans for me. I love it really, though it's bloody hard graft. I applied to be foreman of the Garden because no one else wanted the responsibility. I had to go before a Board and I thought my tongue might let me down. I'm a Leo. My tongue's let me down a few times in my life, I can tell you.'

He became foreman in 1976 and since then he has had a few arguments with people, the general public as well as his colleagues. 'I could strangle them sometimes, these visitors. I've seen Arabs get out of their Rolls Royces and go and pick the bloody flowers, watched by their chauffeurs. They're *our* people, these chauffeurs, who should know better.

'My two biggest hates are push-bikes and dogs. I'd ban them both, if I had my way. Bikes aren't supposed to be ridden, but they are. You get some nice old age pensioner, doddering up and down the paths, and wallop, a bike goes right into her. And the skate boards and roller skates, I'd stop them. This garden is meant to be a place where people relax.

'As for the dogs, I don't think the public can read, if you ask me. The notices make it quite plain. Dogs must be on a lead. I tell someone that every day, but it does no good. Their mess is disgusting. I love dogs and have a collie myself, but I wouldn't let them in the gardens at all. There's enough open grass out there for them in the rest of the Park.

'Oh, I've had some abuse, and given it back. The usual thing they say is, "Don't forget we pay your wages," I always say, "Yeh, and it's not bloody good enough." You get a lot of know-alls. Just a few moments ago a bloke told me I was mixing the cement the wrong way. "If you're so clever," I said, "you come and do it." '

'It's only a handful, I suppose. Most people really appreciate what we're doing, but I think 50p at the gate would make them appreciate us more. Teach them a bit of respect. You've come too early for the roses. Wait till next month. They'll be gorgeous, really gorgeous.'

There are at least 20,000 rose bushes in the Queen Mary Gardens, set out in 100 rose beds. Doug Richardson has a staff of 14 to look after them, plus the rest of the garden area, but says he could do with double. 'There's enough work on the roses alone to keep one gang employed permanently, all the year round. People see us in the summer and say what a nice job you've got, but forget we're at it all the time. In the winter we have to lay metal tracks on the ground to work from, and you should try moving some of them. About a dozen complete rose beds have to be dug up every winter and everything slung out. Rose bushes should last 15 years, but some last less. Black spot was very bad last year and mildew, that's always a bugger. Red spider and rust hasn't been so bad recently. The only slack moment is when it's pouring down. Then I do a bit of reading. No, not paper-backs, bloody hell. I read about mildew.

'I was here at 6.45 this morning, picking up rubbish in the waterfall. These young lads think it's a good joke to go to the top and chuck empty tins in and watch them float. Then there's these tough nuts who think it's fun to jump in the fountain. I know what I'd do with them all. Every morning, from eight o'clock to ten, I have two men who do nothing else but paper picking. The public don't realise half the things we do, isn't that right, Dave.'

He turned to another gardener who had just brought him a fresh load of cement for his wall. 'Ta, my old son,' said Doug, still talking non-stop and building his wall at the same time. 'Then, blimey, the stuff that gets nicked. Two rose bushes went not long ago. And I'd dug them in a foot deep.'

Doug first joined the Royal Parks in 1956 as a labourer, aged 16. Now, as a foreman, married with two children, he lives in a park lodge at Richmond Park, fourteen miles away. 'It's gorgeous, really gorgeous. Must be 17th century or 18th century. I don't know. But it's gorgeous, really gorgeous. You must come and see it when you get to Richmond.'

I thanked him for his help and went to look for some refreshments, but the Rose Garden restaurant was closed for alterations, though it looked an interesting building, with some pyramid-shaped roofs, a bit like the Serpentine Restaurant. Instead I found the tea pavilion open beside the tennis courts, where a host of sparrows helped me to eat a rather limp ham sandwich.

Apart from the roses, the big attraction of the Inner Circle gardens is the Open Air Theatre. The entrance is a brightly-painted wooden construction, highly professional-looking. I don't mean this as a slight, but as I had never been to the Regent's Park Theatre before, and had no idea what to look for, I half-expected it might be very amateurish, like a pierrot show, with deckchairs on the grass.

I asked at the box office if the director, David Conville, was at home, apologising for not having made an appointment. He was about to go up to Nottingham, so I was told, but after a short wait I was directed inside where there was a great deal of activity as workmen got the stage and sets ready for the new season and builders finished off some new dressing-rooms. Mr Conville poured me out a glass of wine, which was kind, then proceeded to drink it himself, which was a mistake of course. He was rather busy and preoccupied that day.

He was once an actor and is now perhaps one of the last actor-managers, having been managing director of the company for twenty years. As we toured his little empire, he spoke as if he was still on stage, gesturing and declaiming to the workmen, his secretary and the world at large. It does take an outsize personality to keep such things as an Open Air Theatre alive, especially when there are constant threats of grants being removed. He had recently won his latest battle with the Arts Council and, thanks to successfully raising money from many other sources, they had been able to spend £200,000 on improvements. He now felt that their future was secure and they were all happily getting ready to welcome the Queen, due in a few weeks to celebrate the Theatre's 50th anniversary.

It all began in 1932 with a performance of *Twelfth Night*, directed by Sidney Carroll, with Sir Nigel Playfair as Malvolio and Phyllis Neilson-Terry as Olivia. Many other famous actors and actresses of the day played

David Conville, declaiming, at the Regent's Park Open Air Theatre

there, including Vivien Leigh, Gladys Cooper, Jack Hawkins, Deborah Kerr and Robert Helpman. In 1962, when Mr Conville arrived, the company changed its name to the New Shakespeare Company, a registered charity, and they have managed to attract many more modern stars, such as Jeremy Irons, Gemma Jones, Edward Fox, Penelope Keith, Judi Dench, Wayne Sleep, Michael Crawford.

The site of the theatre is part of the Royal Parks, ultimately administered by the Department of the Environment, but the company has a lease on the premises until 2000 AD. The Department helps to maintain the buildings and gardens, but the company runs itself financially and is proud that 75% of its money comes in from the box office, with the rest from grants and sponsorship. 'The nation really has *two* National Theatres,' boomed Mr Conville, 'the other lot and us.'

The auditorium has been completely rebuilt since 1975 – it was formerly all deckchairs – and is now as modern and well-appointed as any West End theatre, despite being open to the skies, with seating for 1,187 and excellent acoustics and lighting. It is listed as a West End Theatre and you can buy tickets at most booking agencies.

It started to rain slightly as we walked through the rows of seats but Mr Conville refused to shelter. 'It's not raining, my dear,' he shouted across the auditorium to a lady who was painting on the stage. 'You're just imagining it.'

One of their strengths, he explained, is *reality*. If Shakespeare calls for a woodland glade, as he is so very often does, then they have it, laid on by nature, with only a little bit of occasional fiddling. They use real logs and real trees, though, if an actor is called to pick up a log, they might then fake that one, as it could be too heavy.

Although they specialise in Shakespeare, they do other playwrights, such as Bernard Shaw and Pinter. In the winter season, when the Open Air Theatre is closed, they tour abroad. They keep a close eye on the school examination syllabus and most summers they get over 20,000 school children, usually at matinées. Their season lasts only three months – June, July and August – yet they attract over 80,000, of whom 20,000 are foreign tourists. Food and drink are served one hour before the performance. Clement Freud used to organise the catering a few years ago, and turned out four-course gourmet banquets.

But what about the weather?

'Yes, it is obviously best on a fine evening. Then you should get here really early and walk slowly through Queen Mary's Rose Garden. Have a good meal beforehand, one of our excellent suppers, and sit back and enjoy our excellent acting and staging. As daylight fades, you slowly realise that artificial light has taken over the night and the effect is truly magical. If it gets chilly, well, just hire a rug or have another glass of mulled wine.'

They rarely have to cancel, so he says, perhaps at the most six times in any summer. Summer rain in London has a habit of falling, when it does fall, in the afternoons, then clearing up in the evening. You don't get your money back if a play is cancelled or not completed, but are given tickets for another performance. The actors, of course, can get very chilly, if they have a non-speaking, hanging-about part. Even worse, they can be attacked by midges, if it's a hot and clammy evening, but, to a man and a woman, they greatly enjoy the experience of open air acting.

Mr Conville then had to rush off, so I went to see the lady who was working on the stage scenery. She had continued to work during the shower, hammering away, dressed in a strong yellow waterproof and wellington boots. She was Margot Burry, the stage designer, who has also worked at the Regent's Park Theatre for 20 years. 'I like the rain. Everything always looks so much fresher and nicer after a shower. It makes things look more real. The paint fades and little lichens start growing.'

I said how lucky she was to have such a handsome classical building, the one I could see just behind the stage, as it must make a perfect background. Was it part of a villa left over from Nash's days? Her face lit up. 'I built it myself!' She rushed to show me round it and, to my surprise, it was completely a façade, held up at the back with scaffolding. (As you go round the Inner Circle Road, you can see the scaffold from the rear, like catching a model from behind, all clipped together with pins.) We climbed up to the balcony, from which many passionate Shakespearean speeches have been poured over the last four years.

'It's an all-purpose Renaissance building. The trick is one of perspective, helped by polystyrene. It's been a Greek palace, an Italian church and an Irish castle. For one play we put up a date above the door, 1585, and during the day we found Americans taking photographs of it, convinced it was genuine. We're always being asked why we don't open the shutters.'

The fake shutters have been painted on, though even as close as a few feet away they looked genuine. Strips of gauze had been put over the polystyrene walls, to stop it crumbling, and then painted. Natural weathering does the rest.

'The biggest development over the last twenty years has been the arrival of emulsion paint, the ordinary household stuff. Until then, we used scene paint, as in normal theatres, but that comes off in the rain. If we were lucky, we waited till it dried and then varnished it, but usually we weren't lucky and it never got dry and we had to varnish it when it was still damp and it went all misty and funny. Basically, we use builder's materials, tough paints, tough woods, tough glues. We get through gallons of Unibond and Tretobond.'

They have no overhead flies, of course, or any mechanism for lowering sets, so the carpenters have to be very ingenious with gang ropes hidden behind bushes up to a hundred feet away. If there's a shower during a play, they quicky throw a plastic covering over the stage, then mop up before they restart, to stop actors slipping.

'The whole glade *is* our scenery,' she said, pointing to all the bushes and trees which grow naturally round the stage. One tree grows right up through the false Renaissance palace, coming out over the roof. 'We're just paying a compliment to reality.'

There are quite a few other buildings around the Inner Circle Road, some of them rather mysterious, hidden away behind high hedges, with few clues to their use, as if they might be secret Government institutions. Several of them are engaged on Governmental work, such as the

Conservation Studio, which is a Department of the Environment workshop where things like paintings and ceilings are renovated, and the Ornamental Ironsmith, another D. of E. concern, which looks after the wrought-iron work on Government buildings. At least, that was what I was *told* went on inside. The Inner Circle would be a perfect place for clandestine meetings, with only two road entrances which can easily be watched, and then countless bowers and shrubberies for intimate meetings.

It was thanks to the Superintendent that I found the *most* hidden garden in the whole of Regent's Park. Even then, he took some persuading, worried that if I described its location it would become overrun. You have to concentrate hard to find it. First of all, go round the Inner Circle (several times if necessary), until you see a large, handsome, cream-washed villa, St John's Lodge. This was the first of Nash's country house villas to be erected in the Park and is worth going to see anyway, as it gives the best feeling of what the Park in Nash's time was meant to look like. The entrance appears to be private, which is why so few people venture through the gateway, but be bold and carry on, passing the little Gate Lodge, then turn right and there ahead of you, down a broad swathe of beautiful lawn, is a secret Marienbad garden full of elegant statues and ornamental urns. It opens out at the end into a circle, with a fine fountain and a leafy bower, a cul de sac where you can sit and look back down the lawns towards St John's Lodge, yet be seen by no one. It must be the most *private* garden of any public park in London.

I sat and stared, convinced that an unseen eccentric gardener was somewhere at work, hidden behind the trees, creating the garden to his own and special taste, ignoring the municipal patterns which so many of his colleagues are forced to follow. I learned later that a lady gardener is in charge, but I failed to find her, or anyone else. It was just me and the birds, half in a trance, waiting for the Prince Regent and John Nash to stroll past, discussing their latest schemes. I noticed that the bench I was sitting on had been dedicated to a young boy of sixteen who had died in 1980, Nicholas Andrew Bacon, who had found this garden 'a haven of peace'. Commonplace words, which you find even in the noisiest parks, but this time I believed it.

They like to keep this little garden quiet because there are no laid-out paths, only lawns, which would soon suffer if the hordes started trampling through every day. You probably still won't find it, even from my description, as there are no signs to direct you there and no clues to say you have arrived. If you do discover it, handle it with care.

St John's Lodge itself is private, being part of Bedford College, as is another of Nash's villas, just around the Circle, known as The Holme, the second villa to be put up. This is equally splendid, with lawns sloping down to the boating lake, which was constructed for James Burton, a wealthy builder, who had been of great help to Nash, not just supporting him when his plans started going wrong but agreeing to take one of the first sites in the Park, thereby showing public confidence in the whole scheme.

The job of designing Mr Burton's villa was given to his tenth child, a lad then only eighteen years old, called naturally enough, Decimus. How many youngsters have been handed such a plum through their family connections? The answer is quite a lot. It is rare, however, that these chances are grasped in such a way. The young man did such a good job of the design that Nash took him on and gave him a professional training and he went on to design and build many of the most gracious buildings in and around the London Parks.

The main building of Bedford College, which is part of London University, is further around the Inner Circle, that large red brick building on your left as you come in from York Bridge, built in 1913, on the site of an original Nash villa, South Villa, which was pulled down to build the new college. Bedford College had previously been in Bedford Square and was founded in 1849, the country's first college for women. (Arguably, the *world's* first women's college, as its only possible rival is a school in America, not a college of higher education.)

Bedford College students have always given the Park a refreshing atmosphere of youth, mingling with the old buildings and the many older citizens who frequent the rose garden. This, alas, is soon to come to an end. The college is amalgamating with Royal Holloway and they are due to leave Regent's Park for deepest Surrey around 1985. At the time of writing, it is not clear who or what will occupy their Regent's Park premises.

I then left the Inner Circle, and its lush villas and lavish gardens, and came out into open countryside, walking up the Broad Walk in the direction of the Zoo. Turning back, I could see St John's Lodge, looking very impressive, yet alone and isolated, as if surrounded by a moat, with no hints of all the treasures and secret places behind or all the life and exotica going on inside Queen Mary's Gardens.

I stopped at the refreshment pavilion, which was clean and efficient but somehow uninviting. I was about to leave when I noticed that on the counter and in the display cabinets there had been a landing from the Orient, an invasion of little paper umbrellas, all in different colours and shapes, stuck carefully on the sandwiches and cakes. Exotica was obviously not confined to the Inner Circle. Someone had made an attempt to brighten up our little plastic lives. There were no other customers, except two delivery men in blue overalls, sitting at a corner table, filling the air with expletives, and no signs of any staff. Then a young Chinese waitress appeared behind the counter and leant forward on her elbows, lost in space.

I coughed and said a coffee please and I do like your paper decorations. She looked guilty and then smiled, but still worried that I might be an official, come to disrupt her daydreams or her decorations. She said she was from Thailand, not China, but there the conversation ended.

From the Broad Walk, looking to the right, you can see the roofs of Cumberland Terrace. You have to go up close, across the Outer Circle Road, to see Cumberland Terrace in all its glory, the most extravagant of the Nash terraces and one of the finest and most luxuriant architectural façades in the whole of London. It was designed to face the Prince Regent's own pavilion, the one that was never built. For a moment, I imagined that it had been created by one of the stage designers at the Open Air Theatre, working in icing sugar on a rather lavish budget, and that behind it was all scaffold.

The terrace is 800 feet long and has a central block with ten giant Ionic columns and at the top a pediment full of statuary set against a royal blue background. Nash designed it as one unit, to look like the front of an enormous palace, linked by arches. You half-expect a vast mansion to stretch behind, on the scale of Blenheim Palace or at least Buckingham Palace, but the front is basically all there is. Inside, it is simply a row of terraced accommodation, divided into flats, grand flats nonetheless, but not as palatial as the exterior might lead one to believe.

All the Nash terraces around Regent's Park were built to make the Crown some money, which was the whole point of developing and creating Regent's Park in the first place, but Nash got rather carried away and they turned out far more costly than he expected, and tenants were at first hard to find. Over the years, many famous people have lived in them. Mrs Wallis Simpson lived at 7 Hanover Terrace while H. G. Wells lived, and died, at number 13 and Vaughan Williams at number 10. (The last two have appropriate plaques outside, but I found no memento of Mrs Simpson.) Hugh Walpole lived in York Terrace, Admiral Lord Beatty at Hanover Lodge and Herbert and Cynthia Asquith at Sussex Place.

The Terraces, as they stand today, are a triumph of rehabilitation. The Second World War almost finished them off completely, thanks to bomb damage. Most of them were left empty and decaying and by the end of the War, in 1945, a Government report indicated that the neglect was total. 'Scarcely a single Terrace does not give the impression of hopeless dereliction ... there are in fact few more lugubrious experiences in London than to be obtained from a general survey of the Nash Terraces in Regent's Park.'

There was a serious possibility that the whole lot would be pulled down, as being beyond repair, and the site redeveloped once again, but the Crown Commissioners, and their advisers, managed to save them. By the early 1980s, the job of repairing was almost finished, though behind those

Cumberland Terrace, Regent's Park: the most spectacular of all the Nash terraces

majestic façades there are several houses which still need small fortunes spent on them.

I noticed there was one for sale in Cumberland Terrace, number 46, so I rang the estate agent, John Wood, wondering how much, thinking it might be nice to have a pied à terre, right on the Park, especially one named after my home county. It turned out to be a flat of five bedrooms, and I could have the 42-year lease for £225,000. Sounded a bargain. After all, you don't get much change out of a million these days. This was the asking price in 1982. It has probably gone up by now. There was also the little matter of service charges, £6,600 a year, plus £2,000 a year for the rates. Perhaps I'll stay in Kentish Town after all.

The firm had some other properties in the Nash terraces, all of them owned by the Crown Commissioners, with varying lengths of leases on offer. Number 29, Chester Terrace, a five-floor house, was on offer at £500,000 for 79-year lease, while a three-bedroom flat at 14 Ulster Terrace was £380,000 for a 91-year lease. The best bargain sounded a whole house at 8, Hanover Terrace, the next most desirable terrace after Cumberland, which was going for only £34,000. I asked for further details. Perhaps ordinary people after all can live in the Park, but it turned out to be an 18-month lease only. However, a 60-year lease would then be available, on condition you agreed to spend around £400,000 modernising the whole house. Thank you, Mr Wood, I'll let you know.

Back on the Broad Walk, I came to a large and elaborate fountain, built like a little church with an ornate spire on top. A notice said it was the gift of Sir Cowasjee Jehangir, 'a wealthy parsee gentleman of Bombay, in gratitude for protection under the British rule in India'. I wonder if he chose the words himself. Not many people today feel particularly grateful to the British for anything, least of all for protection. Thank you, Sir Cowasjee. For letting us know.

Ahead, I could see the Zoo which no stranger to Regent's Park should miss. It is possible to combine it with an exploration of the Park, though each should really be given a day to itself. The Zoological Society of London was founded in 1824 by Sir Stamford Raffles who became its first President. Several of the founder members lived around the Park and thought it would make a suitable site for an open-air menagerie. They were offered a five-acre site at first, though they later got more, but were forced to restrict themselves to a far corner of the Park, well away from the Inner Circle tranquillity or the fine gentlemen in the Terraces. Our young friend Decimus Burton was commissioned as architect and he designed some elegant buildings for the animals, several of which remain, notably the Giraffe House. Modern designers have included Sir Hugh Casson and Lord Snowdon who created the wire-mesh aviary.

One of the best views of the animals, and certainly the cheapest, is to walk along the inside of the Park, looking over the railings, which of course does not help the Zoo. At the time of writing, they are in great financial difficulty. Their 5,000 animals and 36-acre site are proving so expensive that the Zoo in 1982 was being run at a large loss, despite the high entrance fees. It looks as if one day the Government might lend a hand, with the D. of E. becoming ultimately responsible for the Zoo, as well as the other attractions of Regent's Park.

Behind the Zoo is the Canal, Nash's speculative venture, which was constructed between 1812 and 1820 as a link between Paddington Basin and the Thames at Limehouse. It was being built at the same time as the Terraces and the other buildings and suffered similar problems of finance and local objections. In the last ten years, several miles of the Canal, from Islington to Limehouse, have been opened to the public, landscaped and made into an excellent walk-way, while at the same time the old warehouses around Camden Lock have been rejuvenated and now contain one of the busiest and most popular open-air week-end markets in

London, with many restaurants, antique shops, stalls and specialist shops.

The rebirth of the Regent's Canal for recreational use is a modern success story. The only thing lacking is a map of the canal walk, at least I have so far failed to find one on sale. But you come to expect that when you walk the London Parks. You can find an occasional notice board, which shows a simple diagram of the local amenities, but naturally you can't put that in your pocket. It is so difficult to get hold of any information, either maps or leaflets. Regent's Park particularly, and its surrounds, have so many things to offer which visitors must miss, never knowing what is there. I managed to borrow a map of the Park from the Superintendent, published in 1961 by the Ministry of Works, price 4/6, but I had to return it. It was years out of date, yet it was his last copy. Is it a conspiracy to keep us out of our own parks? Or are they doing a Samuel Smiles and trying to encourage a spirit of Self-Help, making us responsible for finding out our own information?

Part of Regent's Park which is easily missed is Primrose Hill. You have to cross a rather busy road, Prince Albert Road, and it is very much a separate entity, so it is understandable if strangers never reach it. Even residents do not always realise it is part of Regent's Park and run by the same staff. As a Royal Park, it has a relatively recent history, compared with St James's or Hyde Park. The Crown acquired it in 1842 from the Eton College estate who still have several properties, and many associations, in the area.

The main feature of Primrose Hill is the Hill itself, 219 feet high, which provides an excellent panoramic view of London. There is a pretty lamp at the top, a favourite spot for models and photographers to pretend they are in the heart of some grand estate. Primrose Hill has a history of violent and dirty deeds, of bodies in ditches and fiendish plots being hatched, and it still today suffers regular bouts of hooliganism and muggings. It is much smaller than Regent's Park (around 50 acres, as opposed to Regent's Park's 420 acres) yet most years there are more criminal incidents. It is open twenty-four hours a day, which doesn't help, while Regent's Park itself is closed at dusk.

In the last few years, a lively local residents' association has grown up which has become very interested in the protection, and development, of Primrose Hill. They now have a big bonfire for the local community on November 5 and an annual sports day, run like a village green fair. Near the Zoo is a children's playground which boasts an outdoor gymnasium, a rather grand title for a few bars and ropes. A recent addition has been a boules pitch.

There are no flower beds in Primrose Hill, or any notable landscaping features on the lines of Regent's Park, as the Hill is primarily a grassy slope, but there are lots of well-kept paths and enough space and variety for a brisk half-hour walk.

I remember walking there early one Spring day in 1967 with Paul McCartney who lived a couple of streets away. The sun came out after a dull start and Paul said, 'It's getting better.' He was talking about the weather but the phrase made him remember a drummer who had once helped out on an Australian tour, filling in for Ringo who was ill. After every concert, they asked him how he was getting on, and he always replied, 'It's getting better.' It became their joke phrase during the tour. Later that Spring day, when Lennon joined McCartney to work in the studio nearby at Abbey Road, they turned the phrase into a song on the Sergeant Pepper album. They have blue plaques all around Regent's Park, recording that a famous person once lived there. Perhaps one day some fan club will put up a notice in Primrose Hill, saying that a Beatle song was begun here.

Despite its name, Primrose Hill has no primroses, and no one knows when they were last seen there, if ever, but there is a plan at present to establish them on the Hill somewhere. They want to grow wild primroses, naturally enough, but they are hard to grow in captivity. It would be cheating to introduce any of the cultivated forms. Only 'primula vulgaris' will do. The Regent's Park nursery has been engaged on this delicate work – they have their own greenhouses, separate from the ones in Hyde Park – and it is hoped that by 1983 they will have successfully bred the right strain and introduced it into the Park. The exact location is being kept a secret.

The northern reaches of Regent's Park consist mainly of football pitches, stretching almost as far as the eye can see across a flat and featureless grassy plain. It was now May, and the football season had just finished, but the worn patches which had been the goals could be clearly seen, soon to be covered in fresh grass, another season's games and arguments gone for ever. Over a thousand sports teams are registered at Regent's Park and there's a clerk in the Superintendent's office whose job it is to allocate the permits for the 19 football pitches, 16 cricket squares, 5 hockey pitches and one rugby pitch. The London Baseball Society, usually full of exiled Americans, also plays regularly in the Park.

The American Ambassador has his residence in Regent's Park, very handy for the odd baseball game, over in the north-west corner of the Park. It is called Winfield House which is a name you might have seen on those cheap paper bags you get in Woolworth's, though the connection might not be immediately obvious. Originally, there had been one of Nash's villas on the site, built by Decimus Burton and named St Dunstan's Villa, but this was demolished in 1937 when the present mansion was built for the Countess Haugwitz-Reventlow, as she was called at one time, before she married Cary Grant. Her better-known name was Barbara Hutton, and she was the daughter of the founder of the famous store Frank Winfield

Woolworth. She called her new house after her father. When her marriage to Cary Grant was dissolved in 1945, she gave up the house and, in 1946, it was presented to the US Government for the use of the Ambassador. Every name tells a story.

Not far from Winfield House is Regent's Park Lake which twists and curls in strange shapes so that a walk along its banks, following the various tendrils, gives an ever-changing perspective of the Park and of the London skyline. There are boats for hire, from the same firm which looks after Hyde Park, and as at St James's Park there is a Bird Man and a bird island containing a famous Heronry. There were six pairs of herons breeding the day I was there.

I stood for a long time on the Bandstand, a very handsome one, admiring the views over the Lake. This was the scene, just a few weeks later, in the summer of 1982, of an IRA outrage when a bomb explosion killed seven people. That same day, another bomb went off on the edge of Hyde Park, killing four soldiers and seven horses. In all their history, the Royal Parks had never known such a massacre. It is planned, so the Royal Bailiff later told me, to plant eleven trees in Regent's Park, a memory of the dead.

There is one strange view which all visitors to Regent's Park must now look out for, as exciting in its way as the Nash Terraces, but a totally foreign sight which almost appears unreal, a mirage from another world. I had caught glimpses of this unusual object while walking on the flat of the sports fields, its copper dome gleaming through the trees, then as I went round the Lake it seemed to dazzle like a beacon, beckoning me towards it. So I now set off, hoping to get my first close-up inspection of the Central London Mosque.

I didn't know whether I would be allowed in. Nobody I had talked to in the Park, either in the Superintendent's office or at the Department of the Environment, seemed to know anything about its rules and regulations or if it was open to the public. I approached it with caution, scared of being a trespasser, working my way round to the front entrance from Hanover Gate. I found myself in a huge inner courtyard surrounded by tall arched windows and doorways, and realised that the site was much bigger than I had imagined. The flashing copper dome is only one part of it, though the major one. There was a lot more concrete and glass than I had expected, which gives the buildings the feeling of a modern hotel, despite its Middle Eastern architecture.

The Islamic connection with Regent's Park started in 1944 when the British Government helped to establish an Islamic Cultural Centre in an existing villa, then known as Regent's Lodge. British Governments have for a long time been keen supporters of the need for some centre of Islamic culture in London, if only because London was the capital of the British

The Central London Mosque with Regent's Park behind

Empire, an Empire containing more Muslims than Christians. Work on the present buildings began in 1974, after the British architect Sir Frederick Gibberd had won an international competition to design a new mosque. The builders were John Laing and it cost over £6 million by the time it was opened in 1972. It is a study and education centre, with library and teaching facilities, as well as a place of worship.

I went up carefully to what appeared to be the main door and read the notices. 'Dress modestly and behave appropriately. *No* smoking or alcohol drinks allowed. Ladies must not uncover any part of their bodies except their hands and faces.' I opened the door and entered a long, cool foyer. Two gentlemen in white robes and embroidered white hats were talking together in what sounded like Arabic. I noticed a bookstall and went across and found it was selling souvenirs of the mosque, religious books, postcards, texts, for adults and for children. I looked at some mats which contained a compass in the middle, to help worshippers find the direction of Mecca, price £7.50, made in West Germany, but decided against them. Instead, I bought a shawl, price £2.20, as it was my wife's birthday next day.

I then looked through a doorway into the main prayer hall of the mosque which was covered in a rather lurid carpet. The high ceiling, underneath the dome, was equally garish, bright blue with lots of stars, like something from the London Planetarium. The walls and the rest of the hall were, however, stark and bare, clear and uncluttered, which gave an overall atmosphere of peace and holiness. Under Islamic law, no pictures or statues are allowed in a mosque.

There was a wire-mesh rack at the entrance for shoes, like a school dressing-room, so I took mine off and went inside. I could hear prayers being chanted through a loudspeaker in a corner but could not make out whether the noise was taped or live. About half a dozen men in bare feet were on their knees, bending over double in the direction of a carved wooden pulpit in the far corner. Two were wearing white robes and hats but the other four were in jeans and dirty T-shirts as if they had just come from a building site, which they probably had.

I listened and watched for a while, then put my shoes back on and set off to explore the rest of the building. I studied a notice board which contained an appeal for the East London Mosque, a job going for an Experienced Meat Man to work in Northern Ireland and a request for someone to give a home to three Muslim children. Upstairs, I came to an enormous library, full of Arabic newspapers, magazines and books. There were two silent attendants and one girl who was sitting reading. No one spoke or asked me what I wanted, but as I came out one of the attendants asked me to sign the visitors' book.

Downstairs once again, I noticed for the first time a sign saying Enquiry Office, so I asked a gentleman in a dark, European suit if he could show me round, apologising if perhaps so far I had been trespassing. He said he was Mr Ali, the house manager, and he gave me a selection of books on the Islamic faith, including a timetable of prayers held at the mosque. There are five prayers every day, which vary in time, depending on the sunrise. The timetable went on for several pages, like a list of seaside tides. Friday is their Sabbath and, on that day, they hold the main congregation of the week (1–2.30 in summer, 12.30–1.30 in winter) at which over 6,000 Muslims can turn up. There are often so many, said Mr Ali, that they fill the main hall and the overflow stands out in the courtyard, the prayers being re-layed by microphone. For a big festival, they have had crowds of up to 15,000.

He handed me a book which listed all the mosques in Britain, many of them very simple, without a minaret and a dome, but still places of worship for the country's Moslems. I counted 165 which included 14 in

Birmingham, 8 in Bradford, 5 in Manchester, 4 in Cardiff, 4 in Blackburn, plus individual mosques in Oxford, Cambridge, Brighton, Kidderminister, Worcester and Dublin. In Greater London there are 30.

There is a director general in charge of the Centre and three Imams in residence to lead prayers, but Mr Ali explained that Islam was a simple religion. Anyone could lead prayers and anyone could call for prayers to begin. The noise I had heard in the mosque was the sound of an ordinary worshipper, not taped music, calling for prayers. I admired the copper dome and he said it had been covered with a plastic coating to protect it from the weather. Would it ever change colour and perhaps turn green, which is what usually happens to copper? 'In a hundred years perhaps. One should live to see it . . .'

He said they were keen on visitors coming to the Centre, Muslims or not, as long as they obeyed the rules. The prayer hall was open to anyone. Women, however, had to go upstairs to a ladies' gallery. They were now getting around 2,000 visitors a week, apart from Muslim worshippers. 'Religion is satisfaction,' he said, smiling. He seemed friendly, if slightly cool and distant, so I asked if I could go up to the top of the tower, the Mosque's Minaret, which looks over the whole building. Minarets in Islamic Mosques are supposed to be functional as it is from the top that by tradition the faithful in the neighbourhood are called to prayer. The spire on a Christian church is, by comparison, purely symbolic.

'It is not open to the public,' he said, jangling his keys. I said I understood this, and would certainly not give any impression to the contrary, but it would be very interesting for me to be able to see the view of Regent's Park. He paused for a long time, thinking, then he set off quickly through the building and I followed. 'The ablutions,' he said, pointing to some stairs leading to a basement. I could see a shower room and rows of little wooden stools and a mound of plastic flip-flops, left by worshippers who had washed their feet before going to pray.

We came to a lift and up we shot, some 140 feet, to the top of the Minaret where we stepped out on a twelve-sided platform. The view even as the lift door opened was sensational – right across the whole expanse of Regent's Park. I could see every detail of the buildings and places I had been visiting that day – and a lot more I had not been aware of, such as the private garden of the American Ambassador's home at Winfield House, a view totally hidden from the ground. No wonder the public are not allowed up the Minaret. What havoc a sniper could cause. The far horizon was rather hazy, but even so I could clearly see across London and picked out St Paul's, Big Ben, and the GPO Tower. In the other direction, there was a good view down and into Lord's Cricket Ground and then beyond to Alexandra Palace.

'I do a little run to the Zoo every morning,' said Mr Ali, 'about 6.30. I always look out for the herons when I run past the Lake. It is very nice. London is very nice.'

I noticed a loudspeaker on the platform, facing down towards the large courtyard below, but the wires seemed to be disconnected.

'We did use if for calling the faithful,' said Mr Ali, 'but not any more. For two reasons. There are not many Muslims living just in this neighbourhood, and two, they could not hear the noise anyway. The road and the traffic and the wind is too noisy.'

The fountain in Queen Mary's Gardens, Regent's Park

We came down in the lift and I thanked him for all his help and returned to the Park, wondering what John Nash would have thought of this shining new addition to his master plan. He might well have approved. Sussex Place, which is very near the mosque, is not quite in the same neo-classical style of Cumberland Terrace and the other Nash terraces, but is distinguished by the fact that it has ten pointed domes, grouped in pairs. The domes were disliked by several architectural experts of the time, dismissed as being eccentric and too experimental. Now, they rather complement the dome of the mosque, as if, 150 years earlier, John Nash knew what the future might bring.

CHAPTER FIVE

Greenwich Park

I arrived at Charing Cross Pier at ten o'clock, ready to catch the first boat, whenever that might be. I had not been down the river for several years, since my children were very young, but my memory told me that the boats ran frequently and my other memory told me that it would be a waste of time looking for a phone number. You can spend for ever trying to find Charing Cross Pier in the directory.

A notice said that the first boat to Greenwich was at 10.30, which was neat, and I bought a return ticket for £2.10. I found I was going on a boat called the *Pride of Greenwich* and with a company called Greenwich Pleasure Craft Ltd. There are around thirty different boat operators on the Thames and, as with the London Parks, it is hard to get overall information, but they are surprisingly easy to use. You just turn up at Charing Cross, Westminster or Tower Bridge piers and a boat will take you down the River to Greenwich every 30 minutes, from 10.30 each morning. The last boat back is usually around five o'clock. (You can also go up-river to Kew and Hampton Court but these are less frequent and take much longer.)

Just over two million passengers used the Thames pleasure boats in 1982, compared with 2.5 million in 1980. The recession, so they say, has meant that native Londoners have had less money to spend on their day-outs, but they think the tide has turned as petrol or train fares for a day at Brighton or Southend have now become so expensive. As for foreign or provincial visitors, Greenwich has continued to be a major attraction throughout the last ten years, coming after Westminster Abbey and the Tower in order of popularity with the organised tours.

I asked the man taking the tickets for any leaflets and he gave me a bundle of brochures about the special chartering facilities his company offers. They have six boats and all can be hired for parties, with catering and amusements laid on, the most expensive boat being the *Elizabethan*, price £625 for an evening. He offered to let me see it, but I was worried I might miss my boat. No problem, he said. The *Pride of Greenwich* wouldn't leave without us. He was the skipper.

The *Elizabethan* was at the end of the pier, a scene of great activity as smartly dressed hostesses and busy executives with clip-boards rushed around and barmen and caterers prepared tables and displays of lavish food. The boat is a reproduction Victorian paddle steamer, with mock chimneys and paddles, chintzy décor and arty furnishing, built by the company at Greenwich in 1980. It has proved very popular with big companies entertaining important visitors. There's a sliding roof, so bulky video equipment can be loaded in. Recently, they had had on board representatives of the Zimbabwe Air Force, who were being encouraged to place some big orders with British Air Space. That morning, so the place settings revealed, the boat was being hired by the Provincial Insurance Company. Some folks have all the luck. Or at least some good expenses.

Climbing aboard the *Pride of Greenwich* seemed rather plebeian and bus-like by comparison, but there was a jolly atmosphere as we set sail. The boat can hold 270 and has a crew of three and a barman. It was early June and we were about half-full, mostly with foreign school children, either French or German, plus one large group of Japanese. I sat beside an elderly couple from Australia who asked me if I'd been to Singapore. That was really lovely, you should go there, what a stop-over they had.

As soon as we set off, a running commentary began which I could see was being done by my friend the skipper, standing beside the wheel, talking into a microphone. It was very good indeed. My memory of previous Thames trips is of the commentaries being rather poor. They are always done unofficially, by the crew themselves, so you can hear some choice Cockney accents, quite a bit of information you can't possibly believe and, now and again, a few good jokes. You take your chance, which is part of the fun. I'd rather have a live commentary any time than pre-recorded tapes which some boats now provide.

I learned that Churchill went to the City of London School (which I didn't believe, but it was true); that Waterloo Bridge was built with the aid of women during the war which explains why it leans slightly to one side (which I took to be a joke); and that the new riverside post office telephone exchange is known by the staff as Busby's Birdcage. The skipper came round afterwards with a hat, smiling and beaming, saying thank you ever so much, and then invited me to join him on the bridge.

His name was Eddie Smith and he comes from four generations of Thames watermen and lightermen. He started on the River in 1952, became a tug skipper, but the work ran out and he gave up the commercial boats for the pleasure trips five years ago. He had a packet of cough sweets in front of him, 'The Fisherman's Friend, Extra Strong', as he feared his voice was going. 'There's just so much to talk about on every trip. The problem is getting it all in.'

Was it true about the women having worked on Waterloo Bridge? Yes, he said, but the lean was just his little joke. 'One person refused to put anything in the hat yesterday. He said I was sexist.' His mate, who was

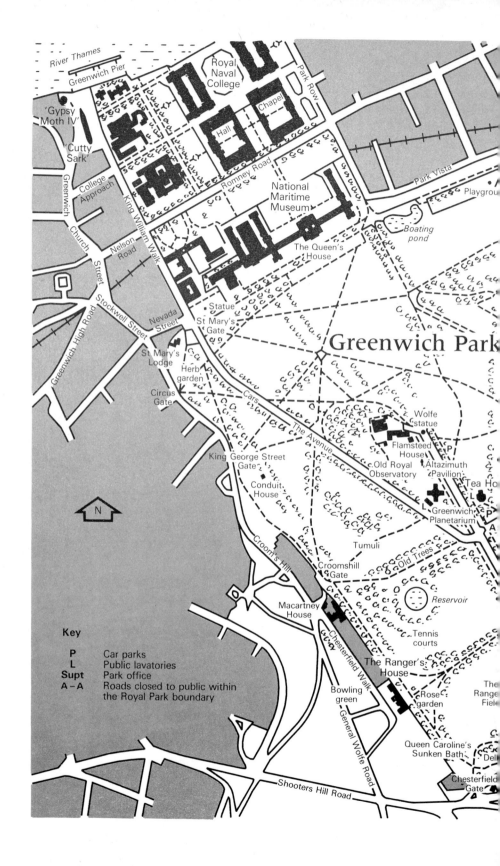

River Thames

Greenwich Pier

Royal Naval College

Park Row

Chapel

'Gypsy Moth IV'

'Cutty Sark'

Hall

Romney Road

Park Vista

College Approach

National Maritime Museum

Playgrou

Greenwich Church Street

King William Walk

Nelson Road

The Queen's House

Boating pond

Nevada Street

Statue

St Mary's Gate

Greenwich High Road

Stockwell Street

St Mary's Lodge

Herb garden

Greenwich Park

Circus Gate

Cars

Wolfe statue

The Avenue

Flamsteed House

P

King George Street Gate

Old Royal Observatory

Altazimuth Pavilion

Tea Ho

N

Conduit House

Greenwich Planetarium

P

A

Tumuli

Old Trees

Croom's Hill

Croomshill Gate

Reservoir

Macartney House

Tennis courts

Key

P	Car parks
L	Public lavatories
Supt	Park office
A – A	Roads closed to public within the Royal Park boundary

Chesterfield Walk

The Ranger's House

The Range Fiel

Bowling green

General Wolfe Road

Rose garden

Queen Caroline's Sunken Bath

Del

Chesterfield Gate

Shooters Hill Road

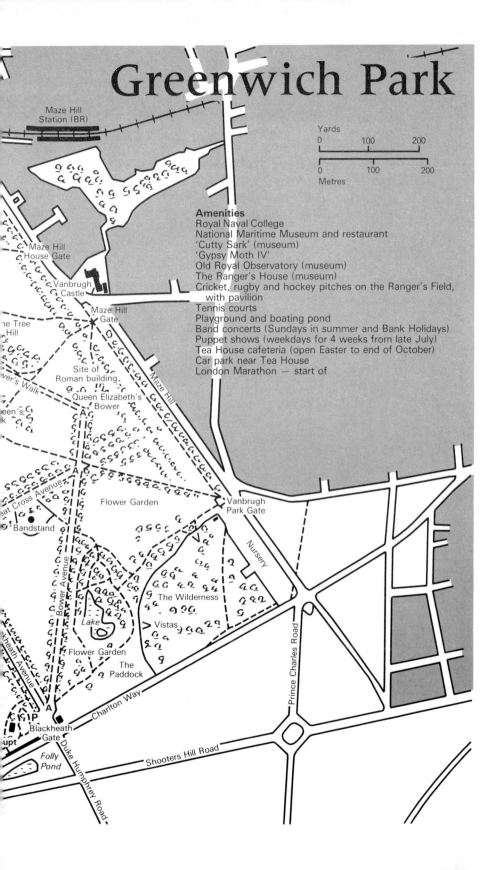

Greenwich Park

Maze Hill
Station (BR)

Yards
0   100   200

0   100   200
Metres

Amenities
Royal Naval College
National Maritime Museum and restaurant
'Cutty Sark' (museum)
'Gypsy Moth IV'
Old Royal Observatory (museum)
The Ranger's House (museum)
Cricket, rugby and hockey pitches on the Ranger's Field,
   with pavilion
Tennis courts
Playground and boating pond
Band concerts (Sundays in summer and Bank Holidays)
Puppet shows (weekdays for 4 weeks from late July)
Tea House cafeteria (open Easter to end of October)
Car park near Tea House
London Marathon — start of

Maze Hill
House Gate

Vanbrugh
Castle

Maze Hill
Gate

Tree
Hill

Site of
Roman building

er's Walk

Queen Elizabeth's
Bower

een's

Maze Hill

at Cross Avenue

Flower Garden

Vanbrugh
Park Gate

Bandstand

Nursery

Bower Avenue

The Wilderness

Vistas

Lake

kheath Avenue

Flower Garden

The
Paddock

Blackheath
Gate

Charlton Way

Prince Charles Road

upt

Folly
Pond

Duke Humphrey Road

Shooters Hill Road

steering the boat, burst out laughing. His mate, called Del, said he has a joke when he does the commentary about the Traitors Gate at the Tower. 'I say it's no longer used, but they're thinking of opening it again, especially for Margaret Thatcher . . . I cut that out during the Falkland Crisis.'

I got off the boat at Greenwich and noticed how well-painted and attractive the pier was, compared with my last visit. There is a rather good tourist information centre and souvenir shop right on the quay, another improvement, and something which would be of great use at the entrance to all the major London Parks. Hordes of foreign school children from the boat had beaten me into it, and were scrambling and pushing to spend their money on tourist badges and Union Jack tat.

I went first to *Gypsy Moth*, as it looked empty and rather small and forlorn, far too insignificant for its own stirring legends. This was the boat, *Gypsy Moth IV*, in which Sir Francis Chichester did his famous single-handed voyage in 1967, sailing 29,630 miles in 226 days, at the age of 65 and already suffering from cancer. He arrived in Greenwich in July 1967, and it was here, at the waterside, that he was knighted by the Queen, using the same sword with which her ancestor Elizabeth I had knighted Sir Francis Drake. The boat is preserved as it was on the voyage and has been on show at Greenwich since 1968.

There was more space inside than I expected. In fact it seemed rather comfortable and well appointed. I was inspecting an empty bottle of champagne, drunk on board to celebrate his 65th birthday, and his choice of reading material, which included a book about Alfred Hitchcock, some detective stories and some Shakespeare, all of them pre-war volumes, when I was knocked over by some English school children who rushed down the steps behind me. It was then I realised how small *Gypsy Moth* really is, only 53 feet long. They were from the West Country, by their accents 'Look, he's got his own loo,' said one girl. 'Is he still alive?' asked another.

The big boat nearby is the *Cutty Sark* which absolutely dwarfs the *Gypsy Moth* and its enormous masts can be seen for miles around. This is the last survivor of the early 19th-century sailing boats which raced each other back from China to be first with the new season's tea crop. 'To go at a clip' meant to go very fast, a term used from the earliest coaching days, and these sleek boats became known as China Clippers, the fastest sailing ships the world had ever seen, capable of doing 17 knots in a good wind and up to 360 miles a day.

The *Cutty Sark* was built in 1869 at Dumbarton on the Clyde and the name comes from a phrase in the Burns poem, 'Tam O'Shanter'. (Cutty Sark, a Scottish derivation of the French *courte chemise*, was a short shift, which you can see the lady on the figurehead is wearing.) It was fitted out with great lavishness, gilded with gold leaf, as the owner wanted a symbol he could be proud of, not just a fast ship. In the process, the original shipyard went bankrupt and no sooner had the ship herself started on the China run than the whole trade collapsed. Steam had arrived and steam boats could slip through the Suez Canal, opened in 1869, while the sailing boats had to make the long passage round Cape Horn. However, the *Cutty Sark* was changed to the Australia wool run for the next twenty-five years, on which she sailed with great success, till in turn the steamers took over that route.

I did a quick tour, as the hordes of school children had now become an avalanche, but enough to see the collection of ships' figureheads, to marvel at all the holds and cabins, and then stand high on deck, looking up at the masts and swaying ropes and imagine for a moment that we were about to set sail down-river for the China seas. I decided I'd better get my legs going at a clip, if I wanted to fit in all the other treasures of Greenwich. First the boats, then the buildings.

The buildings at Greenwich are a study in themselves, and many books have been devoted to them. Their history is complicated, but fascinating, not only because they represent the work of some of the greatest British architects but because at the same time they tell the story of the British monarchy, particularly of the Tudors and Stuarts. It is usual to describe them by starting at the beginning, which is utterly confusing for someone exploring on the ground, following present-day signs, as no sooner do you have the image of a Tudor Palace firmly in your head, working out which bit must be which, than you discover that it was either completely demolished, and there is nothing now to be seen, or that it was later drastically changed. So let us start by stating very simply what the groups of buildings are *today*, always remembering that in the past they were either Royal residences, or created by the Royals for some other purpose, usually with some other name.

There are three distinct groups of buildings which you come to in turn as you progress up the hill from Greenwich Pier. The first is the Royal Naval College, designed by Sir Christopher Wren in 1695. Hawksmoor and Vanbrugh were also involved in several of the buildings and the whole is considered a Baroque masterpiece. The second grand series of buildings is the National Maritime Museum which has two wings, and in the middle is the Queen's House, designed by Inigo Jones. Thirdly, once you have entered Greenwich Park proper, there is another more domestic group of buildings perched on top of the hill, the Royal Observatory, which includes Wren's Flamsteed House. The professional Observers have moved elsewhere, and it is the tourists who now observe each other, and the many objects around. The buildings are in fact part of the Maritime Museum, though it is still called the Old Observatory. One College then, plus a Museum and an Observatory, those are the buildings which we see today.

The National Maritime Museum at Greenwich: London's most stately public buildings

Now, let us move back to 1433, when Greenwich was a little fishing village. This was the year that Humphrey, Duke of Gloucester, uncle of Henry VI, got Royal permission to enclose 200 acres of open heath and build himself a crenellated manor house beside the River. As the Park was physically enclosed, if only with a wooden fence, Greenwich to this day boasts that their Park was the *first* Royal Park of all. (St James's Park was not fenced off till 1530.)

The Park and house passed to the Tudor Monarchs and it became their favourite residence, till in time they tore down the old mansion house and built their own palace. Four Tudor monarchs were born at Greenwich, Henry VIII, Edward VI, Queen Mary and Queen Elizabeth. Henry VIII married two of his wives at Greenwich Palace, known then as the Placentia. Elizabeth used the Palace when she became Queen and it was here that Sir Walter Raleigh is reputed to have thrown down his cloak for Elizabeth, a nice example for the gentlemen of the Royal Naval College who inhabit the site today.

I decided to visit the College first, as those are the buildings you see on arrival by boat, a dramatic and breathtaking sight, though I had forgotten how after that first impact there are several rather annoying roads to work your way around and for a while you lose sight of the whole. It is such a shame that you can't somehow go from the River straight into the College grounds and then directly into the Park.

I failed to get into the College. Not a good start, but one all visitors must expect as it is a working College, not a museum, and is open only in the afternoons, from 2.30 to 5. It would at least give me something to look forward to for the end of the day. I hurriedly crossed the busy Romney Road and made instead for the next stage, the National Maritime Museum.

I asked the uniformed attendant on the door, a small Scotsman with a precise accent and a meticulous moustache, what he would recommend for a quick visit. 'I would recommend, Sir, the Cook display, the Nelson display and the Royal Barges as perhaps the most interesting three places. Then I would visit the Queen's House. That is quite exquisite, Sir. It is generally said to be a Palladian building, but I personally would call it Tudor, with a Palladian façade. Others might disagree, Sir.'

I thanked him profusely, thinking how unusual to have such a knowledgeable person on the front door. As I walked away, I heard him give a little cough. 'But,' he added stiffly, 'the Queen's House is closed today for decorating. I am most sorry, Sir.'

The Captain Cook display was very impressive, especially his instruments set up in a tent. Lord Nelson's belongings were equally interesting and there was a large crowd looking and wondering at the uniform in which he was mortally wounded. I enjoyed the barges, particularly a gold-leafed, highly-decorated Royal barge from 1732, but I found the room next to the Barge Room, Neptune Hall, the most exciting of all. It is the biggest gallery in the whole museum and contains a full-sized paddle steamer, the *Reliant*, in full working order.

I then went along an open colonnade towards the Queen's House, passing a fashion model striking a beautifully bored pose beside one of the pillars, while a photographer and two assistants shouted great, trific, really great, just one more. I was able to walk through part of the Queen's House, despite the main rooms being closed. (On average, I don't think I visited any London Park without finding at least a part of one building closed for some reason or another.)

The Queen in question was Anne of Denmark, wife of James I, who had the house designed by Inigo Jones as her summer palace, though she had died before it was completed in 1635 by Charles I. Today the Queen's House has been restored to give a feeling of regal life under the Stuarts. It is said to have inspired the White House in Washington and has been much admired, and copied, over the centuries. I walked round it carefully, noting the spectacular view of the River. The National Maritime Museum took it over in 1937, plus other once-Royal buildings. Today, the Museum has

*National   Maritime
Museum: along the cool
Colonnade   to   the
Queen's House*

over 1½ million visitors a year and is the world's largest and most comprehensive maritime museum.

The Museum grounds lead right into the Park which I entered near St Mary's Gate, passing a statue of William IV who carries a staff, or it might be a telescope, at a rather unfortunate angle above his groin. On the right, as you go into the Park, there is a herb garden noted for its smell but I was unable to get near and smell very much because of a fence.

I then strolled up the hill along a road called the Avenue, which is a public motor way, enabling cars to cut right through Greenwich Park and out the other side at the Blackheath Gate, which of course we visitors who arrive by boat, as those Tudor and Stuart Monarchs used to do, do not approve of. Sailing to Greenwich is a hundred times more pleasant than driving there.

To my right I could see the handsome houses in Crooms Hill, some of the most desirable residences in London. I once visited the journalist Nicholas Tomalin when he had a house there and also the Poet Laureate, Cecil Day Lewis, and I envied their homes, but I remember thinking would I *really* want to live so far away from Central London. Much more convenient to have a house overlooking Regent's Park, but of course there would then be no river to admire. Everyone can fantasise on his or her ideal London house, which is what the Royals did. The fact that they could hire the best architects, organise the choicest views, rope in the pleasantest bits of park, didn't stop them changing their mind, suffering from river mists, falling out with the builder or, even more inconvenient, dying before all the wonderful schemes had been completed.

The name Crooms Hill is thought to come from the Celtic *crom* or *crum* meaning crooked and you can see clearly how the road does wind its way up the hillside. It probably pre-dates the Romans, as they always built their roads very straight, and if so it could be the oldest human thoroughfare in the country which is still in use.

On the grassy slopes the recent hot weather had dried out the soil and the thousands of children who regularly roll down this hill had worn away several bare patches. I watched a group of Cockney families having picnics, with the Mums asleep on the grass, their summer frocks half off and the empty plastic bottles of pop all around.

Once I was on the top, the people changed and it was like being in a foreign country. The ridge was swarming with French, German and other nationalities, all queueing up to visit the Royal Observatory and take photographs of each other on a bit of metal marked in the ground, proving they had one foot in the Western Hemisphere and one in the Eastern. Organised parties do the three major sites, but rarely have time or interest for the parkland in between.

The Royal Observatory was founded in 1675 by Charles II who appointed the Rev. John Flamsteed as the first Astronomer Royal and commissioned Christopher Wren to design the building. The King wanted to help his sailors and navigators and had heard that Flamsteed, who had delivered a report to the Royal Society, was convinced that the longitude of places could be established, and navigation made easy, when the skies had been properly surveyed.

Flamsteed, who had been born near Derby in 1646, suffered from poor health, and lack of funds, and hoped that the King's handsome offer would solve all his problems. Wren was an amateur astronomer himself, and looked forward to designing the new building which, as he neatly put it, had two purposes – 'for the Observator's habitation and a little for Pompe'. The job had to be done cheaply, using the foundations of an ancient tower, and the money was raised by selling some old gunpowder for £520. But the King seems to have lost interest after his initial enthusiasm and Flamsteed found that when he moved in he had to buy his own instruments and that his salary of £100 was not enough to live on and he had to take in pupils.

His researches over the next forty years proved of vital importance for the whole world and the results were eagerly awaited. On occasions, some people could not wait for them to appear. 'How unworthily, nay treacherously, I am dealt by Sir I. Newton,' so Flamsteed complained. Newton urgently needed some of Flamsteed's researches for his own work

Astride the world at Greenwich Observatory: East and West, and ever the twain shall meet

on gravity and decided in the end, after endless rows, to publish them himself, even in an incomplete form. 400 copies were printed, much to Flamsteed's fury, but he managed to get hold of all 300 unsold copies and burned them. Scientific rows today are just not the same.

The research at Greenwich went on after his death, the second Astronomer Royal being Edmond Halley, and it was in 1767 that the Greenwich Meridian, the standard line from which the world's longitude is measured, first began to be used by British sailors and British map-makers. Greenwich also laid down a basic time system, Greenwich Mean Time, but it was some years before this was generally used, even in Britain. Until the coming of the railways, most communities had their own local time, but from the 1840s Greenwich time became 'railway time' and standard throughout the country.

With the enormous expansion and increased speed of world-wide communications over the next forty years, it became essential for all countries to agree on a zero mark, for both longitude and time. Any meridian could have been chosen, but a World Conference in 1884 chose the Greenwich Meridian, mainly because 72% of the world's ships had by then got the Greenwich Meridian on their charts. The North American railroads were already using time zones based on Greenwich Mean Time and this too became standard practice throughout the world. So by the 1880s the world followed Britain and adopted the Greenwich rules for both time and longitude.

It is strange to realise that this little building, one hundred years ago, dictated two such basic principles which the whole world follows to this day. Britain itself of course only uses GMT half the year these days, now that British Summer Time has come in, but every school child in every country still learns in his or her geography lessons about longitude and that 0 is at Greenwich, even if they do get rather confused about time differences, and forget that Greenwich is still the standard. No wonder then that all visitors like to put one foot either side of Greenwich's little brass line in the Observatory's courtyard.

Flamsteed House, the Observatory's oldest building, is arranged much as it was in Flamsteed's day, 300 years ago, with the main attraction being the Octagon room designed by Wren, one of the few surviving unspoilt Wren interiors. There are other buildings to see, and the route through them is very well marked, containing old clocks and astronomical instruments. The Astronomer Royal and his assistants are today down in Hurstmonceux in Sussex, after it was decided in the 1930s that the London smog and street lighting were making observations of the heavens rather too difficult. (Perhaps if they had waited for the Clean Air acts of the last twenty years to come into force, and the end of smog, their vision might have been improved.)

I noticed a telescope set up in a courtyard outside Flamsteed House – which was free, just like everything else in the Museum – and I waited for a party of Germans in shorts to finish before I had a quick look. The view down the River was absolutely clear. Several miles away, I could clearly see the repro-paddle steamer, *Elizabeth*, the one I'd inspected earlier that morning at Charing Cross Pier, steaming down towards Greenwich.

The best view of all in Greenwich Park is from the nearby statue of General Wolfe which commemorates his victory at Quebec in 1759, winning Canada for Britain. Wolfe lived and is buried in Greenwich, his home being Macartney House, just beside the Park, and standing by his statue you feel you have really stormed the heights. The buildings around the Park are set out below you, both the Museum and the College, indeed all London spreads out before you.

On most maps of Greenwich Park there are no contours, so you do not realise that the Observatory buildings are on a steep escarpment. It separates two sorts of park, each with its own atmosphere. Down below, on the flat, is the popular part, where the people play and besport themselves. On the top, once you have left the Observatory and the foreign tourists, you are on a plateau which has a completely different feeling, much more formal and tasteful, full of ancient trees and paths and well-laid-out flower gardens.

Parts of Greenwich Park were originally based on designs by the Frenchman André Le Nôtre who had worked on Versailles, as well as St James's Park. Charles II invited him to do some landscaping and he produced a rather formal plan, criss-crossed with avenues, but he never visited the Park personally. It would seem that he worked from a map, and his schemes did look excellent on paper, but most of them proved not to work so well in reality. His main grand avenue was meant to go right down the hill to the Queen's House, but it never got further than the edge of the steep escarpment beside the Wolfe statue. It still is a magnificent walk, even if it suddenly stops, leaving you suspended in the sky.

The ancient trees include some Spanish chestnuts which stand in line like some grand family retainers, gnarled and twisted, but still tall and proud, which began their life here in 1663. The old cypress trees, usually standing on their own, give the feeling of a dark green Mediterranean cemetery. I searched for a tree known as Queen Elizabeth's Oak which turned out to be no more than a large trunk, about 30 feet high, but it looked alive as it is covered in vines and creepers and surrounded by shrubs and ferns, the sort of place where Robin Hood might have hidden, at least in a Christmas pantomime. According to tradition, Henry VIII danced round it with Anne Boleyn when they lived at Greenwich. Queen Elizabeth is said to have taken picnics inside, which is also possible, as it is a good six feet in diameter. Later on, it was used to imprison wrong-doers in

The Old Royal Observatory at Greenwich

the Park. Now there's a little fence round it, which you can peer over, and read a little notice full of bad grammar.

At the end of the plateau is a flower garden, with a fence all the way round. It felt like a miniature Kew with its open lawns, fine specimens of trees and plants and a little lake. Hidden behind it is an area of some 13 acres known as the Wilderness which is not open to the public. It is very easy to miss completely as trees and shrubs and a fence obscure it and there are only two viewing points. This is where the Park's herd of deer is kept, about 30 in all, a feature of the Park since the 16th century. There are nice historic reasons for still keeping them, but it seems an empty gesture as they are almost unseeable by the public.

Beside the impressive Blackheath Gate entrance to the Park stands the Superintendent's office and yard, so I went in, hoping for some explanation of the deer, but the new Superintendent had taken over only a few weeks previously and was still learning about the Park.

Jim Buttress is one of the more extrovert of the Royal Parks Superintendents. He was previously at Hyde Park and says he was the first to coin that rather rude description of the Henry Moore statue. 'Lovely bloke, old Henry, but I dunno what he's trying to do, bloody hell, you tell me. We once had several of his sculptures on display and we were told we'd erected one upside down, so I went to see the Curator and he didn't know which way up it was, so we asked one of his own assistants, but he said he was on holiday when Henry did that one. In the end only Henry himself could tell us which way was up.'

Mr Buttress is 37, unmarried, with three dogs called Crystal, Selhurst and Terry, the derivation of which any footbal fan should quickly be able to explain. (He's a supporter of Crystal Palace who play at Selhurst Park and were managed by Terry Venables, though Mr Buttress has now gone off him, since he left Palace.)

'I was once in Kensington Gardens with Selhurst and this posh woman came across and said, "I heard you shouting Sandhurst, you must have Army connections." It was too complicated to explain, so I just replied "Yes, Madam."'

He was still living in a lodge in Hyde Park, though hoping eventually to move to the Superintendent's lodge at Greenwich. 'My Hyde Park lodge is beautiful, right near Speakers' Corner. The only trouble is that people think it's a public convenience. Selhurst usually frightens them off. If he'd been human, he'd be in a mental institution. I used to have a rabbit which came to my front door every day, but the huge crowds for the Royal Wedding fireworks put him off for good. I had about 200 climbing on my roof, trying to get a good view.

'Rubbish was the bane of my life at Hyde Park. After the Royal Fireworks, we took away 60 tons of rubbish — and we didn't find a 2p amongst it. Oh, yes we always have a look at the rubbish. That's how Terry was found. He'd been left in a Hyde Park bin in a paper bag, a six-week-old mongrel.

'You hardly ever feel Hyde Park belongs to you, with all those public events. Now here, I can already feel this *is* a Park. Have you seen those lovely flowers? They're already telling me that their rose garden is as good as Queen Mary's. And those terrific old trees. Marvellous. And the cricket square. I couldn't believe that. I feel when I close the gates here it is *our* park. You can never feel that at Hyde Park.'

Greenwich in the last couple of years has become more of a public park since the arrival of the London Marathon. Millions of people must have seen on TV that magnificent sight when 15,000 runners start the race by coming through the St Mary's Gate entrance. Mr Buttress says there have been no complaints. All the locals have told him that the Marathon has been excellently organised, with no rubbish left.

He has no plans to make any changes, and approves of everything the previous Superintendent had done over the years. Well, perhaps he might put in a few more Parrot tulips rather than Darwin tulips, as a personal preference, but that's about all.

'The Royal Parks should not be changed. Every time we do so we're endangering our heritage. They must remain as they always have been. We're just curators. No country in the world can match our parks.'

As I left his office, I noticed on his desk a sign which said, I'D LIKE TO HELP YOU OUT. Underneath, in smaller letters, it said, 'Which way did you come in?' Full of fun, some of our parkies.

The cricket square when he mentioned is officially called the Ranger's Field, and it was a surprising sight. I had seen quite a few acres so far of London parkland grass, some of it quite attractive, but this was so utterly verdant and immaculate it looked like a perfect meadow. I never thought I would stand in London and get pleasure out of just gazing at some grass. It is well-used, by two local cricket clubs, and has its own little pavilion.

In a corner, against the Park wall, I came to a hole in the ground, lined with slabs of stone and a few old tiles, which is reputed to have been a bath used by Queen Caroline. At the bottom was some stagnant water. Two ladies with prams were staring into it. 'Is it Roman?' said one lady. 'No, too modern for that,' replied the other. 'I think it was for kitchen slops. Look at the rubbish at the bottom.'

Nearby stands the Ranger's House, overlooking the Ranger's Field, with a delightful rose garden in front. The house dates back to the early 18th century and in 1748 it became the property of Philip Stanhope, the Earl of Chesterfield, famous for his *Letters* to his son. (The *Letters* did not impress Dr Johnson who said they encouraged the 'manners of a dancing master and the morals of a whore'.) In 1815, the house became the official residence of the Ranger of Greenwich Park, usually a member of the Royal Family.

It is now a museum, but I had come across very few references to it and had no idea what to expect. I entered the back way, through a half-door from the rose garden, which opened like a stable, and surprised a couple of attendants who were idly looking out of the front door, as if hoping for customers. I asked if I could buy a guide but there was none on sale, which was a disappointment, so I had to pick up information from notices and captions. The house contains the Suffolk collection of Jacobean and Stuart paintings which were given to the GLC in 1974, most of them family portraits connected with the Earls of Suffolk and Berkshire. None of the artists is particularly famous, but the details in the paintings are invaluable, showing the styles of the period. Roy Strong of the V. and A. is a great fan of them.

I met no other visitors as I walked round the various rooms, all of them immaculate and gleaming. So were the attendants, each in a crisp white shirt despite the sultry weather. The lavatories were particularly pristine. Do ordinary members of the public ever go round the house?

'Oh, it's not usually as empty as this,' said one attendant at the postcard stall in the hall. 'We usually have, let me see, about six people at this time of day. It is a shame, I know, but I think it will take us ten years to establish ourselves. By 1984 we should be on the map. We're GLC, you see. We don't get advertised in the Royal Parks. We see the crowds going past to the Observatory and we wonder what we have to do to attract them. But some people come to see us just for the carpets.'

I looked around, convinced the floors throughout the house had been polished wood, and apologised for having missed any special carpets.

'No, no, carpets *in* the paintings. And the costumes. Students of the period love that sort of thing.'

I hurried down the hill towards the Royal Naval College to catch the last of its slender opening hours. You have to follow a line of railings, and not trespass on the naval parts, till you come to the two parts of the College which can be examined, the Painted Hall and the Chapel. It is an interesting-enough walk through the College grounds, passing some handsome Baroque buildings, yet the final view still caught me by surprise. Standing between the Chapel and the Hall, which are two separate buildings, each with a dome like St Paul's, mirror images of each other, there is a magnificent view of the Queen's House, beautifully framed, with behind, peeping over its shoulders, the Royal Observatory. You have to ignore, if you can, the traffic crossing the canvas in the foreground (on Romney Road, between the College and the Museum) but this is easily done. Then, if you turn the other way, you see the Thames, equally cleverly framed.

In many ways, such perfect views, so immediately appreciated by any eye, do not need an explanation. Is it not sufficient to say that Christopher Wren created these two buildings? Who needs further information? There is a school of thought which says that art should always stand on its own. 'Daffodils' is a good poem, or a bad poem, depending on your taste, so does it matter if you know of Wordsworth's relationship with his sister Dorothy and what was happening the day she wrote down their first impressions of those daffodils? Personally, I think it does. It certainly added to my pleasure

The Royal Naval College, Greenwich, from the Queen's House

of that view to know the struggles that poor Wren went to in order to achieve it.

You will remember there was a Tudor Palace on this site, where all those Tudor Monarchs were born. That decayed and was finally demolished by Charles II and work was started on some new buildings, to complement the Queen's House, but this new palace was never completed as money ran out. William of Orange, who was liable to asthma, and his wife Mary preferred living in Kensington Palace or Hampton Court and had no interest in Greenwich Park or their Royal residences at Greenwich and decided to turn the palace site over for a Royal Naval Hospital. Wren was given the job of conversion by Queen Mary in 1695.

Wren originally wanted to have as the central point one main building, containing the Hall and the Chapel, topped by a great dome, which would outshine anything in Europe as a piece of monumental architecture. It is hard to appreciate all this now, as a home for sick and elderly sailors does not sound such a marvellous commission, but it was a *Royal* creation, at a time when the country was celebrating some naval victories, and it seemed to Wren and his fellow architects that in proclaiming William and Mary as saviours of Europe they could also create something truly magnificent, a glorious monument which would be admired for ever. Wren spent twenty years on the Greenwich buildings, and is said to have charged no fees during that time. It was another thirty years before everything was finished.

Queen Mary hated Wren's first plan. She said its situation would ruin the view of the River from the Queen's House and she simply would not have it. Wren then proposed moving his central building to one side, knocking down an existing building to accommodate it (the so-called King Charles block), but she refused to have that either. In the end, Wren was forced to split his magnificent idea in two, putting the Hall and Chapel in separate but identical buildings, facing each other across a courtyard, leaving the Queen, should she be sitting in the old Queen's House, with a clear view of the River. To help still further, he altered the course of the River, to line nature up exactly.

I much prefer the result of his rearrangement. Each building is a masterpiece in its own right, and could hardly have been bettered by being bigger, but it also created another element, that perfectly framed view, one which can be enjoyed from every angle. Dr Johnson didn't agree. He told Boswell that Greenwich for his taste was 'too detached to make one great whole'.

The interior of the Painted Hall, the first of the two buildings which visitors can enter, is certainly magnificent, but not to my taste. On the whole, I prefer outside architectural glories to interior decorations. In Venice, I would rather be outside the Frari, enjoying the skyline, than inside, trying to examine the Titians on the dark walls.

Unlike so many Venetian buildings, however, the Painted Hall is light and airy with windows up to the ceiling and you can at least see everything, even if you can't appreciate all the 17th-century political alusions. The use of space and colour and light is very clever, and the various scenes painted on the ceiling and walls are dramatic, but despite a little booklet which explains the contents of paintings, I failed to pick out John Flamsteed who is supposed to be in the corner of one painting, or a symbolic figure of old Father River Tyne carrying a bag of coal. My eyes, and my patience, were not up to it. It is all a bit overwhelming.

How on earth did those poor injured sailors find solace in such gilded and ornate surroundings? As a Hospital, it was ridiculous, which was what one old sailor observed, rather bitterly. 'Columns, colonnades and friezes ill accord with bull beef and sour beer mixed with water.' Such love and artistic lavishness had gone into the building, but when the inmates arrived they received cold charity. Later, there were tales of corruption and controversy and eventually several investigations into maladministration until finally it closed as a Hospital.

In 1873, the Admiralty took it over and it became the Royal Naval College. Today, it has 175 students, all of them serving officers, working mainly on post-graduate research, in a building which has become in effect the Navy's university. The inmates now at long last are much more suited to their surroundings.

The long banqueting tables were set for dinner, with some fine candelabra. Behind a screen were some pigeon-holes full of napkins and rings. I asked a butler figure, who was bustling in a dark corner, carrying some cups, if perhaps there was going to be some special dinner this evening. He said no. This was normal. All the naval officers have their breakfast, lunch and dinner in this Hall every day, which explains why the public have such short visiting hours. 'It is *not* a museum, sir. This is a dining room.' On my way out, I happened to touch one of the pillars, wondering if the fluted bits were real or painted (they were painted) and the butler's voice followed me down the stairs. 'Don't touch the paintings, Sir. Thank you.'

The Chapel was another surprise, and probably would be to Wren, as the original heavy Baroque interior was destroyed by a fire in 1779 and the present design is more Georgian in style, clean and clear with a predominance of cool Wedgwood pastel colours. The focal point is a large canvas over the altar, showing the shipwreck of St Paul at Malta, painted by the American-born painter, Benjamin West.

There were few people in either of the two College buildings, compared with the hordes traipsing round the Royal Observatory up on the Hill, or the parties next door going round the Maritime Museum. I suppose the shorter opening hours put people off, or perhaps the lack of publicity. The Royal Naval College is alone certainly worth a trip to Greenwich.

I caught the last boat back at five o'clock, queueing up with various hot and angry foreign tourists who did not appear to understand the system. You have to go back with the boat company you came with, which is annoying. Return tickets are not interchangeable on other boats.

On the way back, I sat beside a middle-aged French couple who had several large cases at their feet. They asked if I knew where we were and I told them. Green-wich, they repeated several times, finally finding it on their London tourist map. They had arrived that morning from Paris and the weather had been so lovely they had decided, before even finding a hotel, to walk along the Embankment. When they suddenly came to a pier, they had jumped on the first boat, not knowing where it was going.

'This Green-wich,' said the man, as the boat pulled away from the pier and I caught my final sight of the Wren masterpiece, 'is there anything to see there?'

CHAPTER SIX

Richmond Park

Richmond Park is different. You don't find any statues in Richmond Park, or museums or stately homes to visit, and few of those neat little tarmac paths for pedestrians which criss-cross other London Parks. Throughout most of it, you are on your own, walking on unmade tracks which look little more than wide sheep tracks. Richmond Park is more natural than many so called countryside areas of England, at least outside the National Parks. Bring your wellies.

There are public roads in the Park, alas, which are regretted by the purist walker, but they stick mainly to the perimeter, providing a circular tour for the lazy driver who wants to see the main sights. The best-known sight in Richmond Park is of course the deer which even on the briefest of walks, or the quickest of drives, can easily be spotted.

I had always assumed from my own previous fleeting visits that the Richmond Park deer were accessories, a passing amusement for the passing public, luxury extras to brighten up the landscape, something for the kiddies. The deer are in fact the most important thing in the Park and everything is organised for their welfare. They have been there for 350 years. The gamekeepers still do their own culling and their own gralloching (or disembowelling) on the premises to provide haunches of venison for the Royal Table. Looking after Richmond's 700 deer is a very serious business, not something put on by the English Tourist Board. Richmond Park *is* a deer park, some 2,500 acres in area, where the deer are allowed to roam wild. By comparison every other London park is just a big garden.

It is an enormous Park, some 13 miles round the boundaries, and its size and its wildness make it hard to believe that the centre of London is just ten miles away. Charles I chose it specially for its wildness when he decided to enclose it in 1637, building a brick wall all the way round, to give himself a bigger and more natural hunting ground. He was worried that Hyde Park was not secluded or private enough.

There had been Royal connections in the area since the 12th century and various Royal Palaces or mansions had been erected over the centuries, all of them now gone, demolished or abandoned. Richard II in 1394 actually *ordered* his manor at Shene to be burned down. His wife, Queen Anne, had

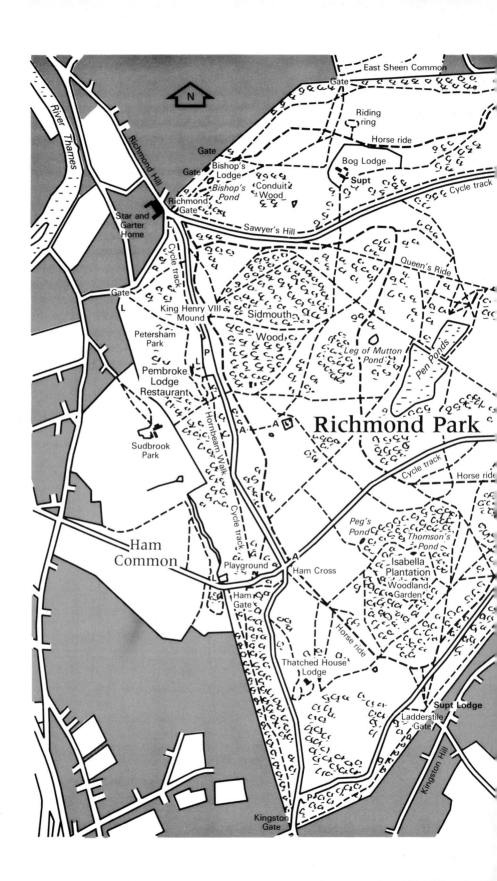

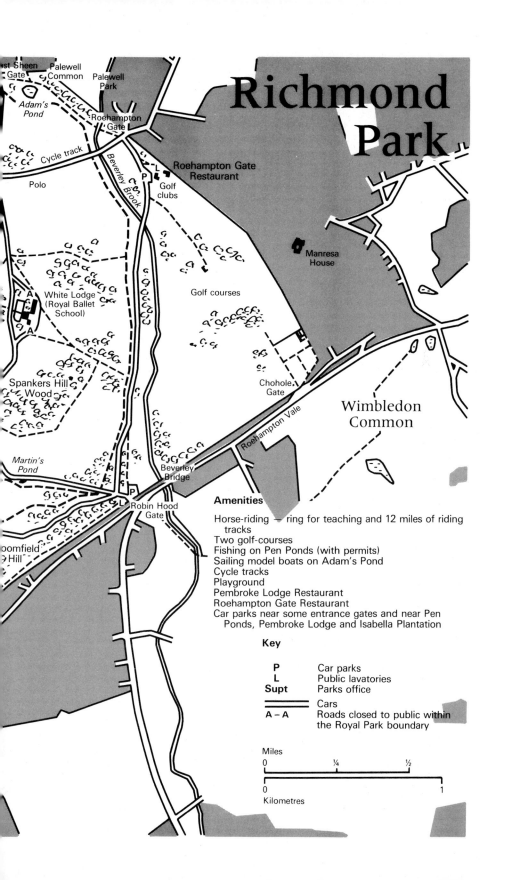

Richmond Park

st Sheen
Gate
Palewell
Common
Palewell
Park

Adam's
Pond

Roehampton
Gate

Cycle track

Polo

Beverley Brook

L
P

Golf
clubs

Roehampton Gate
Restaurant

Golf courses

Manresa
House

White Lodge
(Royal Ballet
School)

A

A

Spankers Hill
Wood

Chohole
Gate

Martin's
Pond

Beverley
Bridge

Roehampton Vale

Wimbledon
Common

P
L

Robin Hood
Gate

oomfield
Hill

Amenities

Horse-riding — ring for teaching and 12 miles of riding
     tracks
Two golf-courses
Fishing on Pen Ponds (with permits)
Sailing model boats on Adam's Pond
Cycle tracks
Playground
Pembroke Lodge Restaurant
Roehampton Gate Restaurant
Car parks near some entrance gates and near Pen
     Ponds, Pembroke Lodge and Isabella Plantation

Key

P	Car parks
L	Public lavatories
Supt	Parks office
═══	Cars
A – A	Roads closed to public within the Royal Park boundary

Miles
0   ¼   ½

0   1
Kilometres

Deer at Richmond Park

died of the plague and he was so grief-stricken that he couldn't bear to be reminded of the happy days they had spent there together.

The area was generally known as Shene until the late 15th century when Henry VII decided in turn to build himself a Palace, near the same bend in the Thames, but instead of another Shene Palace he called it Richmond Palace, after one of his Yorkshire titles, Earl of Richmond. The immediate area eventually became known as Richmond, after the Palace, which it is to this day, while Shene has been reduced in size, though it still has its own Common. Richmond Palace was well used by the Tudors, and Elizabeth I died there in 1603, but in 1660 it too was demolished and now only part of the Palace gateway remains.

Charles I did not build himself a Palace when he took over the 2,500 acres for his own hunting in 1637, but he was sensible enough to build six gateways in the walls to allow local people right of way. There had been some ill feeling about the way in which he had forcibly taken over the Park, much of which had been common land. He put up ladders over his new wall, where it crossed existing paths or thoroughfares, and one of the entrances to Richmond Park is today still called Ladderstile Gate. He also agreed that the poor should be allowed to carry away firewood as they had done before the enclosure.

There was a battle over entry to the Park in 1751 when Princess Amelia, daughter of George II, became Ranger and tried to exclude the public from entering, making her gatekeepers close all the foot gates. A local brewer called John Lewis brought a test case and after various and lengthy legal actions he won his point. Princess Amelia was virtually hounded out of Richmond and retreated across the Thames to Gunnersbury, giving up her Rangership in exchange for some lands in Ireland. John Lewis is still remembered in Richmond and his portrait is on show in a pub in the middle of Richmond Green, the Cricketers. Richmond still has an active local association, the Friends of Richmond Park, who make sure nothing like that can ever happen again.

There is no Ranger today, but Michael Brown, the Superintendent, and his staff of seventy would not dare to ban any of the public, though road traffic through the Park is one of the banes of his life. He estimates that between 30 and 35 deer a year are injured or killed through motor car accidents. He is not necessarily blaming the motorists themselves as he realises that very often the deer rush in front of cars, or are chased by dogs.

'It's very difficult to prove that a motorist has injured a deer. We just find it lying on the road, with its ribs stoved in, and it has to be destroyed. I admit the fallow deer can be a bit nervy, liable to make a sudden dash, but red deer have more traffic sense.'

Mr Brown is a lean, rather sombre Scotsman. He did a diploma in Horticulture in Edinburgh, went off to India for seven years as a tea planter, returned to Britain and worked for the Sports Turf Research Institute, then landscaped with the Economic Forestry Group. He saw the Richmond job advertised in 1971 and applied on the off chance, little realising how well his varied career had equipped him. Running Richmond is greatly different from the normal parks job and getting the right person can take time, but the open spaces of Richmond were nothing new to him. He knew about deer from his forestry work, and even his turf expertise had not been wasted as Richmond Park includes two 18-hole golf courses. Most Superintendents, when they have had outside experience, which is not always the case, have usually worked in commercial nurseries. Mr Brown sees himself generally as not being the same as most of his colleagues. He looked different for a start, wearing a rather strong tweed jacket, more like a laird than a municipal official, and he has become an expert, known throughout the country, on one particular subject.

He was asked to do a talk a few years ago to the British Deer Society about the Richmond deer and found afterwards that he had done so much research that he decided to go on and write a book. He had recently finished it when I met him, an opus of some 40,000 words. Two London publishers had just turned it down as being too specialised but he was hoping some local firm might be interested. If not, he might have to publish it himself in the end. Mr Brown does care about his deer.

At present, they have 400 fallow and 300 red, which is slightly more red than normal. The fallow can be any shade, from black to white, but they are normally chestnut and usually spotted. A fallow family consists of a buck, a doe and the fawns and they are smaller than the red deer. The adult red deer have no spots or patches, but they're not necessarily a reddy shade of brown, though most are. They are called stags, hinds and calves. The two species of deer have been there since Charles I's time and have traditionally been looked upon as perfect park deer. They do not interbreed.

All the males have antlers, right from their second year, which they shed every year around March and April. It is a bit like humans losing their milk teeth, except it happens every year throughout their life. Twenty-four hours after they drop, you can see the new antlers pushing through. Locals keep an eye out for this happening, and try to pick up the fallen antlers as trophies, though official policy is to collect all antlers, either fallen or from dead deer, and sell them to contractors and not to individual members of the public.

They also sell any venison which is left over, once the Royal Warrant list has been gone through. Apart from the Royal Family, there are about a hundred dignitaries on the Royal Warrant which dates back to the time of Magna Carta. There are the Prime Minister and various other members of the Government, the Archbishops of Canterbury and York, the Lord Chief Justice, Lord Mayor of London, the Grand Falconer of England, the Master of the Horse and other strange-sounding worthies. Most of them, around two-thirds, take up their allotment each year. At one time, in the early 19th century, they needed 400 deer a year to supply the needs, but today around 40 deer are enough. It is always the fallow deer they use for venison as their meat is thought to be preferable for eating. Any surplus is sold by contract and prices vary with the season, but they can usually make in excess of £10,000 a year from venison sales, with a lot going to Germany where the market is very big.

Richmond Park could, if required, accommodate a herd of up to 1,600 deer, but the norm today is 400 fallow and 250 red which they have found is enough deer to be easily seen by the public, enough to provide the venison, enough for the two gamekeepers to cope with and cull and enough to withstand any losses, either by accident or disease. The Richmond deer, touch wood, have always been very healthy. There is an image in the public mind that deer should be out in the wilds of the Scottish highlands, standing on a high crag amidst the Scots firs, but Mr Brown says this is a legend created by the Victorian painters. 'Deer's natural habitat is the sort of open oak woods we have here. They have had to adapt themselves to the Scottish highlands.'

There is a new development in deer husbandry which they have started at Richmond and they do not know yet how successful it will be. They had just completed a year during which the deer pastures have been treated with special sewage, Thamesgro, put down by the Thames Water Authority. It is pathogen-free, but full of nutrients which are released slowly into the ground and encourage good grass to grow right into November. The rutting season, when the deer mate, starts in October, and some of them become a bit exhausted, so they need good and easy grazing. The sewage comes free. The Thames Water scientists want a good home for it because up to now they have spent a fortune taking it out in barges to the North Sea and dumping it.

From Bog Lodge, where the Superintendent has his office, I walked round to Richmond Gate, the most impressive of the entrances into the Park and the one most people use. Just outside I could see the large red brick Star and Garter home with the flag of St George flying over it. There is a good view, once you get into the Park, looking towards the Thames down the wooded slopes of Petersham Park. This has been part of Richmond Park since 1834 when 59 acres were bought for £14,500, a high price for those days, but a bargain today.

Pembroke Lodge on the ridge of Petersham is a honeypot area, as Mr Brown always calls it, which attracts lots of tourists. It has restaurant facilities, a big car park and well-laid-out gardens. Having said Richmond Park is different, I have to admit this corner is very much like a normal Royal Park, back in central London, Although many visitors do not realise it, the ones who never venture further than the car park and café, this is untypical of Richmond Park. The *real* Park, the wild and open expanses, are out there, just waiting to be explored.

Meanwhile, in the interests of research, I came into the Pembroke Lodge gardens through a large set of side gates, set up to keep out the deer, and stood to admire a large wooden notice board which contained some lines of poetry, beautifully painted in gold letters on dark, varnished wood. The lines were in honour of 'James Thomson, 1700–1748, author of The Seasons'. He was a poet I had never heard of, a Scotsman who lived in Richmond for twelve years. I wrote some of the lines down nonetheless.

> Ye, who from London's smoke and turmoil fly
> To see a purer and a Brighter Sky,
> Think of the Bard who dwelt in Yonder Dell.

I wondered which dell it was and who had paid for such a handsome memorial. I made a note to ask the Friends of Richmond Park for details. One of the things about all London Parks is that you come across minor monuments and mementoes hidden away which are often in excellent condition, cared for by unseen hands. You also come across items which have been left to rot, generations of park keepers getting into the habit of ignoring them, taking the mower up only so far, then moving on quickly.

I asked a lady with a dog if she knew who James Thomson had been but she shook her head. 'I only come here for one thing. The air. Isn't it wonderful?' She looked down towards the River and took several deep breaths. 'I must always be high,' she said. I knew the Thames was out there somewhere, meandering in the plain between Twickenham and Teddington, no more than a mile away, but my eyes were not up to picking out any definite stretches. I caught a couple of brief flashes through the trees, but they might well have been shiny roofs rather than water.

I walked through a brand-new bower in the gardens, a walkway made of wrought-iron with some young laburnum saplings being trained to grow over and along it, all well-behaved so far, young and very fragile, sticking to their alloted places. One day it will be a long dark tunnel, strong and resolute, a cool refuge on a hot day, a trysting place for lovers. When so much in the Royal Parks is very old it is refreshing to come across new creations and wonder about their future.

There is a large and strange Mound in the gardens, known as the King Henry VIII Mound, with a path winding up to the top. One park keeper told me that this was the vantage spot where Henry stood to watch a rocket being fired from the Tower of London, a signal that Anne Boleyn had been duly beheaded. This would therefore have been in 1536, leaving him free to have his wicked but legal way with Jane Seymour, the next wife on the waiting list. There's no proof of this, though the King might have stood here once. Perhaps when taking easy pot shots at the deer. More likely, the mound was originally a barrow, an ancient burial place.

Pembroke Lodge is a long, two-storey, white-washed building which is today partly divided into flats for the park officials and the rest used as a restaurant and cafeteria. It takes its name from Elizabeth, Countess of Pembroke, who died here in 1831. Its most famous resident was Bertrand Russell. His grandfather, Lord John Russell, the Prime Minister, had been given it as a grace and favour home by Queen Victoria in 1847 and lived in it till his death in 1878. Young Bertrand came to live with his grandparents in 1876, aged four, after he had become an orphan, and it was his home till 1890. His father had wanted him to be brought up as an agnostic but he was made a ward of court and his grandmother brought him up on traditional lines.

The restaurant is quite smart, as Park restaurants go. There is a dining room, with rather elderly waitresses in uniform and a nice Adam fireplace, and two equally attractive rooms, overlooking the steep terraced gardens, where you can take snacks from the self-service cafeteria. The dining room set lunch menu looked reasonable, £3.80 for soup, roast beef and crumble, but I decided on a sandwich and a glass of milk from the self-service, as I still had a long day's walking ahead. The room was filled with a party of old ladies and gentlemen with sketch pads, out for a day's drawing.

The skies opened the moment I left the restaurant so I sheltered at an ice cream caravan, beside the gate leading into the Park proper, and got talking to a lady who turned out to be the wife of a park keeper. The young man in charge of the ice cream was reading a paperback copy of Kafka's *The Castle*, a student on vacation, getting some study done, thanks to the bad weather. The lady was a mine of information about the Park, not all of it correct. She swore Pembroke Lodge had been lived in by Queen Victoria's boy friend. 'You know, John Brown, that bloke she fancied.' She was a great enthusiast for Richmond Park and said how proud she was to live in it and that her husband worked for the *Royal* Parks. 'We definitely feel superior to places like Wimbledon Common.' She instructed me that when I got to the Plantation I should look out for a gardener and ask about the fox. That was all. Just Ask about the Fox. She promised me I would be amazed.

'Personally,' said the boy, taking a quick break from Kafka, 'I much prefer the woods in Bushy Park . . .'

I left the two of them arguing and headed for Ham Gate, a pleasanter entrance than Richmond Gate, far less busy, with a steep winding road leading from the gate, past ferns and up a hill, as if you were about to enter the Scottish Highlands. Not far away is Thatched House Lodge, the home of Princess Alexandra and Angus Ogilvy since 1963. Richmond Park might not have the stately buildings of Greenwich but it has retained one Royal Residence. I walked round, noting that it is not thatched, trying hard to get a glimpse of their swimming pool. My friend at the ice cream stall had told me to look out for it. 'Lovely pool,' she had said. 'And they paid for it themselves.'

The present house was built about 1727 (possibly from the shell of a previous building) by Sir Robert Walpole, our first Prime Minister, who had another house in the Park, now demolished. He was responsible for a lot of improvements and developments in Richmond Park and retreated there most weekends, avoiding the noise and bustle of Whitehall, cutting himself off from the public.

The best-known and the best-loved of the honeypot areas of Richmond Park is the Isabella Plantation. There are lots of signs leading you to its various entrances but the best way to approach it is from Broomfield Hill where there is a good car park. On a previous visit to Richmond Park, several years ago, I had noticed this clump of tall trees in the middle of the open parkland but had studiously avoided it, not wanting to go into some dark wood. By doing so, I had missed something quite unexpected and unusual, unlike anything I had so far seen in any London Park.

Floral gardens are easy to explain and even easier to appreciate and there are fine ones in many public parks round the country, though the central Royal Parks always like to think they have the best ones. But a *woodland* garden is something different, something much more unusual. The object of a woodland garden, where the overwhelming colour is green for most of the year, is to look natural. You don't get that regimented look of a flower garden, or those line-ups of lurid colours which keep changing, just as long as the gardeners keep emptying more pots and shoving in more plants. Woodland gardens are very subtle. It is only when you walk slowly through and examine the profusion of shrubs and plants and trees, most of them hidden away, as if completely lost in the undergrowth, that you realise the artifice, the love and care and attention that has taken place. City folk never see such delights in their urban parks. There is never the space, the time, or even the need as grass and flowers are what most people demand. It would also be a hostage to fortune. Think of the footpads who could hide in an urban wood.

The Isabella Plantation is about 42 acres, and was originally just a plantation, enclosed and planted with trees by Lord Sidmouth in 1831, then for the next 120 years left to become a natural wood. The reason for the name is obscure. There could have been a lady called Isabella, possibly a Ranger's wife, or perhaps the name comes from 'Isabell slade', which appears on a map of the Park in 1771, meaning a yellow valley.

It was not until 1951 that the old wood began to be transformed through the inspiration of the then Superintendent, George Thomson, and his head gardener, Wally Miller. They opened up the wood and created little grassy clearings, put in three ponds and introduced three streams, each fed by pumps from the Pen Ponds. There was no master plan, no landscape design created on an architect's board. It was developed on the ground over the next twenty years by the staff themselves, adding to it, piece by piece. George Thomson used to crawl through the undergrowth on his hands and knees, a ball of twine unwinding behind him, to mark the route which his latest stream would follow. There have been additions since, such as an island in Peg's Pond in 1976, called Wally's Island, after the head gardener.

The Plantation is now predominantly a mass of flowering shrubs, mainly rhododendron, azalea, camellia and heather. Around the ponds and along the streams are many varieties of water plants and ferns. There are still of course many trees, and it looks outside as if it is simply a wood, but the feeling inside is more of a series of glades than a wood with paths and sudden open patches. The present plantation has been schemed to provide a different vista at almost every angle, though there are no seats, just the odd log left lying around where you can sit and enjoy the clever arrangement of nature's own foliage. In many ways, this *is* open-air theatre, a theatre of the open air.

A notice at the entrance says a leaflet can be bought, price 20p, from the office, but doesn't tell you how to get to the office. Richmond Park, yet again, is a Park that keeps itself to itself. Finding the Superintendent's office is an expedition in itself. I had already been there, and bought a leaflet from his Secretary, so with its aid I was able to identify the leading specimens. There are little numbers at the foot of around 30 of the main or most interesting trees and shrubs, if you can find them, and the leaflet, written like a Nature Trail, gives their names, in English and Latin. Very handy for keen gardeners.

I seemed to have the whole wood to myself. I felt so privileged, as if I'd discovered it and could claim ownership, a secret forest no one else knew about. Then across a grassy glade, beside Thomson's Pond (named after the old Superintendent), I caught a glimpse of a policeman in uniform, one of the Royal Parks' police force, carrying a plant pot. He kept on disappearing behind high shrubs, then round trees, re-appearing in flashes through the ferns and bushes. He looked like an actor, on his way to take part in some sylvan play.

I dashed after him and eventually caught up. He stopped, without looking at all surprised. I suppose policemen spend their life being suddenly accosted by strangers. I said I was looking for the fox, the tame fox, which I'd been told lives in the wood. He smiled and directed me to the gardeners' huts in a corner of the Plantation which is enclosed and kept private from the public. On the way, I met a young gardener who said I could follow him, and, if I was very quiet, he would take me to where the fox lived, but he couldn't promise it would come out. He was called Mark and he had been working in the Isabella Plantation for three years, since

The Isabella Plantation, Richmond Park

leaving school. Soon, he was going to train as a psychiatric nurse. It was becoming a bit repetitious, working in the wood, though he still enjoyed it. He was in the best gang in the whole of the Park. Everyone wanted to work in the Isabella Plantation. It was so famous, wasn't it.

'People always say the best time to come is in April and May when the azaleas and rhodos are in full bloom. The crowds are enormous and the whole wood is ablaze. People then come in June and you hear them saying, 'Oh, we've missed it all.' I don't think there is any 'best time'. Personally, I think the colours are a bit calendarish in April and May. I much prefer it later. The autumn is wonderful. But there are no bad times for this wood. Late in the year is a good time to see the marsh plants and you get fewer people around.'

We came to the gardeners' huts and he pointed to a tree stump beside a thicket of beech and birch, half hidden by dense ferns. This was where the fox usually appeared, but she might not today. It most often was the vixen, though they had seen other members of the family. As we watched, the vixen did emerge, as if on cue, and then the male, followed by two younger foxes. They looked and listened, scraped the earth and found a bit of old bread, a gardener's sandwich which had been thrown away. They were only ten yards away so I stood motionless and watched them. The two adults were big and handsome, not wicked or scrawny or nasty-looking, as I had imagined a wild fox might look. They were more like brown dogs, similar in build and colour to the fox-hunting hounds who normally chase them on the Lakeland fells. Very slowly, having sniffed around, stared towards us, looked at the huts, listened to the world ticking, felt the air, they gracefully went back into the underground.

Mark then took me to meet the present Head Gardener, Eric Davey, who has worked in the plantation for 26 years. He has a staff of seven who devote their whole working life to that one little wood. Inside it, he has his own nursery, growing mainly azaleas. He estimated they had 100 different species of azaleas and several hundred varieties of rhododendron. He asked another gardener, called Mike, a bird expert, to help Mark take me round the rest of the wood, show me all the latest work that was being done.

They took me first to a new stream, which had only just been dug, so the bare earth around was still like a building site. They worried that the pumping mechanism would not be up to sending even more water round the wood and whether it would spoil George's streams. They talked continually about the old Superintendent George and Wally the head gardener as though both were still working there. Stored in this little wood, amongst the trees and shrubs, are human stories, legends of people now gone, handed down only by word of mouth.

They took me proudly to see a badger's set which is easy to find – marked Badger Gate on the Leaflet – but the occupants are harder to observe, unless you have a night to spare. Their set is nearby under an ancient oak, which also houses three types of woodpecker, Lesser, Greater and Green. They showed me a swamp cypress, some strange reeds, and a heather garden round Peg's Pond. 'We've put some trout in the pond, but I think the herons are getting them.'

There was little smell in the wood, which was strange, but the trees are mostly oak, beech and birch with very few pine. I had meant it as an observation, not a criticism, but they insisted on finding me a species of azalea which does smell, luteum, though it had already flowered for that year. Mark pointed out a shrub he thought was called Euonymus, though he wasn't sure of the spelling, which had very strange bark, shaped like fish fins. 'I always think this is a prehistoric shrub, the sort which must have grown before history began. I just love looking at it.'

'Don't look at those oaks,' said Mike suddenly. 'Look the other way.' All I could see were several lines of youngish oaks, laid out in a large rectangle. 'They were meant to be planted out *before* they got to that height, but it was never done. Now, I'm afraid, it's too late . . .' The symmetry of the oaks was obviously what had offended his eye. In the Isabella Plantation, everything is meant to look natural, thanks to a little bit of help from nature's friends.

I worked my way back to Broomfield Hill, after leaving the Isabella, to see if a view I'd been told about was worth the effort. It is a surprisingly steep hill, with the land suddenly falling away below, and the views are extensive, over the north-eastern section of the Park, but on the far horizon is a row of monster tower blocks at Roehampton, concrete warders guarding the Park. I kept spotting them from then on, weird space age glimpses through the trees or across the plains, just when you are convinced you are back in a mediaeval hunting park, alone but for the deer.

Now and again, in the distance, I could see a lone walker with a dog, but they passed quickly like ships out of sight. In a central London Park, you can *feel* alone at certain times, but a few yards ahead, round the bend, behind that tree, there is always the chance of meeting someone face to face. In Richmond, the skies do seem enormous and the Park appears to stretch away for ever. With careful timing, you could bring Charles I back for an hour or two and persuade him nothing had changed since 1637. Almost. Those occasional aeroplanes overhead would have to be explained as God playing tricks, hanging toys from the sky, and those strange blocks on the horizon must be your imagination playing tricks, creating castles in the air.

I headed towards Pen Ponds, the focal point at the centre of the Park. They are not as remote as they might look from the map, as there is a public road which ends in a car park, just half a mile away. On summer weekends, they become Mr Brown's final honey pot. Along with Pembroke Lodge and the Isabella Plantation, they are the three most popular tourist spots in the Park.

The weather was still dull and the car park was almost empty, but for an ice cream van, one of several dotted round the various car parks. Its windows were closed but I could see another student and a girl inside, mouthing to some music on a transistor, their feet up, staring into space, wondering where all the crowds had gone, creating their own world to make up for the emptiness outside.

The Pen Ponds are artificial and there was only a little stream here when Charles I enclosed the Park, but work began on them not long afterwards and over the years they were enlarged until by 1746 they took on the shape they have today. They do look like an old-fashioned pen nib, if you turn the map sideways, but the name probably comes from pen as in sheep pen or cattle pen. I found them a bit bare and featureless, but it was a windswept day with some realistic waves whipping along the shores and no doubt the ducks and other wild life were sheltering somewhere. The Pen Ponds are well stocked with fish, notably bream, carp, pike and perch, and the plantation at the end has become a bird sanctuary.

I walked up a broad grassy path, known as Queen's Ride, towards White Lodge, the only house in the middle of the Park, built in 1727 as a hunting lodge for George II. From 1801 to 1844 it was occupied by Henry Addington, later Viscount Sidmouth, who has a wood in the Park named after him (now a bird sanctuary, not open to the public), and he was visited here by Walter Scott, Nelson, Sheridan, William Pitt (he succeeded Pitt as Prime Minister in 1801) and other distinguished people. It then became a Royal home again, after Sidmouth's death, and Queen Victoria herself used it for a while. The Duke of Windsor (Edward VIII) was born here on June 23, 1894, and the Queen Mother lived here for a while after her marriage in 1923 to the Duke of York, later George VI.

I had a good look at the house through some wooden palings, but from that angle it appeared rather grey and uncared-for. I decided it must be the rear of the house, although the extensive view from it across the Park right to Richmond Gate was an excellent one. When I worked my way round to the front of the house, white-painted and in excellent condition, I could see that their front view was much inferior. There, once again, were the dreaded Roehampton tower blocks on the horizon.

There are no Royals today crouching inside, trying to avoid that view, but there are Royal connections, of a sort, as the White Lodge is now used by the Royal Ballet School. I could see lots of cars parked inside a courtyard, but no signs of any dancers. The heavens opened so I sheltered under a tree outside the gates, thinking of all the famous people who had once ridden up to this fine house. Two rabbits raced towards me, hoping for shelter under the same tree, then stopped and raced away again. When the sky cleared, I sat on a chair on a hill overlooking the Pen Ponds, a seat donated by W. P. Cubitt, another to add to my collection of inscriptions, and decided that this was the best view of all in the whole Park. I could see right over the ponds towards Richmond with no buildings whatsoever to be seen, even on the far horizon, something you can rarely say about any view in Greater London.

Coming down the hill, just before the car park, I met a lady with a pram and two dogs. She was struggling to push the pram across the grass, which seemed rather pointless, as there are proper paths at this point, but she said she *always* walked on the grass. She lived near Sheen Common and did two grassy walks every day. 'This is the most interesting part of the Park. I never come here at weekends of course. Pen Ponds are murder at weekends in the summer.'

She had been frightened by a deer on her walk that day, one of the hazards of walking on the grassy parts. She never fears humans. 'We don't get those sorts of ruffians. People in Richmond Park are more interested in themselves than other people. But the deer can be dangerous. It was a red deer which came for me, though the fallow deer are said to be the worst. This is the time of year when they drop their fawns. They just leave them there, in the grass for twenty-four hours, and you can stumble across the damn things by mistake. The mother's usually not far away, and if she sees you near the fawn, or even worse, if she sees your dog, she comes for you. Some deer are out to kill. I have several friends who have had their dogs killed by deer. They must get about ten a year. If they do come at you, then you must stand up to them and not be frightened. It's really the dogs they're after.'

I told her that according to the Superintendent it was the dogs who caused all the trouble, not the other way round. 'Regulars don't let their dogs upset the deer, but I suppose you do get strangers who come into the Park at weekends with things like Alsatians and let them chase the deer. That's when they stampede and go wild, and that's when accidents happen.'

We chatted and I happened to mention that I had found the Pen Ponds a bit barren. *That* was precisely the quality she liked about them. 'Far better than those pretty little ponds in the London parks,' she said with a sneer. 'Pen Ponds are wonderful in winter when there's no one around and the wild geese arrive.

'We moved from Central London three years ago. I wanted to live out in the country but my husband didn't want to commute forty miles. So we compromised on Richmond. I now think it's *better* than the real countryside. You can't get such open walks in the countryside, because of the farmers.

'I wouldn't walk on Wimbledon Common, not on my own, because of all the assaults. I have heard Barnes Common is even worse. In Sheen Woods we now get lots of flashers. Richmond is so open, yet so well patrolled.'

Her baby had wakened and was now crying so I said goodbye and she headed back for her car in the car park. I offered to help her de-camp, when I saw her struggling to take the pram to pieces and get it into the boot, and control the two dogs who were rushing around, but she said she could manage, thank you very much. Very independent, these young wives of Richmond Park.

I finished my walk at the Roehampton Gate end of the Park, which I had been putting off, but I felt I had to see the two public golf courses which the Park authorities are very proud of. This is the artisans' end of the Park, at least that word is used on a plaque outside the golf course. It marks the club's foundation in 1923 by the 'Artisan Golfers Association'.

The club house was very busy, despite the bad weather, and the prices seemed very reasonable, £2 a round weekdays, £3 at weekends. A man at the ticket office said that they were the fourth or fifth most popular municipal golf course in Britain. 'One in St Andrews is first, then Beckenham, then one in Birmingham. We're usually about next.'

I followed the signs to the Golf Course Restaurant, as after a hard day's walking, my longest so far, I felt in need of some refreshment, but it was closed for renovation. Nearby was a kiosk selling food, with a few youths hanging about, throwing litter on the ground, and I asked what was on the menu. An uninterested girl behind the counter pointed to a notice: 'We regret due to a break-in and theft of our micro oven that we are at present unable to supply hot food.' Not the micro oven. Some thieves these days have no respect.

I walked back towards Sheen Gate where I had entered early that morning, leaving the tower blocks behind me, and was soon back in the lush and open grass and woodlands. On the way I passed a polo pitch. It seemed to be deserted. Not a toff or an artisan in sight. Just me and the deer.

CHAPTER SEVEN

Hampton Court and Bushy Parks

However did Thomas Wolsey manage it? For a butcher's son from Ipswich, he did awfully well. Starting as a humble priest in 1498, he had worked his way up till in 1515 he had become Archbishop of York, a Cardinal and Henry VIII's Lord Chancellor, the second most powerful man in the Kingdom. So much for the basic facts, which you can read in any history book.

It is only when you *see* with your own eyes one of his possessions that history takes on a reality, a flesh and blood proof of his incredible achievement. Or should one say his insatiable greed? Hampton Court Palace is still today one of the most magnificent houses in Great Britain — yet it was just *one* of Cardinal Wolsey's houses, his country home, which he popped down to for the weekend from London as a break from running the country. His London home was York House, which later became Whitehall, the sovereign's main Palace, till it was accidentally burned down in 1698, due to the carelessness of a Dutch washerwoman.

Cardinal Wolsey had been looking for something a bit special when in 1514 he decided it was time to acquire for himself a country estate. First of all, he employed the best physicians in England, and even called in doctors from Padua, to select for him the healthiest spot within 20 miles of London. The Hampton Court estate was chosen for its 'extraordinary salubrity'. Another priority was easy access to London. Being on the river was a great advantage, for Wolsey and for subsequent Royal residents and visitors. Terribly handy for Whitehall, Richmond or Greenwich. (Today, a country estate might be advertised as being handy for the Motorway. Then, access to the Thames was what mattered.)

Wolsey bought in all 2,000 acres of parkland and this is there still and basically intact, although a road through the middle now cuts it roughly in half, the northern section being called Bushy Park and the southern Home Park, the name generally given for the parkland immediately outside Hampton Court Palace.

Having bought the Park, Wolsey's next task was to build himself a suitable house, something which would be imposing enough for the man who was known by his contemporaries as 'the proudest prelate that ever

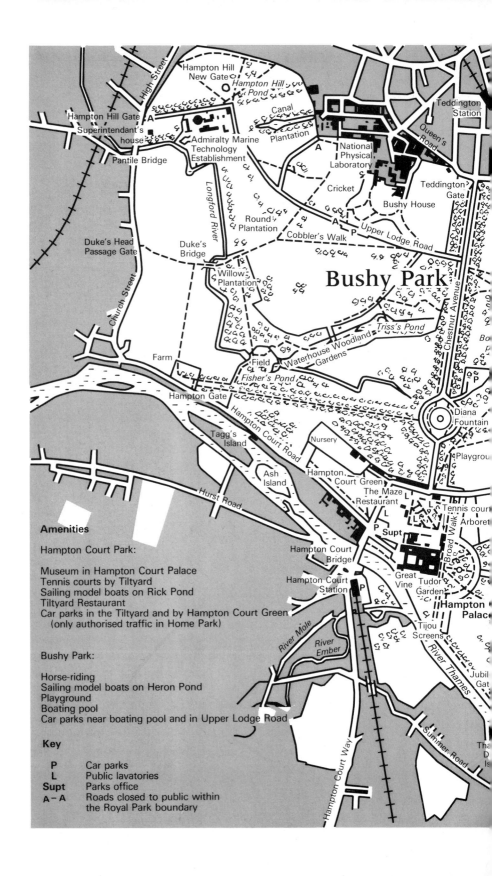

Teddington
Station

Hampton Hill
New Gate

High Street

Hampton Hill
Pond

Canal
Plantation

Queen's
Road

Hampton Hill Gate
Superintendant's
house

Admiralty Marine
Technology
Establishment

National
Physical
Laboratory

Teddington
Gate

Pantile Bridge

Longford River

Cricket

Bushy House

Duke's Head
Passage Gate

Duke's
Bridge

Round
Plantation

Cobbler's Walk

Upper Lodge Road

Bushy Park

Church Street

Willow
Plantation

Triss's Pond

Bo

Chestnut Avenue

Farm

Field

Waterhouse Woodland
Gardens

Fisher's Pond

Hampton Gate

Hampton Court Road

Diana
Fountain

Tagg's
Island

Nursery

Playgrou

Hurst Road

Ash
Island

Hampton
Court Green

The Maze
Restaurant

Tennis court

Arboret

Amenities

Hampton Court Park:

Museum in Hampton Court Palace
Tennis courts by Tiltyard
Sailing model boats on Rick Pond
Tiltyard Restaurant
Car parks in the Tiltyard and by Hampton Court Green
   (only authorised traffic in Home Park)

Bushy Park:

Horse-riding
Sailing model boats on Heron Pond
Playground
Boating pool
Car parks near boating pool and in Upper Lodge Road

Key

P	Car parks
L	Public lavatories
Supt	Parks office
A–A	Roads closed to public within the Royal Park boundary

Supt

Hampton Court
Bridge

Hampton Court
Station

Great
Vine

Tudor
Garden

Broad Walk

**Hampton
Palac**

River Mole

River
Ember

Tijou
Screens

River Thames

Jubil
Gat

Hampton Court Way

Summer Road

Tha
D
Is

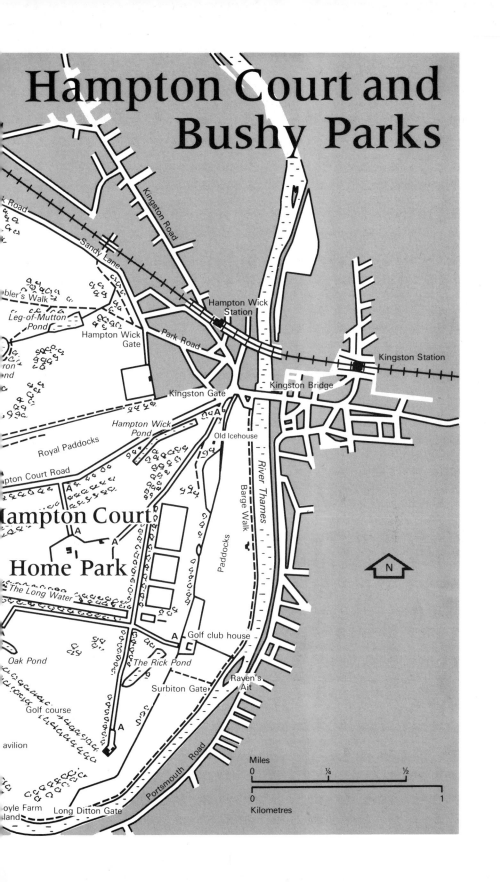

Hampton Court and Bushy Parks

k Road

Kingston Road

Sandy Lane

bler's Walk

Leg-of-Mutton
Pond

Hampton Wick
Station

Hampton Wick
Gate

Park Road

ron
nd

Kingston Gate

Kingston Station

Kingston Bridge

Hampton Wick
Pond

A

Old Icehouse

Royal Paddocks

River Thames

pton Court Road

A

Barge Walk

Hampton Court

A

Home Park

Paddocks

The Long Water

N

Oak Pond

A

Golf club house

The Rick Pond

Raven's
Ait

Surbiton Gate

Golf course

A

Portsmouth Road

avilion

oyle Farm   Long Ditton Gate
land

Miles

0   ¼   ½

0   1

Kilometres

Hampton Court Palace: the country house that Wolsey built for himself

breathed'. His house turned out rather big, even by Royal Standards, with 1,000 rooms, 280 silken beds and a household staff of 500. When he entertained the French Ambassador, he was able to sleep 100 French noblemen at a time, accommodating them with the utmost luxury and providing three days of non-stop hunting and entertainment, all on his own estate. The Venetian Ambassador, when he came to pay court, wrote an account of 'Wolsey's Closet', the Cardinal's personal room, which is still on show in the Palace. 'One has to traverse eight rooms before one reaches his audience chamber, and they are all hung with tapestry which is changed once a week.'

Hampton Court Palace is still today one of the most royal of all the Royal Palaces and Castles and homes. I would rather live there any time than in Buckingham Palace. Think of all the traffic noise they have to put up with, not to mention intruders, and even in their private garden, which is rather small anyway, only 40 acres, you can still hear the throb from Hyde Park

Corner. Hampton Court Palace is not only architecturally more distinguished, it has a real park, where you can stretch your legs. It is the only one of today's Royal Parks which the Royals got second-hand – St James's, Hyde, Kensington, Regent's, Greenwich, and Richmond Parks were all enclosed in the first place by Royal proclamation – and was entirely the work of a jumped-up cleric, a provincial on the make.

The English nobles were naturally jealous that such a low-born person had grown so powerful, and once things started to go wrong for him, they worked hard at turning the King against him. The immediate cause of his downfall was his failure to persuade the Pope to annul Henry's marriage to Catharine of Aragon. He himself had been decidedly worldly, turning his enormous legal and political and ecclesiastical powers to his own advantage, and had been far from chaste, despite his clerical vows, having an illegitimate son and daughter. He decided in 1525 to hand over Hampton Court to the King, hoping perhaps that he could keep the King's favours for a while longer. Four years later, in 1529, all his lands were taken from him and he was eventually stripped of all his offices.

Henry VIII stocked the park with deer and over the centuries various other monarchs made alterations, some of them major, but in essence the Palace is still Wolsey's creation. It has survived remarkably well, unchanged and un-ruined, as long as you do not consider that a surfeit of tourists is a ruination. They flock there for very good reasons. While Greenwich and its associated buildings is perhaps a more splendid sight, though maybe a trifle austere for some tastes, Hampton Court with its Palace and Gardens is more luxuriant. Would I choose it as my number one setting in all the London Parks? It's a hard decision, but how lucky we are, having such treasures to argue about.

I started with the Palace, though determined not to spend too long inside, as the day was so fine and the intention was to walk the Parks not the corridors. I knew from previous experience that you can spend a whole day looking at the Palace, yet still feel you've missed something. Most of all, you can still feel lost. There are so many rooms and corridors and courtyards, all interconnecting, but leading you on in such a way that it is easy to walk straight past the entrance to something even more interesting, and never know it was there. The gardens around the Palace are equally confusing. Even now, sitting trying to recollect in tranquillity, I fear there are vital bits I probably never saw. Hampton Court's best-known feature is its Maze, and it is as if they have taken this image and applied it to the site as a whole, setting the public the puzzle of finding their own way around.

The official guides are of little help. Inside the Palace, there's a busy bookshop, which was full of school children and tourists, and I bought a nicely-produced and well-written HMSO booklet on the Parks and Gardens, but the only map in it was completely inadequate. The little

Hampton Court Palace: statues and security

formal gardens were on the same scale as the open parks, all 2,000 acres of them. So I bought a Palace guide, also full of pretty colour photographs, but the map there gave only the State Apartments. I stood inside one of the many internal courtyards, wondering how I'd got in, which was the main entrance, how to get out and which exits might lead to the Gardens. I felt exceptionally stupid. All around me were large parties with professional guides trotting out their set speeches, then rushing on to the next excitement. An attendant told me later that the average coachload spends only twenty minutes inside the Palace, which must be a slight exaggeration, but I would think that the 700,000 people who do visit the Palace every year see very little of it, and even less of the formal Gardens outside, which is the greatest pity of all.

The Tudor connection is what appeals most. I followed a group of Americans, as they seemed to have a very good guide, but when they had been shown Anne Boleyn's Gateway, they decided it was time to move on. They therefore missed the fun of looking for signs of Henry's other wives. Anne Boleyn's coat of arms had to be quickly obliterated, when she lost her head, and workmen had to start carving JS instead of AB in the Queen's apartments when Jane Seymour took her place. The so-called Haunted Gallery is supposed to be visited by the ghost of Jane Seymour and also by

Catherine Howard, Henry's fifth wife, who was dragged screaming through the Palace, before ending up on the scaffold. The Tudors will probably pull them in for ever, not just those who have read their history books but the many other millions who have thrilled to the sagas on their television screen.

The most important Monarch in the Palace's history after the Tudors was William III, not as glamorous a figure as Henry VIII but it was he who brought in Christopher Wren, whose ghost, or at least his drawings, hover behind so many of our Royal Parks. Wren built new apartments and re-schemed much of the Gardens. Alternate Monarchs seemed to like and then dislike Hampton Court, depending on their personal fancy or their finances. Queen Anne never cared for it, preferring small rooms in smaller houses, which was why she liked Kensington Palace.

George III as a young boy was walking through the state apartments one day with his grandfather, George II, then a rather irascible old man. The young boy apparently made some remark which angered the old King and he got his ears soundly boxed. When George III took over in 1760, he refused to live there. That was the end. Since then, no reigning monarch has lived at Hampton Court, though it was not until 1838 that Queen Victoria opened it to the public. (There are still some Royal grace and favour apartments, fourteen in all, privately occupied, one of them by the Chief Steward of Hampton Court Palace, General Sir Rodney Moore.)

I eventually found a door at the East Wing of the Palace which led out into the Gardens, and went in search of the Park's Superintendent. He had told me previously on the phone that his office and yard were in the Wilderness, which was no help, as I could find no signs or arrows leading me to it. I did however see some rather attractive wheelbarrows being used by the gardeners, painted brown and green with rubber wheels, which carried various place-names on the side, such as 'East Front' and 'Wilderness', so that proved I was on the right track.

Wilderness is in fact the ancient name for one of the larger gardens, which includes the Maze, on the north side of the Palace. It was originally an orchard in Henry VIII's time, then after William III it became more of a wild garden. It is certainly not a wilderness today, although it is kept very informal, with the grass allowed to grow fairly long, and in springtime it is a mass of wild daffodils, harebells and primroses.

George Cooke became Superintendent in 1974 after ten years as Apprentice Master and two years as Deputy Superintendent. There were 25 apprentices recruited each year at that time, now they take only 15. Mr Cooke is a Welshman from Bridgend and took a diploma in horticulture in Wales and also at Wisley. He then went on to gain a teacher's certificate, which makes him very unusual amongst parks people, and taught in ordinary schools for three years before joining the Royal Parks in 1963. He still has a no-nonsense, schoolmasterly approach, keen on discipline and standards and not above shouting out any shirkers. Like any good head, he is absolutely convinced that his school, I mean his Royal Park, is the finest of them all. 'The standards of horticulture at Hampton Court are higher than anywhere else. We have *more* things here and can offer the widest range of experience and the best possible training.' I asked for some examples and he reeled off a long list, starting with his half-mile-long herbaceous border.

His opinion of Hyde Park did not appear to be very high, but then most Superintendents shudder at the thought of being responsible for that Park, and all the rubbish that has to be picked up after every event, nor was he envious of their large nursery. 'We have our own 2½-acre nursery here and we produce 250,000 plants every year. Our Grower, Ken Evans, is one of the best in the country . . .' He was beginning to sound more like a Texan than a Welshman. But he does have a lot to boast about.

He got out from a bookshelf an ancient book on the Gardens, produced in 1926 by Ernest Law, which he kindly let me borrow, and an introductory sentence jumped out at me. 'The History of the Gardens at Hampton Court is in fact the history of English gardenage . . .' There were other equally lavish claims. 'There is no garden in England so rich in such embellishments as stone gate piers, vases, urns, pedestals, stone steps, ornamental iron gates, screens and balustrades, decorative brick work and pilasters, fountains, sundials, etc.' It would seem that the history of boasting about Hampton Court goes back a long way.

He has a staff of 95, plus 14 apprentices. When he arrived in 1974 the total complement was 149, but he maintains that he has not allowed standards to drop. If anything, they are expanding their gardening work all the time. Their total area of *intensive* gardening, mainly around the Palace, is 60 acres, an incredible amount to have to deal with, far greater than any other Royal Park. (I suppose a comparable piece of intensive gardening would be Queen Mary's Gardens in Regent's Park, which is about half that area.) According to the 1926 book, the formal gardens covered 50 acres, so the area has increased.

We started in the herbaceous border, George Cooke's pride and joy, which runs along the East Front of the Palace. Calling it a border does it a disservice, implying a little strip of flowers, as it is in fact a long garden, about 10 feet wide, which stretches for half a mile along the Broad Walk, though for some reason this walk is not named in the official guide book.

The Broad Walk, some 40 feet wide, was laid out in 1700 at a cost of £7,000. It was Queen Caroline who first started planting flowers against the warm, red brick of the Palace walls in 1735, so beginning the present herbaceous border.

From the Broad Walk you look out at arguably the most magnificent landscaped garden in the whole of Great Britain. Sissinghurst has nothing on this scale, delightful though it is, nor has Blenheim. Only Versailles can compete and there are many deliberate similarities between the Hampton Court Gardens and those at Versailles.

It is officially known as the Great Fountain Garden and armies of gardeners have devoted their lives to these 24 acres over the last 300 years, tending the geometrically-laid-out avenues of yew trees and the equally geometric lines of the ornamental canals. There is a master plan, but you would really have to be a bird, or standing on the roof of the Palace, fully to appreciate the intricacies of the vast design. Very simply, it has been set out in the shape of an immense bird's foot, a *patte d'oie*, or goose foot pattern, as it was known in ancient gardenage manuals. If you stand at the Great Fountain, the focal point of the garden, with the semi-circular ornamental canal ahead you are at the heel of the goose, but its three long toes stretch on and into the distance, beyond the formal part of the Garden, for well over a mile. The middle toe comprises a long straight canal known as the Long Water, while at either side, going off at exact angles, the other toes become avenues of lime trees.

In old prints of Hampton Court, dating from the early 1730s, the toe-lines

Hampton Court Palace Gardens: Britain's answer to Versailles

of yew trees in the formal garden look so doll-like, little statues, no taller than a man's shoulder. Now they are enormous, 'black pyramids' as Virginia Woolf called them, mostly 30 feet high. It takes two men two days to prune each one. Ideally, it needs scaffolding to cut them properly, as the moment you lean a ladder against them, their shape changes, but traditionally they have been done from ladders – one man holding, one man pruning.

Mr Cooke then led me round to the South Front of the Palace to the oldest parts of the Gardens, the Old Tudor Gardens, originally laid out by Cardinal Wolsey and Henry VIII. We came first to the Knot Garden, a curious arrangement of low box hedges, arranged in intricate patterns, many of them in the shape of complicated knots, interspaced with traditional English flowers, thyme and lavender. Their present formation was done in 1924 by Ernest Law, author of that old book about the Gardens, following some similar work he had done four years earlier for a Knot Garden at Shakespeare's house in Stratford upon Avon, copying exactly designs used by master gardeners in the reign of Elizabeth I. Such Knot Gardens were in vogue throughout the Tudor and Stuart periods, and most noblemen had one, usually by the walls of their stately home, but they died out completely after the Stuarts, until Law revived them in the 1920s.

Near the Knot Garden, Mr Cooke inspected some very fancy flower urns and noticed that several plants were wilting. He put his hand in one urn, then shouted in the direction of some tall hedges. 'Charlie, get someone to water these heliotropes! They're dying.' It was a Monday after a very hot weekend, when there are few gardeners on duty, but even so, standards have to be maintained.

The Tudor Gardens contain several other elements, including a sunken garden, similar to the one in Kensington Gardens, though with more turf. At the end of it is a statue of Venus, sheltering artistically in a yew arbor. In the guide book it is referred to as the Pond Garden though Mr Cooke, in talking about it, called it the Sunken Garden. Beside it is another Pond Garden slightly smaller, and not mentioned in Mr Law's 1926 book, which Mr Cooke called the New Pond Garden.

We then moved on to a brand-new garden, one not yet seen by the public, though he had plans for it to be opened by 1984. We reached it by going back along the Broad Walk, through the gardens, along a canal, where he unlocked a gate and took me into an area which on the map is marked as Paddock. This, ladies and gentlemen, is Mr Cooke's very own creation, the Arboretum. Five years ago, it was used for grazing cattle, but Mr Cooke has gradually taken it over and planted as many different specimens of trees as he can find, though nothing too exotic or tropical, as he wants hardy trees which will grow for ever. One tree already doing well is a variegated horse chestnut, a variety bred in their own nursery and called the Hampton Court Gold. Most of the work in this new garden has

The Pond Garden at Hampton Court

been done by his apprentices as part of their training, giving them the chance to work on something new.

His other bit of expansion so far during his term as Superintendent is a stretch at the front of the Palace, on the Hampton Court Road, where he has grassed in a paved area, between the Palace walls and the road, and planted it with bulbs. He referred to this as the Frog Walk, which was what he had been told it is called. 'I suppose it's French.' Perhaps that French Ambassador and his 100 fine noblemen who had come as guests of Wolsey paraded up and down along here.

He then had to return to his office to work on the bedding schemes for next July, exactly one year ahead. One look at that half-mile of herbaceous border would explain why it takes such time. In the 1926 book, it listed details of all its 73 different beds, including the names in English and in Latin of the types of autumn- and summer-flowering plants growing in *each* bed that particular year. ('Annuals, for the most part, are not given,' so it noted.)

We had passed near the Privy Garden on our little walk but it seemed rather hidden away, obscured by foliage, and I had not been able to get a feeling of it, so I returned to the Tudor Gardens to look at it properly. It was originally laid out as the King's Privy Garden, for Henry VIII, who often needed quite a bit of privy time when strolling with his ladies. It turned out to be a much bigger garden than I expected, stretching right down to the River, full of high yew hedges and secret little grassy paths, lilac and magnolia trees, statues glimpsed down narrow avenues, fountains at cross-sections, and little bowers and seats at discreet intervals. Several people were in the Privy Garden, but sitting so still in quiet corners, lost in their own worlds, regulars who always came to sit in the same spot, or so I imagined, judging from their lack of cameras and tourist booklets.

I admire a statue of a young girl clutching a garland of spring flowers with a lamb at her feet which I discovered, from the Ernest Law book, was called Flora. She was given a new nose in 1926, after she had lived with a broken one for fifteen years. I took a snap of it, to give to my own daughter called Flora. We tourists do that sort of thing.

At the end of the Privy Garden, right beside the River, I at last found some of the greatest treasures of the Hampton Court Gardens, the *Tijou screens*. I had them all to myself. There was no plaque in sight to name or explain them, which obviously makes it even harder for those who have read about them to track them down. It is said that nothing more princely nor more beautiful has ever been made in iron. I could quite believe it. They consist of 12 gateways, all linked together, which form a screen separating the Privy Gardens from the tow path along the River. Each gate is about ten feet high and thirteen feet across and contains a different design, such as heraldic shields, faces, birds, instruments, thistles, flowers, panels, foliage. I gave up trying to identify all the various elements but simply stood back to wonder at the work that must have gone into them. They were part of William III's grandiose schemes, aided by Wren, for reshaping Hampton Court, in order to create his own château style gardens. After all, why should Louis XIV be the only monarch capable of such extravagance and artistry? The screens were designed by Jean Tijou in 1694 and for a time, during Victoria's reign, they were sent to the Victoria and Albert Museum, but re-erected on their present site in 1902, which is where it is thought they originally stood. Tijou's bill for them, in 1694, came to £2,160, a huge sum, even for those days.

Henry VIII was a great all-round sportsman, playing hearty games with the gentlemen as well as the ladies, and he had his own tennis court at Hampton. This is along the East Front of the Palace, and a very fine court too, built in 1530, the oldest ball game court in the world still in use. Real tennis (or Royal Tennis) was played throughout Europe from the Middle Ages until the 17th century. At one time, France had two courts to every church and Charles VIII of France died while playing on a tennis court.

According to a little booklet on sale at the Palace bookshop, beautifully handwritten, it says that Henry 'heard of the execution of Queen Anne Boleyn as he played tennis at Hampton Court Palace'. More confusion.

Real tennis is the father of the modern game, though it has slightly different rules and involves knocking the ball around the interior walls. There are sixteen Real Tennis clubs in Great Britain today, seven in the USA, two in France and three in Australia. It is very active at Hampton Court and visitors are allowed to enter the court, even during a match, free of charge. I watched two middle-aged gentlemen, one with his knees heavily strapped, playing a very fierce game, then I opened a side door, trying to find some further information about the club, but could find no one to ask. On a notice board I saw a letter from the Royal Melbourne Tennis Club and some ties for sale, for club members only, which displayed crossed Real Tennis rackets and the year 1530. Beside it was a scarf in a similar design, for lady members. In Henry's day, quite a few of the Real Tennis champions were ladies.

The most popular sport at Hampton Court today is getting lost in the Maze which I finally decided to look at, though I have never been one of its fans. It always looks so small and the outside hedges are rather tatty, but I suppose this is to be expected when over 500,000 people go round it every year, most of them school children, quite a few of them rather unruly. At one time, they used to have an observation platform in the middle, with a park keeper aloft, to help anyone lost and sort out any rowdies, but now security is based on an emergency telephone at the gate where you pay your entrance fee. I stood and watched a party of excited Americans who were crouching over what appeared to be a crib, a little map showing how to get *out* of the Maze. What cheats.

Hampton Court Maze is the best-known and by far the most-visited Maze in the world. In 1926 it was getting 220,000 visitors a year who paid 1d each, and it was estimated that 10 million had been round it in the previous 200 years. It is quite small, covering only one third of an acre, but inside there is half a mile of walks divided by yew, privet and hornbeam hedges. Its original date is uncertain, but references to it go back to 1670 and a published plan exists from 1749. It acquired mass popularity in the Victorian age and most of the famous people of the day took it in as part of their Hampton Court tour. In 1828, Sir Walter Scott met up with Wordsworth by chance in London and they joined with their respective families in doing Hampton and the Maze.

Today, it is looked upon more as a children's amusement. 'It's perfect for teachers,' so Mr Cooke the Superintendent told me. 'They can dump the kids there while they go to the pub.' I saw that the White Lion pub was only a few yards away, a perfect distance, right beside the Lion Gate entrance.

I was about to leave the gardens at last, determined not to ignore the

The Lion Gate entrance at Hampton Court: one of Tijou's masterpieces in wrought iron

open parkland, like most tourists, when I noticed a sign pointing to something called the Great Vine. I had never heard of it until that day, but I was glad I didn't miss it as it proved to be one of the most fascinating and eccentric attractions I had come across in any of the London Parks.

It is simply one old vine, first planted in 1768, which over the last 200 years has taken on a life and a legend of its own. Its longest branch is 114 feet and it is now housed in its own greenhouse, a long arch of glass, about 70 feet in length, which goes over it like a tunnel. There is a little viewing section at one end where the public can stand in respectful silence and gaze at the vine.

The Keeper of the Vine, whose sole job is to care for this one plant, has for the last 21 years been a lady called Mary Peto. She not only devotes her working life to the vine but she lives on the job, able to pop in at nighttime, should it be necessary. The Vine is at the end of the South Front of the Palace, just past the Pond Gardens. Her house is next-door.

She is sixty years old and left school in Hampton at fourteen to work in a local commercial nursery. In 1957, she saw an advert in the local paper for a woman gardener at Hampton Court, applied and got the job, to her surprise. 'I've never been to college. I'm useless at learning things from books. I'm only good at practical things.' She is a tall, rather angular lady, who looks rather tense one moment, then bursts into laughter the next, usually when running herself down.

She did ordinary gardening work for two years, then one day she was told that the old Vine Keeper, a man, was about to retire, and she was being put in on a temporary basis. 'I didn't really want it. I'd spent my life until then under glass. I felt like staying outside for the rest of my working life. I didn't think they would want a woman anyway. Six men did apply, but each withdrew in the end. I think they were scared, frightened of its age. What if it should die when they were in charge, after growing since 1768. It was the old Superintendent who talked me into applying. I never dreamt they'd take *me*. Now, I love it. I don't want to work anywhere else.'

She was that day busy pricking out the smaller grapes on each bunch to let the others grow to a better size. There were over 600 bunches hanging from the vine above my head, most of them still green, as it was only early July, though a few had already begun to turn purple. The grapes are a black Hamburg variety, a dessert grape, not used for making wine. All of them are sold to the public when they're ripe in late August, but you have to come early as they go quickly. 'I can sell 70 pounds an hour if I suddenly gets lots of coachloads, then I ration them, one pound per person.' Her best year so far was in Jubilee year, 1977, when she sold 700 pounds. 'I feel this year will be another good year, and I hope to get over 700 pounds again.'

Her hardest part of the year, from a manual point of view, is in November, once the growing season is over, when she trims off the old bark and dead wood and painstakingly removes each little branch from its position, untying its support rods, paints each branch with insecticide, then ties it up again. This job, working from ladders, takes her two whole months.

'Touch wood, it's never had any diseases. The worst is a spot of mildew and I spray for that with flowers of sulphur.' I noticed that a few of the older branches seemed to have lots of woodworm holes, like an old piece of furniture. 'Don't look at them,' she said. 'Just ignore it. That's what I do.

Perhaps it is woodworm, but it doesn't seem to do any harm. I just cut off any old branches when they get completely dead. I have enough new shoots coming through every year.'

She chain-smoked throughout our little chat, but said the vine wouldn't mind. It was used to it. Anyway, it was her lunch break. She didn't like to smoke when on duty, especially with the public watching. That was one of the problems about the job which worried her in the early days, being watched all the time. 'It's like being a fish in a goldfish bowl, but I've got used to it now. The only worry is when I'm up a high ladder and they start taking photographs. The flash lights blind me and I worry I might fall off. They can't talk to me, luckily, but they often come round to my door and ask me to come to their homes and look at their vines. But I can't leave my vine, can I?'

Her proudest moment as a Vine Keeper happened almost twenty years ago, though she can remember every moment. That was the day she appeared on 'What's My Line'. 'I had to go up to the TV studios at two o'clock, and do you know, I didn't get back here till 11 at night. I had my hair done specially the day before, but when I got there, they said it wouldn't do. I'd paid the earth for it as well. It had to be altered for the cameras and I had to put special make-up on. It was black and white, of course, back in those days, dear.

'Barbara Kelly got near when she asked if you could eat and drink whatever it was I did. Eamon Andrews whispered at me to say no. Well, that wasn't quite true, was it? I've thought ever since that it was a bit unfair. You *can* eat the grapes, but you don't drink this variety. I suppose he was half-right. Anyway, that put them right off the scent and none of them could get it. Lady Barnett, David Nixon, they all started asking silly questions, like can you take it into the bedroom. I won in the end and beat the panel and I have the certificate. But I still feel a little bit guilty about that answer . . .'

It was rather strange to start exploring the open pastures of Home Park after all those formal, rather fussy gardens. It seemed so empty, not just of people but of traces of human activity, and I had to re-focus my eyes to the new scales and new horizons.

Home Park is terribly select, very like a private estate, with no attempt at entertaining or providing amenities for the public. There is no road through it and very few entrances and it tends to have mainly local use, people cutting through from Kingston. I walked down the Long Water till I reached the golf club (which is private) and then back along one of the avenues of lime trees, a distance of over two miles, and saw only one elderly couple. The Long Water, despite its symmetry and stillness, has a mesmeric quality. I began to imagine that I could walk across it, stepping on the flowering water lilies. I would not have come to much harm as the water is very shallow, despite the enormous size of some of the fish I could see arrogantly swimming slowly up and down.

This broad canal was created by Charles II, a reminder of the sort of Dutch scenery he had come to enjoy while in exile. He also re-stocked the Park with game and I kept on coming across groups of young deer throughout the Park. It is often forgotten that Home Park and Bushy Park are also deer Parks. There are 200 fallow deer in Home Park and 320 fallow and red in Bushy with two gamekeepers to look after them. They join with Richmond in supplying the needs of the Royal Venison warrant.

Bushy Park, the final but largest section of the Hampton Court estate, is much busier than Home Park. It is divided from it by Hampton Court Road and if you enter through the nearest entrance to the Palace, opposite Lion Gates and the Maze, there does at first seem to be a similar, rather formal atmosphere. A broad avenue stretches ahead, going round a large circular pond, which contains the Diana Fountain, then leads into Chestnut Avenue, a mile-long broad boulevard lined with chestnut trees.

This part of Bushy Park was designed by Wren for William III. Chestnut Avenue was meticulously laid out with 274 chestnuts, planted 42 feet apart, and conceived to form part of a grand new vista. A northern wing of the Palace was being planned, and the view from it down Chestnut Avenue was meant to rival the view from the East Front over the Long Water and Home Park. The view was completed, but the wing was never built. The avenue is still intact, however, and from a map you can see how it was meant to link directly with the Palace.

During the 19th century, the avenue was a popular meeting place for Londoners who came out every May on Chestnut Sunday, when all the blossom was out, and rode up and down in their carriages. Later, they came in their motor cars and omnibuses, but that event has now long since fallen out of fashion. So too have the Bicycle Meets which used to congregate here in the 1870s.

Bushy Park, once you leave the Diana Fountain area, soon becomes a more public, informal park with lots of activities, such as fishing and sailing boats on a line of ponds which stretch up towards Hampton Wick. There is one part which is private, the Royal Paddocks. This was at one time a Royal Stud but now is more of a grazing and pasture area for Royal horses, giving them a rest from ceremonial duties.

Bushy not only has deer to rival Richmond but also has its own Woodland area which Mr Cooke assured me was as fine as the Isabella Plantation. Alas, they don't have a leaflet for it, or even any notice board map which I could see, so it took me some time to find the entrance.

I had just got into the Woodland Garden, and was beginning to jot down a few notes, when a gardener emerged from behind a tree and asked if I was writing a book. I explained my purpose, and immediately he asked if I

The Diana Fountain in Bushy Park

could help him to get his book published, an opus of some 1,000 photographs, plus 30,000 words, all about the deer in Bushy Park. Not another one. There must be more unpublished works on London deer than on any other subject. He said he was called Caleb William George Buckingham and I congratulated him; a name impressive enough to grace any title-page.

He kindly handed me over to another gardener, called Mick, who happened to be going through the wood and promised to guide me. Mr Cooke had called this whole area, which stretches for more than a mile, all of it planned to look as natural as possible, the Woodland Gardens, which is probably the neatest way to describe it, though in fact it is in three sections, each with a slightly different identity.

The first stretch, the Woodland Garden proper, was begun in 1949, around the same time as the Isabella Plantation was being re-schemed in its present state. It is basically a rhododendron and azalea wood, but not as dense or as luxurious as the Isabella. We came to a pond which he said was called Triss's Pond, named after a relative of a previous Bailiff of the Royal Parks.

We left the first woodland part, all neatly fenced off, and went down a short, connecting avenue of newly-planted ash trees which he said, proudly, was called the Ash Walk. Thank you, Mick. We were now in the Waterhouse Garden, an older plantation, by the look of the age of the trees. The third section is the Willow Plantation which follows the course of the River Longford.

The Longford River is a curious creation which twists and turns, burbles and flows, but is a completely man-made river. It was cut long before the ornamental canals were thought of, another of Charles I's schemes, providing his parkland with running water, but as naturally as possible. It was quite a feat of engineering as a link had to be formed through his estate from the River Colne to the Thames. It still supplies running water for various canals, fountains, waterfalls, and ponds throughout the park and gardens. Mick swore it was a real river, and was willing to take bets, but, having read the history books, I declined to take his money. Its name has nothing to do with Lord Longford but betrays its purpose – the long ford.

We worked our way along the river bank which was tough going as tall rhubarb-like plants, which Mick said were called gunneras, had taken over the path. We almost fell over a rather suspicious-looking man who jumped up and furtively hid his copy of the *Sun* and turned off a transistor radio. He was the first person we had seen in a mile of walking. What a strange place to rest. Perhaps he had been planning to do some illegal fishing in the River.

At the end of the Willow Plantation we came to a bridge, Duke's Bridge, which leads to a footpath through the meadows towards Hampton Hill. The meadows themselves, being part of the Royal Park's own farm, are not open to the public. There are no cattle these days but the farm grows hay and barley to help feed the deer in winter.

I thanked Mick for his help and left him to retrace his steps back into the wood to rejoin the Woodland Gardening team. Was it nicer than Richmond Park's Isabella? It is bigger, more spread out, more natural, but I probably would have to choose the Isabella. My joy at first seeing it had been so spontaneous. Bushy's Woodland Garden is well worth seeing and I would rather wander round it any time, despite the lack of directions or guide lines, taking my chance on being lost, but likely to be surprised by joy, than wander round that mangy old Maze and be surprised only by unruly school children.

Overleaf: Epping Forest: London's unique nature reserve, a woodland untouched by man since the Ice Age

CHAPTER EIGHT

Epping Forest

Epping Forest is not a Royal Park, despite some definite Royal Connections, so who owns it? No, it is not run by Epping Borough Council or any local authority masquerading under some other modern name. I admit I did not know the answer until I decided to go there. In fact I knew very little about Epping Forest at all, though I have driven through it several times over the years, always in a hurry, trying to escape the awful North Circular and then as quickly as possible get through those dreary suburban flat lands where London becomes Essex, though who can tell the difference, or even want to?

We people who live in Inner London tend to feel slightly superior about our brothers in Outer London while those in Central London, who live beside a real Royal Park, are definitely snooty, never venturing out to such uncouth places. It's where those dreadful East End people go to leave their litter, isn't that the place, or dump their bodies? Epping does have a poor reputation amongst people who have never been there. It only ever seems to impinge on popular consciousness when something horrible happens. There was that lesbian prostitute whose body was found there, cut up in several pieces and left in plastic bags. Then Harry Roberts, one of the most wanted men of the Sixties, hid out in Epping Forest for several days and avoided the police. Not the sort of place to send Nanny. Let's stick to Kensington Gardens.

It was when I looked at a map of Greater London that I first realised the extent of Epping Forest, by far the biggest splurge of green that there is, well over twice the area of Richmond Park, equal in size to all the Royal Parks put together. It covers 6,000 acres, stretching for 12 miles from the edges of the East End right up to beyond Epping. The first six miles or so (about a third of the total area) is in the GLC boundary, before it runs into Essex, so it can fairly be classed as a London Park, though technically it should always be called a forest.

In some ways, it is the *most* Londonish of all London's open spaces. Those Royal Parks are national parks, internationally famous monuments, visited as much by foreigners as by locals. Epping Forest is peculiarly a London lung, a breathing space for those people who happen to live around its

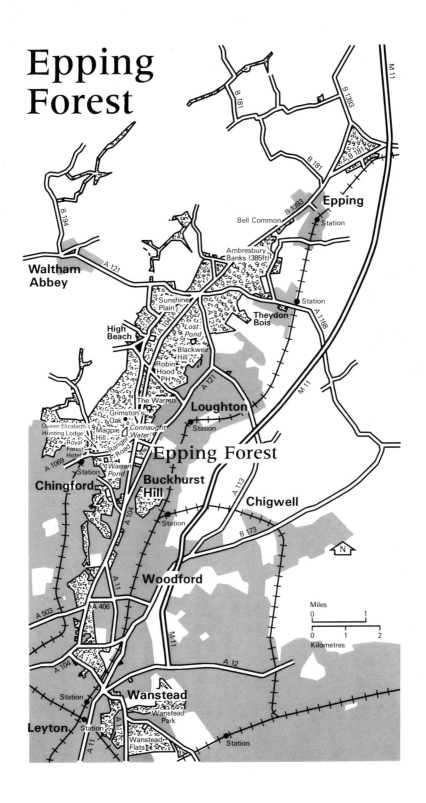

Epping Forest

Epping

Bell Common
Station

Ambresbury
Banks (385ft)

B 181

B 1393

M 11

B 181

B 194

Waltham
Abbey

A 121

Sunshine
Plain

High
Beach

Lost
Pond

Blackweir
Hill

Robin
Hood
PH

The Warren

Grimston's
Oak

Queen Elizabeth's
Hunting Lodge
Royal
Forest
Hotel

Magpie
Hill

Connaught
Water

Ranger Road

Warren
Pond

Station

Chingford

A 1069

A 104

Theydon
Bois

Station

A 1168

Loughton

Station

A 127

Epping Forest

Buckhurst
Hill

Chigwell

A 113

Station

B 173

M 11

Woodford

A 11

A 503

A 406

M 11

A 12

A 104

A 114

Station

Wanstead

Wanstead
Park

Leyton

Station

A 11

A 117

Wanstead
Flats

Station

Miles
0   1

0   1   2
Kilometres

N

boundaries, and is hardly used by people who live elsewhere in London or in the world outside. By doing so, they are missing a unique nature reserve, a forest with a history that goes back well beyond the Royal Parks and, perhaps best of all, some of the finest and definitely the longest walks to be had anywhere in the London area. I will never again make nasty remarks about Epping Forest.

My first impression, however, was not at all propitious. As usual, it was very hard to get any good information in advance. Throughout my walk, I did eventually pick up various leaflets, some of them excellent, but I failed completely to get a map of the Forest, all on one sheet, which gives the paths and main features.

I started at Chingford, which by the look of the OS maps, seemed to be the beginning of the densest part of the Forest. I could have begun a lot further south, down at Wanstead Flats, which is just a mile from Stratford East, but that would have meant crossing the North Circular on my way north. I discovered later that there is a route which covers the entire length called the Centenary Walk, some 15 miles long, worked out by two members of the Ramblers Association and published in a little leaflet, price 15p. (See Appendix for details.) It does entail some road-crossing and dodging. Once at Chingford, it is possible to leave all roads behind and walk for miles along Forest paths and glades.

Chingford, that rural gem beside the Ching Brook. I suppose it must have been at some time. If you come out of the station at Chingford today you could be in the middle of any London suburban high street, part of metroland, or should it be centroland, which seems to go on for ever, but don't despair. Turn right quickly, down Station Road, and in minutes you see the Forest, full of real trees, stretching on into the horizon, and, even more surprisingly, a vast open plain in the foreground, Chingford Plain. The contrast is quite dramatic. How did they ever manage to stop the urban sprawl taking over? You have of course to overlook the cars on the road running beside the Forest, and avert one's gaze from odd bits of litter on the verges, but in essence the view is as it was in the Middle Ages, untouched by man. You can't say that about the Royal Parks. Epping is natural wood-land which has had continuous tree cover since the glaciers retreated at the end of the Ice Age. The word to stress is *natural*. There have never been plantations in Epping Forest. That's what makes it unique.

Queen Boadicea is supposed to have fought her last battles in this area, yet another unprovable story. The Anglo-Saxons established communities on the fringes, along the River Lea to the west and the River Roding to the east, but left the Forest unaltered. After the Normans, it became part of the area known as the Royal Forest of Essex, then Waltham Forest and finally Epping Forest. The deer in the Forest were protected for the benefit of the Monarch, and there were savage penalties handed out at Forest Courts for any poaching or other infringements, but certain local people were allowed to graze their cattle freely in the Forest and collect wood.

A system known as pollarding was used for wood conservation. Every tree could be cut from above head height on a fifteen-year cycle. The new shoots were then left to grow again, out of reach of the deer. You can see still lots of pollarded trees in the Forest, strangely stunted with thick, fat trunks up to about seven feet high, then a mass of thinner branches above. The other ancient system of harvesting natural trees to provide fuel is coppicing, which meants cutting the tree right down to the base, allowing the new shoots to grow directly up from ground level. In a deer forest, of course, such as Epping, coppicing results in deer and other animals eating the young, fresh shoots, unless they are protected.

It is often easy to forget that, throughout the history of the universe, wood has until recent times been the prime source of fuel. Look at the fuss we now make about oil supplies, an energy source which has been with us only a few moments. Over the centuries, rules and regulations for gathering wood grew up in every forested region. In Epping, only the chosen folk were allowed the privilege of getting their bill hooks out and lopping off those branches above seven feet. 'By hook or by crook' they could bring the stuff down, giving us a phrase which has passed into the language.

The Tudor Monarchs were fond of hunting in Epping Forest, though it meant a longer journey than hunting in the Royal Parks on their doorstep, but later Monarchs gradually lost interest. All those Forest laws were basically a means of raising Royal finances, augmented by selling off various concessions to local Lords of the Manor.

By the middle of the 19th century, a forestral property, once as vast as an English country, which in 1641 had covered 60,000 acres and stretched all the way to the sea, was down to 6,000 acres and in danger of shrinking away to nothing. Officially and unofficially, land had been enclosed by local people for their private use or by property speculators for building houses. The ownership and rights over what was left were very complicated, bogged down in feudal customs and tradition, while the trees themselves became increasingly abused or allowed to grow completely wild.

It was the action of an elderly wood-cutter called Tom Willingale which drew attention to what was happening. He was living in the parish of Loughton, one of those local people who traditionally had rights to lop wood. The Lord of the Manor said the land had now been enclosed and Willingale no longer had these rights. Encouraged by local action groups, Willingale took his protest to court.

Meanwhile, another body with rights in the Forest had become very interested in these legal battles. This was the Corporation of London who had purchased 200 acres in 1854, a plot known as Aldersbrook Farm, to turn it into the City of London Cemetery, which it is to this day. They had therefore become Commoners and as such they were very keen to guard their rights, and those of other Commoners. The result was that the City took it upon itself to save Epping Forest. After even more complicated battles, the Master of the Rolls in 1874 decided in favour of the City. Not only did they win their case, they won the entire Forest, which must have been something of a surprise to some of the other individual Commoners who could not have envisaged what the final outcome would be when the battles had first begun some twenty years earlier. The City paid £250,000 in compensation to those who were losing their rights in the Forest, plus £25,000 in legal fees. In 1878, an Act of Parliament, the Epping Forest Act, constituted the City as 'conservators' of Epping Forest and laid down the terms on which they have to preserve the Forest for ever and ever.

At the same time as the City was fighting to save Epping Forest, it acquired powers under Parliament to purchase other lands within 25 miles of the City, 'for the recreation and enjoyment of the public'. They had quite a killing during the last few decades of the 19th century and today they have ended up with over 7,000 acres of forest and parkland, more even than the GLC. A lot of this is outside the Greater London boundaries, such as Burnham Beeches, but they still have considerable acres inside London, such as Highgate Wood and Queen's Park in Kilburn. (See Appendix for full details.)

This all explains, therefore, how the owners of Epping Forest come to be a body based in the Guildhall, some 14 miles away, a situation which strikes many visitors today as rather anomalous. Inside the City's own square mile it has only 35 acres of open space (the biggest chunk being the little gardens in Finsbury Circus), while *outside* they have 7,000 acres of forest and grass land, but they do very kindly allow the general public to have full access to them. They are excellent landlords and we should be thankful for their past and present work. It is not generally realised, even by local residents, that the cost of running Epping Forest, and their other open spaces, is paid totally by the City, using what is called 'City Cash'. Nothing at all comes from the local rates.

The first building you come to along Ranger's Road from Chingford, as you proceed towards the Forest, is a very large hostelry called the Royal Forest. It was built in the 1880s at a time when the masses had just begun to pour out of the East End in their omnibuses for a day in the Forest, encouraged by Queen Victoria who made an official visit to the Forest on May 6, 1882, to formally dedicate it for public use. (They staged some centenary celebrations in 1982, but did not manage to get a present member of the Royal Family to turn up, making do instead with an effigy of Victoria.)

The architecture of the hotel is a cross between Mock Tudor and Austrian Schloss. Today, it seems to have been turned into a Berni Inn, judging by a notice, and I could see several commercial-looking travellers sitting outside in company cars, waiting for opening time, or clients, or other more personal meetings, so I passed quickly on, looking for the building next door, the first object of my Epping Walk.

This is Queen Elizabeth's Hunting Lodge, a genuine Tudor building, but easily missed by many visitors who think the pub is not only older and more impressive but much more important. It is now the Epping Forest Museum, the only historic building in the Forest, and one which all visitors should try to get inside. I nearly failed. It was a Monday, and a notice outside said Closed Mondays and Tuesdays. I was about to turn away when I heard children inside on a school outing so I knocked and was allowed in.

Despite its name, it was built by Henry VIII, probably in 1543, but it fell into disrepair after Henry's death and was renovated by his daughter Elizabeth in 1589. It was originally known as the Great Standing, a grandstand or pavilion from which Henry and his party could watch the hunt. 'This was his Camp David,' said Jeff Seddon, the Curator, a young

Queen Elizabeth's Hunting Lodge: the oldest building in Epping Forest

bearded gentleman who used to stuff birds at Hull Museum before being appointed seven years ago. 'Henry would invite all the important Ambassadors into the Forest for a weekend's hunting. This Lodge would be one of the things built to impress them. You can see by the timbers that it was a very expensive building.'

Under Elizabeth, it seems likely that the Lodge was used as a shooting gallery, the deer being driven underneath the walls, in range of the crossbows. The Queen was 56 by the time she took it over, no doubt feeling her age, not up to all that chasing round the Forest. The Stuarts continued to use the Lodge, but its history after that is vague until the 18th century when it had become a keeper's lodge. Not long after the City of London took over, it was turned into a Museum, part of their campaign to give the masses something worthwhile and noble to occupy their minds in their leisure moments. Things had become pretty rough and plebeian around the Chingford area towards the end of the 19th century, especially when the trains arrived in 1873 and crowds of up to 13,000 a day were being disgorged and let loose on the Plain and in the Forest, riding on donkeys and fairground swings. The new hostelries and tea gardens did a roaring business.

'The presence of such an Institution at Chingford,' wrote Edward Buxton, one of the instigators of the plan to turn the Lodge into a Museum, in 1883, 'would tend to raise the tone of the visitors to the Forest. It is to the poor of the East of London what the sea side is to the middle classes for even the roughest and most uncultivated man or woman must leave its beautiful glades in some measure refined by what they have seen.' How pure and simple the Victorians could be.

According to Mr Seddon, the days of the mass exodus from the East End have long gone. The huge, boisterous crowds ended with the War. Since then, even East End poor managed to have cars and drive themselves to Southend or Clacton for a Sunday spin in the country, at least for the last two decades. That all might change once again, of course, as both the working and middle classes find it harder to afford the petrol.

The building is on three floors, broader and more spacious than it looks from outside. The oak staircase is said to have been wide enough for Queen Elizabeth to ride upstairs to the top gallery and watch the hunt, though Mr Seddon fears this might be pure legend. 'It's a story that's been around for centuries. In the 1890s there was a man who hired out donkeys who charged sixpence to anyone who wanted to try to "emulate the Queen's feat".'

The Museum gets 24,000 visitors a year, a third of them school parties. They love all the gory details about the penalties exacted by the Forest Courts, such as castration or getting your arms cut off. Mr Seddon says those penalties existed but most people paid a fine instead. Children also enjoy the illustrations showing the King at breakfast in the Forest during one of his hunts, having the droppings from the deer laid before him. 'The droppings were called "croteyes" and, depending on how thick or big they were, an expert could tell whether the deer was worth hunting. When the King chose a particular dropping, the dogs were then put on the scent.'

When he first arrived from Hull, Mr Seddon was very taken by all the traditions of the Forest. 'It did seem to be truly Romantic, the idea of an Ancient Woodland, unchanged since the Ice Age, being looked after by Keepers in dapper uniforms and controlled from the City like a Medieval institution, with Verderers and Commoners. I am more used to it now, but it still is a very special place.'

I crossed the road to have a glimpse at the southern section of the Forest, just in case I had unfairly dismissed it, and came to a pond called the Warren Pond which was so scruffy, so surrounded by litter, so stagnant and unattractive, that I hurried quickly on. I found myself outside a building on the far side which appeared to be the entrance to a rather exclusive tennis club, judging by the number of notices saying private, keep out. There was a boy on one of the courts playing on his own, the balls being served to him from an electric serving machine, as if being fired from a cannon. When all the balls had been served, a trim-looking woman filled up the machine again. 'Get on your toes and *bounce*,' she shouted at him.

She saw me watching and came across to ask what I wanted. I explained I was just wandering round, doing no harm, trying not to disturb the animals. She said she was the manager of the club, the Connaught, and that was her son and the machine was called a lobster. There were no vacancies, but I could put my name down, though there was no chance of *anyone* on the waiting list being considered before next October.

'Oh, we're terribly popular and successful. That's because we're the best. We've won a lot of awards. We have a lovely setting and set very high standards. We're terribly strict here about wearing all white. For one year we did allow pastels, but people simply didn't seem to know what a pastel shade was. They turned up in so many different shades. No we're back to all white. We find it's easier all round.'

She took me proudly round the club, pointing out the record board with names of champions going back to 1892, though she said the club was much older than that and had been founded in the 1870s as a croquet club. Before that, she said, the site had been a market garden.

I mentioned the scruffy pond outside and she groaned. They had a running battle every year with the fishermen. 'After the drought of 1976, it was cleaned out completely, but now it's as filthy again. You wouldn't believe the vandalism. We've had five break-ins. Our fence is always being knocked down and if I tell them to get off the bank of the Pond, because at this end it belongs to us, I just get a mouth full. They even ride their motor bikes along it. "It's our bleeding water," so they always say. Some of these people are just so uncouth.' Ah well, if you create a People's Forest you have to put up with all sorts and conditions of people.

I then began my walk north through the Forest, cutting across the thick grassy pastures of Chingford Plain till I came to a broad track into the Forest, the Green Ride, one of many paths in the Forest laid out for horses. There was a flurry of black and white wings ahead and about a dozen magpies rose from the path ahead of me. I had rarely seen so many in a group before. I looked at one of my maps and found that a spot called Magpie Hill was just ahead, a rare example of nomenclature being correct. Perhaps they had imported them to please the map-makers, just as those primroses are being introduced to Primrose Hill. Calling it a hill was a slight liberty, as the path hardly rises. Epping Forest is only ever gently undulating, the highest point being 385 feet, close to Ambresbury Banks.

The first pleasant surprise, now that I was in the Forest proper, was to find it was not dense, which was what I had feared. Walking those man-made National Forests in Wales, the Lake District or Scotland, can be very monotonous and depressing. It is not just the uniform arrangement of the trees, all the same and all in straight lines, but the lack of clearings and the limited view of the sky above. Throughout Epping Forest, you can always clearly see the open sky and you rarely have to walk far without coming to some sort of clearing or a bit of scrub, heath or grassland, making every walk full of variety. Out of the total acreage, 4,000 acres consist of trees and the other 2,000 acres are open space.

The trees, being self-sown, grow randomly and are all types, just as nature intended, with beech and birch the main ones on the lighter soils and oak and hornbeam on the heavier clays. A sign of the age of the Forest is the number of ancient trees, such as wild service and field maple, which are not found in modern plantations. There are many types of fungi, thanks to centuries of rotting wood and accumulated leaf mould, and the grass and scrubland has a rich variety of flora and fauna.

A narrow path took me towards Connaught Water, the biggest pond in the northern part of the Forest, a little lake in fact, with several islands, covering about 12 acres. It has a regal name, after the Duke of Connaught who opened it in the 1880s, and despite the fact that it is basically artificial, being the remains of an old gravel pit, like many of the ponds in the Forest, it seemed to have a great deal of natural atmosphere, marshy and moody, like one of the Everglades, a mysterious swamp in which crocodiles might be lurking.

As I got close and then walked round it, I realised how wrong I was. My first glimpse had been through the trees from a remote angle. It turned out to be even more squalid than the Warren Pond, especially on the side nearest the road where there is a large car park. It always strikes me as strange that fishermen can be so filthy. One would have thought that they loved nature and tranquillity, being so willing to sit silently, communing with the spirits, yet they leave litter and debris everywhere, turning ponds and rivers into caravan sites, making beauty spots resemble the terraces of a football ground.

There was an elderly couple arguing. The woman had her line caught in a tree and the man was shouting at her not to be so stupid, but at the same time saying he couldn't come and help her as he might have a bite. So I talked to a younger man, a motor mechanic, fishing on his own. He said he lived in Chingford and fished in the Water at least once a month. 'Usually, I come evenings, when there's nothing on the box. Seems to be better then. Things are quieter and there's more fish, but this week I'm on holiday, so I'm having a whole day's fishing.' What for? 'Anything that wants to oblige. Bream or roach, I don't care.' His young son also fishes, but he makes sure that either he or his wife drives him there and back, and he's never allowed to fish in the dark or after nine in the summer. 'I won't let kids loose in the Forest on their own. You hear some funny stories.'

Sometimes he takes an evening walk in the Forest, driving up the Epping Road and pulling off the roadside. 'It's very handy. I'm just two miles away. I might bring my camera and do a bit of shooting. It's not as nice as the Yorkshire Dales, but it's very handy.' He denied that fishermen left litter, apart from the yobboes. He blamed the pony-riders 'It's them that's spoiling the park, not the fishermen. There's so many of them, now they've put down all these new pony tracks. It used to be unspoiled when I first came to live round here eight years ago.'

It was only the area immediately round Connaught Water which was so untidy. Once back on the Forest paths, everything was clear of litter and I soon began to feel I was the only person in the Forest, with not even a pony-rider in sight. You are free to walk anywhere, but the undergrowth can be fairly dense, once you leave the paths and the clearings. I wondered how many bodies there were out there, waiting to be found. There must surely be stretches of the Forest which no one has penetrated for years.

'Miss, Miss! Where are you, Miss?' A teenage girl, dressed in tight jeans and a jumper, was standing behind a tree. I did not know whether to walk on, pretending I hadn't seen her, or ask if she wanted help and perhaps be told to get lost. She ran ahead of me and I saw she was part of a school party. They were from William Fitt School at Walthamstow, doing some orienteering, but had lost the next clue. 'I'm *not* lost,' said the teacher, '*they* are.' I walked with them a few hundred yards till we came to a massive oak tree, a well-known landmark in the Forest, known as Grimston's Oak. It stands in an open space, with wide-spreading branches, near the junction of several paths. I left them trying to climb up it, convinced the next message would be hidden there.

For the next hour, I met nobody at all, except two cyclists who suddenly tore past me, giving me a fright as I had not heard them coming, then vanishing in seconds into the Forest ahead. I failed to see any deer, though I kept looking for them. Their disappearance from the Forest has been something of a mystery. In 1902 there were 270 deer, now there are rarely more than half a dozen in the annual count. They have apparently moved into private woods and estates bordering the Forest, where they are breeding fairly successfully and probably number about 200. It is suggested in the official booklet about the Forest, by Alfred Qvist, a former Superintendent, that dogs might be to blame, or the increasing number of cars on the various roads which cut through the Forest. Having recently been to Richmond and Bushy, where both dogs and the cars are much more in evidence, this would seem to be only part of the explanation. Probably the Richmond Superintendent was right when he said that a forest is not the best habitat for deer. They like open grassland with ample pasture. The Epping deer, when they are seen, are black fallow deer, descendants of the herd which has been there for centuries. They are not literally black, more a dark brown, and you can see some of them (stuffed) at the Museum in the Queen Elizabeth Lodge.

At High Beach, on the western edge of the Forest, I came to another large pub, the King's Oak, where the area round the car park was again strewn with litter and debris. This has remained one of the most popular parts of the Forest, but now it has also become a rendezvous for motor cyclists. Groups of up to 200 gather here, all in their black leathers, then roar through the Forest roads which are very smooth and straight, ideal for roaring along. They have a legal right to gather anywhere and in fact they spend most of their time standing still, admiring each other's machines, till a few start racing each other up the roads. It is only when they leave the roads and roar into the Forest itself, which a few of the wilder ones do, that the forest authorities can apprehend them.

I was looking for the High Beach Conservation Centre which is in the Forest behind the pub, an attractive white-washed, one-storey arrangement of buildings, used as an educational centre and the main information office for the Forest. Paul Moxey is the Warden and Director of Studies and his wife Tricia is the Bursar. They came here when it opened in 1970, both previously having been teachers. She was a biology mistress and he was a geography master. They have three classrooms, a library, theatre, exhibition areas and a full-time staff of five. It operates like a mini-University with several post-graduate and other students working on research projects.

Most of their work is devoted to school children from Inner London or the surrounding Boroughs who come on field courses to study ecology, geography, environmental studies and other subjects. The previous year,

10,000 children had used the Centre, but they were worried that the new education cuts would reduce their numbers. They are funded by a charity called the Field Studies Council and organise courses and lectures for ordinary members of the public, not just schools. 'I'm running at present a 26-week evening course on the Forest,' said Mrs Moxey. 'I could do a longer course as there is just so much to talk about in the Forest.'

They had a slice from a 236-year-old beech displayed, with the ring for every year absolutely clear. Rings very close together are sure signs that pollarding has taken place, reducing the growth for a few years, while the new shoots become established. I bought various leaflets, including some postcards, special offer, of the Queen Elizabeth Lodge, reduced to 4p for a quick sale. The Lodge had recently had some of its timbers removed, when it was found they were not genuine Tudor but Victorian additions, and so these old photographs were now out of date.

I also bought an excellent 16-page booklet, price £1.35, which seemed rather steep, but they included handsome maps designed and drawn by Mandy Johnson. I asked who she was, thinking she might be some old Victorian lady, long gone, though the name Mandy seemed rather modern. Mrs Moxey said follow me and she took me into the Library and there was young Mandy, sitting working.

Mandy is now at the University of East Anglia, reading Environmental Sciences, but she had previously taken a year off, between leaving Woodford County High School and going to University, to do a year's research at the Centre, working for nine whole months on the maps. 'The hardest part was stopping my hand from shaking when I was drawing the paths. I had to keep them the same width, you see.'

The ten maps, showing the paths and other features in each section of the northern part of the Forest, from Chingford to Epping, had originally been done in 1950 by James Brimble, but the Centre decided they needed updating, now that so many horse tracks had been added and because of other changes. It seemed a shame that they could not be reduced to a single sheet and perhaps sold more cheaply. She thought perhaps there was too much detail for them to be reduced into one, but hoped one day some sort of single map could be produced.

To draw the maps, she had walked all the paths, without getting bored once. 'I never walked the same way twice. When I approached a place I knew, I always came at it from a different angle. I got lost a few times, but mainly in the snow.'

I asked her for her favourite bit and she thought hard and said perhaps the Lost Pond area, that was very nice and very remote. Brimble himself had named it the Lost Pond – though it is also known as Blackweir Pond. 'After he'd first found it, he couldn't find it again, so he called it the Lost

Pond.' She pointed out on her maps where it was, near the middle of map nine, so I set off in that direction.

I soon lost the Lost Pond. I started well enough, or so I thought, working my way east and safely across the main Epping Road, managing not to be run down by any roaring motor cyclists. Immediately, the foliage felt different, somehow richer, with more ferns and lusher undergrowth, and it did indeed seem more remote, as Mandy had promised. I found myself ploughing along a new horse track, laid with some sort of wood chippings, but full of mud which dragged at the ankles. After about an hour, I heard the sound of crashing behind some bushes and saw through the trees four people walking. They were on a narrow path I hadn't noticed, just fifty yards away, thus avoiding the horse track.

It was an elderly couple and two young ladies and they were amused to find I had become lost looking for the Lost Pond. 'You're walking completely in the wrong direction,' said the gentleman. They were heading towards the Pond themselves and said I could follow them. He was called James Arnold, a retired draughtsman, and his wife Evelyn, daughter Susan and Susan's friend, a French girl from Chartres called Anne-Marie. Mr and Mrs Arnold live near Chingford and do a six- or seven-mile walk in the Forest every day. She prefers the Forest but he prefers a mixed walk with some open countryside thrown in. Their favourite walk, combining all pleasures, is round Copped Hall. He spelled it out for me and then we looked it up on my maps to find Mandy had spelled it Copt Hall.

They both said that all the new horse rides had made walking much more difficult. The clay ruts set like concrete in dry weather and in wet weather they became bogs. We discussed the joys of walking in other parts of Great Britain, including Hadrian's Wall, where they had recently walked, helped by an *excellent* guide book by some chap or other. He could not believe that I had never walked in Epping Forest before. How could I possibly call myself a Londoner and a Walker.

'Now, just about here,' announced Mr Arnold, 'if we head through those trees, we should hit the Lost Pond.' And so we did. So useful to fall in with an expert. I had never needed a guide in any of the London Parks so far, even ones which were new to me, as it is possible with a simple map to figure out in an hour or two the boundaries and the general shape, even in a Park as extensive as Richmond. I think Epping Forest, however, would take me a week's walking to begin to feel confident of my whereabouts. By the look of Mandy's maps, there must be several hundred miles of different paths and routes.

The Lost Pond was suitably lost-looking, with not a crisp packet in sight. I thanked the Arnolds who continued north while I turned back, heading south again, making my way down the east side of the Forest, heading for a spot on the map called the Warren and the office of the Forest's Superintendent.

On the telephone, the Superintendent, John Besent, had told me he would not be back until late in the afternoon, and feared he might be very late, which he was, held up by tube troubles. He had been to the Guildhall in the City of London for his monthly meeting with his masters, the Conservators, a body constituted under the 1878 Epping Forest Act. They consist of twelve people appointed by the City's Common Council and four Verderers, elected by the Commoners of the Forest. There are not many Commoners these days, as you have to be fairly well off to own a half-acre garden, even in the outer suburbs. But a Commoner can still exercise his right of pannage (putting swine in the Forest) or grazing his cattle, horses and sheep, which is handy for farmers but not so vital for commuters.

Mr Besent is a tall, rather aristocratic-looking gentleman who went to Mill Hill School, the Royal Agricultural College at Cirencester and then qualified as a chartered surveyor and land agent. As an estate manager, he has worked for various local authorities, such as Leicester and Mid-Glamorgan, before coming to Epping in 1978. He expects to remain here. There are not many big private estates left for professional chartered surveyors like him to manage, so getting a job which is in a sense a private appointment, financed from private funds, yet serving the general public, is worth hanging on to. It must be reassuring not to have to weather changing political parties which happens when you work for a local council or Government body.

There have been only five Superintendents of Epping Forest in the last 100 years. Mr Qvist, his predecessor, had the job for 29 years. Before him, from 1879 to 1949, three generations of a family called McKenzie had the job, grandfather, father, then son. 'Some of the older residents still call this McKenzie's Place. A Forest needs continuity. Managing woodland is a long term affair. It takes time to make your mark.'

He has a handsome house which goes with the job, and some fine gardens, in a large clearing just off the main Epping Road. There is an office staff whose hours are clearly stated on a notice board near the main road, and they are open in these hours to the public for Forest business. Unlike some Superintendents I had met, he does not hide himself away. 'It is today very much a public relations job.'

His total staff is 51, plus six frozen jobs, which might or might not be filled one day, compared with Mr Qvist's day, according to his 1971 booklet, when there was a staff of 73. They consist of six office staff, four tradesmen, three men on the golf course at Chingford, four on the playing fields at Wanstead Flats, one groom, 14 woodmen, 18 Forest Keepers and one museum curator.

All Keepers wear a brown tweed uniform when on duty patrolling the

Forest, but they also spend half their time on manual duties, such as picking up litter. Three have motor bikes and three are mounted Keepers, which explains the need for a groom. They have four horses in all as Mr Besent is expected to take regular duty rides through the Forest. He likes to go out for a couple of hours every few days, perhaps to inspect a wood gang, or investigate a complaint.

All the Keepers are Special Constables, which they train to become after they have joined the Forest staff. They have police powers to march off any wrong-doers, then they themselves do all the paper work, the summons is issued from their own office, and they have to appear in Court as both prosecutor and witness. Quite a responsibility, well beyond the duties of normal municipal park-keepers. In a year, they probably average sixty prosecutions, the majority against people riding motor bikes in the Forest, carrying weapons or simply dropping litter.

He agrees there is an image of Epping Forest as a fairly violent place, with bodies for ever being dropped from passing cars, but thinks this is unfair. People even tell him it is worse than it was, but he doubts this. 'In the past, attacks in the Forest and other deeds were not as widely reported by the media as they are now. I am sure the Forest is no less safe for females than it was 100 years ago. It has just become fashionable to say so. In 1912 there were so many assaults that plain clothes police had to be drafted in to help. Human nature does not really change. We are the first wild area that you come to from the East End. You wouldn't expect anyone to go and dump a body in Hyde Park. It would quickly be found. So they come out to Epping.'

He estimated that perhaps there is a suicide or some other serious incident once every two months. If that is so, then Hampstead Heath is a more violent place, and much smaller. 'On the other hand,' he added with a smile, if a trifle weary smile, 'far more people are conceived here than die here. People are not officially allowed to stay in their cars in the car parks after dark, but our Keepers cannot be patrolling everywhere. They have much better things to do than march courting couples out of the Forest.'

I moaned about the debris I had seen around Connaught Water and High Beach and he said those were by far the worst places, along with parts of Chingford Plain. 'It's a mammoth task. Five days a week in the summer, all day long, there are five Keepers on duty collecting litter.' Vandalism, however, was not very serious. There is no planting in the Forest, as they rely on natural regeneration, and it is usually new staked plants which attract vandals.

'Down in Wanstead Flats we put in several thousand new trees last year, protected by fencing. They have been almost totally destroyed, the young trees completely chopped down. This autumn, we are putting in 7,000 trees in Wanstead Park, but *none* of them will have stakes. We hope to get away with it this time as our trees will appear to have grown up naturally.'

I asked about the lack of a map of the Forest, on one sheet, and he said they hoped to work on this, in the next year or so. I also passed on the moans about the horse tracks. 'The Conservators have a love-hate relationship with horses. The public has a right to ride in the Forest and we like to see them, but they do do a lot of damage to paths. Our new routes have been constructed with hoggin, which is a sand, gravel and clay mix, which we hope will protect the Forest floor. We've done 17 miles so far. In the wet weather, horses do poach the surface, churning it up the way cattle do in fields.'

He did think the number of horses using the Forest was probably now excessive and that saturation point had been reached. I had hardly seen them all day, though it was a Monday, nor had I spotted a single uniformed Keeper, but I had spent a lot of time getting lost. On Sunday mornings, the Forest becomes awash with horses, numbering many hundreds. 'The whole point of the Forest is informality. There are no fences to shut you out, no laid-out picnic spots, no set nature trails. We want the public to go everywhere and enjoy themselves, but *respect* the Forest.'

The people who least respect the Forest can sometimes be a public authority, who take a quick look at the map and think, perfect, what an easy route for my new pipe line or my new motorway, no buildings to knock down or awkward streets to dig up. The big drama in the last few years has been the threat of the M25, due to open in 1983. The Ministry of Transport wanted to cut across the northern part of the Forest, but there was such an outcry from local preservation and other bodies that a long battle ensued and a Public Inquiry was set up. In the end, it was decided that the M25 could go *under* part of the Forest at a spot called Bell Common. It has meant the construction of a special quarter-mile-long tunnel, adding millions of pounds to the total bill, but keeping the Forest above intact. The work is due to be completed in 1984, and the mess all cleared up, including replacing a cricket pitch which had to be dug up on top of the tunnel.

All these human problems, from litter to horse riders, from vandalism to road-builders, all caused by pressures from the public, are only a minor part of Mr Besent's day-to-day worries, and he appears to take them in his stride. The bigggest problem of all about being Superintendent of Epping Forest as we move through the 1980s is the Battle with Nature.

Although the Forest is natural and unplanted, it does not mean they ignore it and let the elements simply get on with it. Nature needs a helping hand, if only to protect it from itself. Under the 1878 Act, they are instructed to preserve a *balance* of Nature in the Forest, to maintain a wide spectrum of animal and plant life, keeping the Forest interesting and enjoyable for all visitors, experts and the general public alike.

'Nature has got to be manipulated. Grasslands would go back to scrub and in some cases to trees, unless we interfered and did systematic cutting and clearing. The Conservators consider this our most important work. The decline in deer and rabbits is linked with the decline of grazing lands and the disappearance locally of many farms and cattle as Metropolitan London has moved nearer all the time.

'We want scrubland, grassland, heathland, heather and Forest, but we want to keep the balance between them all. If we do nothing, trees will win. Forest ponds have got to be kept alive. They dry up and silt and lose their plant and animal life. Most of them were gravel pits and are not fed by natural streams.

'So much of our energies and labour has been spent in the last ten years with clearing dead elms. Routine thinning had not been done and the Forest has become unbalanced in certain areas. My achievement as Superintendent in the years ahead will be to put back the Balance of Nature.'

Before leaving, I asked him for his favourite bits of the Forest, the places he would take a visitor. His choices show his interest in woodland rather than in crowds of people, which is why he personally would not go to Connaught Water or Chingford Plain. He shuddered at the very idea.

'I would take someone firstly to Broadstood, part of the Forest near Theydon Bois. We have achieved excellent continuity of tree cover in this area. The old trees have been thinned out and new ones encouraged and we now have a perfect mixed woodland, with all age groups represented.

'Queen Elizabeth Lodge. I know it is in a very popular area, and gets very crowded, but the displays in the Museum are so well worth going to see.

'For a grassland area, I would choose Sunshine Plain. This is a wet, heathland section with some very interesting plants, especially an insect-eating plant called the Sundew plant.'

I had visited the Lodge and been near his woodland choice, though without realising it, but I decided to save his grassland for another day. Having lost the Lost Pond, I would probably stumble upon the insect-eating plant straightaway . . .

CHAPTER NINE

Hampstead Heath

After all those Royal Parks, or parks with Royal connections, Hampstead Heath is by comparison a commoner. Its history is very much anti-establishment and it represents the struggles of ordinary locals against the inherited wealthy. The people of Hampstead *made* their own Heath, saving it for themselves when all could easily have been lost. Since they rescued it for public use, just over a hundred years ago, it has increased in size fourfold – and it is still growing, all the time. There have been many great battles over the centuries in and around all the London Parks, but Hampstead Heath is perhaps the greatest achievement that any preservation lobby has ever had.

By *ordinary* Hampstead people we are not of course talking about the same breed as ordinary Wigan people or ordinary Scunthorpe people. Ordinary Hampstead folk tend to be eminent lawyers, successful publishers, well-known broadcasters, famous journalists, best-selling authors, international musicians, established politicians, Harley Street doctors, stars of the silver screen and pillars of the West End stage and oh, all those ordinary folk one meets every day in Hampstead High Street. With such people on your committee, how could anyone ever lose? The answer is, very easily. Saving the Heath has taken, and still takes, constant vigilance.

I have to declare an interest. It is my local park. I have lived beside the Heath since 1960 and I estimate I have put in 10,000 walking hours, doing a morning and afternoon walk each day, plus three hours on Sunday playing football. (We play on a far pitch, Number 9, beside the Tumulus, and as I get older it takes me longer to walk there, and even longer to crawl back.) It was strange, therefore, to set off to walk round it professionally, to make notes and a try to see it with cold, clear eyes.

I worried if perhaps I had short-changed all those previous parks. We regular Heath-walkers, we like to think we know everything and everyone, we nod and smile, without knowing names or background, recognising each other by an angle of the body, the dog on the lead, the time of the day, that path they always come down. We see it in all weathers, all seasons, and know what used to be beside that pond, behind

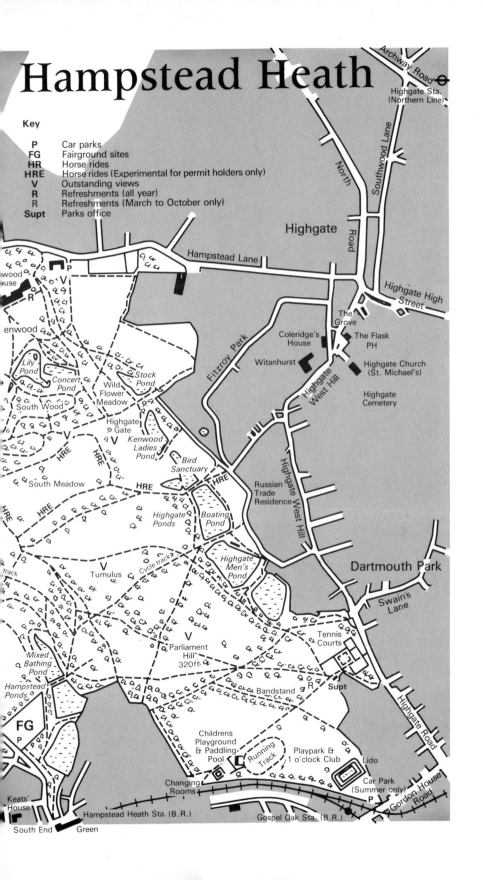

Hampstead Heath

Key

P	Car parks
FG	Fairground sites
HR	Horse rides
HRE	Horse rides (Experimental for permit holders only)
V	Outstanding views
R	Refreshments (all year)
R	Refreshments (March to October only)
Supt	Parks office

Archway Road

Highgate Sta.
(Northern Line)

North Road

Southwood Lane

Highgate

Hampstead Lane

Highgate High Street

enwood

wood ouse

P

V

R

The Grove

Coleridge's House

The Flask PH

Witanhurst

Highgate Church (St. Michael's)

Fitzroy Park

Highgate West Hill

Highgate Cemetery

Lily Pond

Concert Pond

Stock Pond

Wild Flower Meadow

South Wood

Highgate Gate

Kenwood Ladies Pond

Bird Sanctuary

Russian Trade Residence

HRE

South Meadow

HRE

Highgate Ponds

Boating Pond

Highgate West Hill

track

Tumulus

Cycle track

Highgate Men's Pond

Dartmouth Park

Swain's Lane

Mixed Bathing Pond

Parliament Hill 320ft

Tennis Courts

Highgate Road

Hampstead Ponds

Bandstand

R

Supt

FG

P

Childrens Playground & Paddling Pool

Running Track

Playpark & 1 o'clock Club

Lido

Changing Rooms

Car Park (Summer only)

P

Gordon House Road

Keats' House

Hampstead Heath Sta. (B.R.)

Gospel Oak Sta. (B.R.)

South End

Green

those trees, what will happen in the coming season to those meadows, what will appear on that hill, where the dragonflies play, changes for the better, changes for the worse, we've seen them come, we've seen them go. I was a stranger in all those other parks, so what did I miss? I could only report what I saw as I passed through or what people told me. The Heath is a second home, and I like to think I wear it like a skin, but by having gone round those other parks I felt I would be able to tell how it differs in feeling and facilities. Who knows Hampstead who only Hampstead knows? By going away, I might discover what I have always had at home.

The name Hampstead comes from the Saxon Hamstede, meaning homestead, meaning farm, and until well after the Middle Ages that seems to have been the main activity, especially pig farming. By the 16th century it had become a small community, known for its laundresses, where the London gentry and aristocracy, including Royalty, sent their washing. A colony of washerwomen had established itself, using the natural springs on the Heath and the various streams, many of them the sources of rivers flowing down into London, such as the River Fleet. On a dry day, it was said that the heights of Hampstead was turned into a snow-capped mountain with the lines of flapping linen.

In the early 18th century, Hampstead suddenly became a fashionable watering place when people flocked to spas near Well Walk which were said to have medicinal qualities. The first period of development in Hampstead then began, with fine houses being built around Church Row and the High Street. Hampstead became a bustling, lively, sometimes bawdy little tourist centre, not just with people taking the waters but with those attracted by a racecourse on the Heath and other less wholesome entertainments.

By the early 19th century, this first wave of popularity was long over, but the gentry who had been attracted by the spas stayed on and made Hampstead a more refined enclave, with wealthy professional men, especially from the City and from Bloomsbury, settling down with their families. So started the second wave of development and the village once again began to grow. As the village grew, the Heath began to shrink.

In 1680, Hampstead Heath had measured around 330 acres but this was down to 250 acres by 1818 as various enclosures and housing developments had taken place. The Heath, in those days, was a wild, scrubland area, full of gorse, with odd bits of common grazing ground and several large sandpits, all of it just outside the Village, centred on those parts we now call West Heath and East Heath.

The Lord of the Manor was Sir Thomas Maryon Wilson and he maintained he had all rights over the whole Heath, including the right to enclose unused parts of it. In 1829 he tried to cash in on his inheritance and take advantage of the enormous building development going on all over

North London. Heaths, or commons, which had formerly been much bigger than Hampstead Heath, such as Finchley Common and Highgate Common, soon disappeared completely, and appear on no maps today, but in Hampstead the local citizens were determined to fight and to exercise their common rights, and over the next forty-two years, from 1829 to 1871, they waged a guerrilla war. If Sir Thomas had been more circumspect, gradually selling or developing little bits of the Heath, keeping the various factions happy, he might in the end have got away with his whole plan, but he was obstinate and bull-headed and demanded all or nothing. His opponents took legal action and stopped several of his attempts to get his enabling bill through Parliament. He then started his own campaign against the locals, installing a permanent land agent (he himself was an absentee landlord), and charged the local washerwomen for using his Heath, farmers for letting loose geese, putting in any fences, or for taking away sand, all customs which had gone on for centuries. Just to annoy, he planted a few thousand willows and oaks, simply to prove his own right to plant willows and oaks.

His most ambitious move, as a dire warning to all the protesters, was in 1845 when he built a road across the edge of the Heath (East Heath Road), a large Viaduct and a Viaduct Pond, all of which are still there, the first stage, so he said, in a large development of villas which would soon take place, once he had got his Act through Parliament. He was attacked nationally in the Press as the ultimate arrogant landlord and an article in *Household Words* in 1857, thought to have been from the pen of Charles Dickens, a frequent visitor to Hampstead Heath, lambasted him without actually spelling out his name. 'Did not some say that somebody – we forgot and do not care who – tried to enclose Hampstead Heath? If he does, may his heirs find a quick road to their inheritence. It must have been some half fledged baronet, the second of the family . . . Whoever he is, may visions of angry laundresses scald his brain with weak tea . . .'

Sir Thomas never gave up, despite an attempt to buy the Heath from him for public use. This fell through when the price was said to be £400,000, a sum no one could afford. Ten years later, in 1865, he had put it up to £2,500,000 which he said was now a reasonable figure for a building plot. His death in 1869 proved to be the only solution. His brother, who inherited the title, quickly gave in and the Hampstead Heath Act was passed in 1871 and his manorial rights to the Heath sold for £45,000. They were bought by the Metropolitan Board of Works, subsequently the London County Council and, today, the GLC, who are the present owners.

A new battle then began to extend the Heath by further purchases and acquisitions. In 1886, Parliament Hill and its surrounding fields were taken over for £302,000, and in 1899 Golders Hill was purchased for £38,000. The most spectacular acquisition was the Kenwood estate which happened as recently as the 1920s. Since then, further additions have been made, and are still going on, and today the Heath covers 800 acres compared with 200 acres in 1871 when the Act was passed.

The main protector today is the Heath and Old Hampstead Society, an impressive organisation founded in 1895, now under the chairmanship of the redoubtable Peggy Jay, JP, who could make any GLC official quake. They have 430 members, many of the names being familiar to any reader of *Who's Who*. Casting my eye down the present membership list, I counted 24 titles (ranging from Sirs, Lords, Earls, to one Princess), plus assorted Professors and Rt. Hons. The literary and artistic names include Dame Peggy Ashcroft, Peter Barkworth, Melvyn Bragg, Robert Dougal, John Hillaby, Marghanita Laski, Yehudi Menuhin, Nicholas Parsons, Nikolaus Pevsner, Sir Ralph Richardson.

They hold regular walks across the Heath, arrange lectures and talks and are ever alert for new buildings going up around the perimeter, watching for any which might destroy the views. They get valuable houses listed, to prevent future development, and keep an eye on every move which Camden (the local Borough) or the GLC makes, knowing that, for all their fine public words, officialdom can very quickly bend or change the rules to suit itself.

Their biggest campaign in the last twelve years has been directed against the development of Witanhurst, a stately home with twenty acres on the flanks of Highgate, adjoining the Heath. Since 1969, a joint group with the Highgate Society has held over 100 committee meetings, collected a petition which now has over 18,000 signatures and forced various legal enquiries. They have managed to reduce the proposed development and now only 24 instead of 70 houses are going to be built on the site.

The day I set off, on my own official little walk, I learned from the local paper, the *Hampstead and Highgate Express*, that the Heath had just acquired another one acre of garden, from Manor House Hospital, which is over on the West Heath part of the Heath, traditionally the smarter end. I live at the other side, beside Highgate Road, in what is known as Parliament Hill Fields – though outsiders never know where that is, so depending on whom we're trying to impress we either say Highgate or Kentish Town. Kentish Town was formerly the wrong end, the working-class end, till quite recently. Now, when even ordinary terrace houses on the Kentish Town side of the Heath are going for £100,000, it would be hard to call any of it undesirable any more.

All the same, this is still the popular, most-used-by-the-masses part of the Heath, thanks to the running track, cross-country championships, the playgrounds, the tennis courts, football pitches, bandstand, bowling green, kite-flying and the fishing ponds which bring in thousands of ordinary Londoners every weekend. In summer, the grass gets worn quickly, litter gets left, the cafeteria gets scruffy, easily achieved as it is one of the most unattractive tea houses in any London Park, though there are reports that it might change soon. It faces the wrong way for a start and the inside is equally grim.

I know people who live on the Hampstead side who never walk on our side, always keeping on the heights, avoiding the hoi polloi down below near Highgate Road. John Le Carré and John Hillaby are both regular Heath-walkers, but I have never seen them on the Kentish Town side. Michael Foot, with his Welsh terrier Disraeli, does venture our way, on his marathon Heath walks, but he has had other things to occupy him recently. A. J. P. Taylor lives on our side and is one of the masses. He goes everywhere, including regular dips in the open air pond.

The GLC produces a very good map of the Heath which is not just the best but the *only* one-sheet map of any of the Parks I walked. The price is 50p, a bargain, but they do keep it rather quiet and you have to barge into the Superintendent's office and demand one. On it, there are five walks suggested by Ralph Wade, all very useful, but not one starts from or even takes in our end of the Heath. Oh well, we can take it.

I had an appointment with the Superintendent, whose office and yard are just on the left as you enter from Highgate Road, but I was a trifle early, so I had a drink at the fountain, which was working for once, after endless acts of vandalism, when I noticed a youth bent almost double looking for something in the grass. Over the previous few months, I had seen several young people, often in groups, scouring this end of the Heath very intently. He said he was looking for magic mushrooms. In his hand he had an empty crisp packet filled with about fifty very small mushrooms, very grey and wispy, with long thin stalks and heads little bigger than a drawing pin. No wonder you have to bend double to find them. I would never have noticed them myself.

'They're really good,' he said. 'You dry them for about two or three days, then eat them. No, you don't cook them. Eat them raw, with a cup of tea, that's what I do. I usually take about eighty at a time. Me and my mate once had a hundred each. After about an hour you start to hallucinate. It lasts for two hours. It's really good. No, there are no after-effects.'

He looked a clean and presentable-enough young man, not haggard or ill. He thought the correct name for them was something like Silly Bum, but he didn't know how to spell it (presumably Psilocybin). His mate had shown him which ones to pick. He wasn't scared about poisoning himself, but his back did ache with looking for them. It was all very simple, he said. You got a high, all for free, better than buying drugs or booze. S'natural, innit.

Then I went to look for Mr King, our friendly superintendent. We were a bit worried when Dave King took over in 1976 that he might do awful things to the Heath, such as putting in flower beds. His background is horticultural and some feared he might try to turn the Heath into a municipal park. Even the word 'Park' has the Hampstead purist reaching for his blue pencil. The GLC just has to let that word slip into any conversations or on to notice boards – and a few years ago they did have an offensive notice which said 'Welcome to Your Park' – and there will be angry protests. The Heath is a Heath.

Mr King has turned out to be a success, well in tune, so far, with the wishes of the local preservation societies. He is a well-built, rather gentle Irishman, still with a very strong accent, despite his many years in London. He was born in 1934 in the village of Shillelagh, where the sticks originated, in County Wicklow, and brought up on a large country estate owned by Lord Fitzwilliam where his father and grandfather worked as shepherds. He left school at fourteen, worked on the estate's gardens for two years, then moved to Cork in a commercial nursery. In 1952, aged 17½, he joined the RAF with a friend, a sudden whim to see a bit of the world, spread their wings a bit. He signed on for five years, during which time he served in Suez and Cyprus.

In 1957 he joined the LCC Parks department, filling in time as he was about to emigrate to the United States, to join his parents who had already moved there, but in London he met his wife on a blind date through an old friend from Shillelagh, and they have stayed in London ever since. She is from the Falls Road area of Belfast and they have four children. He worked in the nurseries at Kennington Park, became a foreman at Victoria Embankment Gardens, till in 1970 he took over his first proper park, Alexandra Park, which has around 200 acres. The jump to the Heath was quite a big one, but he says he did not apply for it. All his promotions have been suggested to him.

It still says Superintendent on his office door, and this is what most people call him, but the GLC for clerical reasons insist he should be called the Park Manager. He is in charge of most of Hampstead Heath, some 560 acres, which include Parliament Hill, East Heath and Kenwood. The remaining 240 acres – West Heath, Sandy Heath and Golders Hill – are managed by Peter Challen who is based at Golders Hill. The terms for the various parts of the Heath can be very confusing. Just because they appear on the map does not mean they are always used, either by the park-keepers or by local people, who often have their own names for their favourite bits. Older residents on the Kentish Town side still talk about going over the Fields, rather than the Heath.

Mr King has a staff of 65, 34 of them Keepers, 20 gardeners and the rest are attendants, in charge of things like toilets, playgrounds and the Lido. He had just been interviewing for Keepers, a job I would have thought would have had them queueing down Highgate Road. Imagine having an outdoor job in rural surroundings, right in the middle of London. He said it was a disaster. Only three applicants were suitable, all of whom he took, yet he could have taken on six. 'I can't understand it, yet we've got over three million unemployed.'

One reason could be the salary, which is not very good and has to be made up with overtime, at unsociable hours. 'It should be paid better, but the clerical workers, who push paper around in the background, now get better money than the park-keepers on the front line.' Half the job is manual, picking up litter, marking out football pitches, and the rest is patrolling, and this is apparently what people do not like today. 'You do have to remind people of the bye-laws of the Heath and stop them doing certain things, which can result in abuse or even assault. There is no respect for people in authority these days, so people don't want to do it. They don't want the aggravation, so the calibre of people who apply for the job is not as good as it was. This is one of my biggest problems.' In the Royal Parks of course, the job is completely separated, with the Royal Parks Constabulary doing the patrolling, except for Hyde Park which the Metropolitan Police control direct.

One other major problem for every Heath Superintendent over the last hundred years has been the number of action groups looking over his shoulder, but Mr King says he has no complaints about them. When he took over, the previous Superintendent told him he would have thirteen different societies to worry about, but with amalgamations there are now only seven, the most important being the Heath and Old Hampstead Society. They have set up a sub-committee which he meets every three months, to tell them what he plans to do. He listens to all their comments and suggestions, and invites them to site-meetings when any important work is about to take place. What he won't agree to – and there are probably one or two passionate people who would have liked it – are day-to-day meetings.

The present harmony has been helped by a permanent conservation unit which was set up in 1979. This consists of six men, including two foremen, who attend to the specific conservation areas throughout the whole of the Heath, not just Mr King's domain. In the old days, when some special reclamation or clearing work had to be done, gardeners would be taken off other jobs, depending on who was free, and sent with their machines and told to get started. They were often unskilled, and sometimes uncaring, and naturally, when the preservationists saw what was happening, it led to screams and shouts and arguments.

The work on South Meadow, on the left as you enter the Highgate gate to Kenwood, is their biggest success so far. This was an overgrown, scrubland area, hardly used, except by unsavoury people, hiding in the thick bushes. It has been judiciously cleared and provides splendid views down over the Highgate Ponds, yet still retains a natural, country feeling, with many trees and a special riding track for horses. 'Some people wanted it left completely wild of course. I see my job as trying to serve the needs of the people as a whole, not just of Hampstead, but all of London, giving them a Heath they can enjoy in safety.'

The only trouble now is that his conservation unit should be bigger, with up to ten men, as there is so much for them to do. That day, they were working over on the Heath Extension, clearing out a series of small ponds which had become overgrown. They were then due back on the main part of the Heath to start ploughing a two-acre meadow on the east side of Kenwood which it is planned to sow with wild flowers.

Everyone is very excited about this project, part of a wild flower campaign that has been going on since 1979. Every year, Mr King's men plant up to 10,000 bluebells. They have also been planting gorse bushes to counter soil erosion on over-used paths, such as the one at the Hampstead Gate entrance to Kenwood. Then they have a long list of sycamore trees to take down, especially around the Viaduct. 'Sycamores are no good for wild life, but they grow like mad everywhere. We have a ten to fifteen year plan to replace them with approved trees and shrubs.'

During an average year, between ten and twelve dead bodies have to be dealt with on the Heath. Some are accidental deaths, caused by drowning, by people swimming in ponds they're not supposed to use, or in winter by skating on forbidden ice. There are suicides, most of which also end up in one of the ponds. Then there are murders and assaults. Judging from the local paper, there would appear in recent months to have been an incident of rape almost every week, but Mr King says it goes in spells. Clearing the denser undergrowth has helped, and using mounted policemen, park-keepers with dogs as well as the ordinary keepers on patrol. 'At the moment we have somebody attacking women round the Vale of Health. The last serious spell was about three years ago when it was happening round Kenwood. It was one of my keepers who helped to catch him. He heard screams from the wood and ran to investigate. A man ran out and he gave chase and caught him up. He took out a knife and my keeper got a branch and they struggled but the man got away. He then chased him across the Heath and saw him get into a car at Gospel Oak. He only got part of the number, but that was enough. A few weeks later the police saw the car in the car park on East Heath Road and arrested him. He admitted everything.'

Two minor things which have recently puzzled me about the Heath are the amount of hay which is left to rot, now that the fashion is to increase the number of long meadows, and the wastage of good logs. Was this the GLC being profligate or just disorganised? 'It is bad grass management to let it rot, as it changes the nature of the soil, but there's not a lot we can do with our long grass. It makes very poor quality hay and farmers won't even take it away. The best we can do is hope the police will take some of it for their horses, but they need to have it baled.' As for the logs, I have seen them being thrown on bonfires. This seems ridiculous when all round the Heath there are commercial nurseries selling logs at £8 a hundred which people buy for their winter fires. (Illegal, of course, since smokeless zones came in, but every right-thinking Hampstead type is now opening up his old drawing-room fireplace, the one he blocked up ten years ago.) Mr King says that much of the timber is now going to be left to rot in special enclosures to serve as an ecosystem for wildlife, insects and fungi. He is also thinking of investing in a wood chipping machine, which will grind the branches into a mulch, suitable for flower beds.

I then started my walk proper round the Heath, heading first for the Highgate Ponds. There are six, strung out on a long string like conkers, or eight if you count the two which curve into Kenwood, and each has a different use and a different atmosphere.

Near the first Highgate Pond I caught sight of a lady with a pair of binoculars who was watching some bird movement on a raft in the far corner. It was Kate Springett, the GLC's Bird Observer. She is a familiar figure on the Heath, plodding round in all weathers, in her sensible shoes and coat, usually carrying a little rucksack and her binoculars. She can look very severe and preoccupied, deep in some worrying thought when she's busy, but her face lights up when you bring her back to human life.

She was a milliner by profession, now retired, but ornithology has always been her hobby and she taught it at evening classes. She got the position, which is honorary, in 1958. 'Oh, you just have to be recommended to the GLC, then they check you out.' She lives in a council flat near the Heath, on the Parliament Hill Fields side. She does an annual report of all her bird observations which is published in the local paper and in the Heath and Old Hampstead Society's newsletter.

I asked her what those ducks were, over there, the ones she was watching, and she said they were Canada geese, but very nicely, not putting me in my place. They are a new breed on the Heath, having arrived in the last year or so and now seem here to stay. Another newcomer in the last few years has been the great crested grebe. This makes up for a couple of breeds which seem to have deserted the Heath, notably the hawfinch. On the whole, bird life is doing very well. Last year she reported 83 different species, with around half of them having bred on the Heath. She thinks the Conservation unit has helped, restoring hedgerows, planting trees and shrubs, clearing out the swamps.

Regular sightings include kestrels, tawny owls, black-caps, willow warblers, shovelers, and the lesser spotted woodpecker, the most elusive of all the woodpeckers. The previous year a pair of goosanders were seen, the first known sighting on the Heath. Mute swans, once residents, are now irregular visitors. Two stayed for a long time the previous year, then the adult was found dead on the raft. The finger of suspicion fell on the fishermen. Some discarded fishing tackle had possibly caught in the swan's throat as it had been seen having difficulty eating.

The best ponds for observing the Heath's birds are, rather surprisingly, the two nearest the main roads – the Number One Highgate Pond, the first on your right as you come in from Highgate Road, and the Number One Hampstead Pond, again the first pond you see when you enter from South End Green. The reason is quite simple. They each have bird rafts, thanks to Miss Springett having proposed them some years ago.

The next Highgate pond is the Men's Pond, reserved for male swimmers, though it is also a fishing pond and a bird pond. Men have swum there for a hundred years without any harm, though the water round the edges can look very murky and uninviting, especially where the fishermen sit. They swim there all the year round, breaking the ice on Boxing Day for a race, and there is a strong nucleus of daily swimmers and keep-fit fanatics, some so old and gnarled-looking you can hardly believe they have the energy to get into their track-suits. The pond is also used by a group of professional boxers in training. John Conteh used to be one of them. Now they mainly seem to be Nigerian. You see them staggering back after a long run, crinkling in their grey Lonsdale sweat-suits, their hoods up, throwing occasional punches at the empty air, looking completely shattered. They have a shower or a swim and walk home, very very slowly, to their soulless digs in some nearby terrace, the long afternoon to put in, miles from their homeland, before it's time for training once again. Some live in our street and I often hear them in the afternoon, listening to the children's programmes. In the summer, these two groups of regulars are out-numbered by an influx of more exotic creatures, beautifully-tanned males who lie around naked, admiring each other and themselves.

The Men's Pond looks nothing when viewed from the other side, especially its grim little changing room, merely a wooden enclosure, open to the heavens, with no amenities, not even hot water, simply a concrete floor and some old wooden benches round the walls. Yet for many of those different groups of men it is the centre of their social life, where they meet and play, exercise and gossip every day.

The best view of the ponds is from the top of Kite Hill, or Parliament Hill, or Parly as most locals call it. Highgate from that position looks positively Mediterranean with the green dome of St Joseph's and the spire of St Michael's dominating the sky line. It appears to be a terraced hill slope, incredibly green and lush, as if Highgate was totally rural. You can see why Heath-lovers worry so much about any alterations or developments on the fringes. The other London Parks are flat and could survive if the fringes were altered, though no one wants that to happen, but the Heath is the only central Park with height. What happens on its borders is vital to the whole.

Parliament Hill is a natural adventure playground, with kites all the year round, skiing and sledging in the winter, plus occasional Druids and other groups regularly assembling. The view over London is the best natural one anywhere in London. Parliament Hill is 320 feet high, not the highest point on the Heath – Whitestone Pond is 443 feet – but it has a perfect situation and you can see clearly all the major buildings, St Paul's, the Palace of Westminster, the GPO Tower, right across to Kent.

I had always assumed that it was called Parliament Hill because Cromwell set up some sort of Parliament there, but Mr King the Superintendent says the name comes from Guy Fawkes. On the night he thought he was going to blow up Parliament, he arranged for some of his supporters to stand on the hill and enjoy the blaze. They were rounded up, but their vantage point became known as Parliament Hill. No doubt there are other explanations. At least Henry VIII does not appear in any of them.

The next Highgate Pond, Number Three, is the Boating Pond, for model boats only, either sail or motor. Pond Number Four is out of bounds, as it is a bird sanctuary, and so is the next pond, except to ladies. This is their own swimming area and by all accounts it is much nicer than the men's, with better changing facilities, cleaner and more attractive. The final pond before Kenwood is also enclosed, used as a stock pond.

I always walk the length of the Highgate ponds first thing in the morning, just after nine o'clock, right to the end and back, taking a neighbour's dog with me. On my afternoon walk, I always go for the heights. While Miss Springett is on the look out for birds, I am always trying to spot my first Russian of the morning. They tend to move in pairs, usually with heavy but cheap shopping bags, with a distinctive walk and distinctive dress and I give myself marks if I can identify them a long way away. They live in their Official Residence belonging to the Russian Trade Delegation, that large modern apartment block on Millfield Lane, overlooking the Boating Pond. They have been warned not to smile – I met a defector once who told me that – which of course is completely against their nature, or to converse with the natives, though I do exchange eyes with several of them, having passed them on the same spot every morning for years. I did know a few to actually speak to, when there were some Russian children in my daughter's class at the local Primary school, but they have now returned home. On Sunday mornings, the men play football on the top, near the Tumulus, and have often joined in our games.

As I was walking up the hill to Kenwood, I suddenly heard the sound of bagpipes floating down the slopes. Over the previous few months, I had

The sound of music on Hampstead Heath: a lone bagpiper practises his pibrochs

twice raced up the hill to see who or what it was, but never managed to get there in time. As I ran towards the sound, it seemed to fade. Perhaps he was walking away, marching back to Hampstead. Then it grew louder and I decided he was walking the other way, towards South End Green. It stopped completely and I thought, curses, I might never hear him again for months. Who will believe I ever heard him? Official Bird Observers have to be believed when they present their report. My family will say I have been imagining a bagpiper.

It started again and I doubled my speed and reached a plateau near the Tumulus and there was a young bearded man in a tweed sports jacket slowly walking up and down, tracing out a large rectangle on the grass, turning carefully at each corner, playing his bagpipes as he marched. I sat on the grass and listened, not wanting to interrupt. I remember once at Uig on the Isle of Skye hearing a lone piper on a hillside across a bay and feeling almost emotional. In a corner I could see where he had neatly laid his music case and a scarf. He had very short hair, brushed back on top like a French crew cut, and looked very fit.

Eventually, when he had finished and was packing away his pipes, I went over and talked to him. He was called Dave Brooks and he lives in a flat on Christ Church Hill, Hampstead. 'It's hard to practise in the house. The woman upstairs is deaf. I don't know if it's because of me she's deaf, but I don't like playing indoors anyway. You get a much better sound in the open air.'

He had not played on the Heath for two months, which was why I had begun to think that haunting sound had gone for good. 'I've been waiting for a chanter. This new one's just come today, but it'll have to go back. Cost me £30. It's not right, look.' I didn't understand the technicalities but I could see where he had stuck on some black tape. He likes to practise at some time on the Heath most days, unless it's too cold and his fingers go numb. 'I usually aim for 8.30 in the morning. Then I go down to the pond, leave my case in the Men's Pool, have a two-mile run, and then a swim, and I feel really great.'

He is English-born but has a Scottish mother and therefore feels qualified to wear the kilt which he often does, even when practising. He is self-taught on the bagpipes but plays the saxophone professionally as a member of a modern jazz group called Silly Boy Lemon. 'We play pubs mainly. Come and hear us at the Bird in the Hand. Turd in the Hand, we call it. It's a good pub. I'm an amateur piper really, but I'm practising hard and I intend to go in for some piping competitions. I've done a few gigs on my pipes, things like Burns Suppers. I hope to get more in the future.'

I walked with him down the hill, on the way to his post-bagpipe swim, and then I headed for Kenwood.

The acquisition of the Kenwood estate was the greatest achievement in the long saga of Hampstead Heath, second only in importance to the original purchase from the Maryon Wilson family. There was a house there as early as 1616, but the present house is mostly associated with the First Earl of Mansfield, a Scottish-born lawyer who became Lord Chief Justice. He bought the house and estate in 1754 and commissioned another eminent Scotsman, Robert Adam, to enlarge and improve it, both inside and outside. Successive Mansfields lived there until the First World War when they decided they preferred their Scottish home at Scone. The entire estate looked as if it would be sold to speculators, but there was a local and national outcry and in various stages the land was saved, 100 acres being added to the Heath in 1922, with another 32 acres in 1924, at a total cost of some £152,000.

Kenwood House, Hampstead Heath: the greatest art treasures of any London Park

It still seemed likely, however, that the house itself would eventually go to a developer, having been let out to tenants and then stripped and left empty for some time, but in 1925 along came Edward Cecil Guinness, the first Earl of Iveagh, an Irish gentleman then aged 78, who had conceived a marvellous plan which has resulted in his title being remembered for ever. His own family surname has, of course, been known to be good for us all for many generations. It was he who put Guinness on the world map, inheriting the family brewery in Dublin at the age of 21 and then building up its international importance.

Lord Iveagh bought the derelict house plus 74 acres, the remainder of the estate, for £107,000, and proceeded to put in his own art collection which he had studiously built up in the 1880s and 1890s, most of it being purchased through Agnews. He re-created the house in its original 18th-century manner, filling it with English paintings, and then, without ever living there himself, he handed the whole lot over to the nation on his death in 1927. The GLC is now responsible for handling The Iveagh Bequest, Kenwood, an architectural and artistic masterpiece, the GLC's most prized possession in any of their Parks, perhaps the finest *house* in the whole of London. Certainly, it is the one I would most like to live in, as long as they left all the contents. On the open market, which of course is not the sort of thing Curators like to talk about, I estimate the contents are probably worth about £20 million while the house and grounds would easily fetch £10 million.

There's Rembrandt's 'Self Portrait', worth £3 million, and Vermeer's 'The Guitar Player' (the one which was stolen a few years ago, then found, unharmed), which must be worth about £2 million. The main strength is in English painting and they have what is considered Gainsborough's finest work, 'Lady Howe', plus many others by him and by Reynolds, Lawrence, Raeburn and Turner.

The Curator of The Iveagh Bequest is John Jacob. It was from him that I learned that the correct pronunciation is 'Iv-agh' not Ivy, which is what I've always said, and that the good Earl did in fact spend five nights there.

Mr Jacob comes from Carshalton. He was educated at Cambridge and picked up a taste for radio work during National Service when he did Forces Broadcasts. He still regularly broadcasts, mainly for Radio Four's 'Kaleidoscope' on art topics. He arrived at Kenwood in 1967 from the Walker Gallery in Liverpool and one of his main aims since then has been to track down the Adam furniture which was originally in the House, before the Mansfield family emptied it. He and his assistants scour furniture catalogues round the world, knowing from contemporary drawings what their Adam bits look like, but hoping no one else will realise and put up the prices. He had recently retrieved a table and some pedestal cabinets from the USA and he took me down to the workshop where their resident craftsman was repairing them, before they go on show in the House.

He has little money to spend, so he needs bargains or gifts. The Iveagh Bequest, handsome though it was in 1927, now does not provide nearly enough to run the house, bringing in only around £15,000. It is hard to work out exactly how much Kenwood House *does* cost the GLC, as their accounts lump it with Ranger's House at Greenwich and Marble Hill House in Twickenham, both of which Mr Jacob also administers. The total expenditure on the three in 1982 came to £780,000. You can see why certain politicians sometimes think the money, and capital, could be better spent. Tories often want to impose admission charges while Socialists say sell the lot and put the money into community projects. The public, 150,000 of whom visit the House every year, obviously like it as it is.

Mr Jacob has built up Kenwood's reputation as an academic centre, with scholarly catalogues for their regular special exhibitions, and he has expanded the bookstall. I have regularly taken visitors to Kenwood over the years and I always encourage them to buy the postcards and reproductions, all excellent value. (The GLC is usually more reluctant than commercial shops to put up prices.) They make far better souvenirs of a London visit than lurid postcards from newsagents or Union Jack junk from Carnaby Street.

He lives on the premises, in a flat with his wife and young daughter aged seven. The other day, a member of the public complained about his child's pop music being too loud. 'He was perfectly right to complain, but I wonder if this were a stately home, and it had been the young Lady Charlotte, daughter of the Earl, whether he would simply have smiled and gone away and told his friends? We are public servants, part of the Bureaucracy, and people are always quicker to complain about us.

He was engaged that day in lengthy legal complications to buy a Gainsborough for £100,000, a painting in private hands, though it had been on show in Kenwood. His annual allocation for new works, for all three houses, is £15,000, hence the complications. The Government gives tax concessions for paintings sold to public galleries, and there are also special Art Funds he can go to, but that day he was still £20,000 short. 'I could wait for April, and a new financial year, and start again, but I've raised so much already that I must carry on. I'm sure we'll do it.' (And they did – in January 1983. The painting is of John Joseph Merlin, inventor of the double manual harpsichord, and also of roller skates.)

We went on a brief tour of the paintings which I have looked at scores of times before, but they appeared in a new light, with an expert to guide me, especially one so conscious of every kind of light. There are often complaints from visitors more used to the big-city galleries like the Tate and the National, or those in Paris and Amsterdam, that they can't *see* the

Kenwood paintings. Mr Jacob refuses all artificial or overhead lights. He prefers natural light, with just a normal central light in the middle of the room.

'I *hate* all spotlights. They make paintings look like colour transparencies. You may as well have a gallery which uses a cinema screen to show them. I have seen the "Night Watch" in Amsterdam, but I have never *experienced* it. Our "Self-Portrait" I have both seen and experienced. I often go and look at the Old Boy, the way other people might play a favourite piece of music, and I sometimes come away thinking, no, the Old Boy's not on today. It can be my fault, the way I feel, the time of day, or the light, the reflections, the season, other people in the room. Paintings are not stable. They are not meant to always look the same, which is what a spotlight does to them. After all, we are a *domestic* gallery. This is an 18th-century gentleman's villa. You should walk through the greenery of Hampstead Heath to come and see us. We would throw all those advantages away, if we then plunged you into artificial light.'

I examined the Rembrandt and although it was a dull afternoon, and the Old Boy was not on top form, Mr Jacob pointed out something I had never seen before, something which is not yet mentioned in the catalogue. If you look carefully, at the right of the painting, you can see where Rembrandt had painted in his left arm, holding the brush. He was working from a mirror and it was only when he finished for the day that he realised it made him look left-handed. So he painted out this arm, moving it further down, giving the body an almost abstract pyramid effect. This was discovered a few years ago, after an X-ray study, though with the naked eye you can detect a different shade where the arm used to be.

The Rembrandt, the Vermeer and Gainsborough's 'Lady Howe' are perhaps the Kenwood's three most famous paintings, which everyone wants to see, so I asked him for two more choices, lesser-known works which he thinks the public should include on their Kenwood tour. He chose one for amusement, at least it always amuses him, and that was the right-hand half of 'Old London Bridge' by Claude de Jongh. 'Look at it,' he said, 'that does look like Kodachrome, even without strip lighting.' More seriously, he chose a self-portrait by Angelica Kauffmann, one of the earliest women painters in England. 'It's a charming neo-classical portrait. It is inscribed to the man who commissioned her, which is of interest. It has emotional contact with the past which I like.'

No one, of course, should miss the Adam decorations, particularly in the Library, possibly the finest Adam room in existence, and the pieces of furniture now displayed round the House, and the Adam exteriors, especially the South front. The Coach House is open all the year round, except Christmas Day, as a cafeteria, and now has slightly better coffee than in the old days, plus good welsh rarebit and macaroni cheese. The Old

Kitchen, next door, is open only on Sundays for lunch, which is a shame. With its setting, it could be the most attractive restaurant in Hampstead. In the gardens there is a Barbara Hepworth, soon to be joined by a Henry Moore, when it emerges from the GLC pipeline, and nearby is a little thatched and wooden summer house, once used by Dr Johnson, which was moved to Kenwood in 1968.

On the way out of the Kenwood gardens, I met an old man, ill-shaven and wearing a dirty raincoat, a familiar figure, one I have talked to for years. He always walks very quickly, talking to himself, as if in a great hurry. It is usually the state of the country which upsets him, a topic I always get off quickly. The Heath is full of such eccentric figures, most of them harmless. There's one on a bicycle who carries his worldly possessions with him, including a transistor tied with string to his handlebars, always tuned to classical music. Then there is an old lady who carries all her possessions in plastic shopping bags and takes her meals almost genteelly on a park bench, spreading out her things, opening little plastic tubs, carefully buttering bits of stale bread.

'We've had it now,' said the old man. 'Gone to the dogs.'

'Have you heard about the wild flowers?' I replied. 'They're going to plough that bit outside Kenwood and plant it with wild flowers, isn't that good?'

'We don't want wild flowers. We want f—houses. Houses we can *buy*. Do you get my meaning? Houses we can buy.'

Down on the lawns below the house I could see workmen dismantling the open-air stage, putting it away for the winter. This is where the open-air orchestral concerts are held in June, July and August every year, on the other side of a little lake. All the best-known orchestras have played there, and many famous soloists, and crowds of up to 10,000 gather, sitting on the grass or on deckchairs, with blankets for the colder evenings and bottles of wine. I have regularly taken friends there over the last twenty years, from the north or abroad, showing off one of the many delights of London life. It never fails to impress.

From Kenwood I walked round to the Hampstead Gate and sat for a while beside a pine tree, near the entrance to the woods, which is my favourite view of Kenwood, glimpsed in the distance through the trees. Then I cut round and over Spaniards Road, the main road into Sandy Heath, one of three sections, divided by roads, which look from a map like later additions, although it is today's main part of the Heath, between Parliament Hill and Kenwood, which are the later additions.

Sandy Heath is mainly wooded with a few deep glades, left-over sand-pits, and it always seems damp and rather mysterious. I hurried through and across Wildwood Road into the Heath Extension, such an unattractive name for a very pleasant corner of the Heath. It is a long,

The Open Air orchestral platform at Kenwood, Hampstead Heath

rectangular slice of parkland, good for horse-riding, with a few small ponds at the Hampstead end and at the far corner a large area of football pitches. There was a great battle to acquire it at the turn of the century. Thanks to Miss Henrietta Barnett, who had a cottage nearby, and others, it was finally taken over in 1904 at a cost of £43,000. The basic purchase was an 80-acre farm, Wyldes Farm, bought from Eton College who had at one time wanted to sell it for building development. There was also a plan to open a new tube station at the Bull and Bush which would have meant further development in the area. The shafts were dug but the station was never opened and is now kept for railway archives.

You can still see the shape of the old fields and the lines of the hedges as you walk through the Heath Extension. I went right to the north corner, the furthest point of the Heath, which I suppose is only about 2½ miles as the crow flies from where I had begun, but it is possible, by doing the whole circumference, walking in and around all the various elements, to have a walk of up to ten miles, giving a good three- to four-hour stroll, pausing for refreshments and taking in an enormous variety of landscape and greenery, sights and views.

I crossed over the road at North End, near the Bull and Bush, trying as usual to see where that tube station might have been, but failed once again, and entered the main gates of Golders Hill where I had the best cup of coffee to be had anywhere in the London Parks. Golders Hill has always had the finest flower garden in the whole of the Heath, very popular with the elderly, and a deer and animal enclosure, very popular with the young, a handsome bandstand, two ponds, lots of ducks, flamingoes and tennis courts, but these days it is the little tea house which gives as much pleasure as anything else.

The café has nothing intrinsically attractive about it, unlike the large one at Kenwood, being a basic little modern building, but over the last ten years an Italian called Tony Pazlenti has put his own individual stamp on it, dispensing with the usual plastic cups and plastic-wrapped, sliced-bread sandwiches, providing home-made salads, quiches and gâteaux. He even has a wine licence, but on the whole tea-time food or coffee and goodies are best. The interior décor might not be to everyone's taste with some rather heavy ornaments and garish paintings which look as if they might have been won at a fair or taken from the cabin shrine of a long-distance lorry driver, but it shows a definite personality. Even under the GLC, an individual can still flourish.

I came back slowly through West Heath, which is densely wooded, like Sandy Heath, but it contains a beautiful secret garden, one I discovered relatively recently. It is high up on the North End side of West Heath, called The Hill, and it became part of the Heath in 1960. It makes a sharp contrast to the wildness of West Heath to wander amongst its pools and colonnades. It was formerly owned by Lord Leverhulme. Hampstead Village proper has of course housed many famous people over the years, but so have these Heath fringes, away from the Georgian streets and brighter lights, especially those seeking a more countryside life in cottage-style houses, with back doors opening straight on to the Heath. William Pitt, first Earl of Chatham, lived nearby at North End as did Anna Pavlova, William Blake, John Linnell and Raymond Unwin, architect of Hampstead Garden Suburb.

Jack Straw's Castle is at the summit of the Heath, the very heights of Hampstead, these days an exceedingly busy road junction. The inn dates back to 1713 and its name refers to Jack Straw, leader of the Peasants' Revolt in 1381. There's a bar named after Wat Tyler, another after Dick Turpin who haunted these parts, and a Dickens Room. The present building, with its wooden castellations, is new, rebuilt in 1962 after serious bomb damage.

There are three other famous pubs around Hampstead Heath which are well-known throughout London. The Bull and Bush is even older, 1645, and was made famous by Florrie Ford's song. It was at one time Hogarth's country house where he used to entertain Reynolds, Gainsborough, Constable and Romney. Yes, it now has a Florrie Ford Bar and a Hogarth Bar. Not far away is the Spaniards which claims to be the oldest inn, going back to the 1600s when a Spanish Ambassador is said to have lived there. Mr Pickwick had one of his numerous mishaps in the inn's gardens. The fourth ancient inn is on the other side of the Heath, the Flask in Highgate, at the top of West Hill, though it is not quite as big as the other three. All of them are interesting buildings, with literary and historic connections, well-furnished in posh pub style, with many genuine features, but personally I never go in any of them. They are just too big and impersonal, full of tourists and visitors.

It was a relief to get away from the traffic round Whitestone Pond and on to the open Heath again, especially to see the familiar chimneys of the Vale of Health stretching below, that strange little enclave, right inside the Heath. My wife and I lived here in a flat when we got married in 1960. I was so proud of it, so thrilled to start married life in such a beautiful and famous spot. We were at 9, Heath Villas and our bedroom overlooked the Vale of Health Pond. There was an old Victorian pub beside the pond, now replaced by a block of modern flats, but everything else is the same, even the fairground caravans.

When we lived in the Vale of Health we used to boast to visitors that the name arose during the Great Plague of 1665 because this was the only oasis in London where people survived. All utter nonsense. There is no reference to it being called the Vale of Health before 1801. Until 1777, it was decidedly unhealthy, little more than a mosquito-ridden swamp, till the marsh was drained and a new pond created. Since then it has gradually become a very desirable spot, the home of many writers and artists. Shelley is supposed to have sailed paper boats on the pond, another non-proven story, but Leigh Hunt did live there, so did D. H. Lawrence, Rabindranath Tagore, Stanley Spencer, Edgar Wallace, Compton Mackenzie, Alfred and Harold Harmsworth. The best-known resident today is probably Trevor Nunn of the Royal Shakespeare Company. The origin of the name is still uncertain. It could have been to indicate it was now healthy, once that swamp had been cleared, or more likely it was a misspelling of the Vale of Heath. Although I enjoyed my two years living there, I was glad in one respect to leave the Vale of Health. In the end it had made me ill. That pond brought on my asthma, something I had not had since my childhood.

I walked over the Viaduct, Wilson's Folly as it was once called, after he failed to get his wicked way with those villas, and into what I have always called the Avenue of Trees, though I now discover, looking at the GLC map, it is called Boundary Path. It is a splendid avenue, lined with limes. Nearby is a little football pitch with a tin hut, used as a changing room, which featured in John le Carré's *Smiley's People*. You might have seen it in

Boundary Path, Hampstead Heath: lined with limes and memories of Le Carré

the television adaptation. It was where the messages were left and where the murder took place in the first episode. On the rear of the hut I noticed the letters METS, graffiti left behind perhaps by a baseball-loving TV technician.

I then walked back up Parliament Hill, to cast my eyes again on all things lovely, another Heath walk over, thinking back over all the other London Parks I had recently walked. From flood-lit running to open-air orchestras,

Bank Holiday fairs to Rembrandt, the range on Hampstead Heath is enormous, far greater than any other London Park.

All London Parks like to boast that really, deep down, they are a bit of real countryside, a rural shelter from the urban world, and it is true that even in St James's Park, small though it is, you can position yourself and see only trees and water. But it was only on Hampstead Heath that I could really feel I was *not* in Central London. It is easier of course if you go much further out, fourteen miles away to Richmond or Epping, but Hampstead's ruralness is remarkable, considering it is only four miles from the centre.

It is the hills and the slopes and the undulating pastures which make the Heath a perfect escape. On the flatlands of Hyde Park, Kensington Gardens or Regent's Park, you always feel you can be seen. The Heath is London's answer to the Lake District, though the Ponds are puny compared with Windermere and Parliament Hill is but a ripple on a carpet compared with Skiddaw. Roll on the next 10,000 hours.

CHAPTER TEN

Burgess Park

Burgess Park is unbelievable. Is that too strong a word? I think not. I would go further and call Burgess Park the most incredible park in the whole of London, probably in the world. Experts arrive regularly on official visits from almost every major city just to stare at it. To a man and to a woman, they make the same remarks. 'However was it done . . . we could never do it at home . . . only London could get away with it.'

They don't come to look at Burgess Park for its astounding natural beauty. If you want prettiness, you go to St James's Park, Regent's Park or

Burgess Park, London's most surprising open space: a hundred acre park being created out of an urban landscape

Burgess Park

Key

F   Factory

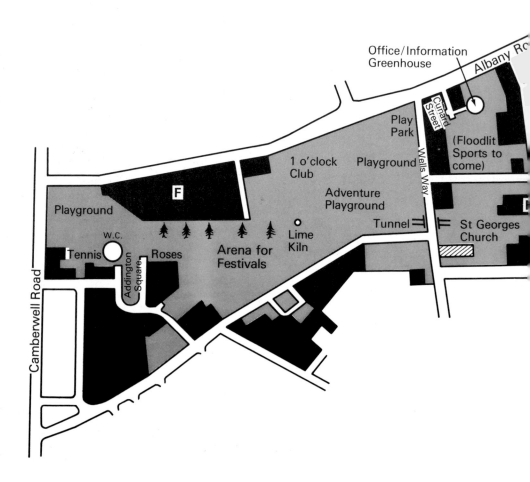

Houses/Buildings

Park — green space

1983 — 88 acres in use as Park

Still in use inside perimeter —

2 Churches

2 Schools

7 Factories

10 Roads

200+ Dwellings

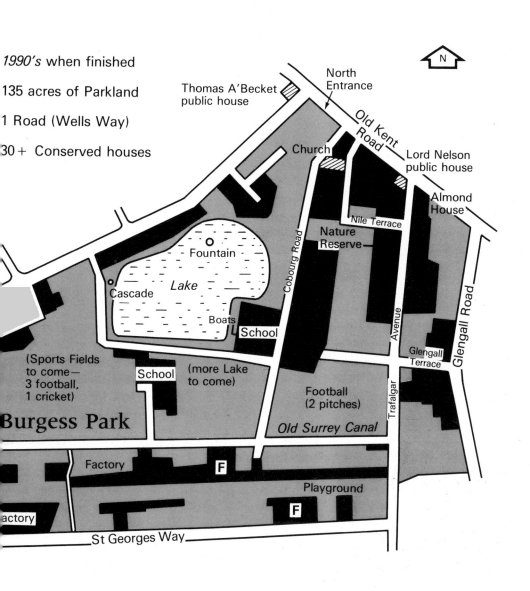

1990's when finished

135 acres of Parkland

1 Road (Wells Way)

30+ Conserved houses

Thomas A'Becket public house

North Entrance

Church

Old Kent Road

Lord Nelson public house

Almond House

Nile Terrace

Cobourg Road

Nature Reserve

Fountain

Lake

Cascade

Boats

School

Avenue

Glengall Terrace

Glengall Road

(Sports Fields to come— 3 football, 1 cricket)

School

(more Lake to come)

Burgess Park

Football (2 pitches)

Trafalgar

Old Surrey Canal

Factory

F

Playground

F

actory

St Georges Way

Miles
0 ¼

0 ½
Kilometres

Kensington Gardens. If you want wide open spaces you go to Richmond. If you want trees, go to Epping Forest. If you want historic connections, go to Greenwich or Hampton Court. Or if you are after literary associations, then try Hampstead Heath. Burgess Park has none of those qualities or attractions to offer, at least not so far. Yet Burgess is unique.

You have probably never heard of Burgess Park for the simple reason that it is brand new, and therein lies its uniqueness. While other Parks have striven over the centuries to save their virgin open spaces from the advance of the surburban estates or the high-rise blocks, Burgess Park has turned the whole process upside down. They have created a Park, where previously there was no open parkland, by *demolishing* all the existing buildings. In the very heart of one of South London's densest urban areas they are at this moment carving out a park which will ultimately be 135 acres in size, complete with all the facilities and foliage, green spaces and gardens, play areas and pastures which we traditionally associate with a Park – plus a great deal more which those Monarchs who first enclosed and created the Royal Parks never dreamt about. No one, anywhere in the world, has ever bulldozed the urban landscape on such a scale before, just to produce a bit of open space.

Dave Sadler, Manager of Burgess Park: some day, all this will be yours, when the bulldozers have turned the slums into sylvan glades

They are already two-thirds finished, with 88 acres in full use, which is about the area of St James's Park. They have a brand new eight-acre Lake (with more to come) on a site which only five years ago consisted of ten streets. Their opening celebrations for the Lake in 1982 were not quite on the scale of the Serpentine opening in 1730 when the whole Royal Family came to watch and two yachts were launched for their diversion, but it did result in quite a few subsequent dramas and incidents.

When you write about Hyde Park or Hampstead Heath you know you are following in the footsteps of countless writers and diarists, observers and researchers, artists and poets, who have trodden the same literal and metaphorical paths over the centuries. One tries to offer first-hand impressions, facts and comments about the people and places and the problems today, but when it comes to their history, it has all been said before, not once but umpteen times. As far as I can discover, no one has so far written about Burgess Park in a book. Hurrah then for Burgess, a new star in the London firmament.

To whom does the credit go? It would be nice to point to one person, a new Capability Brown with the vision and resources of a Hollywood mogul and the power of a Tudor Monarch. Instead, we have to thank the Greater London Council. The GLC is continually berated for a multitude of crimes and excesses, real and imagined, so you can imagine how much they enjoy standing up and shouting about Burgess Park. It seldom happens in the life of local government officials that they can point to something new which they have helped to *create*, a monument which will last for ever.

I went first to County Hall for a half-hour appointment in the crowded schedule of Lord Birkett, the Director of Recreation and the Arts, a grand-sounding mouthful but a very informal and approachable gentleman. It turned into tea and then, after I'd been there three hours, the whisky came out to celebrate. I cannot remember now what we were celebrating, apart from Burgess Park.

Along with the Royal Bailiff, whom we met in Chapter One, Lord Birkett is the most important person in the London Parks. He is responsible for around 30 London Parks, and a great deal else, twenty-two of them being major Parks, known and visited by all, such as Hampstead Heath. Equally important and interesting are Battersea Park and Victoria Park. Then there is Dulwich Park, Blackheath, Holland Park, Marble Hill, Hainault Forest, Trent Park, and many others. (See Appendix for complete list.) Altogether, the GLC has 5,484 acres, about the same as the Royal Parks. They had a great deal more till they transferred control of a number of their Parks to the local Boroughs in 1971. His staff number 1,700 and he has a budget of £40 million a year. He is ultimately in charge of all those famous paintings in Kenwood House, all those concerts at the Festival Hall, plus countless festivals and exhibitions, from art to ballet, in GLC theatres and halls all over London. By comparison, Burgess Park is small beer, in size and in the number of the public so far being catered for. It is the concept which is so exciting, as Lord Birkett well knows.

Michael Birkett was born in 1929, son of the famous lawyer, and he succeeded to his father's title in 1962. He spent most of his early working life in films, starting as an assistant director at Ealing Studios, then becoming a producer in his own right (*King Lear, The Caretaker*) and a director (*Overture and Beginners, The Soldier's Tale*). In 1975 he joined the National Theatre as Deputy Director to Peter Hall, helping to open and launch the new theatre.

After three years, by which time he felt his main work was done, he saw an advertisement one day in the *Sunday Times* for the GLC job and applied, only to be told that he was three months too late. He had happened to be looking at an old *Sunday Times* that day, one stuck on an ironing board. Several months later, he was contacted again and told the job was being re-advertised, as they had not found anyone suitable, and that if he wanted to apply properly this time, he should do so at once. It was a new position, as Parks and the Arts were being put together for the first time. His knowledge of the Arts was obviously first class, but at the interview all he could say about Parks was that he had always loved them. 'No one could be completely qualified. All I could offer was a width of sympathies.

'By comparison, I now realise that the movies were a tea party. This is one hard slog, but I'm loving it. I don't miss the movies, but if I ever get the sack from here, I could go back to being a producer. A technical person, like a cameraman, couldn't go back after a long break as everything changes, but a producer can. I'm producing now. Instead of finding finance for films I'm encouraging the politicians to spend the ratepayers' money.

'There is no political problem in running the Parks. No political party ever comes in and says we're against Parks. Everyone loves them, but the trouble is making them *push* the Parks, put a really big drive into them. You can see the problem. A local politician is not going to get a half-page in his local paper for doing something good in the park.

'I see the parks as basically having two purposes, each on a different level. There's all the obvious *doing* things, the activities, sports, playing, walking. Then on another level parks act as a mirror of our distant selves, reminding us about those parts of our country which we might never visit, perhaps never have visited, such as the great marsh lands of East Anglia or the hills of the Lake District. We should hear echoes of those sorts of countrysides, catching them here, right in the middle of London. The Thames is really London's biggest Park. That is also a mirror image, to remind us of the sea, that we are an island race.'

Perhaps that is why he is so enthusiastic about Burgess Park. Now that the Lake has taken shape, the first new lake in Inner London to be created this century, South London has its own bit of rural and marine life, to remind us of ourselves.

'The story of Burgess Park starts back in 1943 at the height of the London bombing. Some planners were sheltering from the bombs and they said to themselves, "When all this is over, we'll make this a better place to live in. We'll give some greenery to people who haven't't got any, making up for what they've been through . . ."'

The plans started to take shape by 1947, outlined in a report called 'County of London Plan' by Farshaw and Abercrombie, and the LCC, as it was then called, started buying up the bomb sites, old houses, factories, railways, slums and general industrial buildings in a mile-long wedge between the Old Kent Road and Camberwell Road in what is now the Borough of Southwark. There was no public park in the area, no stretches of greenery, no football pitches or open spaces at all, apart from a couple of small gardens at either end. It was one long, decaying, in-dustrial sprawl.

The master plans have changed over the years since 1947, as new ideas, new aims were realised or abandoned, but the original concept of a 135-acre Park to be built within 50 years has been kept to. The actual work started in 1950. By 1965, the first 15 acres had been laid out, then known as North Camberwell Open Space. Then it became St George's Park. In 1974 it was christened Burgess Park, after the late Jessie Burgess, a long-time Councillor and Alderman in Camberwell; by that time the Park had grown to over 40 acres. All should be completed on schedule by the year 2000, or just before.

'It will never be possible again. No one in London, not even a huge Council authority, will ever be able to buy or to afford 100 acres of space ever again.'

How much has it cost? He said he would have to get someone else to work that out. It was almost an impossible job to compute. So many different departments have been working on it solidly for over 30 years, buying up land when it became free, making compulsory purchases, flattening slums, rehousing residents. No, perhaps he had better not try to work it out. Suffice to say that the buying was still going on. The present running costs, including legal work and all the new amenities now being installed, was about £2 million a year.

I set off for darkest Camberwell, prepared for disappointment. How could a load of flattened bomb sites and slum clearance live up to such advance enthusiasm? I should really have waited till the year 2000 for a proper look, when everything would be ready, but at Hamish Hamilton they said they could not wait that long.

The Manager of Burgess Park, David Sadler, told me on the phone where to find his office. Go down Albany Road, he said, and turn into Cunard

Dave Sadler, Manager of Burgess Park: the shape of things to come

Street. (A little street which by the time you read this will exist no more.) Like most Parks' offices, it was hard to find, though in this case he had a good excuse. The immediate area around that side of Albany Road is still like a bomb site.

Burgess Park is still not on any map, even the most modern, and that whole stretch of South London, around Walworth, Elephant and Castle, Kennington, still appears to be a completely greenless area. Until now, the locals have had to drag themselves up to three miles for any real greenery, either south to Dulwich Park or Peckham Rye, or west to Battersea Park. Burgess Park will be the last important bit in the GLC's jigsaw puzzle. 'When it is filled in, there should be nobody in the whole of the GLC area,' says Lord Birkett, 'who will not be within a short bus ride at least of a green park.'

Having finally found Cunard Street, I came face to face with a notice saying Information Centre, which was a welcome surprise. Mr Sadler's yard and offices seemed to be turned into a public service area, with displays and exhibitions open to all, such a change from those park officials who are determined to hide from the public whom they almost see as enemies, hoping they will keep away. Mr Sadler is very keen on being available to the public, as of course he should be. Burgess Park could never have been created otherwise.

Dave Sadler has lived his whole life round Burgess Park. He was born in Camberwell and joined the LCC as an apprentice gardener at fifteen. In those days, the LCC ran 148 London Parks. He was involved in the very first bits of planting at Burgess Park when as a young apprentice in the early 1950s he put in some shrubs at one of the playgrounds. In 1963, he became Deputy Manager, then after a spell at Kilburn and Hammersmith he returned in 1971 as Manager with a staff of 26 and an acreage of 38 acres. Today, his staff is 42.

In the last twelve years, he has been a community relations worker as much as a park manager. There were 30 streets and over 900 dwellings in the Park perimeter when he arrived, plus numerous factories and other buildings. The job of explaining to those 3,000 or so people that over the next twenty years their homes would go has been very difficult and time-consuming.

Now, there are only around 200 dwellings and about 600 people left, but many of those people are even more unhappy. They have had to live there during all the construction work. Now they have to put up with the new sporting activities which have suddenly begun around them. Meanwhile, in a giant ring outside the Park, there are around 100,000 living in monster high-rise council flats, all of them desperate for the Park to be finished, so they can play on the football pitches or fish in the lake, which is what the Council has been promising them since 1950. Which lot should he care about most – the 600 fed-up old residents or the 100,000 newer people outside?

For his efforts to strike the right balance, and keep everyone happy, and at the same time push on with creating and running the Park, Mr Sadler was awarded the MBE in 1977. It hangs on the wall of his little office. He is 46, open and friendly, painstaking and frank, but with a determined, perhaps stoical air about him. You feel he has seen a lot of human nature, and probably experienced far too many protest meetings over the last twelve years to be surprised by very much. Yet his enthusiasm for the Park is undiminished and his capacity for listening to every complaint and observation is still intact.

In retrospect, the biggest excitement since he arrived, until the new Lake, was the completion of the Play Park area in 1979. This was the first *permanent* fixture. Until then, all the amenities, even a floodlit football pitch, had been temporary, plonked down when a space became clear, in the knowledge that in the next ten years they would have to be moved when their final resting place, as laid down in the master plan, became empty. It must have been mentally very confusing to have to work or walk in a Park which was never the same two years running. First you see a football pitch, then you don't. Look, three streets away, it's now over there. How comforting to work in a Royal Park where little has changed for 400 years.

We went first to look at the famous Lake, and I was glad of his company. Even with the aid of his latest sketch map of the Park, things are very hard to find. You have to keep crossing half-streets, working out what all the strange new empty bits might be. It was quite a shock to turn off Albany Road, go over a grassy mound and see before me a massive expanse of dark water, enclosed in the far corner by a large, Victorian school, but with cars still driving round on one side. There was a feeling of concrete newness as if it was going to be a reservoir rather than a pleasure lake. The surrounds are a bit barren, as most of the grass and saplings have yet to become established, but yes, it was undeniably a lake. On the far side, I could see some pedalo boats tied up in a cluster, but nothing was on the Lake that particular morning, not even any bird life. There was great excitement a few months previously, just before the opening, when some crested grebes arrived, then a couple of swans, then some mallard ducks, but sadly they have all moved on. Perhaps they will return next year. One year, in the distant future, the GLC will appoint an Official Bird Observer for Burgess Park, just like their older brother in Hampstead.

'Look up there,' said Mr Sadler, suddenly. 'See those swifts – and there's some swallows!' What a relief. Proof of nature's intent. It was not an indoor pool after all.

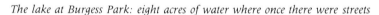

The lake at Burgess Park: eight acres of water where once there were streets

The Lake covers eight acres but it will eventually increase by another five acres when the school opposite, and another one, are demolished. At the moment, it does look rather hemmed-in but, once the landscaping is complete, it should be very convincing. Before then, they hope it will have made the *Guinness Book of Records*. The huge sheets of thick black plastic called polyethylene (a sample can be seen in the information centre), which were laid across the floor of the Lake, are said to be the biggest sheets of plastic in the world. They were welded together so that the lake is securely lined, then a thick layer of gravel put on top as a protection, almost like a modern flat roof. The water is clear so far, as it was when it came out of the taps, and you can still see the gravel at the bottom. The average depth is six feet, but there are three big pockets up to eleven feet deep in the middle where fish can hide. They have stocked the lake with 11,000 fish, mostly roach, carp and rudd, but no fishing is being allowed until 1984. Ultimately, they hope the Lake will support 100,000 fish. Mr Sadler pointed out proudly little concrete ramps beside the Lake where disabled fishermen, in wheel chairs, can secure themselves.

There is a fountain in the Lake, though that day it was not working, and there will be sailing dinghies soon as well as the pedalos. Mr Sadler was currently on a course, being taught how to sail. 'I like to know about everything I have to manage.' We walked round to the Cascade, a little waterfall into the Lake which was gently gurgling away, a refreshing sound after all the traffic noises. Not far away was a bed of reeds, roped off to give them a chance to grow. Eventually, when the fish and water plants and water snails have all established themselves, the Lake should be teeming with natural life.

'But no matter how inviting it looks,' so said a Burgess Park news release in November 1981, 'the water will never be suitable for swimming. We shall not be treating it with chemicals.'

That was the GLC's plan, still in operation on the official opening of the Lake in May 1982. Those who remember that month will recall that London suddenly had two weeks of almost unbroken sun with temperatures each day up to the 80s.

'Just as the Park opened, the heatwave started,' said Lord Birkett. 'We suddenly got 3 to 4,000 people at the Lake every day – 300 to 400 of whom decided to have a dip. We tried to stop them, but our staff could not cope. It was Mums and Dads and children, not just lads, and it was all night long. We pointed out the dangers to health, then let them go ahead. What else could we do?

'Meanwhile, the boats have been taken over and everyone thinks they are Venetian pirates. They attack Don John of Austria while Othello is trying to board the chief pedalo which of course gets sunk. Everyone is having a marvellous time, but our men in the brown uniforms are in a dreadful state. What happens if people get drowned? Yet we're only giving them what the rest of the world already has – a lake, sporting facilities, woods, wild life. Nothing brilliant about that.

'If we ever needed a sign that this Park was *needed*, that was it. The pressure on that Lake every summer from now on is going to be enormous, so we have had to completely rethink our plans.'

The first thing was that Mr Sadler had to double his staff round the Lake. When the heat wave expired, he started sending as many of his staff as possible to pass their bronze medal for life-saving. As for the health risk, the health authorities are still busily investigating, working out what can be done. It is not known, at the present time, what the future will be for swimming. No chlorine is ever put in the Hampstead ponds, but they at least have a natural mud base, full of fish life, and have been swum for decades.

The Lakeside was almost deserted, except for a couple at the far side walking with a dog and a youth sitting alone on a bench reading the sports pages of the *Daily Mirror*. I sat and chatted to him and he said he was from Sierra Leone and lived in a high-rise block not far away. He was out of work and every morning he came to the Lake to read his paper. 'It's brightened up the whole area, this park. I only wish I could swim. When I get a job and get a bit of money, I think I'll buy a life jacket. If I get a job, I might even take up tennis, when they get round to building the tennis courts.' Mr Sadler heard the last observation and came over to say there already were some tennis courts, at the other end of the Park, at Addington Square. The boy said he never knew they existed. He'd never been that far. Mr Sadler also pointed out that those out of work were allowed to pay reduced fees on the tennis courts.

The boat house has a large and attractive wooden landing quay and a brightly-painted hut for the boatman. He was taking his break, sitting in a large and gleaming motorboat reading a science fiction novel by Arthur C. Clarke. The boat is for security purposes, to patrol the Lake in emergencies.

We then walked down Cobourg Road, a road adjoining the Lake, a row of Victorian terrace houses, most of them very neat and tidy, which will all eventually come down. There was an elderly lady in an apron cutting her front lawn at number 69 who waved to Mr Sadler. He said I might find it interesting to talk to her. There was no point in his hiding things from visitors. She was Mrs Grace Cattermole and she had lived in the house for 64 years. I admired her neat lawn and said it must be nice for her to have such a good view of the Lake, just twenty yards away. That started it. She hardly paused for breath for the next twenty minutes.

'I hate it! I wish it had never been built. It might look nice to *you*, with nobody around, but you should come when it's sunny or at night times. There was one morning I didn't get to sleep till five in the morning. The noise and swearing was dreadful. It shouldn't be allowed. These hooligans just climb over, shouting and screaming, then chuck each other in. Really, it was five o'clock and I could still hear them going "One, two, three . . ." and then a splash. And the effing and blinding. Disgusting. So don't ask me what I think. I think it's a pain in the neck.

'And your speed boat, Mr Sadler, must he go round the Lake joy-riding every morning? The noise is shocking. I stand in the garden and I can't concentrate on anything for the blessed roar of that boat . . .'

'I'm very sorry,' said Mr Sadler. 'He's not joy-riding. We've been told we have to burn up oil every morning, so it means doing a fairly fast circuit. We're all new to this, and it's a new boat, so we're just finding our feet. I can understand your worries . . .'

'And the transistors! Why do you allow it? I'm not racist, but where do they all come from? They don't belong round here, making all this noise. Why don't you control them? I've seen them climb over at night after your men have just locked up. They tell them not to go in, but then do nothing about it . . .'

'Most of our men are new to this sort of job,' explained Mr Sadler. 'It will take time before we all know the best way to run things.'

'I don't want time! I want to move now. I'd go tomorrow if they'd give me another house. There's no use living here any more. The old houses opposite were lovely houses. We were all respectable people. There was no trouble round here. Now for the past 30 years we've lived on a knife edge. We don't know if it's worth doing any work in the house. Nobody has any interest in us any more.

'And the cold, you wouldn't believe it. Since that Lake was built, we get this terrific wind whipping right across. It's going to put my fuel bills up in the winter. I'm not against parks as such, it's just that blessed Lake. Why did you have to build it? It's that water, that's what attracts all the people.'

'There will be worse to come, I'm afraid,' said Mr Sadler. 'We're getting the sailing boats next week. The schools will eventually be using the Lake for sailing, almost every day.'

She sighed heavily and I broke in to suggest there must be *some* advantages. Surely the view had been improved, with that splendid new Lake and all that landscaping. She was not impressed. 'I had two roofing men in yesterday, and they said exactly the same. I soon told them off. It's not my house. I don't gain by the view. I rent it from the GLC. They don't care about it any more.'

Well, didn't she feel that, for the good of the community as a whole, the Lake and a Park were a blessing, especially for those living in high-rise blocks?

'No, I don't. They should have left all the old houses as they were. We were happy then. I went to that school across there and it was a lovely school. There was no aggro in those days. I admit people have deteriorated since then, and that's partly to blame, but they still should not have changed anything. I liked everything as it was. I don't want any changes.'

'I can't help but sympathise, Mrs Cattermole,' said Mr Sadler. 'I hope you'll go to all the meetings and express your opinions . . .'

'And the mosquitoes!' she exclaimed, returning to the attack just as we were moving away. 'That's *your* Lake what's done that. We never had *them* in the old days. I get bitten every time I go in the garden. And they come in the house at night. The night before last I saw huge columns of them above those trees, like columns of smoke, sort of spirals of them, hanging over the trees. Never in sixty-four years in this street have I seen *that*, Mr Sadler.'

'Yes, well, they are a worry. Our experts are not absolutely convinced the Lake is to blame. They could be breeding in old drains . . .'

'Oh yes it is, Mr Sadler. We never had them *before* your Lake was built. So answer me that.'

'When the fish start growing, they'll start eating all the mosquitoes,' said Mr Sadler.

'Well,' said Mrs Cattermole, suddenly smiling and stopping for breath. 'I have had a right old go at him, haven't I. Poor old Mr Sadler.' He said, no, she had a right to her opinion.

I finally thanked her for her comments and we walked on.

'But I won't change my mind! That Lake is a pain in the neck . . .'

It was one of hundreds of conversations he has had with many of the older residents in the last twelve years. He pointed to all the high-rise flats not far away, full of people with the opposite complaints, desperate for more activities and amenities. He obviously feels sorry for the old residents and knows that until the Park becomes a whole and therefore easier to run and patrol, the pressures and the noise will get worse not better for those still living on the site.

There is now a further complication. Inside the Park are a couple of old streets containing Georgian and Regency houses (Trafalgar Avenue and Glengall Road) which various preservation bodies have decided, naturally enough, they would like to see conserved. Mr Sadler would ideally like the whole site cleared quickly, but he can see the point of keeping some of them, as they would enhance the views, yet he worries that living in them won't be a lot of fun for the residents. Discussions are still going on.

Everything to do with Burgess Park is endlessly debated, all of it out in the open. There are fourteen residents' associations involved and one overall steering committee. Over the last thirty years, as the political control of the local Council has changed, different attitudes to the public have come and gone. Some councils have refused to discuss things, saying, we know what's best. Others have debated every move.

As we were talking, another lady came running down the road after Mr

Sadler, a younger woman this time, much more aggressive, smoking a cigarette as she proceeded to harangue him. The argument was over a meeting he had not turned up at. He said he had not been told in time, yet they had put his name on the handout, pushing it through the letter boxes, announcing he 'would be in attendance', which was embarrassing for him, as if he'd *deliberately* not turned up. She said she had mentioned it to him in time. He said she had not, and so it went on.

'If you had told me in time, I couldn't have made it anyway. I can't make Tuesday meetings at the moment. You know that. It's my sailing course day.'

'We'll be having others then, Dave,' said the woman. 'Don't you worry. We'll let you know *well* in time for the next one . . .'

We then went into a little nature reserve, which Mr Sadler carefully unlocked. It looked at first glance hardly more than an overgrown bomb site but he explained that it had been cleared of refuse by his gardeners in 1972, then sown with wild-flower seeds and bulbs, and allowed to be overgrown. Old people in the district liked to visit it at bluebell time and school children made regular visits to chart the mosses and fungi and collect broken bits of wood. 'You'd be surprised how many of them don't realise wood comes from trees.'

At his Information Centre, they have a permanent display of local school children's work. One school survey charts the most popular game in the Burgess Park playground. Gym rings (which you can swing from) were number one, followed by the slide, paddling pool, swings and then finally the see-saw. The see-saw, apparently, was the least popular because you always needed a partner. There is also a lot of art work done by the children, including a life-size painting of Mr Sadler by a West Indian boy. In this particular portrait, Mr Sadler is a black man.

From his arrival, he has tried to get all local children involved in the Park. There are nine primary schools in the area, two of which are in the Park itself, the ones which will eventually close. Many of the trees in the Park have been planted by the children, who are encouraged to keep an eye on progress and chart the insects and growth. They have a greenhouse in their Information Centre which is open to schools and the general public. 'It grows only indoor flowers and plants. That's all they can do in a high-rise block. We give free information at any time on people's plant problems and we allow schools to borrow displays or take cuttings from our plants for their school greenhouse.'

It can all sound rather idyllic, almost rural and village-like, but the Park, even when completed, will still be the centre of a concrete jungle, even if they will be providing a large green oasis in the middle. The pressures on the Park in the next decade will get much worse, and so will vandalism. They have already had lads on motorbikes charging round at night, something even Mrs Cattermole forgot to complain about. At first, they put the Park lights out at night, to make it look closed, then the police made them leave them on to help them spot any hooligans. The best system has still to be settled on.

'It is a tough area, but one of our aims is to help these people, to soak up these pressures and provide a means of escape. Behind those big flats there's the railway line. They can't go that way. They've got to come here.'

So far, walking round the Park, we had been dodging from one clearing to another, some quite big and green, large enough for a couple of football pitches, but when we got to the far end of the Park, beside St George's Way, I could at last see a long clear stretch of greenery ahead. This follows the route of the old Surrey Canal and is about a mile long, a perfect length for fast running or a good brisk walk, without having to cross any roads. (You have to go under a little tunnel beneath Wells Way, the only road which will remain inside the Park, according to the master plan.) There are still half a dozen little factories along the way, but there is a clear grassy path between and around them, including a new children's playground, just about to be opened, to serve the large blocks of flats along St George's Way. 'They have been on at us for a long time to do something for *them*, not just for the people living over by the Lake or near the Big Playground.'

The Big Playground, on the other side of Wells Road, is an enormous, well-established fun area, containing a large playground, the One O'Clock Club and an Adventure Playground. It was very crowded and I estimated that between 300 and 400 children, including organised groups of school children, were playing some sorts of games. It has been well landscaped, with lots of hills and slopes and little copses of lime, white willow, and ash. In the middle there is an old lime kiln which has been preserved, the sort of old monument one often finds in most London Parks, but it was a surprise to see it in such a modern place as Burgess. 'It's the last Parker kiln left in London,' said Mr Sadler. 'So I'm told. It used to make a type of cement called Roman cement.'

They see this end of the Park being used in the future for local festivals, such as the Walworth Festival, providing for South London the sort of public meeting place which Hyde Park provides for the nation as a whole. Already they have found that people are coming from as far away as Lambeth and Lewisham, a catchment area of eight miles, twice as far as they had anticipated.

The final bit of the Park, ending at Camberwell Road, is the nicer end, slightly quieter, more refined, less boisterous, though of course all these terms are comparative. Burgess Park is never going to be Kensington Gardens. Camberwell Road is still a decidedly working class area, but there are quite a few enclaves of gentility. After all, Princess Margaret's daughter had just started at the local Art College.

Near the tennis courts are some flower beds and roses, the first I'd seen in the whole Park, and there is a further garden in the middle of Addington Square, a handsome Georgian square which is where Mr Sadler himself lives, in a GLC house that goes with the job.

Mr Sadler then took me round the corner, a few yards down Camberwell Road, where he led me through a crowded antique shop called Franklin's which turned out to contain a little restaurant at the back, and we sat in the garden eating a late lunch. We had freshly-made chilli con carne, salad and our choice from six home-made puddings, plus a large glass of apple juice each and coffee. The surroundings were delightful and so were the staff, most of them resting actresses. I mention all these details as it was such a surprise – and the bill for the two came to only £4.80. I had expected to find nowhere to eat all day, as the restaurant complex in Burgess Park, which will probably also include a pub, will not be ready for years, nor will the Entertainment Centre, nor the golf nets, car park, sports changing-rooms, and the new and bigger information centre, horse-rides, stables, nature trails, study centre and a village green. All these good things are yet to come.

It was the most enjoyable meal I had had in the whole of my walks through the London Parks, which is not saying a lot. It was of course not technically inside the Park boundary, just a few yards away. I later asked Lord Birkett if and when the time comes to decide the franchise for Burgess Park he will try and give it to some enterprising little firm, perhaps a family genuinely interested in cooking, not one of the motorway chains interested in profits.

Naturally, he pointed out all the problems. There is not a great rush to tender for catering in the London Parks, and the authorities do impose some strict conditions. They often want, for example, a restaurant to open *all* the year round, regardless of the weather or the lack of customers, which means that a little firm can easily go out of business in the winter. 'I'd love to get *real* cooking in the London Parks, but you are faced with a choice of three sorts of firms – a large catering chain, a spiv trying to make a quick buck and thirdly some little person who *could* be a three star chef in the making and one day will turn it into a Gavroche or Ma Cuisine. But how do you *know*? We have to play safe and go for proven service.'

My other recurring complaint about the London Parks, after a year walking round them, is the lack of information. They erect a notice board at the entrance with a diagram of the Park and hope that everyone can memorise it. There are no proper information kiosks inside any of the Parks I visited, apart from Greenwich with its Tourist Centre on the quayside and Epping's educational centre. The Royal Parks people are the worst offenders. The Department of the Environment does produce some good booklets, on things like Bird Life in the Royal Parks, but they market them as if they were under the Official Secrets Act. You have to trail to the HMSO bookshop in Holborn, hoping that the one you want is still in print. The GLC is a bit better, and they produce many good leaflets, but you have to be lucky to find a Superintendent who is interested, or allowed to release them. I can appreciate that special information kiosks would be impossible in the present economic climate, but every café and restaurant in every Park, even under an outside franchise, should have to carry all the published local literature, keeping it openly on sale, and every Superintendent should have one person on his staff whose job it is to provide information, to act as a local public relations officer, able to go out and talk to schools.

Those are my only two serious moans and they would disappear under a welter of praise if I had to list again all the good things about the London Parks, their marvellous facilities, their beauty and history, the countless pleasures they provide for all sorts and conditions of Londoners and visitors.

It was reassuring to end at Burgess Park, a new and unknown Park, one which will take another sixty years to come to maturity. It is experiencing many of the growing pains which those older, more famous Parks have gone through in the past, plus several new ones which they will have to find their own way of solving. One day, it will doubtless have its own Friends of Burgess Park, a preservation group like those who care for Hampstead Heath, Greenwich, Richmond and all the others, who will be screaming should anyone dare to alter that ancient plastic Lake or remove that genuine 20th-century artificial football pitch. It must come.

We forget it now, but Burgess Park's present problems have all happened before, in some degree. Remember the protests from the locals when Chares I in 1673 enclosed Richmond Park. The older residents were terribly upset. Where would they get their firewood from? How could they walk their dogs or take their exercise or cross the Park? Today it is noisy transistors and motorboats, but in essence it is the same. There are always people who will be discomfited by the creation of any Park.

'It's either a good thing, or it wasn't worth doing in the first place,' said Mr Sadler. 'You have to keep remembering it *is* a good thing. When all the problems start coming in, you have to stand back and look at the whole. Walworth School spends £25,000 a year bussing pupils to play football. That's just one school. Very soon, *all* the local schools can come here and use this Park, night and day.

'I get visitors from every country. Professor Jim Fuerst, Professor of Urban Studies at Chicago, comes to see us almost every year and monitors progress. He always says the same thing, "No bugger would let us have all the real estate."'

Their progress so far appears to be on the right lines, providing new solutions to old problems and offering different amenities which – one never knows – the older-established Parks might one day care to copy. They have made an excellent start, for example, by creating an Information Centre, right from the beginning, and by installing a Park Manager who sees his job as being constantly available to the community at large. It does, of course, make it a tough job. 'It means they have somebody to shout and scream at. I am not a faceless person. My policy is never to lie and never to hide. Parks are for people.'

Further Reading, Further Information, Chapter Notes

General Publications

There are two first-class general guide books on London which include some good information on some of the London Parks:

The Penguin Guide to London, by F. R. Banks, first published 1958, 1982 edition £2.95.

The Companion Guide to London, by David Piper, Collins £6.50.

Also recommended:

Discovering London's Parks and Squares, by John Wittich, Shire Publications, 1981, £1.25.

Discovering London's Statues and Monuments, by Margaret Baker, Shire Publications, 1980, 85p.

Old London Gardens, by Gladys Taylor, Ian Henry Publications, 1977, £4.55.

Green London Walks, by William Bagley, Gerard Publications, 1975, £1.75.

Royal Parks

They are run by the Department of the Environment from 2 Marsham Street, SW1, 212–3434. Government publications covering the Royal Parks are on sale from the HMSO bookshop at 49 High Holborn, WC1, 928–6977.

Official Guide to the Royal Parks of London, by Sean Jennett, HMSO, 1979, £2.50.

Wild Life in the Royal Parks, by Eric Simms, HMSO, 1974, 50p.

Bird Life in the Royal Parks, Annual Reports, normally about 30p.

The Royal Parks of London, by Guy Williams, Constable, 1978, £6.95.

General Advice

Going for a walk in a London Park is simple. They are always there. But if you also want to take in a museum or a gallery, it is best to check opening times beforehand. The opening hours below, though correct when going to press, can occasionally be subject to alteration, especially in winter.

For all London information, including Parks, ring or write to the London Tourist Board, 26 Grosvenor Gardens SW1 – 730–0791. Or visit their Information Centres at Victoria Station, Selfridges (ground floor); Harrods (4th floor) or Heathrow Central station.

Maps

Maps of the individual Parks are almost impossible to get, hence the rather detailed ones we have had drawn for each chapter. The few which exist are usually out of print, except for the one of Hampstead Heath. Start by getting a free London map, from any tube station or from the London Tourist Board. (They will also send you one; include 40p for postage.) For Royal Parks, the official guide book (see above) does include maps, but now rather out of date.

Chapter 1 The Royal Bailiff, St James's Park and Green Park

Supt.'s Office 930–1793

Changing of the Guard – 11.30–12 every summer morning; alternate days in winter. The new guard, complete with band, comes from either Wellington or Chelsea Barracks, and takes over from the old guard in the forecourt of the Palace. A less spectacular change-over takes place each morning at 11, and 10 am on Sundays, at Horse Guards Parade in Whitehall.

Chapter 2   Hyde Park

Supt.'s Office 262–5484
Serpentine Restaurant – 723–8784
Boathouse (to hire boats) – 262–3751
Horse Riding – Ross Nye Riding Stables, 8 Bathurst Mews – 262–3791.

Chapter 3   Kensington Gardens

Supt.'s Office – 723–3509
Serpentine Gallery – 402–6075
Kensington Palace. State Apartments open from 10 weekdays, from 2 on Sundays; closes at 6 in the summer and 4 in the winter. Booklets, cards, souvenirs available in Palace bookstall.

Chapter 4   Regent's Park and Primrose Hill

Supt.'s Office – 486–7905
Open Air Theatre – Open June, July and August; 935–5756
Nash Terraces: To buy a nice little property, try John Wood estate agents, 103 Parkway, NW1 – 267–3267.
London Central Mosque, 146 Park Road, NW8 – 724–3363.
Visitors welcome, but ladies not allowed into the prayer hall; book stall souvenirs. Islamic Cultural Centre Library, open to students.
Zoo – all enquiries ring 722–3333.
Recommended specialist book: *Regent's Park*, by Ann Saunders, published by Bedford College, 1969, price £3.50.

Chapter 5   Greenwich Park

Supt.'s Office – 858–2608
Thames Steamers – every day from 10.30 at Charing Cross, Westminster and Tower Bridge Piers. Time, about 50 mins from Charing Cross to Greenwich. Last return boat, about 4.30. You must return with the company you sailed with. Enquiries – 930–2074; or London Tourist Board River Boat Information Centre – 730–4812
Royal Naval College – open 2.30–5, except Thursdays, Good Friday and Christmas.
National Maritime Museum – open 10–6, 2.30–6 on Sundays. (Closes winter weekdays at 5) 858–4422.
Old Royal Observatory – 858 4422. Opening hours as Maritime Museum.
Ranger's House, Chesterfield Walk, SE10. Open 10–5 daily.
Cutty Sark – Open 11–5; Sundays 2.30–5.
Gypsy Moth – Open 11–5, Sundays 2.30–5.
HMSO leaflet on Greenwich Park, 9p. Good Tourist shop on Greenwich Pier.
Recommended Book – 'Guide to Greenwich', by Nigel Hamilton, Greenwich Bookshop, 1972, £1.99.

Chapter 6   Richmond Park

Supts.'s Office – 948–3209
Isabella Plantation – leaflet from Supt.'s Office or HMSO, 20p.
Leaflet on Richmond Park by HMSO, price 6p.
Two 18-hole Golf Courses open to public – 876–3205.
Pembroke Lodge, Restaurant and Cafeteria.
Friends of Richmond Park – Sec. Arnold Francis, 22 Woodlands Avenue, New Malden, 942–6125.

Chapter 7   Hampton Court and Bushy Parks

Supt.'s Office – 997–1328
Hampton Court Palace – State Apartments open daily 9.30–6 in summer, Sundays 11–6;
shorter hours in winter.
Royal Tennis Court – members only can play but public can view. Booklet – *Royal Tennis Court*, 30p.
Recommended specialist book – *Hampton Court Gardens*, by Ernest Law, Bell and Son, 1926.

Chapter 8   Epping Forest

Supt.'s Office – The Warren, Loughton, Essex – 508–2266
Epping Forest is run by the City of London from the Guildhall, EC2 606–3030
Queen Elizabeth's Hunting Lodge (Forest Museum), Ranger's Road, E.4; open daily, 2–6,
except Mondays and Tuesdays, 529–6681
Epping Forest Conservation Centre, High Beach, Loughton, Essex, 508–7714. Main
information office for the Forest; also education centre.
Booklets: *Epping Forest*, by Alfred Quist, published by Corporation of London. *Epping Forest,
Centenary Walk*, by Fred Mathews and Harry Bitten, published by the Conservators of Epping
Forest, 15p.
Short Walks in London's Epping Forest, by Fred Mathews, £1.
Brimble's Guide to Epping Forest, revised by Mandy Johnson, 1982, £1.35.
Friends of Epping Forest – Sec. Mrs Georgina Green, 39 Smeaton Road, Woodford Bridge,
Essex – 505–2159.

Chapter 9   Hampstead Heath

Managers Office –
Parliament Hill 485–4491
Golders Hill 455–5183
Old Heath and Hampstead Society, Sec. Annetta Bynum, 54 Gayton Road, NW3, 435 4465.
Highgate Society, Sec. Brian Holland, 6 Cholmely Court, Southwood Lane, N6 348 1571.
Kenwood House (The Iveagh Bequest), open daily 10–7 (till 4 in winter), 348–1286
Open Air Concerts – Booking Office, GLC, Dept. for Recreation and the Arts, County Hall,
SE1 633–1707
Restaurant, Cafeteria – Kenwood Old Kitchen and Coach House, open daily; 348–4286.
Recommended books: *Streets of Old Hampstead*, by Christopher Wade, High Hill Press, 1972,
75p
Hampstead: London Hill Village, by Dorothy Bohm and Ian Norrie, Wildwood House, 1982,
£8.95
Map – text by Ralph Wade, 50p, GLC.

Chapter Ten   Burgess Park

Manager's Office – 703–3911
Franklin's, Restaurant and Antiques, 159 Camberwell Road, 703–8089

The Parks of London over Twenty Acres

Greater London stretches at its broadest point 34 miles across and encloses an area of 610 square miles. Inside this giant blob there are some 45,000 acres of Parks and open space, ranging from massive Parks like Richmond Park, 2,500 acres in size, to one-acre open spaces which are little more than large gardens or playgrounds. There are around 1,000 stretches of grass throughout London which are known as Parks, some quite small, but it would take another book to list and describe them all. No one has yet done so. The main problem is that they are run by so many different bodies. In the meantime, the following is a list of all the Parks and open spaces over 20 acres and their respective owners.

Royal Parks   Total acreage, 6,000 acres

St James's Pk — 93 acres
Green Pk — 53
Hyde Pk — 360
Kensington Gdns — 275
Regent's Pk — 472

Greenwich Pk — 200
Richmond Pk — 2,500
Hampton Court Home Pk — 1,000
Bushy Pk — 1,100

GLC   Total acreage, 5,484 acres

Avery Hill — 86
Battersea Pk — 200
Birchmere Pk — 36
Blackheath — 272
Bostall Heath and Woods — 158
Burgess Pk — 80
Crystal Palace Pk — 106
Dulwich Pk — 72
Finsbury Pk — 115
Hackney Marsh — 335
Hainault Forest — 958
Hampstead Heath — 800
Havering Country Pk — 167
Holland Park — 54

Horniman Gardens — 25
Hounslow Heath — 204
Eltham Pk — 122
Lesnes Abbey Wood — 215
Marble Hill — 66
Mile End Pk — 51
Oxleas Wood — 252
Stanmore Country Pk — 78
Southmene Pk — 41
Trent Pk — 413
Tower Hamlets Cemetery — 28
Victoria Pk — 218
Wormwood Scrubs — 192
Woodland Way — 43

City of London   Total acreage, 7,000 acres, of which 2,736 acres are in the GLC boundary.

Burnham Beeches, Bucks — 504
Coulsdon Common, Surrey — 430
Epping Forest — 6,000
Highgate Wood — 70

Queen's Park, Kilburn — 30
Spring Pk, West Wickham Common, Kent — 76
West Ham — 77.

Within the City itself, there are only 35 acres of open space, mainly gardens, squares, walks, churchyards. The largest are the Barbican (8 acres in all of open space), Finsbury Circus Garden (3 acres) and St Paul's Churchyard (2 acres).

London Boroughs   Total acreage – 28,000 acres

Between them, the 32 London Boroughs control well over half of London's Parks and open spaces. These are their parks over 20 acres, plus the total acreage of parks in each Borough.

1. *Barking and Dagenham*   Total acreage, 708 acres

Barking Pk – 76
Castle Green – 42
Central Pk – 135
Goresbrook Pk – 37
Mayesbrook Pk – 116

Old Dagenham Pk – 70
Parsloes Pk – 148
St Chads Pk – 41
Valence Pk – 24

2. *Barnet*   Total acreage, 1,226 acres

Arrandene – 55
Barnet Playing Fields – 82
Bethune Rec. – 32
Brook Farm – 56
Brinswick Pk – 24
Clitterhouse Pk – 47
Copthall Sports – 140
Edgwarebury Pk – 39
Friary Pk – 23
Glebe Lands – 46

Hendon Pk – 29
Lyttleton Pk – 35
Mill Hill Pk – 51
Montrose Pk – 26
Oak Hill Pk – 90
Sunny Hill Pk – 54
Tudor Sports – 24
Watling Pk – 21
West Hendon – 70
Woodfield Pk – 39

3. *Bexley*   Total acreage, 1,163 acres

Bexley Woods – 27
Bursted Woods – 30
Chalk Wood – 69
Danson Pk – 185
East Wickham – 60
Franks Pk – 41
Footscray Meadows – 48

Hall Place – 146
Martens Grove – 29
Mayplace Sports Field – 36
North Cray Meadows – 60
Northumberland Heath – 23
Sidcup Place – 37

4. *Brent*   Total acreage, 1,036 acres

Roe Green Pk – 38.1
Silver Jubilee Pk – 32.1
Barn Hill, Fryent Way Open Space – 253.2
Woodcock Pk – 28.0
Northwick Pk – 65.8
Welsh Harp – 38.5
King Edward VII Pk – 26.3
Vale Farm – 63.8

Barham Pk – 25.2
One-tree Hill – 26.4
Alperton Rec. – 22.7
Neasden Rec – 37.4
Gladstone Pk – 93.2
St Raphael's Way Open Space – 20.2
Roundwood Pk – 35.4
Willesden Sports Centre – 31.1

5. *Bromley*   Total acreage, 2,000 acres

Croydon Road Rec. – 23
Coney Hall Rec. – 24
Harvington Sports – 47
High Broom Wood – 20
Kelsey Park – 32
Sparrows Den – 31
Well Wood – 43
Martins Hill – 23

Marvels Wood – 22
Norman Pk – 56
Parkfield Rec. – 44
Hayes Common – 207
Keston Common – 55
Chislehurst Rec. – 28
Elmstead Wood – 61
Hoblingwell Wood – 87

Mottingham Sports – 30
Goddington Pk – 64
High Elms Estate – 350
Riverside Gdns, St Mary Cray – 21

Leaves Green Common – 20
Jubilee Pk, Bickley – 82
Pauls Cray Hill Pk – 82
Ravensbourne Open Space – 27

Note – Bromley is by far the largest Borough in area in the GLC covering 38,000 acres. The next biggest are Harrow and Hillingdon with 28,000 acres each. The rest average about 12,000 acres each.

6. *Camden*   Total acreage, 101 acres

Waterlow Pk – 27

Note: Camden Borough's total looks very small but inside the Borough they do have the GLC's Hampstead Heath and the Royal Parks' Primrose Hill and part of Regent's Park. The Borough itself owns only two Parks – Waterlow Park and the much smaller Kilburn Grange Park (8 acres). The rest of its open spaces are gardens or squares, including London's biggest square, Lincoln's Inn Fields, 7 acres.

7. *Croydon*   Total acreage, 2,583 acres

Addington Hills – 130
Addington Pk – 24
Addington Vale – 48
Ashburton Playing Fields – 49
Betts Mead – 30
Birch Wood – 37
Bramley Bank – 23
Croham Hurst – 84
Coulsdon Court – 146
Croydon Sports Arena – 27
Duppas Hill – 34
Foxley Wood – 26
Grangewood Pk – 28
Happy Valley Pk – 246
Hawkhirst – 35
Jewel's Wood – 38
King's Wood – 147
Littleheath Wood – 64

Lloyd Pk – 114
Millstock – 57
Norbury Pk – 28
North Down – 33
Norwood Grove – 34
Purley Way Playing Fields – 108
Purley Way West – 21
Riddlesdown – 37
Rowdown Fields – 29
Rowdon Wood – 34
Sanderstead Plantation – 21
Sanderstead Rec – 20
Shirley Hth – 68
South Norwood Lake – 28
Threehalfpenny Wood – 25
Upper Norwood Rec – 20
Wandle Pk – 21

8. *Ealing*   Total acreage, 1,957 acres

Acton Pk – 28
Belvue Pk – 25
Churchfields Rec – 20
Ealing Central Sports – 37
Ealing Common – 50
Elthorne Pk – 37
Glade Lane – 26
Gunnersby Pk – 188
(Jointly owned with L.B. of Hounslow)
Hanger Hill Pk – 20
Horsenden Hill – 245
Islip Manor Pk – 63

King George's Field – 25
Lammas Pk – 27
Lime Tree Pk – 75
North Acton Playing Fields – 23
Perivale Pk – 110
Pitshanger Pk – 50
Ravenor Pk – 32
Rectory Pk – 63
Southall Sports – 20
Southall Pk – 26
Walpole Pk – 30
Greenford Pk – 33

9. *Enfield* Total acreage, 1,658 acres

Church Street Rec – 24
Firs Farm Rec – 50
Jubilee Pk – 37
Pymmes Pk – 53
Town Pk – 23
Albany Pk – 45
Durants Pk – 54
Bush Hill Pk – 27
Whitewebbs Pk – 232

Forty Hill – 262
Hill Fields Pk – 66
Enfield Play Flds – 128
Hadley Wood – 33
Broomfield Pk – 54
Arnos Pk – 44
Bramley Sports Gnd – 20
Oakwood Pk – 64
Grovelands Pk – 91

10. *Greenwich* Total acreage, 539 acres

Charlton Pk – 43
Hornfair Pk – 26
Maryon Pk – 29
Maryon Wilson Pk – 32

Plumstead Common – 103
Shrewbury Pk – 32
Sidcup Open Space – 20
Sutcliffe Pk – 52

11. *Hackney* Total acreage, 352 acres

Abney Pk Cemetery – 32
Clissold Pk – 54
Hackney Downs – 42
London Fields – 31

Millfields Open Space – 64
Springfield Pk – 38
Well Street Common – 21

12. *Hammersmith and Fulham* Total acreage, 300 acres

Ravenscourt Pk – 35

Bishop's Pk – 25

13. *Haringey* Total acreage, 613 acres

Alexandra Pk – 200
Bruce Castle Pk – 20
Coldfall Wood – 32
Lordship Rec Ground – 123

Markfield Rec – 25
Muswell Hill Playing Field – 25
New River Sports – 31

14. *Harrow* Total acreage, 1,239 acres

Alexandra Pk – 21
Bentley Priory – 163
Byron Rec – 30
Canons Pk – 48
Centenary Pk – 23
Chandos Rec – 27
Harrow Rec – 27
Harrow Weald Common – 47

Headstone Manor Rec – 57
Kenton Rec – 52
Montesole Playing Flds – 20
Newton Pk – 25
Pinner Pk – 250
Roxbourne Pk – 54
Stanmore Common – 120
West Harrow Rec – 26

15. *Havering* Total acreage, 1,938 acres

Bedfords Pk – 214
Bretons Pk – 184
Ingrebourne Valley Country Pk (being developed) – 160
Bridge Avenue, Parkways – 59
Dagham Park – 146
Harrow Lodge Pk – 129
Little Hatters Wood – 94
Oldchurch Pk – 50
Raphael Pk – 55

Brittons Playing Flds – 26
Cranham Playing Flds – 22
Grenfell Pk – 27
Harold Wood Rec Grd – 45
Haynes Pk – 27
Mawney Pk – 24
Rise Pk – 23
Upminster Hall Playing Flds – 35
Duck Wood – 20

16. *Hillingdon*   Total acreage, 3,314 acres

Bayhurst Wood Country Pk – 98
Bridgewater Road Rec – 20
Brookside – 45
Copse Wood – 157
Cranford Pk – 148
Dawley Tip – 42
Field End Rec – 27
Grange Pk – 30
Greenway – 41
Hayes End Rec – 23
Hillington Court Pk – 56
Kings College Flds – 54
Lawn Flds – 33

Little Harlington Flds – 20
Mad Bess Wood – 186
New Pond Playing Flds – 20
Northwood Rec – 24
Park Woods – 238
Pole Hill Open Space – 46
Poors Fld – 40
Stonefield Pk – 98
The Closes – 23
Ruislip Lido – 77
Town Hall Pk – 20
Yeading Brook Open Space – 113

(Hillingdon owns more parkland and open space than any other Borough)

17. *Hounslow*   Total acreage, 1,323 acres

Bedfont Road Open Space – 20
Dukes Meadow – 25
Boston Manor Pk – 35
Feltham Arena – 38
Lampton Pk – 43

Chiswick House Gdns – 67
Hanworth Pk – 145
Avenue Pk – 20
Gunnersby Pk
(Jointly owned by LB of Ealing) – 188

18. *Islington*   Total acreage, 174 acres

Caledonian Pk – 20

Highbury Fields – 29

19. *Royal Borough of Kensington and Chelsea*   Total acreage, 44 acres

There are no Borough parks as large as 20 acres. The biggest are the Royal Hospital South Grounds, 13 acres, and the Kensington Memorial Park, 7 acres.
(Inside the Borough there is Holland Park, owned by the GLC, and Kensington Gardens, which is a Royal Park.)

20. *Royal Borough of Kingston upon Thames*   Total acreage, 236 acres

Alexandra Rec. Ground – 20
Churchfields Rec – 22

King George's Playing Field – 33
Manor Pk – 20

21. *Lambeth*   Total acreage, 623 acres

Kennington Pk – 37
Ruskin Pk – 36
Clapham Common – 206

Brockwell Pk – 127
Norwood Pk – 38
Streatham Common and the Rookery – 61

22. *Lewisham*   Total acreage, – 532 acres

Blyth Hill Flds – 20
Chinbrook Meadows – 31
Downham Flds – 37
Forster Memorial Pk – 43
Hilly Flds – 46

Ladywell Flds – 52
Mayow Pk – 20
Mountsfield Pk – 28
Summerhouse Flds – 20
Sydenham Wells Pk – 20

23. *Merton*   Total acreage, 742 acres

Cannizaro Pk – 34
Cannon Hill Common – 53

Commons Extension – 79
Figges Marsh – 25

Joseph Hood Rec – 21
King George's Fld – 20
Morden Pk – 98

Sir Joseph Hood Playing Flds – 31
Wimbledon Pk – 66

Plus Mitcham Common, 442 acres, which Merton maintain as agents for the Conservators of Mitcham Common.

24. *Newham*   Total acreage, 358 acres

Central Pk – 25
Canning Town Rec – 22
Beckton District Pk – 47

Plashet Pk – 20
Memorial Gardens – 26

25. *Redbridge*   Total acreage, 631 acres

Ashton Playing Fields – 52
Clayhall Pk – 34
Forest Road Playing Fld – 40
Goodmayes Pk – 69
Hainault Rec Grd – 46
Loxford Pk – 20
Ray Pk – 30

Roding Lane North Sports Grnd – 26
Seven Kings Pk – 34
South Pk – 32
Valentines Pk – 136
Roding Valley Linear Pk – 196
Fairlop Country Pk (being developed) – 300

(Redbridge Borough also contains 1,250 acres of Epping Forest, owned by the City of London, and Hainault Forest, owned by the GLC)

26. *Richmond*   Total acreage, 1,116 acres

Palewell Common – 39
Sheen Common – 53
Ham Common – 126
Ham Riverside lands – 124

Hatherop Rec Ground —20
Old Deer Park, Twickenham – 80
Crane Pk – 72
Fulwell Pk – 70

(Richmond Borough also includes the Royal Parks of Richmond, Bushy and Hampton, plus Kew Gardens, which brings the total parks' space in the Borough up to 5,500 acres)

27. *Southwark*   Total acreage, 443 acres

Belair Park – 25
Southwark Pk – 63

Peckham Rye – 112
Russia Dock Pk – 25

Note: 88 acres of Southwark's open space has been laid out since 1975, such as Russia Dock Park, part of their plan to re-develop the old Surrey Docks.

28. *Sutton*   Total acreage, 930 acres

Beddington Park, Wallington – 140
Rosehill Pk – 79
Cheam Pk – 65
Poulter Pk, Carshalton – 51

Sears Pk and Perretts Field – 27
Cuddington Recreation Ground – 25
Carshalton Pk – 23
Mellows Pk, Wallington – 20

29. *Tower Hamlets*   Total acreage, 214 acres

There are no Borough parks in Tower Hamlets over 20 acres. The largest open space is Weavers Fields, 16 acres. The rest are mainly recreation grounds, gardens or churchyards. Half of Victoria Park is in the Borough, but that is GLC owned.

30. *Waltham Forest*   Total acreage, 383 acres

Mansfield Pk – 23
Highams Pk – 24
Lloyd Pk – 36
Larswood – 42

Lee Valley Playing Fields – 21
Low Hall Sports Ground – 46
Marsh Lane Playing Fields – 39

31. *Wandsworth* Total acreage, 554 acres

Wandsworth Common – 175
Tooting Common – 144

King George's Pk – 49
Wandsworth Pk – 20

32. *City of Westminster* Total acreage, 116 acres

Paddington Rec – 27

Finally, there are two other types of organisations which control or run London Parks:

Conservators: Total acreage, 1,500 acres

Mitcham Common – 440

Wimbledon Common – 1,100

These 1,500 acres are open to the public but owned independently, financed by a rate levied on local residents living in the nearby area and managed by an elected body called Conservators. The prime example of this is Wimbledon Common. The Clerk to the Conservators is in effect the Ranger and lives on the Common. (Commander Peter Dean, Manor Cottage, Wimbledon Common, 789–7619). The Conservators of Mitcham Common have a different system. They have appointed Merton Borough Council as their agents to maintain the Common, along with the other Borough parks.

National Trust Total acreage, 892 acres.

Hawkwood, near Chislehurst – 245
Selsdon Wood, Croydon – 198 (Managed by London Borough of Croydon)
Osterley Pk – 140
Petts Woods, Chislehurst – 171
Morden Hall, Morden – 124
East Sheen Common – 53 (Managed by London Borough of Richmond)
Ham House, Richmond – 21

Experts' Opinions

So much for the facts, now finally for some opinions. I asked the head of the Royal Parks and the head of the GLC Parks to nominate their own favourite places, allowing them to select from their own domain, knowing they would not care to comment publicly on their rivals, then I asked a leading London writer for his personal choices from amongst all the London Parks.

Ashley Stephenson, Royal Bailiff

He was loath to pick his favourite Park, as they all have things he likes, but if forced he would choose Hyde Park for personal reasons, as that is where he lives and where he has spent most of his gardening career. 'There's no rhyme or reason to it. I'm a horticulturalist by training, yet Hyde Park is the least horticultural of the Central Parks, apart from Green Park. I just love the feeling of Hyde Park.'

If, however, he had some VIP guests from abroad, and only a set amount of time to show them the glories of the Royal Parks, this would be his choice, depending on the season of the year.

Spring 1. The Waterhouse plantation in Bushy Park at Hampton Court, or

2. The Isabella Plantation at Richmond Park. 'Each Superintendent thinks theirs is the best plantation in London.'

Summer 1. Queen Mary's Rose Gardens and the Broad Walk in Regent's Park, or

2. Duck Island in St James's Park, to look at the flower beds and the water birds.

Autumn 'I'd go for water and colour in the autumn.'

1. The Isabella Plantation again, or

2. The Wolfe Statue and the Lake gardens at Greenwich.

Winter 'They are all much the same in winter, but I think I'd take someone to see the animals, especially the deer, so that would mean going to Richmond or Bushy.'

Lord Birkett, Director of Recreation and the Arts, GLC

'I was driving past St James's Park the other day, and I noticed all the new shrubs coming through and I thought that's a bloody marvellous show, are we in the same league as the Royal Parks? We're not at some places, such as Wormwood Scrubs.

'Wormwood Scrubs, when I first saw it, looked like a bald hole in the middle of the world. All you can see from it is a prison, a hospital, a Motorway and a 48-track railway complex. We started by planting like crazy, but chestnut and oak and other hard woods all failed. The soil is so impoverished. Now we're trying willows and poplars. I insisted that every fifth tree should be a poplar trichocarpa. This gives a lovely balsam smell. You and I will be very old before anyone gets a sniff, but, in the fullness of time, people will walk on Wormwood Scrubs and say, what is that marvellous smell? So I have to mention it on any list.

'In the meantime, we *do* have some parks to equal the Royal Parks, such as Dulwich Park and Holland Park. But it depends of course what you mean by best parks. We don't have show gardens, like the Royal Parks. Once you have a show place, reserves get poured into it and other parts are deprived. We try to spread our resources around. All our parks are so different anyway. If you mean places to get lovely photographs, then in that case I would take a visitor to:

1. Lesnes Abbey, Bostall Heath. This is the ruin of a 12th-century Abbey and there's 20 acres around it which in daffodil time are marvellous.
2. Holland Park, especially the woods in autumn.
3. Dulwich Park, the woodland area.
4. Trent Park – it is now a real country park.
5. Avery Hill – my own particular favourite bit is behind the storage shed at Avery Hill nursery. There's a eucalyptus tree there that someone put in at some time and then forgot. It's now taken root and can never be moved. Its bark is unspeakably beautiful. I go to Avery Hill, just to see it.'

Tom Pocock, author and writer on London topics for the London Standard

Battersea Park 'My favourite and one I have known intimately since 1925. The artificial waterfall above the lake has been dry for years and the little hill from which it fell is now worn by bicycle tyres, but it was once – before 1939 – a most exotic (indeed, erotic) place. Then the waterfall came splashing down through subtropical plants but, as the whole planted area was fenced off, one could not see its source. I once scaled the fence and climbed the hill to find a lovely, limpid (artificial) rock pool on the top. It was an enchanted, secret place and many was the teenage seduction I planned to take place at its brink (but, alas, never achieved).'

St James's Park. 'The famous bridge and its view of Whitehall and Buckingham Palace across the lake, of course. The former suspension bridge, so needlessly replaced, was a great trysting place of mine at the end of the war. On VE-day, or thereabouts, we watched the first post-war floodlighting reflected in the water from there. Then, a night or so later, we returned to find the bridge fenced off – they had found an unexploded bomb in the lake beside it that had been lying there for a year or more.'

Green Park 'Anywhere near that mysterious tunnel that dives into the discrete recesses of St James's. It was surely a bolt-hole for well-heeled chaps with astrakhan collars and spats on their way to assignations in bachelor apartments off St James's Street.'

Regent's Park 'Somewhere in the middle of all that grass where you can see the volcano-like chimneys of the Mappin Terraces, the minaret of the mosque and the gleam of stucco from a Regency villa amongst the trees – and hear the occasional lion's roar above the distant hum of traffic.'

Hampstead Heath 'The famous view of Kenwood from the tall beech above the oak wood. And also the rough meadows just below Kenwood and above the Highgate ponds where you expect to find cowslips.'

Greenwich Park 'The point where the cosiness of well-kept flower beds and ancient oaks suddenly falls away to that stunning view of London. An Olympian view.'

Marion Park, Woolwich 'Anywhere here for the quirkiness so brilliantly caught in *Blow Up.*'

Kensington Gardens 'The sunken garden in front of Kensington Palace in contrast to the open, windy space around the Round Pond nearby.'

Chiswick House Park 'Looking down a thickly-hedged walk to a Georgian folly, where you half-expect to catch the whisk of a disappearing crinoline out of the corner of the eye.'

Index

Numerals in *italics* refer to captions